D0040213

What people are saying about …

CLAIM

"*Claim* drew me in to the Colorado setting with characters who had much to overcome and the courage to stand up for their beliefs. I laughed and cried, cheered, and held my breath until the very end when I had to pull myself into the twenty-first century. This is clearly a masterful work of fiction with explosive emotive conflict."

DiAnn Mills, author of *Sworn to Protect* and *A Woman Called Sage*

What people are saying about …

BREATHE

"Lisa Bergren's *Breathe* is a sweet and sensitive tale of faith, love, and devilry on a raw frontier just coming into its own."

Kristen Heitzmann, best-selling author of *The Edge of Recall* and Christy-award winner *Secrets*

"This book grabbed me from the very first page and kept me reading way past my bedtime—for me, a sure mark of a terrific read. Lisa T.

Bergren is an excellent writer. I highly recommend *Breathe,* and I can't wait for the next book in the trilogy."

Cindy Swanson, blogging at
Notes in the Key of Life

"*Breathe* riveted me with its fascinating peek into Colorado Springs history and well-drawn characters I quickly grew to love. I couldn't put it down! Bergren is one of my favorite authors."

Colleen Coble, author of the Rock Harbor series

"Aptly titled, this is a superb historical medical thriller that brings to life victims of consumption (Tuberculosis) as they struggle to BREATHE."

Harriet Klausner, Genre Go Round Reviews

CLAIM

Also by Lisa T. Bergren:

CHILDREN'S BOOKS:

God Gave Us You
God Gave Us Two
God Gave Us Christmas
God Gave Us Heaven
God Gave Us Love
How Big Is God?
God Found Us You

NONFICTION:

The Busy Mom's Devotional
What Women Want
Life on Planet Mom

NOVELS:

The Bridge
Christmas Every Morning

The Northern Lights series:
The Captain's Bride
Deep Harbor
Midnight Sun

The Gifted series:
The Begotten
The Betrayed
The Blessed

The Homeward Trilogy:
Breathe
Sing
Claim

CLAIM

A Novel of Colorado

LISA T. BERGREN

BOOK 3 of THE HOMEWARD TRILOGY

David C Cook®

transforming lives together

CLAIM
Published by David C. Cook
4050 Lee Vance View
Colorado Springs, CO 80918 U.S.A.

David C. Cook Distribution Canada
55 Woodslee Avenue, Paris, Ontario, Canada N3L 3E5

David C. Cook U.K., Kingsway Communications
Eastbourne, East Sussex BN23 6NT, England

David C. Cook and the graphic circle C logo
are registered trademarks of Cook Communications Ministries.

The Web site addresses recommended throughout this book are offered as a
resource to you. These Web sites are not intended in any way to be or imply an
endorsement on the part of David C. Cook, nor do we vouch for their content.

This story is a work of fiction. All characters and events are the product of the author's
imagination. Any resemblance to any person, living or dead, is coincidental.

All Scripture quotations, unless otherwise noted, are taken from the *Holy Bible,
New International Version*. *NIV*. Copyright © 1973, 1978, 1984 by International
Bible Society. Used by permission of Zondervan. All rights reserved.

LCCN 2010924061
ISBN 978-1-4347-6706-6
eISBN 978-1-4347-0224-1

The Team: Don Pape, Traci DePree, Amy Kiechlin, Sarah
Schultz, Caitlyn York, and Karen Athen
Cover Design: DogEared Design, Kirk DouPonce
Cover Photos: iStockphoto

Printed in the United States of America
First Edition 2010

2 3 4 5 6 7 8 9 10 11

051410

For Traci, friend and editor extraordinaire … thank you for all your hard work on this series. I couldn't have done it without you, sis.

If we claim to have fellowship with him yet walk in the darkness, we lie and do not live by the truth. (1 John 1:6)

CHAPTER ONE

1 August 1888
Gunnison, Colorado

"Keep doing that you'll get yourself killed," Nic said to the boy. Panting, Nic paused and wiped his forehead of sweat. For an hour now, as he moved sacks of grain from a wagon to a wheelbarrow and into the warehouse, he'd glimpsed the boy daring fate as he ran across the busy street, narrowly escaping horse hooves and wagon wheels.

"Where's your mother?"

The brown-haired boy paused. "Don't have a mother."

"Well then, where's your father?"

The boy cast him an impish grin and shrugged one shoulder. "Around."

"Is he coming back soon?" Nic persisted.

"Soon enough. You won't tell 'im, will ya?"

"Tell him what?" Nic tossed back with a small smile. "Long as you stop doing whatever you're not supposed to be doing."

The boy wandered closer and climbed up to perch on the wagon's edge, watching Nic with eyes that were as dark as his hair. Nic relaxed a bit, relieved that the kid wasn't in imminent danger.

Nic hefted a sack onto his shoulder and carried it to the cart. It felt good to be working again. He liked this sort of heavy labor, the feel of muscles straining, the way he had to suck in his breath to heave a sack, then release it with a long *whoosh*. A full day of this sort of work allowed him to drop off into dreamless sleep—something he hungered for more than anything else these days.

The boy was silent, but Nic could feel him staring, watching his every move like an artist studying a subject he was about to paint. "How'd you get so strong?" the boy said at last.

"Always been pretty strong," Nic said, pulling the next sack across the wooden planks of the wagon, positioning it. "How'd you get so fast?"

"Always been pretty fast," said the boy, in the same measured tone Nic had used.

Nic smiled again, heaved the sack to his shoulder, hauled it five steps to the cart, and then dropped it.

"This your job?" the boy asked.

"For today," Nic said.

Nic loaded another sack, and the boy was silent for a moment. "My dad's looking for help. At our mine."

"Hmm," Nic said.

"Needs a partner to help haul rock. He's been asking around here for days."

"Miner, huh? I don't care much for mining."

"Why not? You could be rich."

"More miners turn out dead than rich." He winced inwardly, as a shadow crossed the boy's face. It'd been a while since he'd been around a kid this age. He was maybe ten or eleven max, all wiry muscle and sinew. Reminded him of a boy he knew in Brazil.

Nic carried the next sack over to the wagon, remembering the heat there, so different from what Colorado's summer held. Here it was bone dry. He was sweating now, after the morning's work, but not a lot. In Brazil a man soaked his sheets as he slept.

"Listen, kid," he said, turning back around to the wagon, intending to apologize for upsetting him. But the boy was gone.

Nic sighed and set to finishing his work. As the sun climbed high in the sky, he paused to take a drink from his canteen and eat a hunk of bread and cheese, watching the busy street at the end of the alleyway. He wondered if he'd see the boy again, back to his antics of racing teams of horses. The child was probably letting off steam, just as Nic had done all his life—he'd been about the child's age when he'd first starting scrapping with others.

But that was in the past. Not since his voyage aboard the *Mirabella* had Nic indulged the need, succumbed to the desire to enter a fight. Several times now, he'd had the opportunity—and enough cause—to take another man down. But he had walked away. He knew, deep down he knew, that if he was ever to face his sisters, Odessa and Moira, again, if he was to come to them and admit he was penniless, everything would somehow be all right if he was settled inside. If he could come to a place of peace within, the kind of peace Manuel had known. It was the kind of thing that allowed a man to stand up straight, shoulders back, the kind of thing that gave a man's gut peace. Regardless of what he accomplished, or had in the past. Thing was, he hadn't found that place of comfort inside, and he didn't want what Manuel tried to sell him—God.

There had to be another way, another path. Something like this work. Hard manual labor. That might be what he needed most.

Nic heard a man calling, his voice a loud whisper, and his eyes narrowed as the man came limping around the corner, obviously in pain, his arm in a sling. "You, there!" he called to Nic. "Seen a boy around? About yea big?" he said, gesturing to about chest height.

"Yeah, he was here," Nic called back. He set his canteen inside the empty wagon and walked to the end of the alleyway.

"Where'd he go?" the man said. Nic could see the same widow's peak in the man's brown hair that the boy had, the same curve of the eyes … the boy's father, clearly.

"Not sure. One minute he was watching me at work, the next he was gone."

"That's my boy, all right."

"I'll help you find him."

The man glanced back at him and then gave him a small smile. He stuck out his good arm and offered his hand. "I'd appreciate that. Name's Vaughn. Peter Vaughn."

"Dominic St. Clair," he replied. "You can call me Nic."

Peter smiled. His dimples were in the exact same spot as the boy's. "Sure you can leave your work?"

"I'm nearly done. Let's find your boy."

"Go on," Moira's sister urged, gazing out the window. "He's been waiting on you for a good bit now."

"I don't know what he sees in me," Moira said, wrapping the veil around her head and across her shoulder again. It left most of her face visible but covered the burns at her neck, ear, and scalp. Did it cover them enough? She nervously patted it, making sure it was in place.

Odessa stepped away from washing dishes and joined her. "He might wonder what *you* see in him. Do you know what his story is? He seems wary." Their eyes met and Odessa backtracked. "Daniel's a good man, Moira. I think highly of him. But I'd like to know what has burdened him so. Besides you." She nudged her sister with her hip.

Moira wiped her hands on the dish towel and glanced out at him as he strode across the lawn with Bryce, Odessa's husband. He was striking in profile, reminding her of the statues of Greek gods the French favored in their lovely tailored gardens. Far too handsome for her—since the fire, anyway. She shook her head a little.

"Moira."

Irritated at being caught in thought, Moira looked at Odessa again.

"Trust him, Moira. He's a good man. I can sense it."

She nodded, but inwardly she sighed as she turned away and wrapped a scarf around her veiled head and shoulders. *A good man.* After Reid and Max and Gavin—could she really trust her choice in men? Odessa was fortunate to have fallen for her husband, Bryce, a good man through and through. Moira's experiences with men had been less than successful. What made Odessa think this one was trustworthy?

But as Daniel ducked his head through the door and inclined it to one side in silent invitation to walk with him, Moira thought about how he had physically saved her more than once. And how his gentle pursuit both bewildered and calmed her. Daniel had done nothing to deserve her suspicions.

She moved over to the door. He glanced at her, and she noticed how his thick lashes made his brown eyes more pronounced. He shuffled his feet as if he were nervous. "You busy?" he asked.

"No." Moira felt a nervous tension tighten her stomach muscles.

"Can we, uh …" His gaze shifted to Odessa, who quickly returned to her dishes. "Go for a walk?" he finally finished.

Moira smoothed her skirts and said, "I'd like that." Then, meeting her sister's surreptitious gaze, she followed him outside. It was a lovely day on the Circle M. The horses pranced in the distance. She could see her brother-in-law riding out with Tabito, the ranch's foreman.

"So, you wanted to talk," she ventured.

"There's not a day that goes by that I don't want to talk to you, Moira," he said.

She looked up at him and then, when she saw the ardor in his gaze, she turned with a sigh.

"Don't look away," he whispered gently, pulling her to face him. He reached to touch her veil, as if he longed to cradle her cheek instead.

"No, Daniel, don't," she said and ran a nervous hand over the cover. He was tall and broad, and she did not feel physically menaced—it was her heart that threatened to pound directly out of her chest. Perhaps she wasn't ready for this … the intimacies that a courtship brought.

She'd been dreaming about what it would be like to be kissed by him, held by him, but he never made such advances before. Never took the opportunity, leaving her to think that he was repulsed by her burns, her hair, singed to just a few inches long, her past relationship with Gavin, or her pregnancy—despite what he claimed. Her hand moved to the gentle roundness of her belly, still small yet making itself more and more prominent each day. "I … I'm not even certain why you pursue me at all. Why you consider me worthy. "

He seemed stunned by her words. "Worthy?" he breathed. He let out a hollow, breathy laugh and then looked to the sky, running a hand through his hair. He shook his head and then slowly brought his brown eyes down to meet hers again. "Moira," he said, lifting a hand to cradle her cheek and jaw, this time without hesitation. She froze, wondering if he intended to kiss her at last. "I only hesitate because I am afraid," he whispered.

"Afraid? You think I am not? I come to you scarred in so many ways, when you, you, Daniel, deserve perfection...."

"No," he said, shaking his head too. "It is I who carry the scars. You don't know me. You don't know who I am. Who I once was. What I've done ..."

"So tell me," she pleaded. "Tell me."

He stared at her a moment longer, as if wondering if she was ready, wondering if she could bear it, and Moira's heart pounded again. Then, "No. I can't," he said with a small shake of his head. He sighed heavily and moved up the hill. "Not yet."

An hour after they began their search for Everett Vaughn, Peter sat down on the edge of the boardwalk and looked up to the sky. His face was a mask of pain. "That boy was hard to track when I wasn't hurt."

"He'll turn up," Nic reassured.

Peter nodded and lifted his gaze to the street.

"What happened to you?" Nic said gently, sitting down beside the man. His eyes scanned the crowds for the boy even as he waited for Peter's response.

"Cave-in, at my mine. That's why I'm here. Looking for a good man to partner with me. I'm onto a nice vein, but I'm livin' proof that a man's a fool to mine alone." He looked at Nic and waited until he met his gaze. "You lookin' for work?" He cocked his head to the side. "I'm offering a handsome deal. Fifty-fifty."

Nic let a small smile tug at the corners of his mouth. He glanced at the man, who had to be about his own age. There was an easy way about him that drew Nic, despite the pain evident in the lines of his face. "That *is* a handsome offer." He cocked his own head. "But I don't see you doing half the work, laid up like you are."

"No, not quite. But I've already put a lot of work into it in the past three years, and I'm still good for about a quarter of the labor. To say nothing of the fact that my name's on the claim."

Nic paused, thinking about it, feeling drawn to help this man, but then shook his head. "I'm not very fond of small dark spaces."

"So … make it bigger. Light a lamp."

Nic shook his head, more firmly this time. "No. I'd rather find another line of work."

Just then he spotted the boy, running the street again. "There he is," Nic said, nodding outward. The boy's father followed his gaze and with a grimace, rose to his feet. As they watched, the boy ran under a wagon that had temporarily pulled to a stop. Then he jumped up on the back of another, riding it for about twenty feet until he was passing by them. His face was a mask of elation.

"Everett! Ev! Come on over here!"

Everett's eyes widened in surprise. He jumped down and ran over to them, causing a man on horseback to pull back hard on his reins and swear.

"Sorry, friend," Peter said, raising his good arm up to the rider. The horseman shook his head and then rode on.

Peter grabbed his son's arm and, limping, hauled him over to the boardwalk. "I've told you to stay out of the street."

"So did I," Nic said, meeting the boy's gaze. The child flushed red and glanced away.

"We'd best be on our way," Peter said. "Thanks for helpin' me find my boy." He reached out a hand and Nic rose to shake it. Peter paused. "It's not often a man has a chance at entering a claim agreement once a miner has found a vein that is guaranteed to pay."

Nic hesitated as he dropped Peter's hand. "I've narrowly escaped with my life on more than one occasion, friend. I'm aiming to look up my sisters, but not from a casket."

Peter lifted his chin, but his eyes betrayed his weariness and disappointment. What would it mean for him? For his boy, not to find a willing partner? Would they have to give up the mine just as they were finally on the edge of success? And what of the boy's mother? His unkempt, too-small clothes told him Everett had been without a mother for some time.

He hesitated again, feeling a pang of compassion for them both. "Should I change my mind ... where would I find you?"

A glimmer of hope entered Peter's eyes. "A couple miles out of St. Elmo. Just ask around for the Vaughn claim up in the Gulch and someone'll point you in our direction." He reached out a hand. "I'd be much obliged, Nic. And I'm not half bad at cookin' either. I'd keep you in grub. Give it some thought. But don't be too put out if you get there, and I've found someone else."

"Understood," Nic said with a smile. "Safe journey."

"And to you." He turned away, tugging at his boy's shoulder, but the child looked back at Nic, all big pleading eyes.

Hurriedly, Nic walked away in the opposite direction. He fought the desire to turn and call out to them. Wasn't he looking for work? Something that would allow him to ride on to Bryce and Odessa's ranch without his tail tucked between his legs? The man had said the mine was sure to pay.... *I'm onto a nice vein....*

Was that a miner's optimism or the truth?

"Not yet?" Moira sputtered, following him. She frowned in confusion. He had been coaxing her forward, outward, steadily healing her with his kind attentions these last two months. But now it was as if they were at some strange impasse. What was he talking about? What had happened to him?

She hurried forward and grabbed his arm, forcing him to stop and turn again to face her. Her veil clung to her face in the early evening breeze. "Daniel."

He slowly lifted his dark eyes to meet hers.

"This is about me, isn't it?" she asked. "You attempt to spare my feelings but find me repulsive. I can hardly fault you, but—"

"No," he said, with another hollow laugh. "Contrary to what you believe, Moira St. Clair, not everything boils down to you. You are braver than you think and more beautiful than you dare to believe. I believe we're destined to be together."

Moira held her breath. Then *what*—

"No," he went on. "This is about something I need to resolve.

Something that needs to be done, or at least settled in my mind, my heart, before I can properly court you."

"What? What is it, Daniel?" she tried once more.

He only looked at her helplessly, mouth half open, but mute.

She crossed her arms and turned her back to him, staring out across the pristine valley, the land of the Circle M. It hurt her that he felt he couldn't confide in her as she had with him. She stiffened when he laid his big hands on her shoulders. "I don't need to be rescued, Daniel," she said in a monotone. "God has seen me to this place, this time. He'll see me through to the next … with or without you."

"You don't understand."

"No. I don't. We've been courting all summer, whether you realize it or not. And now you say that there is something else that needs to be resolved? You assume much, Daniel Adams. You think that I'll wait forever?" She let out a scoffing laugh. "It's clear you do not fear that any other man might pursue me. Not that I blame you …" She turned partly away and stared into the distance. "Please. Don't let this linger on. I cannot bear it. Not if you do not intend to claim me as your own."

He was silent for a long minute. Oh, that he would but turn her and meet her lips at last …

But he didn't. "We both have a lot to think through, pray through, Moira," he said quietly.

"Yes, well, let me know when that is accomplished," she said over her shoulder, walking away as fast as she could, lest he see the tears that were already rolling down her cheeks.

CHAPTER TWO

Moira took Daniel's hand and climbed into the wagon, letting go of his warm palm as soon as possible. They moved out to the "barn raising"—which was really more like a "small town raising"—picnic in three wagons.

"Oh, I hate to leave anyone behind for this," Odessa said, settling in beside Moira, with her son, Samuel, in her arms. She glanced back toward Tabito, the ranch's Ute foreman, and two others who would remain on the premises to watch over the herd closest to the house. Three more hands were on the eastern quadrant with the rest of the horses. "It's a shame they'll miss it."

Feeling the hard wall of separation between her and Daniel, Moira wished she could take the place of any one of them.

Odessa glanced at Moira, her eyes softening before she moved the baby to her other side so she could hook her arm through her sister's. "It will be all right, Moira," she whispered. "You'll have fun." She looked up to the wagon bench in front of them, and Moira followed her eyes. Daniel was sitting next to Bryce. They were talking about the lumber that had just been delivered for the snow breaks and stables they'd build over the summer. Daniel and Bryce had an easy rapport, whether it was talking about the ranch or enjoying a hot cup of coffee after supper. Odessa looked quite smug as she looked from one man to another and then over at Moira.

She was matchmaking again. She didn't know yet that it was over, any budding love between Moira and the man before her. Ever since their conversation three days prior, Daniel had stayed as far away from her as possible. The pain of his rejection, his sudden silence, seemed more than she could bear. Seeing him, yet knowing he would never love her. Why did he even remain at the Circle M?

"Stop it, Dess," Moira whispered.

"Did I say anything?" Odessa asked, her blue-green St. Clair eyes, so like Moira's, wide with mock innocence. Moira knew she thought Daniel a fine man, with his sober, steady ways. He was. But she also knew her older sister well enough to know that she'd like to put Moira's life in order—preferably sooner than later, with a baby on the way. Moira's hand moved to her swelling belly hidden beneath the folds of her dress. Four months along, five months to go. It didn't matter, really. Even if Daniel had wanted to marry her, there would be no way to get married and have the baby without the old biddies in town or at church fully understanding that this child was not his babe.

He was not her way out. She was destined to carry this baby by herself with no one to share the load. It was the price she had to pay. As it should be.

She watched the endless rails that marked the northern boundary of the ranch as they passed by. There were knots in the wood, little more than small bumps in the grain; elsewhere there were massive knots that seemed to twist the entire log and change the grain itself, sending it in a new direction. She supposed that was what had happened to her—a couple of massive knots in her life. Her choices with Gavin, her run-in with Reid Bannock, the opera house in Paris closing down, the fire. The pregnancy. *More like a series of massive knots,* she thought.

Moira sensed someone looking at her and glanced up. Daniel's warm eyes were on her, but his gaze was glazed, perfunctory. Simply checking on her, she decided, making sure she was all right. When he turned around again, Odessa squeezed her arm knowingly, as if to say, *See?*

Moira rolled her eyes and then looked to the rail again. God would see her through, raising the child alone. Or at least alongside Odessa and Bryce. But she needed to move out of their house soon, give them their privacy. Perhaps she could purchase one of the cottage lots on the creek, where some of the men were building homes, or maybe in the little town they'd call Conquistador, once it was built.

She tried to summon the courage to face what was ahead and concentrate on the fact that she'd be surrounded by people of the Circle M the whole time—at least for today, if not for the rest of her life—but bile rose in her throat. She hoped she wouldn't be ill. The morning sickness had abated, by and large, but now and again she had a bout of it. It would be mortifying, vomiting here, in this happy company of people. So far, no one besides Odessa, Bryce, and Daniel knew of her pregnancy.

How long could she keep up the charade?

Moira trailed behind her sister, glad to be holding the baby and making herself useful. Odessa moved among friends and neighbors, some of whom had traveled from as far as Westcliffe for what was, in effect, the christening of a new town. Bryce's men had set up a temporary stage on the corner of their ranch that bordered the county road and even set up a couple of outhouses. Around the stage, where the musicians were warming up now, they'd strung cord to hang lanterns, so that come nightfall they could dance.

Some had brought picnic tables and lined them up in several rows. Still others spread blankets about. A good distance away, a group of men were taking turns shooting bottles off a fence post, getting five paces farther out with each shot. Moira glanced their way. Daniel took aim, squeezed off a shot, and hit his target; the crowd of men erupted in shouts. Moira sighed. He was a terrific marksman. She wished she were there instead, shooting things. It might alleviate some of the angst she felt inside.

Moira looked around as Mrs. Moore excused herself to fetch her rolls from her wagon. There were about a hundred or more people in attendance.

Bryce joined her and Odessa, taking the baby from Moira's arms. "It's turned out well, don't you think?"

"Oh, it's wonderful, Bryce," Odessa said. "The boys did a terrific job on the stage—and even outhouses! Very thoughtful."

"Well, it's a long way back to our house," he said, cocking a brow.

"No, it's perfect. It's only that I hadn't thought of it ... and you did." She smiled up at him, and Moira had to look away, tormented, suddenly, by the love they so clearly shared.

"I can't take all the credit," Bryce said. "Tabito was the one who suggested the stage. He said my uncle used to host one of these summer picnics every year and that was how he did things. The stage will, in time, be the main floor of the mercantile."

"And Tabito's not even here to enjoy it," Odessa lamented.

"He's happiest back at the ranch."

"You're certain?"

"I am. As long as we bring him back a heaping plate of food."

"I could take it back for him," Moira offered, seeing an escape.

"No, no," Odessa intoned. "We'll send a man with a whole basket for the boys back at home. You stay here and enjoy the afternoon."

"Oh," Bryce said, looking past them. "They're about to pull the hogs off the spit. I better go help. Want to see?"

"Yes! They smell wonderful."

"You come too, Moira," he said, noticing her hesitation. "I promise," he said, with a sparkle in his eye, "you've never had pork like this." They crossed the field toward a group of the men who hovered by two large smoking pits. They'd dug them out a few days before, started a fire yesterday morning, and placed the hogs— liberally seasoned and filled with onions and apples—inside the glowing, coal-lined cavities last night. They'd been slow-roasting for almost twenty-four hours.

As if drawn by the aroma, everyone began moving toward the two holes and strained to peer over shoulders to get a look. Small children squeezed between legs and hips to make it to the front. Several men talked about Daniel and his marksmanship. One said they should ask him to be the new Westcliffe sheriff.

Moira barely held back a shiver. Bad things happened to lawmen in the West. It would be far better if Daniel stayed on the ranch. Not that he was asking her opinion …

Four men worked at each pit, hands wrapped in cloth to keep from getting burned. They moved aside the smoldering wood and metal at the top, that side of the crowd pressing backward in a wave to give them room. Then, on the count of three, the men lifted the first hog out of the ground. It was on a woven metal mesh, and they set it gently down. It steamed and Moira wondered over the perfect golden-brown skin. The second one emerged then, and the crowd turned its attention to that one, *oohing* and *ahhing* at the sight and smell. Moira thought their bellies might all be rumbling as one.

"Friends and neighbors," Bryce said loudly, so all could hear. "Thank you for coming today, and for bringing all those wonderful pies over there—" he paused to gesture to one of the picnic tables— "that almost make me want to start with dessert."

Men and women laughed. The children grinned as if they thought that was a grand idea.

"Some of you were here on this property when Odessa and I suffered through dark days," he said. He wrapped his arm around her shoulders. "Some of you came to our aid. Some of you offered to help in any way you could afterward. Odessa and I deeply appreciate neighbors that feel like family."

"So, in thanks we offer you this meal. And tomorrow—" he paused to eye Odessa—"we'll raise the foundations of a town I'd like to name Conquistador, because without the gold they left us, it wouldn't be possible."

A cheer went up from the crowd. In the morning, all these people would return, ready to help raise the frames of a tiny new post office, a mercantile, a charity sanatorium for consumption patients, and a church.

"For now," Bryce's voice rang out, "let us give thanks to the Lord for this fine meal we are about to share."

Men pulled off their hats and held them to their chests. All bowed their heads and closed their eyes.

"Lord, thank You for Your deliverance. Thank You for this fellowship and this fine food. We ask that You give us peace in this valley for years to come and Your guidance in all that we do. Amen."

"Amen," said the people.

Immediately they all moved toward the table of food as the men began to carve the first of the hogs. Bowls of potato salad and other side dishes were set out, and families served themselves before heading back to the pits, where the men sliced off hunks of moist, succulent pork and set it atop their plates.

Since the line for food was long and they wanted their guests to be served first, Moira moved with Odessa back to the wagon to help her change the baby and bring back a couple baskets of extra rolls. Judging from the crowd, they would end up needing them. When they got there, they could see four men, lounging in the back of a wagon next to theirs, sipping at a bottle. Drinking, Moira decided. She knew none of them but could feel their heavy stares.

"Mrs. McAllan," said the closest, tipping his hat in her direction. "Thank you kindly for the invitation today."

"Certainly," Odessa said, with the edge of ice in her tone. So she had noted their drinking too. Moira knew none of the Circle M men were given to imbibing. A neighbor's men, perhaps. Or some of the carpentry crew.

"I don't believe we've been properly introduced to your sister," pressed a big man with a dark shadow of stubble across his jaw. "She's as pretty as people say. Can see that, even with that veil on."

Odessa glanced at Moira and then said to them, as briefly as she could, "Forgive me. This is Miss Moira St. Clair."

Moira dragged her eyes to the men and nodded, then started to turn toward their wagon.

"I'm Winston Willaby," said the man, hopping off the back of the wagon and edging to the side, partially blocking her way.

She glanced up at him again. "Pleased to meet you," she said.

Moira stepped to the left, again to move around him, but he reached out and touched her arm. "Please, Miss St. Clair, would you do me the honor of eating with me?"

She glanced at Odessa. Her sister was looking back at them in mild alarm.

"No, thank you," she began.

"Miss St. Clair is with me," Daniel said, suddenly by her side. He pushed past her so fast that she had to take a step backward in order not to fall to the ground. But his attention was not on her. It was on Willaby. He took a hold of the man's shirt in two fistfuls and slammed him up against the side of the wagon.

"Hey!" Willaby cried out, his face a mask of anger. Behind him, two of his friends rose to their feet in the wagon. The third jumped down.

"I'll say this once," Daniel said in a low growl, inches from his face. "If you ever approach Miss St. Clair again, or make her at all uncomfortable, you'll deal with *me*."

"Daniel," Moira said, finding her voice. She took a step closer as a steely look crossed Willaby's face. He was ripe for a brawl. "Daniel, it's all right."

But Daniel didn't move. Did he even hear her? His face was a mask of fury.

Willaby moved and managed to pry one of Daniel's hands off of him. Daniel released his other hold and took a step back, his fists clenched.

"This is hardly the place," Odessa cried. "Gentlemen! I must insist you stop this at once!" Samuel began to cry.

The nearest men in the crowd turned their way. Moira moved to Daniel's side and took one of his hands. "Daniel," she said softly, looking up at him. "*Daniel.*"

After a moment, he wrenched his eyes away from the drunk and glanced down at her.

"Please," she said. "It's all right. I'm all right."

He looked back at Willaby, seeing if the man dared to make another move. Although he looked angry, he remained still.

Moira took a step away, pulling at Daniel's hand. "Come. Come, let's take a walk before supper."

Reluctantly, he turned with her and wrapped a protective arm around her shoulder. She allowed it, solely to get him away from the others. When they were a distance apart, she gently took his hand from her shoulder, let it drop between them. He had no right to touch her at all, not when they'd barely been speaking.

They walked in silence until they entered a small grove of cottonwoods by the creek. "I'm sorry, Moira," he said, pacing. "I don't know what came over me." He leaned against the trunk of a tree and looked upward, then rubbed his face. "I haven't been that angry since ..." He glanced down at her, sorrow and horror and humiliation in his eyes.

"Since ...?" she said.

He looked so lost and afraid and embarrassed, she had to fight to keep herself from wrapping her arms around him.

He stared at her for a long moment, then ran his hand through his hair. "I'm coiled in a twist, Moira. I need to move, do something. A couple men down there—" he paused to hook a thumb over his shoulder, toward the crowd milling below them—"mentioned the open sheriff position in Westcliffe. Maybe it'd do me good, to have something new—"

She shook her head, instantly disagreeing. "No, Daniel, no. Don't you remember?" she pleaded. "Remember that Reid made me ..." She swallowed hard and brought her fist to her lips. *I have no right. No right to ask him.*

Daniel stiffened and frowned down at her. "Moira, that trap, it happened once. It's not likely to happen again."

"You don't know that! Reid's gone, yes, but who will take his place? They killed them, Daniel. Every last one of them. The sheriff. The deputies. Picked them off as surely as you just picked off those bottles."

He stared down at her for several long moments and then lifted his hand to cradle the right side of her face. "I must do this, Moira. It will help me resolve ..." He looked up and away, toward the setting sun.

"Resolve *what*?" she begged, taking his hand, hoping she might urge him to reveal whatever mountain blocked his path.

"No," he said, shaking his head. "Let me fix this. Finish this. Then we can move on."

She dropped his hand and walked down the hill, returning to the line of people awaiting food, knowing he was right behind her. The man who had approached Moira and narrowly missed coming to blows with Daniel stayed on the other side of the long tables from them. Moira and Daniel moved down the line, quickly filling their plates. Across from them, Mr. Weaver, a Westcliffe banker, introduced himself.

"You've been working out at the Circle M, haven't you?" Mr. Weaver asked.

"For the last few months, yes," Daniel returned.

"Bryce has told me about you. Says you're a fine man."

"Well, you can't always believe what you hear," Daniel deflected.

Moira tried to keep her expression blank and continued to fill her plate.

"Well, what I hear is all good. And today, some men have told me that you have good aim too."

Moira stole a glance his way. Daniel raised an eyebrow in Weaver's direction and gave him a slight shrug. "I hold my own."

"Bryce tells me you have a natural ability to lead. That you're a man of integrity and loyalty."

They paused at the end of the line, letting others pass them by. Clearly the man wanted something of him. Moira tried to urge her feet to move, to get away from this conversation and Daniel, but it was as if she were mesmerized.

Daniel's frown deepened. "Is there something you wanted to say, Mr. Weaver?"

"Why yes," Mr. Weaver returned, giving him a jowly smile. "As town council president, I want to officially offer you a job. As our new county sheriff."

CHAPTER THREE

The shot breezed by his head, so close he could feel the heat. Dominic froze, and then slowly lifted his hands as he looked about. "Whoa, whoa," he said, "I'm not looking to do any harm." He could see nothing but the dance of pale green aspen leaves and the massive white trunks of an old stand of trees.

Another bullet came whizzing toward him, this time landing in the dirt at his feet. He jumped and moved deeper into the aspen grove. "My name's St. Clair!" he yelled. "I'm on my way to see Peter Vaughn. He asked me to come!"

He scanned the trees, desperately trying to find his assailant as he eased his revolver from its holster. If someone was going to shoot at him again, they'd best be ready to get shot themselves. He was not one to—

There. His breath left him in a rush as a wild creature came toward him, hair flying in a mass of thick brown waves, backlit by the sun. She was a tiny thing, but her face was a mask of consternation and concentration. "What'd you say your name is?" she called, her eyes still peering at him down the bead of her rifle.

"St. Clair. Dominic St. Clair."

She squinted a bit harder, as if she didn't like his answer. "And you're here at Peter's invitation?" Her tone was clipped, but her words were educated, cultured.

"I am. I met him in Gunnison, him and his boy."

She paused for a breath, then lifted her face off the rifle. From twenty paces away, Nic could see she had an angel's face, with high cheekbones and massive brown eyes and long lashes. "You here to help him on his claim?"

"I hope so."

"So, where is he?"

"He's not here?"

"No," she said indifferently. "He's not." She studied him, and he admired her round eyes wreathed in long lashes. "Sorry about the warning shots. Promised Peter I'd keep any claim jumpers away in his absence." With that, she tucked her rifle in a sheath at her back and turned to move up the hill.

"Wait," Nic called. "Wait!"

She ignored him, trudging up the ravine like a goat on a mountain. He panted and rushed after her, losing her in the trees, then catching sight of her again across a small meadow. "Wait! What's your name?"

She stopped and turned to face him. "It's none of your business. Now quit following me! You've left Vaughn's land and moved onto mine. I'll thank you to return to his."

He gave her his friendliest smile, but his brow knit in consternation as he put both hands out. "Might we not be neighborly? I will be here awhile."

"I have few friends," she said. Then, so softly he could barely hear her, "And you ..." Her words trailed away. He watched as she clamped her lips shut and then turned to walk away, disappearing between the massive pines.

If he hadn't paused, he would have missed her silent companion, an Indian man about his own height, in traditional beaded clothing and long hair, braided to one side. They stood there for a long moment, regarding each other; then the Indian turned and followed the woman into the trees.

He was beginning to see why Vaughn might need another man about.

Nic sighed, turned around, and headed back to the aspens, intent on finding his way to Vaughn's claim. Twenty minutes later, following a sparkling, narrow river that ran clear with sweet water, he reached a tiny cabin. It had to be the Vaughn claim. He called out a greeting, but the place was obviously deserted. Nic tentatively opened the door and peered inside. In the corner was a small stove with a pipe that rose crookedly. Beside it was a table with a washtub, two pans, a tin of coffee, and a tin of salt. Two beds were crammed in the far corner, barely enough room for a father and son. Where was he to sleep? He fingered the doorframe, noting the splintering, rotting wood.

Nic turned to look behind him and his eyes widened and he felt the tug of a small smile. The view was marvelous from here. Mountains of the Divide stretched out before him, barren-topped peaks weaving into thick, green forests. To the right, across a narrow, tight valley floor, a small waterfall fell a good hundred feet, even this late in the summer. Twenty paces away was the creek, easy access for both the cabin and the mine, he hoped. He turned and made his way up a dirt path, through another small grove of trees and around a massive granite boulder.

He pulled up short, before the old mine's entrance. Hand on the top beam, he leaned down and looked in. The tunnel went a good distance into the side of the mountain before disappearing into the dark. Nic reached for the lamp that hung from a peg by the side and shook it. Empty. He looked about. Hopefully Peter was bringing supplies with him.

Nic thought of the cabin beyond the big boulder. Maybe he could add on a room, have a little space of his own. He shook his head. What was he doing here? It was as if he were driven by some unseen force. It was promising, sure, and pretty up here. But mining cabins were rough, lonely places through the cold winter. And deadly. More than one miner had been taken out by an avalanche or frozen solid by week after week of harsh weather.

A shiver ran down his spine. Peter Vaughn had to show up soon, or he'd have no choice but to journey on and face his sister and her husband. He grimaced. No, he wasn't ready for that either. It'd be far better to help Peter dig out his gold for a time and have a decent bundle before he made contact with his sister. No sense in her knowing he'd blown his inheritance.

His eyes moved to the trees, and he thought of the woman and her Indian companion. Who were they? What was their story? And where were the Vaughns? Maybe someone in town could tell him.

Daniel rode with Bryce to the Conquistador site the following day. South and west of them, Generals Palmer and McAllister, founders of Silver Cliff and Westcliffe, were none too happy about the foundations of a new settlement, but Bryce ignored them. Conquistador would serve the residents on this end of the valley, even if it always was "a tiny town with a big name," as Bryce said.

Daniel was still chewing over his words, deciding what to say to Bryce about accepting Mr. Weaver's offer of the position as sheriff. The position had been vacant since Reid Bannock had ambushed and killed Sheriff Olsbo and his men—and made Moira watch—three months prior. Again he felt the tear of anguish, between Moira's fears for his safety and his own increasing desire to take the position and finish the business that kept them apart. It might all be a moot point anyway, he mused. No doubt Palmer and McAllister would offer their own men for the nomination, and once a little digging had occurred, the valley's citizens would know exactly who and what Daniel was. There were certainly many sheriffs in western towns who had less-than-perfect pasts, but was Westcliffe a town that would tolerate what he had done?

"I've been having second thoughts about taking the sheriff position, Bryce," he said at last. "Though I appreciate your backing, I would wager it isn't entirely warranted."

Swaying in the saddle, Bryce frowned and looked over at him. "You're capable, Daniel. Smart and strong—everything we need in a sheriff. Why not go after it?"

"I've done things … things I'm not proud of. It'd come out eventually."

Bryce absorbed his words for a moment; then, "Haven't we all? The question is: Who are you now? What I see is a fine, upstanding man. Someone who went through a lot to save my sister-in-law, as well as aid us, and was wounded himself." He looked forward for a few paces. "You a believer in Christ, Daniel?"

Daniel kept his face as subdued as possible. "I am."

"The power of grace, as best as I understand it, covers us. No matter how far we've roamed, what we've done, if we return to the cross and confess, we're covered."

Daniel continued to stare ahead. "You think it's that simple?"

"That simple. And that convoluted. But it's pretty clear in the Bible."

Memorized verses cascaded through Daniel's mind. "Yeah," he said. "Maybe I'll need to do that."

"How much of your hesitation has to do with Moira?"

"Moira?"

"She didn't seem to take to the idea very well."

"Moira and me …" Daniel said, shaking his head. "I'm not certain we'll ever be anything but friends. I can't let how she feels about it sway me one way or the other."

"I see," Bryce said. But Daniel could see that he did not.

CHAPTER FOUR

With no sign of the Vaughns come morning, Nic hiked down the mountain to retrieve his horse, a strong mare named Daisy, from the mining town's stables. St. Elmo was barely more than a village of three blocks with many vacant lots—overshadowed by her sister city of Alpine farther down the pass—but if the gold continued to flow, she was bound to be something someday.

Daisy had been reshod and seemed perky, full up on fresh hay. "What'd you do, starve that girl?" grumbled the grizzled stable keeper, Jed Salinsky, with the glint of a grin in his blue eyes. "Good you came to get 'er today or I would've had to tie her out back to keep her from eating everything in the stables."

Nic smiled and laid another coin on the shelf between them. "That should cover it."

"Much obliged," said the older man, picking up the money and lifting it in Nic's direction, and then quickly pocketing it. "You make it up to Vaughn's mine yesterday?"

"I did." Nic crossed his arms. "You know anything about his neighbor up there?"

Another smile teased the corner of Jed's eyes. "Mrs. LaCrosse? Sure I do."

Nic frowned. "Mrs.? She's married?"

Jed moved toward him and gestured to two chairs outside the

open door of his tiny office. "Sit a spell with me. Good for a man to know what is at his door, be it a cougar or a kitten."

Daisy whinnied when she saw him, but Nic ignored her, his mind on the woman he'd encountered. Jed was enjoying the attention, reveling in his story. He reminded Nic of the storytellers he'd met in saloon after saloon, drawn there for nothing more than an audience, but he knew the best way to find out what he knew was to wait him out. If one rushed a man like this, he'd clam up and refuse to say another word.

"Sabine LaCrosse was the wife of a miner, up in the Gulch. Was her Indian wit' her?"

"An Indian was with her, yes."

Jed snorted his disgust. "Ain't natural, but the Frenchies, they take to Indians like ducks to water, you know. That'un ain't a Ute, but a Blackfoot. Picked 'im up in Montana territory, when Sabine was but a girl. Story was, the Indian was an orphan, and Sabine's father found him outside a camp that had been run plumb over by the cavalry, every last one of 'em killed."

"He was the lone survivor?"

"Yes. Sabine's pa tried to take him to a reservation, but he refused to stay. Kept sneaking off, following them like a loyal dog. Saved 'em, more than once, over the years. Sabine's pa trapped from here on north until the beaver ran few and far between. He married Sabine off to a miner in Alpine right before he died and the Indian boy was away for a time. But Sabine's man, he was as mean as a ferret caught by the toe. Beat her. She'd show up in town with black eyes. One time he broke her arm." He paused, lowering his voice. "But then he did no more."

Nic glanced over at him. "What happened?"

"No one knows for sure. But Sabine's husband, he went out hunting that winter—'bout four years ago, now—and he never returned."

Nic pursed his lips and slid a foot over his other knee. "Common enough in these parts, right?"

"Right. But that Indian boy, he showed up about then, this time all grown up. He still comes around, now and then. Don't know where he goes in between."

"Do you know the brave's name?"

"Nah. 'Round here, people just call him Sabine's Injun. He's a quiet sort. Like most of 'em. Just studies you, with those black eyes of 'is."

"You think he killed Sabine's husband?"

Jed pursed his lips and raised a brow. He tucked his head to one side. "Many things in these mountains can bring a man to death's door. I'm not one to say. Judge declared 'im dead a couple years ago, and the claim was put in Sabine's name."

Nic stared down the street. Was it simply loyalty that drove the Indian brave to watch over Sabine? He looked at Jed. "She never remarried?"

Jed raised an eyebrow and grinned. He let out a breathy laugh. "Whooo, no, you won't see a man up the Gulch besides Vaughn. She keeps most anybody off her property as well as his. Most likely 'fraid of claim jumpers." He raised a brow. "And for good reason. Not a right place for a gal without a man, 'specially sitting on top a pile o' gold, if Vaughn's onto what people say he is."

"So … Sabine and the Indian are not common-law mates?"

Jed stared at him, as if offended by the idea. "Nah. But they share some sort of bond, I tell you what."

"And she hasn't taken to another man?"

Jed smiled wider, catching on to Nic's interest. Nic shifted in his seat as Jed sat up and then leaned in his direction. "She's pretty enough, but she's a wildcat, that 'un, and her husband, he made her near crazy, wit' his mean ways. Why, she even shot at a traveling parson a couple years back. Poor man only aimed to minister to her lonely soul. It's a wonder folks around here let her—"

Nic held up his hand, deciding he'd heard enough of the town gossip. "As you said, this is a tough place to be a woman alone. Maybe it's best she shoots first, parson or no. Keeps others away, right?"

"Right," said Jed slowly.

Nic rose and put his hat on his head. "Thank you, Jed," he said, reaching out his hand. "I'm much obliged for the information, and for your care of my horse."

"Anytime," said the man, shaking his hand. "Come back 'gain and I'll tell ya more about the folks around these parts."

Nic nodded, moving on before Jed took the gesture as encouragement to launch into a new story. He needed to get his supplies and return to the cabin before sundown. Hopefully the Vaughns would be there before he arrived. There'd be time enough for stories later.

Odessa was packing a lunch to take to Bryce that morning and invited Moira to join her. She planned to leave the baby with Cassie, the redheaded neighbor girl who came to help out each day. "We can picnic together, just the four of us," she said, lifting a teasing brow.

"Dess ..."

"Come on, it will be fun. It's not often I get to dine with a potential lawman."

"You don't understand. I'm not even certain he means to stay here in the valley. Maybe he'll move to Westcliffe."

"With the way he looks at you? Come now. Butter this bread. Make yourself useful."

Moira stepped up beside her and did as she bade. Odessa pulled a steaming chicken from the roasting pan and set it on the counter to cool. "There now. I'll cut that up and we can be on our way. Why don't you put that gold dress on that I got you?"

Moira sighed. "Dess, you're not listening. I don't think Daniel and I will be ... together."

Odessa's smile faded and she narrowed her eyes in Moira's direction. She leaned closer and asked in a hushed tone. "Do you not have feelings for Daniel?"

"I do. It's only that ... things are not as simple as they seem."

Odessa paused. "I had so hoped that you might settle down here, both of you. Be a family, give your baby a father."

"It's a lovely dream. But the beautiful valley is blocked by a couple of mountain passes."

"Well," Odessa said, taking her hand, "let's at least get a little closer to the mountains, shall we? Food always draws a man's thoughts together. Remember how Papa was after a meal?"

"It was always the best time to ask him anything," she said with a sigh. Odessa smiled and nodded. "Let's go and see how your man responds to you today after our picnic lunch."

They rose and gathered their supplies together. Odessa checked on Samuel, who was happily playing with Cassie in the nursery. Tabito rode up to the house, two mares saddled and ready for them. "Guess you assumed I'd be coming?" Moira asked her sister. Odessa answered with an impish smile.

They rode down the lane at a leisurely pace and soon reached the fledgling town of Conquistador. Even in the last twenty-four hours, a remarkable amount of work had been done. Three wagons marked Westcliffe Lumber Co. and laden with lumber waited on one side of the street, and three others passed them, their beds now empty as they headed down the rutted road. Swarms of men were working on each site.

"Dess, look," Moira said, placing a hand over her mouth. Two walls were already framed on the charity sanatorium, which would be a twelve-room establishment to start, with a wraparound, screened-in porch for residents to recline on.

"Oh!" Odessa cried happily, clapping her hands together. "At this rate, the building will be ready months before we find our doctor!" She'd placed an advertisement in several journals, looking for doctors to run the establishment. But most of those were not printed yet.

Bryce, eager to get started on the place, refused to wait to build it until a doctor was hired. "If we're going to do it, let's get it done," he'd said. He'd hired a crew of more than a hundred carpenters. First they worked on the snow breaks and stables for the Circle M, as well as new fencing and corrals. By the time they were done with that, the architects had completed their work for Conquistador and supplies had been ordered.

The activity reminded Moira of a busy colony of ants, all carrying lumber on their shoulders or sawing and hammering away. "This town will be completed in weeks."

"I know it." Odessa looked down the street and then the other way. "I don't see Bryce or Daniel. Do you?"

Moira shook her head.

Odessa called out to a man, asking if he had seen Bryce. The man directed them beyond the framework of the two-story mercantile building, built up from what just yesterday had been their dance floor. "He's out with the surveyor," he said.

They rode on in the direction he had pointed and found Bryce, Daniel, the surveyor, and a couple of other men in the fields beyond. They were marking plots of land and streets, for potential homes and other businesses, in case Conquistador ever became more than a tiny town.

Just that morning, Bryce had decided to add a parsonage behind the church. He gave Odessa a sheepish look as they rode up. "May as well plan for success," he said, as he pinned a rope down in the direction the surveyor pointed.

"What will you name the streets, Mr. Mayor?" Odessa teased.

"I don't know," he said, smiling up at her. "Thought I'd ask a writer I know to help come up with them."

"I'd be delighted. Do you have time to stop for lunch?"

"We will make time," Bryce said. "Let's head over to the brook and the big oaks over there."

"I'm sorry, Odessa, but I need to bow out," Daniel hedged, looking toward town. "I'll catch you back at the Circle M."

"Nonsense. Come and eat first. Breakfast was a long time ago," Odessa tried.

"No, thank you," he said firmly, giving her a gentle smile. He tipped his hat to her and vaguely in Moira's direction, then turned and strode away.

"Well," Odessa said with a sniff.

"Dess. Leave it be," Bryce said. "Come, I'll eat enough for two men. And I'll be dining with two of the loveliest ladies in the valley."

Bryce arranged to meet the other men later. Then he and the ladies walked their horses across the plain, dotted with sage and clumps of desertlike grass, to the shady oaks beside the creek. They set out a couple of blankets and their picnic.

Try as she might to enjoy the meal, the smell of food made Moira's stomach roil. She placed a few small items on her plate, and pretended to be engaged in Bryce's updates on the building progress, but her eyes traced across the field to Conquistador, knowing Daniel was there. Did he truly have something he had to attend to? Or was he merely avoiding her?

Odessa gave her a compassionate glance. "Life will go on for you, Moira," she said in a whisper. "Even if Daniel is not a part of it."

Moira dragged her eyes to the trees above them. It was easy for her sister to say that. She had a husband. A child. A ranch to run.

What was ahead for Moira? At least she wasn't penniless. She had her small share of the gold. It would be enough to hold her and her child for years.

Moira looked up to the trees, the huge old oaks spreading thirty feet wide, with branches as thick as her torso. Life would go on, despite drought and wind and fire.

"Moira? *Moira*," Bryce said.

Caught in her daydream, she glanced with surprise at him. He was holding out an envelope to her.

"This came for you," he said.

Absently, she took it from him, her mind still on her future. "Might I ... do you think I might purchase one of the plots of land?" she said. "Up by the creek, to build a house for me and my baby? Or would you prefer I purchase one in Conquistador? Build here?"

Odessa wrapped her arm around Moira's shoulders. "I think it would be good for you to be with us on the ranch. Near us. In case ..."

"In case I'm alone. And need your help," she finished for her. *I can't count on Daniel for that.*

"It's so pretty up by the creek," Odessa went on, ignoring the bitterness of her sister's tone. "You could have the men build you a darling little house. Cozy."

For two, Moira thought forlornly. *Not three.*

Bryce unfolded an architect's drawing and drew Odessa into conversation about the details for the sanatorium, where many would eventually come and seek the cure for consumption at little or no cost.

Feeling like she was intruding, listening in, Moira looked at the letter in her hand and frowned. She knew no one in New York, other than a few people in the opera business. Had one of them tracked her down, hoping she might come to sing?

She wouldn't go, of course, but it was nice to dream of such things. She stood, walked over to the nearest tree, ripped open the envelope, and slipped out a couple sheets of fine linen paper. It had been the sort of stationery her mother had always chosen, with a

deckled edge at the bottom. She unfolded them and hurriedly began
to read.

> *7 July 1888*
>
> *My Dear Miss St. Clair,*
> *   I am writing to you as a heartbroken mother. We never*
> *had the opportunity to meet, but in Gavin's things—*

Moira sat down on the ground. Gavin's mother.

> *—in Gavin's things that were returned to us, I found*
> *paperwork that detailed your business arrangement. We*
> *were aware, of course, that he was your manager, intent*
> *upon seeing you to fame in the West. But until I read his*
> *journal, I did not know that you and he were intimately*
> *involved. It seems, my dear, that he was quite fond of you.*

So *fond* that he chose to abandon her when she declared she was
more than fond of him.

> *His body was returned to us for burial, and soon afterward,*
> *we learned of the "death" of Moira Colorado, famed*
> *songstress, in a tragic fire. We believed you lost as surely as*
> *our dear son was lost to us. But since then, we have read*
> *of the dramatic occurrences at your sister's ranch and the*
> *brief mention of a certain "Moira St. Clair." From Gavin's*
> *journal I was able to piece together that you and Moira*

*Colorado are one and the same. We are more than glad to
know that you did not perish as was reported earlier, and
were sorry indeed to hear of the injuries you suffered—in
the fire, and at the hands of that foul man, Bannock. You
have endured much indeed.*

Moira frowned. Why so effusive and kind? From what Gavin had
said, she'd thought the woman would never accept her as a potential
bride into the Knapp family. She turned the page.

*My dear, please forgive the indelicacy of this letter. In an
effort to know as much as possible about our beloved son's
last months on this earth, we hired a man to discover all he
could. He's been to Leadville and back and brought back
news that Moira Colorado had been pregnant about the
time of Gavin's departure. I know that Gavin cared deeply
for you. Our man even brought back news that you two
may have been married, although he could discover no
legal record of the union. Dare I hope that you still carry
the babe, even after all your suffering? And that the child
is Gavin's?*

Moira's frown deepened.

*As I'm certain Gavin shared with you, we are an old,
prosperous family, here in New York. And yet in the last
year, we have lost both a son and a daughter. Our daughter
was not fortunate enough to bear a child. And so our line,*

*and the potential for our legacy, has come to an end. Except
for this lone child we pray you still carry.*

*Might I dare hope that you would write back to us
or even consider a visit? Perhaps it could coincide with a
return to your audience; Gavin detailed your success in Paris
and London. Why not in New York as well? In any case,
we would appreciate getting to know you, and having the
opportunity to discuss what the future holds for you and
your babe.*

I will await your reply, with a mother's heart.

Sincerely yours,
Francine Knapp

Moira slowly folded the letter and slid it back into the envelope.
The Knapps wanted to know her, and her baby! The shock of that
realization stunned her even as Francine's tone warmed her heart.
Hadn't Odessa told her of how she herself longed for their mother,
wished that Samuel could know his grandmothers?

She glanced again toward Conquistador, Daniel still nowhere in
sight. Still so far from her. And yet this woman, this stranger, wanted
to know her? Wanted to give her baby a family?

Could this be the best choice for her baby ... and her? Perhaps
God was giving her a way out, toward hope?

Nic led Daisy up the steep ravine to the Vaughn place, lit a fire in
the stove, and opened a can of beans with his knife. In a little while

he added a hunk of salt pork to a pan, and after it started to sizzle, poured the beans on top to warm. His mouth watered at the aroma rising from the pan; it had been a day since his last meal. He pulled the beans off before they were hot, unable to wait any longer, and sat down to eat.

It was then that he heard Daisy whinny. He knew by the sound of it that she either sensed or saw another horse. Wearily, he shoved a heaping bite of beans into his mouth and rose. Perhaps the Vaughns were back at last.

He pulled open the door and stared outward. Rays from the setting sun cast a warm glow across the valley below him, then abruptly ended in shadow. Night was soon upon them. The Vaughns were arriving just in time. Nic squinted and peered down the dark ravine. There was a horse, and by the look of it the Vaughn boy, hunched over, moving in deep response to each roll and pull of his mount. He appeared to be barely holding on, as if injured. Where was his father?

Nic frowned in confusion, looking beyond the boy for any sign of trouble, then slowly reached inside for his rifle. But no one appeared behind or before him. The child reached the cabin, and Nic stepped forward to take the reins. The boy's clothes were torn and covered with brambles, his face bruised and dirty. "Everett?" Nic asked.

The child moved dull eyes over to him. And then he collapsed off the horse and into Nic's arms.

Nic carried him into the cabin and laid him upon the bed. He moved to a pail and dipped a ladle for a bit of water, then went back to the bed to lift the child up and ease some water to his dry, parched lips. Everett came to and drank thirstily, saying with a froggy voice, "More, please."

Nic obliged him, then knelt, waiting beside the bed as Everett closed his eyes. After a long moment he seemed to force them open again. Slowly, he looked over at Nic. "You came. Dad said you would. Said he could see it in your eyes."

Nic shifted uneasily. "Where is your dad, Everett?"

Everett looked up at the ceiling. "He's dead," he said dully.

"Dead," Nic repeated in a shocked whisper. "What happened?"

"We supplied up. Dad didn't want to pay Claude's prices in St. Elmo. But on the way here, about a half day out, we met up against two men. Dad sent me running, into the woods. He put up a fight, but, injured as he was, he couldn't match 'em. They came after me, but my mare is fast. And Sinopa showed me how to—"

"Everett," Nic interrupted gently. He sat down on the edge of the bed. "What happened to your dad?"

"I heard three, maybe four shots. And then they took off with our mule and Dad's horse."

"And did you go back to the road?"

Everett nodded as his face clouded with grief. "I went back. I found him. They'd dragged his body to the side of the road." He reached up and wiped a tear from his dirty cheek with the back of his hand. "Didn't even cover him up. Just set him under some brush. He was too heavy for me to lift. I had to leave him—" Another tear dripped from his other eye, and then he sobbed suddenly, as if it had all caught up with him.

He sat up and flung himself into Nic's arms. Nic slowly, awkwardly held the child as he cried for several long minutes. "I'm sorry,

Everett. Your dad was a good man." He sighed and continued to hold the boy as he cried. What was he to do now? Where was the child's nearest kin?

Anger surged through him, and there was a fierce desire to strike out immediately, hunt the two highwaymen down, and beat each one until dead. His heart pounded as he considered the sweet satisfaction of vigilante justice. Why'd they have to kill the boy's father? Why not take his supplies and leave him be?

After a few more minutes, Everett grew slack with sleep. The boy was clearly exhausted. Gently, Nic laid him back down on the bed and covered him with a blanket, and then he strode to the open doorway and stared out at the mountain valley, now deeply steeped in the shadows of twilight. That was when he saw them, Sabine and her Indian. Slowly, he reached for the rifle again, but the two steadily approached, undeterred.

Sabine came to a halt three steps away. Her hair was pulled back in a loose bun, showcasing fine, high cheekbones and wide eyes. She studied him without blinking. "Sinopa said the boy arrived home, but without his father."

What was it to her? Did they intend to jump Vaughn's claim? He checked himself, noting that she seemed to care about the child. *Maybe she has a relationship with Peter. Had* a relationship.

His eyes moved from the woman to the Indian. Sinopa, she'd called him. The same name Everett had referenced. He had an elongated face and a glossy black braid that fell over his shoulder. The Indian stared back at him unflinchingly. Was that accusation in his eyes? Nic tightened his grip on the shotgun and fingered the cool arc of the trigger.

"Everett did get back today. Said his father was jumped by two highwaymen and killed."

Sabine sucked in her breath, looked away from him, and took a couple steps, gazing out to the valley.

"The boy hid and escaped," Nic continued, speaking mostly to Sinopa now, wondering how much English the man spoke. "The men rode off with the mule and Peter's horse. And all their supplies, of course."

"I need to see Everett," Sabine said, moving toward the cabin door.

"No," Nic said, reaching out a hand. "He's asleep. And worn out. Please, let him sleep."

"The boy was certain that Peter was dead?" Sinopa said softly, his English perfect.

Nic nodded. "Said he tried to lift him but couldn't." He leaned closer, not wanting the sleeping boy to wake and hear what they were discussing. "They left him just off the road, under some brush." He looked over to Sabine and saw that grief filled her wide eyes, and wrinkles of concern pleated her forehead. She and Sinopa shared a long, significant glance.

Nic looked down to the ground, embarrassed at his fascination about this odd pair. Trappers had long taken Indian brides, but he'd never seen a white woman befriend an Indian. Was there anything more than friendship between the two? He tapped his heel. It wasn't any of his business.

"The claim is yours, then," Sabine said.

Nic looked up at her, sharply. "Mine? No … it's Everett's."

"In this county, no mine claim can be passed to a minor."

"So that's it?" Nic said with a scoff. He lowered his voice and leaned toward her. "The boy loses everything, just like that?"

"Just like that," she returned grimly. "And you are the first man to enter the property since Peter's death, so by rights, you can lay claim to the mine. But I'd move quickly."

"Me?" He let out a breath of a laugh. "I was only here to help Peter. I'm no miner."

"If you're fool enough to leave," she said, turning to walk away, "I'll take it. But Peter never befriended fools."

CHAPTER FIVE

Nic awakened to find Everett staring at him from his own cot, two feet away. His hands were together under his chin, making him appear the forlorn orphan. Not a smidgen of the imp he had seen in the streets of Gunnison; this was a lost boy, waking to remember his father was long gone.

Nic sighed, swung his legs over the side of the bed, and rubbed his face vigorously. When he opened his eyes, Everett had done the same thing, his knees but a couple inches from his own. He looked up at Nic, as if waiting.

"Look, kid," Nic said, "I know what it feels like to lose family. My brothers—four of them—died. And my mother … my father's gone too. It's rough, having your dad die. But you won't be alone for long. I'll see to it that you reach your kin. Where do they live?"

Everett glanced down at his hands. His nails were black with dirt and a cut on the back of his hand had scabbed over. The boy needed a mother. Attention. Care. "Everett?"

The boy shook his head. "I don't have any. My mother died when I was born. She had kin in Missouri."

"Which city?"

Everett shrugged his shoulders.

Nic swallowed hard. "And your dad?"

"He had no one."

"No brothers? No sisters?"

"Nah. He came across when he was just a little one, with his father from Germany. Dad always said we were just like him and his own dad, all alone in the world, just the two of us." He looked away, toward the stove, his eyes round with sorrow.

"So that grandfather. He's gone too?"

Everett nodded once.

Nic blew out his cheeks and let out another long breath. "Well, there has to be someone, someplace."

But a fear rose in him that this boy had no one left in the world. No one but him.

Nic led Daisy down the dusty street, Everett sitting on her back. Summer had been long and dry here—even the crusted ruts from the wagon wheels of spring had been ground down to an even layer, several inches deep, that clouded up with each footfall. Once it started raining, this place would be a mud pit, Nic thought. He grimaced as he thought about wagons stuck in the muck, men and horses with caked dirt up their legs.

They pulled up outside the sheriff's office, a tiny five-by-eight-foot room with a jail cell in back. No one was in either the office or the cell. "C'mon, Everett," Nic said, leading him out. They went next door to the St. Elmo Mercantile, leaving Daisy tied to the post in front of the sheriff's office.

The door opened with the jangle of a bell, and a middle-aged man he assumed was the proprietor climbed down a stepladder. "Can I help you, sir?"

"Name's Dominic St. Clair," he said, reaching across the counter. "Friends call me Nic."

"Pleasure to meet you, Nic," he said. "I'm Claude O'Connor." The man was about Nic's height, with a handlebar mustache and crisp white shirt rolled at the sleeves. He looked down at the boy. "Why, Everett, what are you doing in town?"

"He's with me," Nic put in. "We're needing to see the sheriff. Do you know where he is?"

Claude looked from Nic to the boy and back again. "This time of day he's likely up at the stables, yammering with Jed, sharing a cup of coffee." He paused. "Everything all right?"

"No, it's not," Nic said simply, guiding the boy out the door again. They walked the two blocks to the stables. Jed watched his approach, then nodded in their direction. A thin, pale-skinned man with red hair—far too elegant in appearance to be a sheriff—turned their way and straightened. "So you're the newcomer," he said, reaching out a hand. "I'm the sheriff, Drew Nelson."

"Pleased to meet you, Sheriff," Nic said. He introduced himself and watched as the man recognized Everett. "Everett and I have something to tell you. Care to step on over to your office?"

"Sure, sure," said the man, who nodded farewell to the stable keeper.

They walked across the graying boards of the walk to his office, entered, then sat down in two chairs, across the desk from the sheriff.

There was a long, awkward silence. Nic looked to the boy, saw he was on the verge of tears, and told the sheriff what had happened to Peter Vaughn.

The sheriff's red eyebrows dropped lower and lower as Nic went on. He swallowed hard and then looked to Everett. "I'm sorry, son. Your dad was a fine man. A friend I'll miss."

Everett nodded, tears washing down his face. "Me too."

"I bet, I bet. Tell me, boy, do you think you would recognize these men if you saw them again?"

"I–I think so."

Sheriff Nelson rose and went to the corner filing cabinet and pulled a stack of posters from on top. "Look through those, would you? See if any of them are the men you saw."

Everett did as he bade, shuffling through the first ten in rapid succession. On the eleventh he paused, and seemed to hold his breath.

"Everett?" Sheriff Nelson asked.

"Him. He was there." The sheriff looked from the boy over to Nic, then back again. "See if there are any others in that stack."

Nic took the poster from the boy as he continued to look through the remaining stack. The picture was of a tall brown-haired man with a long chin and handlebar mustache, somewhat similar to the mercantile man's. *Chandler Robinson, wanted in Fort Collins and Denver for robbery and murder. Three-hundred-dollar reward, dead or alive.* Dead or alive. Everett reached the end of the stack and shook his head. "No more." He sniffed, handing the rest back across the desk.

"Well, it's something, son," Sheriff Nelson said. "If we find this man, we can find his companion. They'll come to justice. I'll see to it myself."

Everett nodded. Justice was precious little comfort for a grieving son, Nic decided. But it was something.

"I promised Everett we'd get him to kin," Nic said. "Do you know of any family?"

The sheriff sat back in his chair and considered. After a long moment, he shook his head. "The Vaughns have been here since Everett was just a baby. I don't remember hearing Peter talk about any kin—at least not in Colorado."

"No visitors? No letters? Some cousin Everett's too young to remember?"

"I don't think so. But we could check with the postmaster." He paused a moment, fiddling with a sheet on his desk, before looking Nic in the eye. "How did you come to meet up with the Vaughns, Mr. St. Clair?"

Was that a note of suspicion in his voice, heavy in the pause of his sentence? Nic didn't blame the sheriff, with him turning up at the same time Peter turned up dead. "Peter came down to Gunnison looking for help at his mine. Said he'd hit some quality ore, but he was laid up from the accident. Felt he couldn't carry on without a partner. Offered me half of the earnings."

Sheriff Nelson studied him as he spoke, then looked to Everett. "That the truth, son, the best you know it?"

Everett nodded, wiping more tears from his cheek. "Yeah."

Sheriff Nelson nodded slowly and then looked to Nic. "Sorry, friend. Can't be too careful when there's a gold mine involved."

"I understand. Listen, I'm not much of a miner. I think I'll be shoving off since Peter's not here to work it with me."

Everett's head came up, and he stared at Nic in obvious alarm.

Nic ignored him. "Is there someone in town who can take the boy? A woman who can properly see to his care? A clergyman?"

"No!" Everett shouted, rising to his feet, his small hands in fists at his side. "No! My dad asked you to work the mine with him. He's not here. But I'm here! I'll help you. You promised. You *promised.*"

Nic sighed. "I didn't promise, Everett. You said yourself you didn't think I was coming. And I'm not the father type—"

"I don't need a father. Or a mother!" The boy looked over to the sheriff and back to Nic. "My dad's dead. That means I have to man up. I'll work the mine with you. I will. Please, Nic, don't leave. Not now! My dad … all he wanted was to strike gold, and then he did, but then there was the cave-in. You gotta help me. We gotta see it through."

Nic frowned. "Everett, listen. I came to your place against my better judgment. I was counting on your dad to teach me what it meant to be a miner. Promising vein or not, I've never dug, not a day in my life. I'm not going in there without another full-grown man. I'd be a fool."

"My dad chose *you*. We talked to lots of men in Gunnison. But you were the only one he asked. So you might not have thought it was a good idea. But my *dad* did."

He was the only one Peter had asked?

Nic clamped his lips shut. To argue against the child was like arguing with the dead. Futile. Dishonoring Peter's memory, the last thing Everett needed.

"By rights, you could claim the mine," the sheriff said casually to Nic. "There aren't many claims producing quality ore that a man can get to on his own. Most are the big operations, with manpower and machinery that can go thousands of feet. I wouldn't walk away from it. Why not give it a week and see how it goes?"

"That's crazy," Nic said, shaking his head. "The mine should go to Everett. Then he could sell it to someone else, use the funds for a college education or something."

"Everett's too young to inherit the claim."

"So I've heard."

"Only way around it is if you pull out that ore, sell it, or claim it and sell interest in it. Give a portion to Everett, here, in exchange for his help. That'd honor his daddy."

"So I can get myself injured or killed like Peter?"

Both the sheriff and the boy stilled. Once more, Nic wished he could take back his words.

"It doesn't belong to me," Nic said in a conciliatory tone. "It'd feel like stealing."

"Peter offered you half the claim. Gambler's luck, arriving to find you might get more." The sheriff stared at him, hard, as if he were crazy even to think of leaving, but then shrugged his shoulders. "As for folks who could take Everett in, I'm afraid there aren't any. The preacher has a brood of his own. They're bursting at the seams over at the parsonage. Any other women are—" his voice dropped—"not who you'd want the child to be living with."

"Except Sabine," Everett said.

The sheriff looked to him. "Think she'd take you?"

"Maybe," he said.

"And you'd want to stay with her?"

"Maybe," the boy repeated.

The sheriff cocked a brow and glanced at Nic. "It's Sabine," he said, tilting his head to one side, "or I'm afraid it's the orphanage down in Buena Vista."

"Orphanage!" Everett blurted. "No, no, no." He looked over at

Nic with pleading eyes. "Give it a week. Please. Let me show you what I know. See what you think of the work. Please. In honor of my dad."

Nic stared at the child, then closed his eyes and let out a deep breath. What had he gotten himself into?

He puffed out his cheeks, exhaled sharply, and said, "You know enough? To show me the ropes?"

"I know enough."

"Gold mining isn't hard to figure out," the sheriff said. "Just hard work."

Nic knew he couldn't leave, not without giving Everett at least this. "One week."

The boy's eyes lit up.

Nic put up a hand. "Calm yourself. You understand that after a week, I might be taking you down to Buena Vista? And I don't want to be dragging you along, kicking and screaming. I give it a shot. But that's all I'm promising. Deal?"

Everett took his hand and pumped it.

"I'd stop at the county assessor's office on your way out, Nic," the sheriff said. "Tell him you're laying claim to the Vaughn mine." He paused to put up his hands in defense. "However temporary it may be. Tell him to talk to me if he has any questions. But do make it official before you leave." He cocked his head to one side. "Town this size, news will travel fast. And Peter—he was onto something special up in the Gulch. There are folks who won't hesitate to move on it if you don't."

Nic stood and shook his hand. "I'll do it, but I still don't feel right about it."

The sheriff dropped his hand and hooked it around his gun belt.

"You, it seems, are the only way Everett here will ever see any portion of the profits that come out of that mine. Peter set out looking for an honest partner. I hope he found one."

"May I help you find something?" Claude O'Connor asked at the mercantile.

Nic gave him a single nod and looked down at Everett. "Outfitting for a week's work, up at our claim."

Claude looked from him to the boy.

"My dad's passed on," Everett put in, answering the unspoken question.

Claude's mouth dropped open and then he abruptly shut it. "I'm sorry, boy. He was a fine man, a fine man." He didn't ask for details; Nic didn't choose to give them to him.

Everett nodded and looked to the floor.

"I can outfit most miners with anything they need," Claude said, returning his attention to Nic.

"Bet you can," Nic said, picking up a pail and glancing at the tag, then him. "Especially at these prices."

"You know how it goes," Claude said, ignoring his jibe. "I have to pay to get it shipped from the East and then up here via railroad."

"I know how it goes when you're one of the few games in town," Nic said with a small smile. He didn't begrudge the man his good fortune, but he suddenly wished he had won the deed to the St. Elmo Merc—even if he had sworn off retail work forever and ever, amen—rather than falling into a mine claim. Outfitting the mine would cost a fair fortune up here. Not that he had much choice. A trip to Gunnison would take the week he'd promised Everett. "I need sacks of flour, sugar, coffee, baking powder, soda, and salt," he said.

Claude came around the corner and began fetching the items, then stacking them on the counter. "What else?"

"Oil, wicking cloth, a new pick, shovel, and this here triple-priced pail." He moved to one of the display bins as the proprietor gathered the rest of his list. To the pile, Nic added a jar of preserves, four jars of applesauce, a cured ham covered in netting, a tin of sardines, two tins of biscuits, a box of shotgun bullets, and after a moment's consideration, peppercorns. His time in South America had left him with a taste for heat in his food. "Do you have any eggs?"

"Came in this morning," Claude said. "Old man Grover brings them to me every other day or so."

Nic perused the eggs, nestled in dried prairie grass. "I'll take four. Haven't had eggs in … some time."

"Got a pan up there to fry them in?"

"Think so," Nic said, remembering the inside of the spare cabin. He looked over at Everett, and the boy nodded. "I'll take another blanket too." He ran his hands over the thick wool of a Hudson's Bay striped blanket and then over a less expensive one next to it. "I don't know how Everett and Peter have made it so long with what they have," he said, handing the more expensive one to the merchant. Even in summer, these mountains could be cold. Snow often fell atop the highest peaks, given a good storm.

"Dad bought a couple more, down in Gunnison," Everett defended.

Nic considered him, and nodded. He'd have to watch himself. Not say anything disparaging about the boy's dad.

"That'll do it?" Claude asked.

"Better stop there, or I'll owe you my horse too, and I need her to get all this stuff up to the claim."

Claude smiled and began ringing up the purchase on his cast-brass register. Nic leaned over and studied the keys. "Didn't have anything so fancy when I ran a shop a few years ago."

"Ah, so you were a merchant once, eh?"

"For a short time. Didn't suit me."

"What sort of store? If you don't mind me asking."

"A book shop. My father was a publisher."

"Oh? Which one? We carry some books in back—"

"St. Clair Press. It was sold a few years ago."

"I remember St. Clair Press. Fine operation, fine publications."

Nic nodded, not really caring to get into a lengthy conversation about the place. It had been his father's business, not his.

"So a publisher's son, once a merchant, now a miner?"

"And a few things in between," Nic said with a small smile. "What do I owe you?" he asked, cutting off Claude's next question.

"Thirty-nine dollars and twenty-five cents," he said, looking at his register.

Nic coughed. Thirty-nine dollars. He was worried about arriving at Odessa's with nothing in his pockets. But he was about to spend most of what he had left.

Claude, seeming to note his hesitation, said, "You know, I do a good deal of grubstaking around here. In exchange for a portion of the mine's profits, you can take all this out of here now, without paying me a cent."

Nic glanced at Everett. The boy gave him a tiny shake of the head. Claude was making an offer because he knew it was a reasonable risk.

Nic shrugged. "We'd better be pulling gold out of your dad's mine soon if we care to eat anything but venison, eh?" *Or earn back enough money to pay me back.*

Claude raised a brow as he collected Nic's carefully counted cash. "And most of the deer and elk are pretty well hunted out 'round here. Don't go counting on those. Rabbits, squirrel, we still have a fair number of those." He studied him a moment. "But you won't be hunting much, with a mine to dig."

"Probably right," Nic said. He gathered an armful of goods, went to put them on the horse, and stood back. "We'll have to lead her up," he said to Everett. "No room for us." He glanced at the sky, filling with dark gray billowing thunderheads. "We'd better hurry if we want to beat that. I'll be right back."

Claude handed the egg basket to Nic, but he held onto one handle when Nic reached for it. "Nic, these hills have given a fair number of boys some serious trouble. You watch yourself now, you hear me?"

Nic gave him a smile, and he finally released the egg basket. "Hopefully I'm up for the task."

Claude shook his head and began wiping the counter again. "You just watch yourself. I can't afford to lose a good new customer like you." He smiled then, but his eyes were on Everett, who waited on the front porch. The smile quickly faded. "That boy out there's counting on you, now."

Nic stifled a sigh. "I'll watch myself," he said gruffly. He turned and left the mercantile then, a shroud of worry covering him. It felt heavier than a wet blanket in a rainstorm. Which, he thought grimly, staring at the sky and then his new Hudson's Bay, he might soon be wearing.

The claim was a good hour's hike up the narrow, serpentine trail that wove in and out of low-lying scrub oak and groves of aspen and fir—what the locals referred to as the Gulch. In about an hour they reached the creek, Nic ever conscious of the rumbling thunder that drew nearer and nearer. He looked over his shoulder once and saw a fierce bolt of lightning cascade down from the sky. It was followed by a crack of thunder that rumbled in his chest. Had anyone been struck by lightning up here?

The wind came up then, huge gusts that threatened to push them to their knees. The lightning and thunder increased, and then fat raindrops came down, splattering the dry forest and Nic and Everett too. Nic ignored the rain, knowing he could change when he reached the cabin. And his hat kept his head and face dry for the most part. He pulled the brim lower, aware that the wind threatened to send it down the mountainside, and concentrated on each footfall. Already, the path was becoming slick in places.

Soaked through, Everett slipped and fell to his knees. Nic reached down to help him up, but the boy shook off his hand. He was crying again.

Nic glanced back at Daisy, who had her head down, as if she disliked the rain. She was a good mount; nothing pretty to look at, but strong and sure. She easily picked her way forward, finding rocks and flats that Nic wished he had seen himself. He gave her more lead, giving her freedom to take the time she needed.

A bolt of lightning struck then, so close it made his hair stand on end. He felt the jolt of its power from his toes to his scalp, and he instinctively ducked into a ball, right before a second bolt stabbed downward. He let out a gasp as Daisy yanked the reins from his hand, rearing in fear, and then dashed into the creek bed and up ahead of him. She crossed the stream and ran into the trees. He ran through the stream and after her. But she disappeared among the trees, the fading light of afternoon growing dim now. Nic took off his hat, swore, and hit his thigh with it. "Thirty-nine dollars of supplies and she's run off?" he cried.

He remembered Everett then, and glanced over at the boy. He had crossed the stream too, and stared at him, his eyes round with fear.

Nic shook his head and looked up the streambed again, searching for any sign of his horse. He moved upward alongside the stream, glad at least that the lightning seemed to be moving on, the thunder growing more distant.

He hoped Daisy would stop at the clearing by the mine, but it wasn't likely. Nic sighed; he was sure he'd be tracking her come sunup. He fell then, his boots filling with the rushing water. He swore and picked up a rock to throw with fury at the trees. "C'mon!" he cried at no one in particular. Or maybe at God. Only God could be this mean and spiteful.

"Get away from the water," called a man's voice.

Nic glanced up in surprise and saw the Indian, Sabine's Indian, across the stream from him. He scoffed and picked up his drenched boots. "What's it to you if I choose to soak my boots in the stream?" he said with a humorless laugh. "What's it to me?" he added, throwing his hands up.

Everett began clambering over boulders, immediately obeying Sinopa, which made Nic unaccountably irritated. The Indian hadn't signed on for temporary custody—he had.

"Get away from the stream!" Sinopa said to him again, gesturing.

"Do as he says!" Everett shouted.

"Now," the man said.

Nic frowned. "I'm not in the stream! I'm beside it." He was a free man, no longer a sailor under a captain's command. And this man's tone was entirely too close to the captain's…. "Leave me be," he said, staring at the tall brave.

The man straightened and stared back, his mouth in a grim line. Everett was panting, looking between them in confusion.

Nic heard it then. The rumble of what sounded like a cascade. The crack of breaking tree branches, tumbling rocks. He looked up and saw a white mass of water rushing down the creek bed. *Flash flood.* He stood, turned, scrambled for a handhold, missed. The water hit him, and he tumbled feet over head, over twice before hitting a boulder. His breath left him in a whoosh, and he turned to his side, gasping for breath that would not come. White flashing pain threatened to make him pass out.

He was slipping, giving into the torrent of water that pounded against his chest. He tried to gain purchase with his boots, but they only slid off the slick rock beneath him.

Then Sinopa was there beside him. He reached out a hand. "Come out of the stream," he said for the third time.

And this time, Nic reached out.

Moira breathed a sigh of relief when she found him in the stables, mucking stalls. She hadn't seen him at breakfast and was afraid to ask after him, afraid for so many reasons.... But it was time to be brave. Time to try to trust. She couldn't let him leave. Not the way it stood between them, at least.

She wrinkled her nose and then pushed herself forward. Gradually she was becoming more accustomed to the odors that were a part of life on the Circle M—musky sweat, freshly cut hay, overturned earth, and manure were all somehow washed clean by the wind that whistled down the mountains or the mossy scent of the creek. When had that happened, exactly? she wondered. She had been so absorbed with healing from her burns, and Daniel's attentions, and learning to live alongside Odessa again, that she'd barely noticed.

He rose up and regarded her, one hand perched on the top of the pitchfork, the other raised to wipe his forehead of sweat.

She reached out and held on to the nearest post, suddenly tongue-tied.

Still, he waited, his lips parted, panting slightly from exertion. His brown eyes studied her, shifting back and forth as if he hoped to read her thoughts.

"You haven't left yet," she said finally, lamely, wishing she were braver.

"No, I haven't." Was that a touch of tenderness at the corners of his eyes? "Can't seem to make myself go. But they're waiting on me, Moira. I've given them my yes."

Moira swallowed hard. "Daniel, I, uh …" She forced her eyes up again to meet his gaze. "I don't want you to. Go, I mean."

He stilled and remained silent for a couple of breaths. "Why not, Moira?"

"Because ... because of ... whatever *this* is, between you and me."

There. That was hope that sparked in his eyes, just for a moment.

He sighed and then stepped forward. "Can you live with the questions?" he asked softly.

"That depends," she said, shifting nervously. "Are you going to answer them?"

Slowly, he reached up a hand to her face. She tried to step away, realizing he meant to lift her scarf, see her wounds. He reached out and grabbed her arm—not in a rough way, only with a touch that said *stay*.

"Don't. Don't, Daniel."

He dropped his hand. "Perhaps a break would be good for us both, Moira. For me to put my demons to rest. For you to do the same." He stepped closer to her, not touching her, but caressing her with his eyes.

She took a step back, unable to withstand the mounting intense pressure of his gaze. To say nothing of his words. He was going away. He'd made his decision. Why would he not just speak plainly? And who was he to judge her?

"I won't wait for you," she said with a small shake of her head, taking another step away.

He frowned. "Moira—"

"I might go away myself. Leave this place." He needn't know she spoke of a visit only, not a move. She wanted to slash at him, hurt him as he was hurting her.

"You can't leave," he said, stepping forward as she continued to back away. "Not with the baby coming. You need to be here, with Odessa. And Bryce."

With Odessa. Bryce.

But not you.

"Good-bye, Daniel." With that, she turned on her heel and fled the stables.

CHAPTER SIX

In the rain Nic followed the man to the door of Sabine's cabin, wincing with each step. He'd bruised his ankle in the creek, but his shoulder hurt far worse than even his leg. It screamed in agony, though he did his best not to let the pain show on his face.

The storm let up, and Nic realized there was still a fair amount of evening left. Outside, ten paces from the cabin, Daisy was tied to a tree. Nic glanced with relief from the horse to his guide. "You found her?"

"Sabine found her," he replied. Nic studied him for a moment. The man, about his age, had the faintest of accents. He might've been born in Philadelphia as much as the Montana Territory. "She sent me to find you."

"Good thing you did." They shared a long look. Nic hoped it conveyed his appreciation. No telling what would've happened to him if the Indian hadn't come along.... He shifted slightly, noting that even the weight of his clothing hurt his shoulder.

Sabine opened the door then, but didn't invite them in. She came outside, closing the door behind her, before moving to Everett and pulling him into her arms. The boy allowed it. After a moment, she pulled away and cradled the child's face in her small hands. "Sinopa found your father's body," she said slowly, soberly. "I've tended to him. He's inside. We need to bury him, Everett. But first, you need to go in and say good-bye."

Tears flowed down the boy's cheeks, and she pulled him to her again, her face a mask of anguish as he sobbed. They stood there for a couple of long minutes, and Nic had to turn away. Perhaps Everett was right … Sabine might take him in. He studied her, how her hair fell in slight waves over her shoulder, the fine line of her straight nose, the curve of her bottom lip. And then he saw Sinopa staring at him.

He was not looking at Nic as a jealous lover, but more as a protective guardian. *Tread very, very carefully*, his black eyes said.

When he glanced back to Sabine, she was striding toward him. He fought the urge to take a step back, so swiftly did she move. Now that she wasn't standing above him on a hillside, wielding a shotgun, he noted she was short, a few inches shorter than he. She reached up toward his shoulder and this time he did take a step back.

Her hand hovered in the air where his shoulder had been, and her eyes shifted to meet his. "Let me see it," she said, lifting her chin as if calling the shoulder back beneath her hand. "I think it's dislocated."

He realized she was right. It had happened a couple times before to him, in the ring.

"We can reset it," she said, looking over to Sinopa. Behind her, Everett was slowly entering the cabin door, hovering there, peering inside. She followed his glance. "In back, so the boy doesn't hear you cry out."

Nic looked from her to the Indian. Was it a trap? The means to lay claim to the mine? "No," he said. "I'll do it myself." He strode over to the corner of the porch and before he could think better of it, positioned himself, then made a practiced move, twisting the upper arm just so until it corkscrewed back into the socket. He staggered backward, wondering for a moment if he was about to pass out. But then his vision cleared. The pain was still there—but lessened now.

Sabine studied him for a long moment, nonplussed. "I could've done that and caused you far less pain."

"Or you could have put a bullet in my head."

"Is that what you think of us? That we're murderers, ready to pounce on Peter's mine?" she asked, amusement suddenly in her wide brown eyes. She smiled over at Sinopa. "Did he not just save you from a flash flood?"

Nic sighed and looked up into the darkening sky. He glanced back to her. "I don't know what to think. In the space of twenty-four hours I've learned that my partner in a mine, a mine I've yet to *enter*, is *dead*, leaving me a *boy* with no kin behind; that the mine is promising enough for O'Connor to offer to grubstake me; that my *neighbor* is a handsome woman who's more likely to *shoot* me than offer me supper; that a wise man doesn't hover about in the ravine during a rainstorm. Oh, and that I seem to have walked into a whole mess of expectation when I asked for *none* of it." He waved his hand across the air in a cutting motion. "None of it," he repeated.

She studied him a moment longer. "I don't want your mine, St. Clair. My only interest in you is that you might be of help to the child. He needs you to help him get that ore out, give him a start in life, with his father gone."

Nic let out a breathless laugh. "Why me?" He pointed to the cabin over her shoulder. "I didn't even know that child until a week ago!"

"Keep your voice down," she said tightly. Sinopa took a step forward and she lifted a hand up, as if sensing his approach from behind her.

Was she afraid? Of Nic? Nic frowned in confusion. No woman had ever been afraid of him. He thought back. She'd been married to—

"Everett is at an age," she said in her smooth, low tone, "that he needs a man to show him how to be a man. I would do him little good."

"I don't know about that," he said, forcing his own voice an octave lower, calmer. "That child has never had a mother, as far as I understand it. And why can't Sinopa—"

"Sinopa is soon off again. He's a trapper, and these mountains have long been trapped out." She shook her head and clenched her lips. "It is best the boy remains with you. He will be missing his father. When school begins in a month, I'll take him to town with me."

"You–you're the schoolmarm?" He barely contained his laugh.

"I am." She moved slightly, a vague, subtle change. Defensiveness. Nic had spent enough time in the ring to know it anywhere. He tried to recover his composure.

"Well … well," he sputtered, trying to figure out a way to explain his response, "you're … a long way from town." There. That covered his tracks.

She studied him a moment longer, and Nic shifted uneasily. "I live here through the fall, then head down come the first real snows."

Nic hesitated. He didn't know if he'd like being up here in the Gulch, all by himself all winter. He'd seen the schoolhouse. It was across the creek from the main portion of town, in a tall white building. "So … you just give up on your mine come winter? I thought the most stalwart miners worked all winter long."

It was her turn to cover a wry smile. "I'm not a miner. I am here for this.…" She paused, gestured behind him, as if the mountains beyond told him what she wanted to say, then turned and walked into the cabin, Sinopa right behind her.

Nic glanced over his shoulder. It was getting darker by the minute, a few of the brightest stars now visible, the silhouette of the mountains appearing black against the sky's purple. She stayed here because of the view?

He took a few steps, looking back toward the cabin, and then saw Sabine through the open doorway with her arm draped around Everett's shoulders, staring downward alongside him. Probably at Peter's forever-still body, stretched out on the floor.

Nic tried to cut short his shiver.

Who were these people to him? Why not walk away? Why did he feel this strange pull of responsibility, kinship, connection? If he left now, he could get down to town and spend the night, then head out in the morning. He'd be to Odessa's by tomorrow night, or the next day for sure.

He turned and took a few steps toward Daisy, who was still tied to a post out in front of the cabin. If he left now, before Everett or even Sabine was depending on him, it would be better for all of them. Who was he to take on a kid? A mine? All he'd been looking for was work with a promising glimpse of a coming payout. Without Peter, there was no way, no way he could do it. He'd get to town, find a boxing match. Take on a few rounds, win, and at least have some money in his pocket when he left town.

He reached for Daisy's reins and glanced up, to see if his neighbors were watching him out the window. But they weren't. Sinopa stood by the fireplace, staring at the flames. Everett was in Sabine's arms sobbing—he could see the scene now, through the thick panes of glass—as she stroked his small back and held him tight.

Nic stilled, transfixed. There was something about her anguished look, the child's grief that kept him from moving. He remembered crying like that, once. When was the last time?

When his father came to him and told him that his mother was gone. Dead in childbirth.

Father had died himself that day, in a way. It was too much—too much for all of them. But for his father, after four other St. Clair children had been taken by the White Death, it was as if he was just one nail short of a finished coffin. Ever after, his eyes were weary, his last real action to send his remaining children West to chase the cure for Odessa. That action had thrown all three of them on a radically different course than what might have been taken if they had stayed home in Philadelphia. A course that had led Nic to Europe and back, down to the islands and South America, all the way here, back to Colorado. Here, to this mining town. Here. To the Gulch.

He looked down at the toes of his boots, catching the light of the cabin's lamps, and then back inside. Everett pulled away, looked up into Sabine's face and nodded to whatever she had said. He used the back of his hand to rub his dripping nose and then brushed away the tears.

Nic swallowed hard. He couldn't leave them. Not yet. He'd give the mine a week, to see if it was as promising as Peter had made it sound—and fulfill his promise to Everett. He'd find Everett a good home. Surely here, or in neighboring Alpine, there would be someone to take the boy. If need be, Buena Vista was only a few hours away. Then he could move on and find out where this course would take him next.

Daniel was eating breakfast at the table with the men—the only meal served in the main house other than Sunday dinner—when he heard horses riding hard down the lane. From the rumble, there had to be four or more. He glanced at Bryce, then Moira, who was standing by the stove. He rose, wiping his mouth on a napkin. He and Bryce walked down the hallway and through the parlor to the front porch, with several of the other men behind them. Outside in the back, the sunrise was just turning the Sangre de Cristos a deep pink.

It was Mr. Weaver, from Westcliffe, along with several young men. All had gun belts on.

"Is there a problem, Weaver?" Bryce asked.

The men stayed in their saddles.

"Bank was robbed last night," Mr. Weaver said. "These here are three deputies we've hired." He turned his face toward Daniel. "I know I told you that you could wait a week. But we need you in town now, Daniel. The people won't wait any longer."

Bryce, Odessa, and Moira looked at Daniel. He had said nothing, merely reached out a hand to Bryce. "I've thought long and hard on this, Bryce, I appreciate the work here, but as you said, I'd be good at this."

Bryce took his hand and shook it, but his eyes flitted to Moira. She took a step forward.

The others, sensing the tension between them, moved back into the house. The deputies and Mr. Weaver moved off a few respectful paces.

Daniel took Moira's arm and tugged her around the corner of the porch.

She pulled out of his grip. "Stop it. Don't touch me."

"Moira, I have to do this."

"You don't have to do anything. You are choosing to do this. Choosing to leave me. Choosing to put yourself in danger."

He clamped his lips shut and slowly placed his hat on his head. "I'm sorry this hurts you. It wasn't my intention to ever hurt you."

He regretted not finding the right time, the right way to tell her why he must do this. But deep down, he knew she would have objected to him taking the sheriff's job regardless of when she found out. He needed to see this through, resolve the pain that had filled his heart for years.

And the only way to do that was to track down his wife's remaining killer.

CHAPTER SEVEN

Daniel and his deputies tracked the bank robbers to the mountains of New Mexico, but the outlaws made it onto a train there, or so eyewitnesses said, bound for the border. All they could do was telegraph ahead to U.S. Marshals near the Mexico line, but they held out little hope. Lawmen were fewer and farther between, the farther one traveled south.

They began the slow trek back over the Raton Pass, aware that both their mounts and they were weary. In the bustling town of Trinidad they ate a hearty dinner, checked into the hotel, and fell into their beds. The next morning they headed out, hoping to make it to Walsenburg by nightfall. The road was dry, and a hot wind off the mountains to the west blew dust and grit against them, coating one side of their horses. Five stagecoaches passed them during the course of the morning—two headed south, three north—but there was not another soul on the road.

At lunchtime, they paused beside the Apishapa River, little more than the muddy, caked remains common to lesser Colorado waterways in August, and ate venison jerky, bread, and dried fruit. Daniel shook his canteen. "Careful with your water rations, boys," he said. "The next river might not be even this wet," he said, gesturing down to the riverbed.

He looked about at the deputies, all former miners, weary of the drudgery in the Silver Cliff mine, all young enough to consider the job of deputy glamorous. He knew they would vie to be in his position in a heartbeat. There was a redheaded man, Cleveland, sturdy and broad shouldered. Bret had sandy brown hair and a lisp when he spoke, which wasn't often, but he had a wicked draw and better aim. Glen had darker brown hair and steady eyes, taking in everything they passed, always able to recall details that left the others in awe. They'd made a game of it, trying to trick him to pass the time. Never did they stump him.

"So, Sheriff," Glen said, eying Daniel carefully. "What made you leave that pretty girl on the ranch and come out for this?" He waved about.

"Had something I needed to do." Daniel took a bite of jerky and chewed slowly.

"Care to share it?"

"Not yet." He clamped his lips shut.

"Must be important, if you were willing to leave that pretty Miss St. Clair behind you for it."

Daniel met his dark eyes for a moment, letting him know he'd crossed the line. "It is."

Glen pursed his lips and nodded, fiddling with a dried apricot in his dust-encrusted fingers. "Is she your sweetheart?"

Daniel cocked his head and started at him. "Is there something you want to say?"

Glen cocked his head too and winced, as if what he had to say pained him. "Only that if I had a sweetheart on the Circle M, I'd keep a close eye on her."

"And why's that?"

"Plenty of men out there to take my place, for one," he said. "And then there's the small matter of the St. Clair's conquistador gold. Everyone knows how that little town is getting built. And that's only a small portion of their wealth."

"What of it?"

Glen pursed his lips again and raised his eyebrows. "These mountains are full of greedy men. And plenty more than willing to glean the fields after the harvest."

Slowly, carefully, Daniel rose to his feet, his fists clenched. "Are you threatening the St. Clairs?"

Glen raised his hands, fingers splayed, and tucked his chin to his chest in submission. "Not me, boss. Not me. I have a job and I'm becoming partial to it. I'm talking about the bad guys."

Daniel drew in a long breath through his nostrils and let it out. Slowly, he uncurled his fingers. "Bryce is a good man. A wise man. He has a guard 'round the clock out there. He won't be taken by surprise again."

Bret chewed his apricot and then put in, "It only takes a moment to grab someone. Plenty of people know about the gold. And they might think it easier to kidnap a person and demand a ransom, once hidden, rather than rob a bank in the center of town and be chased all the way to Mexico. We'll need to keep an eye out toward the Circle M."

Daniel bit the inside of his cheek, remembering Odessa and Moira, riding out to Conquistador. They'd been on ranch property the whole time. Probably within sight of ranch hands most of the way. But Bret was right. It'd only take a moment. And they were all becoming a bit more lax.

No. These were just the idle thoughts of lawmen too long on a dry, dusty road. And he was willing to entertain them because of what had happened to Mary.

"Come on, mount up," Daniel said, turning on his heel. "I want to make Walsenburg before sundown. Maybe even Farisita."

Nic placed the shovelful of dirt in the bucket of the wheelbarrow and straightened, wincing in pain. He rubbed his shoulder; even after all these days, it was still sore. "This reminds me of shoveling coal in the steam engine of a ship," he grumbled to Everett.

Everett glanced back at him. There were two lamps that lit his face, one on either side of him, and he was chiseling out rock on either side of a section about the size of Nic's fist, riddled with gold dust. "You were on a ship?"

"Yes, one bound from South America."

"South America? That's a long way from home."

"Yes, it is."

He went back to tapping away rock, picking each piece up to examine it before putting it in either a slough or keep pile. "What were you doing down there?"

"Running from home."

Everett leaned against the rock face, so he could see Nic. "Why'd you want to do that?"

Nic sighed and turned away, digging into the pile of dirt again with the front end of his shovel. "I don't rightly know." He dumped a load into the wheelbarrow and sliced into the rocky heap again. "I suppose I was like a candlewick half bent on burning up—" he paused to dump his load and look to the boy—"and half bent on not burning up."

"It's hard to do both," Everett said.

Nic smiled. "You're right about that." He moved over to the boy and offered him a hand up.

"Where'd you live?" Everett asked, brushing off his trousers. It was futile. The mine coated everything in dirt just as clearly as the steam room on the ship had left Nic covered in soot. Every night they heated water from the stream and bathed.

"Buenos Aires," he said.

"Buenos, where?"

"Buenos Aires, in Brazil," he said.

"What were you doing there?"

Nic looked up the shaft to see how much daylight they had left. Fifty feet up, there was an oval opening, and streaks of peach lined high, thin clouds. "Let's call it a day. Get cleaned up. Make some grub."

Everett set aside his pick, blew out the lamps, and followed him to the rough ladder. They began climbing. "What were you doing in Brazil?" the boy asked him again.

"Fighting."

"Fighting? Who? Why?"

Nic sighed and reached for the next rung and then the next before he answered. "I was fighting in the ring. For money."

The boy was silent as they climbed the rest of the way up. Who was he to show a child how to grow up into a man? It was untenable, this situation. Yesterday, he'd just about decided to drop Everett at Sabine's and head toward Westcliffe, when they took in the first bag of gold dust down to Claude's. Turned out, they had pulled more than a hundred dollars worth of ore out in the last five days. Everett had grinned so widely at him, the first smile he'd seen from the child since his dad passed; Nic hadn't the heart to follow through on his plans. Not to mention that he was curious to see just how long this vein would run.

He felt better, clearer headed, the higher he climbed. Being down in that hole was the worst. He couldn't imagine what it was like to have been Peter, in the middle of a cave-in, hurt, wondering where his boy was, if he was okay. Nic knew he was going overboard with the braces, slowing down the rate they could be pulling ore, but there was no way he'd die down in that hole. Not if he could help it anyway.

Nic reached the top and turned to give the boy a hand over the edge. He had no doubt that once Everett headed off to school, he'd miss the child down below. He didn't know if he could do it—force himself below ground, alone. He turned around, dusting off his pant legs and gazing outward, then frowned. "Everett, did you throw a log in the fireplace after noon dinner?"

"Did I—?" The child's eyes followed his, to the small cabin. Smoke was billowing from the chimney. He shook his head.

"Stay here," Nic said, reaching for the rifle. He was walking down the hill to the cabin when she opened the door and smiled tentatively. Sabine. He breathed a sigh of relief and looked over his shoulder at Everett.

But the boy was already running down the hill, a grin on his face. "Sabine!"

Nic looked around, into the grove of trees that lined the creek bed, up above, along the cliff face. There was no sign of Sinopa. He could smell the food the closer they got. He tried to peer over her shoulder, but she put up her hands. "No, no, no," she said, with that lovely accent that gave the word a positive meaning in his mind. Her lush lips were like a flower bud....

"You are not coming in here," she said, lifting a pail of steaming water, "until you clean yourself up with this." She turned aside and then handed Everett a second pail. Then again she turned and handed Nic a stack of clean clothes.

"Dinner and a bath?" Nic said. "Did I step into a dream?"

"I thought you could use a toothsome meal and a woman's touch in the cabin. Peter was always very fastidious. I see that you are not," she said, gesturing behind her.

He lifted his free hand, feeling a bit defensive. "It's not for want of trying. After digging in the dirt all day long, it's a tad hard to keep the white fingernails of a gambler."

"Better to work hard and get your fingernails dirty than go *that* route," she returned. "But a man can try."

"I'll give you that," Nic said, not wishing to argue. The longer they wrangled, the longer it'd take to eat. And his mouth was already watering. "We'll be back, quick-like, because whatever you have cooking in there smells like something I'd do anything to get my hands on."

She shooed them off, hiding a smile, he was sure of it. They hurried down the path to the creek. There, Peter had fashioned a washtub by digging out a long, shallow hole, and lining it with pebbles from the streambed. He'd made a wooden wall for the creek side, with two sluices—one that allowed cold fresh creek water in, then sealed it off—and another to let it flow out. They filled the natural pool with water, then added their buckets of boiled water, which made it lukewarm.

Someday Nic wanted a hot bath, all the way to his chin again, taken indoors, like a civilized man. But for now, it felt good to simply clean off the grime of the day. He and Everett dipped their heads in, lathered up from top to toe, rinsed, then rinsed again—the lye was stubborn, wanting to stick—and then quickly they dried themselves. In the cool of the mountain evening, their skin was covered in gooseflesh. They rubbed harder, and then threw the clean shirts over their heads and quickly pulled on clean underwear and trousers.

Nic tucked his shirt into his waistband, but Everett left his hanging out, making him appear younger, innocent. Nic tried to comb his hair with his fingers, but he needed a proper comb. Then he did the same with the boy. They moved toward the cabin, feeling lighter and looking forward to the evening. Most nights were fairly dismal—opening a can of beans, staring at the fire in a weary stupor, feeling too tired to move. The boy often went to sleep and woke them both up crying. Tonight Nic hoped it might be different.

They reached the door, and Nic fought the urge to knock. Shaking his head in irritation, he lifted the latch and entered. Sabine turned from the stove and wiped her hands on her apron, watching his reaction. "I could not leave it alone," she said.

She meant the cabin. It appeared that she had cleaned it all. Outside on the line were his clothes and Everett's. Inside, every inch of the place had been touched. It felt oddly … intimate.

Everett rushed over to the fireplace and stirred the pot that bubbled above it. Nic covered Sabine in a warm gaze of thanks.

"I did it for the child," she hissed to him, brushing past him to shut the door.

He swallowed a teasing retort. Perhaps the odd sensation of intimacy had struck her too, and she felt caught, exposed. "Thank you," he said, meeting her gaze. "It was kind of you."

She lifted her chin and gave her head a little shake, as if to dismiss the thanks, and moved back to the stove. She grabbed a thick cloth, bent, and opened the grate, pulling out a roasted chicken.

"Chicken!" Everett screeched, rushing over to gawk at it.

Nic had seen the chickens around Sabine's yard. It was generous of her to share one with them. She put a hand on Everett's shoulder. "I thought if Mr. St. Clair could help you build a coop, I might bring some chicks over next week. Then you'd have your own fresh poultry." She turned her gaze upon him in tandem with Everett.

Nic nodded. "Sounds like a wise idea to me," he said. Could he stick around long enough to see chicks mature to slaughter? That remained to be seen.

His eyes shifted to the desk in the corner. In one slot was a letter, addressed to an old friend in Kansas City, Missouri, the biggest city in the state. It was a long shot, but he was going to try—try to see if he could find any of Everett's kin. That was who the boy belonged with. Not some stranger he'd known less than a couple of weeks. Had Sabine seen the letter as she bustled around the tiny cabin, changing bedding, cleaning floors and windowsills, scrubbing the glass? And why did he care if she did? Neither of them should consider this anything more than a temporary situation. He'd promised Everett a week. That week ended tomorrow.

He sat down in a chair by the table, watching as Sabine showed the boy how to carve the chicken. She tore off a hunk of sourdough bread, placed a thick slice of chicken beside it, and then went over to the fireplace. She ladled a thick brown sauce over the chicken, full of carrots and potatoes and what smelled like apples. Then she fixed two more plates and joined Nic and Everett at the table. The child sat, transfixed, staring at the plate. It was obviously taking everything in him not to dive in immediately.

Sabine folded her hands and looked over at Nic expectantly. He glanced from her to the child and saw that Everett had his hands folded and eyes closed. They were waiting for grace. Grace. How long had it been since he had asked a blessing over food? He thought back. Months. More likely years, he thought, bowing his head. He grasped for some memory of how one properly did this and came up with little. "God, I uh … umm … thanks for Sabine's kindness and this food. Amen."

"Amen," Sabine said softly.

"Amen!" said Everett. He immediately stabbed a big potato and thrust it into his mouth. His eyes rounded. "Hot," he mumbled, his mouth full of food.

Nic laughed under his breath and pointed to the boy's tin cup of water. The boy took it and quickly took a sip. He swallowed and took a bite of chicken next. "Slow down, slow down," Nic said, smiling.

He looked over at Sabine and saw that she was smiling too, a warm look in her eyes. There was something about the child that brought out her softer side. Perhaps that was why she was a schoolmarm.

When she caught him looking at her, her smile faded and she looked down at her food. No, she was an undeniably handsome woman, but she was as far out of his bounds as she was out of town. This was a woman who did not want a man. She was sealed off. Injured, somehow.

Nic dug into his own food and chewed, relishing the tastes of delicate seasoning and flavors he had not experienced in months. Not since Buenos Aires had he had such a fine meal. He dared to glance at Sabine and then at Everett, then back to his food. They all ate in silence, lost in their own thoughts.

He didn't know what tomorrow would hold. He was too tired to decide tonight. After a good sleep, that would be when he'd know.

Nic awakened to find Everett sitting up, elbows on knees, chin in hands, staring at him again.

"Ugh, Everett, please don't do that," Nic said, rolling over so his back was to the boy. But he could still feel the child's eyes boring into his back.

"Are you goin' to leave?"

"Not today," Nic said with a groan.

"Tomorrow?"

"I don't know."

"The next day?"

"I don't know."

He was silent for a time; then, "Why would you leave? The mine's producing. Where would you go? For what?"

Nic turned onto his back and stared up at the ceiling, then over at the boy. His hair was rumpled, standing up in all directions. His face still held the indentations of his pillow's seam. But his eyes were clear, bright, focused. "Look, Everett. I told you before, mining's not my game."

"So, you're going to go do what? Where?"

Nic frowned and sat up, rubbed his face, and stared back at the child. "I don't know. I only know that this isn't the thing for me."

"How do you know? You've only given it a week. And it hasn't been that bad this week, has it?"

Besides listening to you cry in your sleep, knowing you're missing your father? Besides being down in that deep, dark hole, feeling like it could swallow us both at any moment? "No," he managed to say, "it hasn't been the worst week of my life."

Everett smiled triumphantly and rose. "Good. This week will be even better." He went to the foot of his bed, pulled off his nightshirt, and pulled on his work shirt and trousers. As he buttoned up the front of the shirt, he peered over at Nic. "You are going to stay, right? For another week? Just to see what the payout might be?"

Nic laughed under his breath and shook his head. He looked up at the child. "Sure you're only ten years old?"

"Pretty sure, yeah."

"Well, you bargain like a man," he said. He rose and reached out a hand. Tentatively, Everett shook it. "I'll give you a week more, maybe even two. But I have to tell you, Ev, I think it'd be good to find kin for you. Your people, they'd want to know you were alone. Once they knew you were, and how great a kid you are, I'm sure they'd send for you."

Everett's hands dropped to his side. "But I want to stay here."

"I understand that. But I don't know if I do. And you can't stay here alone."

"But I could go with Sabine—"

"Sabine thinks you need a man in your life. Someone to show you the ropes. Without, you know, your dad here …"

"Sabine doesn't know everything!" Everett cried. He dropped the sock he had been putting on and ran outside barefoot, letting the door slam behind him.

Nic sighed and put his face in his hands. "What am I doing?" he groaned, emphasizing every syllable. "I don't know how to raise a kid. Am I making it worse, sticking around?"

Who was he asking? God? And since when did he look *there* for advice?

A knock on the door startled him. He threw on his trousers, rose, and walked over to it, half expecting Everett or Sabine.

Two well-dressed men stood outside, hats in hand. "Mr. St. Clair?"

"I am," Nic said, wishing he'd had time to comb his hair.

"I am Mr. Dell," said the shorter one, "and this is Mr. Kazin. May we come in?"

"Certainly." He opened the door wider and gestured to the three small chairs around the table. The men looked around and then sat down, looking smug. Nic knew that expression. They thought they had him. But what did they want?

"We are principals in the Dolly Mae Mine," Mr. Dell said, sitting a little higher in his seat as he did so. The Dolly Mae was a huge producer, a half mile above Alpine, worked by more than a hundred men. Everett had told him how a friend and his dad ran cattle for the mining company, solely to keep the workers in fresh meat. The mine had made the town of Alpine what it was today—a settlement of nearly a thousand.

Nic's eyes narrowed.

"We'll get right to it, Mr. St. Clair," the taller man, Mr. Kazin, said, after glancing around, as if he hoped there was coffee on the stove. His thick mustache twitched. "You very wisely laid claim to the deceased Mr. Vaughn's mine. If we had known that Mr. Vaughn had passed on, we would've done so ourselves."

Nic leaned forward. "What is it you're specifically after, gentlemen?"

The two shared a look and then glanced back to him. "We are prepared to offer you a handsome sum, Mr. St. Clair, for rights to the Vaughn mine. There has been little ore found in this country that didn't require a major operation to extract it. Word has it that you've found quality ore only fifty feet down...."

Nic nodded and forced himself to take slow, even breaths.

"That is fine news, fine news indeed," Mr. Dell put in. "You see, Mr. St. Clair, you might toil down below all winter and bring up perhaps a thousand dollars worth of ore. We can do that in a day or two."

Mr. Kazin leaned forward. "We are offering you shares in our company's work, plus a fine sum for the property itself."

"How fine a sum?" Nic sat back, crossing his arms over his chest.

"If, after a thorough examination, our surveyors approve of it, we are prepared to offer you fifty thousand dollars."

Nic struggled not to gasp. Fifty thousand dollars. That was more than his inheritance had been. Of course, a good portion would have to be put into a trust fund for Everett…. He looked up at the men. "What kind of shares?"

"It's an escalating option," Mr. Dell said, pulling papers out of his jacket pocket. "One percent up front. Sliding up to three percent if the mine produces over a hundred thousand dollars in ore."

Nic stared at the papers blankly, pretending to read but not able to focus on a single word.

"There is a second stipulation," Mr. Kazin said. When Nic met his gaze, he went on, "We need your assistance in convincing Mrs. Sabine LaCrosse to accept our offer as well. As I'm sure you know, our mining operations are quite large."

"Quite."

"Our surveyors believe that the vein you have discovered is likely to run beneath her property."

He ignored the inference that their men had been up here tramping around before they'd had the decency to approach Sabine or Peter. "And are you prepared to offer her similar terms?"

"Potentially. But you see—" the men shared another long look— "Mrs. LaCrosse has declined our initial offer."

"Declined it?" Sabine didn't even intend to mine her property. Why not sell for such a sum?

"Apparently, she has a woman's *attachment* to the property. You know how they can be. Especially women of her kind."

"Hmm," Nic returned, noncommittally. *Her kind? Attached?* He could see why these two had rankled his neighbor. She had probably run them off with her shotgun in hand.

"So we would require, Mr. St. Clair, that you convince Mrs. LaCrosse of the need to comply with the terms of our offer and that you both exit the properties as soon as possible. It is your combined boundary lines that make your land so desirable."

Nic studied him. "As soon as possible? You would immediately begin setting up operations here?"

"As soon as possible," he repeated. He rose and his partner did the same. "It is imperative, Mr. St. Clair, that we move quickly. The Dolly Mae is nearly tapped out and we prefer to move our operation—equipment and crew—at once. We have a maximum of three weeks."

Nic rose. "Three weeks can go rather fast."

"Indeed."

"Well, I suppose it wouldn't hurt to at least have your surveyor do his preliminary work. You did say it had to be done before we could make a deal official...."

"Oh, yes," Mr. Dell said. He reached out a hand. "Can I send him up tomorrow?"

"Tomorrow?" Nic didn't like the feeling of being rushed. And he still had to talk to Sabine. Introduce it in the right way. "No, not tomorrow. Give me three days. Send him up Friday."

Mr. Dell forced a cordial expression to his face. "Good enough. Three days. But I warn you, Mr. St. Clair, if it's as promising as he believes it will be, we'll be urging a rapid sale and move."

"I understand," Nic said. He showed them to the door, then closed it behind them.

Fifty thousand dollars. Peter had promised him half. If he even kept *ten* percent and put the rest in a trust for Everett for when he turned sixteen, he could go a long, long way. He sat down in the chair. He'd be free to move where he wished.

He could go to Odessa, face her with his head held high again.

It had been what he'd wanted all along.

Wasn't it?

Then why didn't it feel … right?

CHAPTER EIGHT

Nic found the boy over at Sabine's—where he'd run, angry with him—eating a bowl of mush. The boy took a long drink of water and casually studied him. "What'd those two dandies from town want?" Everett asked.

"They wanted to buy your dad's land," Nic said evenly. There was no use keeping it a secret. It'd only come back to cause him trouble down the road. He sat down across from the boy, sighing wearily, and then looked up at Sabine. "Your land too."

"Yes," she said. "They were here yesterday." She remained standing, as if bracing herself.

"They're offering a lot of money for the property," Nic said. "Why not take the money, buy another piece of property, and have enough to live on through your old age?"

Her wide eyes narrowed. "They offered me ten thousand dollars. I assume they offered you more?"

He blinked. "Considerably more."

She let out a dismissive noise and turned away, fiddling with a cloth and the teakettle. "That is little surprise."

"But, Sabine," he said, leaning forward on the table, ignoring Everett's wide-eyed look, "we can make them offer you the same amount they offered me. Er, Everett and me."

She glanced back at him. "You would give Everett a portion?"

"Ninety percent. Set him up with a trust fund."

"But I don't need—" Everett began.

"Ninety when Peter promised you half?" Sabine said, cutting off the child.

"I've done little more than tinker around for a few days below ground. The land belongs to Everett. I'm merely a steward, of sorts."

"So, that's it?" Everett broke in. "You'd take your part and leave?"

"Everett, they offered us fifty thousand dollars. Do you know how long it would take for you and me to pull up that amount of ore? You could do a hundred things other than be a miner when you're a man. Your father was looking for a way to make something of himself and make a future for you, right?"

The boy hesitated and then nodded.

Nic looked up at Sabine. "Right?"

She nodded too.

"He succeeded, Everett," Nic went on. "He found the vein that could make you one of the richest boys in the world. We could set up your trust. Get you established in Buena Vista with a nice family, not an orphanage. Someone who would take on your care, feed you, watch after you. Lots of families in need of a little extra. Then, when you're sixteen, you could get a portion of those funds. And another portion when you're twenty-five." He'd seen for himself how fast a trust fund could evaporate. He'd make sure youthful foolishness didn't cause Everett to experience the same. "You could go to college. A fine college, and still have enough to begin a business, launch an expedition, whatever you choose."

"May I speak to you outside?" Sabine asked him, her facial expression tight.

He looked up at her in surprise, paused, and then nodded. "I'll be right back," he told Everett. "Finish your breakfast."

Nic followed Sabine outside. "Where's Sinopa?" he asked. "I haven't seen him for days."

"He left," she said simply.

"To hunt?"

"He'll return when he decides to," she said, ignoring his question.

"I see." He shifted nervously, from one foot to the other, wondering what she needed to say to him.

"I don't want to sell to those men," she said.

He shoved down the flash of anger, the rash words that leaped to his mouth. "W—why?"

She turned and crossed her arms in front of her. "They offered you five times what they offered me. They cannot be trusted."

"So, we won't accept their offer unless they give you the same amount."

"They won't do that, Nic," she said, looking over her shoulder at him. A portion of her long brown hair fell down her back. Nic found himself staring at it.

"Why are you so certain of that?"

"Because I've lived here for years. I know these men. Their kind."

"Rich men? Professional miners?"

"White men."

"Wh—white men?" He stared at her in confusion.

She crossed the few feet between them and tapped his chest with her finger. "Are you blind? I am a half-breed," she spit out, "as those gentlemen of the Dolly Mae so kindly put it, lucky to get anything at all."

Nic stared down at her. All at once he could see the high cheekbones, the wide arc of her dark brows, the brown lashes he assumed were her French heritage. *Sinopa.*

She could see the recognition in his eyes. "Sinopa is my half brother. We shared the same father."

"And that is why he watches over you?"

"If not for him …" She turned and took a few steps away from Nic.

"Sabine?" He dared to take a couple of steps after her.

She gazed at the valley. Far below, smoke rose in serpentine tails from the small cottages that marked the edge of town. "I did not tell Mr. LaCrosse of my heritage. When he found out, he took to beating me. First, once in a while, for burning the bread or not having a meal ready for him when he came out of the mine."

"Then later, more often," he finished for her.

She nodded, chin in hand, still looking away. "I was terribly thin, bruised, my arm in a sling when Sinopa found me." She dared to look at him then. Her look was that of a little girl lost. He fought off the urge to fold her into his arms. Instead he turned away, hand on the back of his head. How many times had he struck out in rage? Not seeing a face, a body, only a means to relinquish the fury inside? If he ever married, would he put his own bride at risk?

Never. *Never.*

He could feel her eyes on him, and slowly he turned. "Your husband died then?"

"Disappeared. He was never seen again."

Nic looked to the ground. "And you've lived up here, all alone, since then?"

"Other than Peter and Everett, yes. Peter was a good neighbor to me. They moved up here and began working the claim just after ... Sinopa arrived."

Nic nodded.

She shook her head, lifted her chin, and looked him in the eye. "I'm a different person than I once was. Which is why I cannot sell to these men. They look at me with the same disdain my husband had in his eyes. To them, I am little more than a dog."

"I understand." After his years in the ring, and as part of a crew aboard a ship, he had seen for himself how a man could be belittled, judged, and found to be lacking.

"Could you consider it?" He dipped his head and met her eyes, seeing the hurt that lingered there. "For Everett? I can handle all the negotiations so you never needed speak to them again. Or would it not be delightful to see them squirm?" He gave her a wink. "To force them to pay you what's right? Nothing hurts men like these more than to let go of their precious money."

She let a small smile tease the corners of her lips.

"Why not take your share and move to wherever you wish, build a fine house? Somewhere with a view that rivals this—" he gestured outward—"but a place that is a little easier to get to come wintertime."

Her smile grew but then quickly faded. "You know that even if we can force their offer to a hundred thousand dollars, we can be certain it's worth ten times more."

"I understand. They also offered me shares. We'll make sure they do that for you as well. If it produces, we continue to gain. From their labor."

She shook her head. "It is much to consider."

"It is. Allow me to go as far as letting their surveyor peruse our mines."

She sniffed and lifted her chin. "If you think it worth the time."

But she was simply preserving her dignity. She was intrigued; he could see it in her eyes. Even with her mixed-blood heritage, she could make a place for herself. Anywhere in the world, regardless of who a person was, money talked. He'd seen it, time and again. Money bought instant respect; character took much longer.

"I don't want to work that mine alone, Sabine," he said, hands on his hips. "There isn't much that could be more dismal than to see you and Everett ride off through the trees toward town, and then have to make myself go down that hole, day in and day out." He cocked his head. "This seems the easy way out."

Even as the words came out of his mouth, his heart twisted. What was wrong with him? Didn't he want out? This was not what he signed up for....

She studied him, glanced down at the town, then back to him. "Sometimes, mon ami, *easy* is not the *best* way. It was easiest for me to marry Mr. LaCrosse, when it would've been better to make my own way, hard though it may have been." She paused for a moment's reflection. "But I shall bless this next step. Find out if all this talk is futile. Or perhaps truly the beginnings of a future path."

Moira sat at Odessa's piano and hit a low F and G flat, over and over again, liking the dissonance. She was thinking of her letter from Francine Knapp. Odessa appeared at last at the top of the stairs. Samuel was in her arms. "Are you going to do that all afternoon?"

"Perhaps," Moira said, not turning around.

"He took a job, Moira," she said, coming down the stairs. "He didn't leave you."

"Perhaps," she said again.

Odessa paused beside her and shifted Samuel to her other arm. "You need to do something. Don't let this suck you into a crater. Let it be your own new chapter."

"Such as?"

"Well, you adore singing. You're a fairly decent pianist, when you're not pecking out the two most sorrowful notes known to man. What if you start practicing again?"

"To sing where? In the carnival?"

She felt Odessa's frown. "Moira, stop that. Turn around and look at me."

Reluctantly, Moira swiveled on the stool and dragged her eyes up to meet her sister's.

"You are not a horror to look at, regardless of what you think. And in your veil, you look even more exotic and mysterious than you did before." She reached out with her free hand to take her sister's. "The fire did not take your voice. That gift from God has not been stolen. What if you gave it back to Him? What if you were the musician in our new church in Conquistador? What if you sang for the patients at the sanatorium, lifted their spirits on occasion? Gave voice lessons?"

Moira's heart began to speed up in response to Odessa's words. She had missed singing. Her voice was rough, but it could be regained through practice.

She glanced up at Odessa, who smiled into her eyes. "There. That's my sister. I've missed that spark. Daniel brought back some of the joy, but there is more yet to come—I can see it. Perhaps that's part of what makes him hesitant … he wants to see you whole."

"Whole? I'll never be whole."

"You *can* be whole again, Moira. Just in a different way. After the consumption, after those years in bed and so nearly dying, and all that happened afterward, I was *different*. I lost my youth in a way. I would never again be innocent. Carefree. But I gained wisdom and awareness and appreciation for life. Why don't you see if you can figure out what *your* new definition of wholeness means?"

Moira looked out the window, thinking again of Daniel's departure.

"Moira."

She glanced back to Odessa.

"If you and Daniel are meant to be together, you will be. You've never been one to avoid taking charge. So take charge of what you can—you. Your life. Seek what God has for you next." She squeezed her hand again and rose, moving toward the kitchen.

Moira turned back to the piano, put her finger over the F key, and paused.

Deciding, she opened a music book before her, hearing the notes in her mind as she scanned them. And she realized she was smiling.

CHAPTER NINE

Word spread among the men that Moira might sing again that night after supper. With fifty extra hands on the premises working on the carpentry needs of the Circle M and, increasingly in Conquistador, they welcomed any activity that didn't include playing round after round of cards. At first, they shyly hung around the yard around the front porch, where the open windows allowed them to hear Moira play and sing.

But Odessa had invited them up to sit on the porch rail the night before, to enjoy a glass of lemonade and have a better opportunity to listen. The men so enjoyed it that she and Cassie generously made pitcher after pitcher the following night— having sent a man to fetch an entire crate of lemons and a bag of sugar.

When Moira discovered the two women among piles of squeezed-out rinds, Odessa responded, "It's my pleasure." She leaned closer so she could add in a whisper, "Your rediscovered joy is mine as well."

Moira helped Odessa finish the dishes that night, trying to ignore her fluttering stomach and the clumping sound of many boots on the front porch.

"Now what's bringing the boys around again tonight?" Bryce said, shooting Moira a teasing glance.

"I have no earthly idea," Odessa joined in, picking up a pitcher of lemonade. "Ready?" she asked.

Moira repositioned her light scarf and straightened the bodice of her dress, then gave her a swift nod. She thought it might be easier tonight than last, but it wasn't. Her heart had returned to her throat. Could she even sing?

Bryce moved out with a tray of glasses, for those who hadn't thought to bring their mugs. "I like this new tradition," he said.

"Me too," Odessa said with a smile.

Shyly, Cassie stood to one side, holding Samuel and watching Moira. Taking a deep breath, Moira entered the hallway, and when a few men caught sight of her, they began to applaud.

Moira's hand went to her belly, willing it to stop turning—or was that the baby?—and gave them a smile and a nod of her head. Bryce and Odessa left the front door open, so more could hear her music better. They stayed outside with the men, only returning for more lemonade, seemingly aware without asking that she needed a little distance, the illusion of being alone, to perform.

Moira went to the piano and opened the music. It was important to her not to sing any of the songs she had sung for Gavin, no matter how the men shouted out requests. To sing the songs of the dance halls and saloons brought back bad memories for her. But in the hymns, she found resonance, words that soothed and strengthened her and melodies that moved her.

She opened a hymnal, having chosen five different pieces for tonight's performance. She sang the first, "Beautiful Savior," remembering her mother sitting at the piano and singing it through her tears after burying each beloved son.

Beautiful Savior, King of creation,
Son of God, and Son of Man!
Truly I love Thee, Truly I serve Thee
Light of my soul, my joy, my crown.
Fair are the meadows, fair are the woodlands,
Robed in flow'rs of blooming spring
Jesus is fairer, Jesus is purer
He makes our sorrowing spirit sing.

Daniel's gelding, pushed well beyond his normal limits, wearily trudged up the Circle M lane. Daniel's shoulders stiffened as he saw the group of men gathered on the porch, with more arriving by the moment. But they were oddly quiet for such a large group of men. What was going on? Had something happened? Gone wrong?

But as he got closer, he relaxed, seeing the smiles and Odessa filling men's mugs from a pitcher. As he eased the horse to a walk, he understood at last what had them all enraptured.

Moira was singing.

A gentle smile tugged at his lips as he dismounted and walked the remaining paces to the edge of the crowd, straining to hear. Men nodded in greeting, but none spoke aloud to him. It was as if no one wanted to disturb her, as if the magical notes might cease altogether if she heard any sound. Bryce moved through the crowd and shook his hand. He leaned close and said, "Good to see you here, brother."

"It's good to be back," he whispered back. "How long has this been going on?"

"Just since last night."

Daniel nodded, and Bryce seemed to understand his desire to stop talking and hear Moira sing.

Then, as if she knew he was listening, the piano abruptly stopped.

But Moira's voice carried on, singing so perfectly on pitch, with such resonance, it was as if the heavens themselves had opened up and an angel were singing in her place. Never had Daniel heard her sound sweeter.

> *Fair is the sunshine, fair is the moonlight,*
> *Bright the sparkling stars on high;*
> *Jesus shines brighter, Jesus shines purer*
> *Than all the angels in the sky.*

It startled him, what came next. A man from the far corner of the porch, a perfect tenor, moved to sing with her on the next verse, and three more quickly did the same. Soon all were singing or at least humming along. The hairs on the back of Daniel's neck rose in exhilaration.

> *Beautiful Savior, Lord of the nations,*
> *Son of God and Son of Man!*
> *Glory and honor, praise, adoration,*
> *Now and forevermore be thine!*

The crowd hushed, waiting. Daniel's eyes moved around the men, their faces in fuzzy silhouette, backlit from a fading sun. But there was an expectancy, a peace in each of them. Moira had that ability—to instill both turmoil and peace in every man she met. It was a gift. A powerful gift. But a tricky one to wield.

Here they all sat, a motley group of Baptists, Lutherans, Episcopalians, and Catholics, many of them probably lapsed from practicing their faith. But they were captured, utterly captured by Moira and the power of her music.

She chose varied hymns afterward, the power of the words evident in her delivery. But the music was what caught and carried her audience. Her last was a Christmas hymn, an ancient hymn that had never failed to move Daniel.

> *Of the Father's love begotten*
> *Ere the worlds began to be*
> *He is Alpha and Omega*
> *He the Source, the Ending He*
> *Of the things that are, that have been,*
> *And that future years shall see,*
> *Evermore and evermore.*
> *Christ, to Thee, with God the Father,*
> *And, O Holy Ghost, to Thee,*
> *Hymn and chant and high thanksgiving*
> *And unending praises be:*
> *Honor, glory, and dominion,*
> *And eternal victory*
> *Evermore and evermore.*

Daniel looked up as she added an "Amen" and was surprised to see many heads bowed, as if in prayer. But then he shouldn't have been surprised, he thought to himself. Wasn't her song as powerful as an angel's own prayer? How could men do anything else in the face of it?

No preacher has ever moved his congregation half as much as she just moved these men, he thought.

The men seemed to sense that the concert was over. They began to move, reluctantly, en masse, out and into the deepening dark in groups of two or three.

A couple of carpenters Daniel recognized from Conquistador walked by him. One said, "I could swear that I've heard her sing before."

Daniel stiffened, listening, but the voices faded as they passed by him. "You never forget a voice like that …" was the last thing he heard them say. What would happen if someone recognized Moira St. Clair as Moira Colorado? Was she ready for that? Daniel shifted his weight, silently urging them all on, hoping that he would soon be able to see Moira alone. But then he shook his head. He was filthy from riding all day. Not that she even wanted to see him.

He'd gained what he came for—the knowledge that Moira was safe, and surrounded by a veritable army. He'd been fretting since the talk with his deputies for nothing. And he would only hurt her since nothing had changed since the last time they'd spoken.

A few men lingered on the porch, talking with Odessa and Bryce. He wrapped his horse's reins around his hand and pulled the gelding into motion, walking alongside him, waiting until he was out of the spreading, warm light of the house and deep into the shadows before mounting up and riding off into the night.

Mr. Dell accompanied the Dolly Mae survey team, a crew of studious-looking men with arms full of equipment. Nic didn't mind the two who wore spectacles—it was the three rough-looking armed men who stayed on their horses just a moment too long, peering down and assessing him and Everett, who bothered him.

Mr. Dell glanced from Nic to the men behind him. "Security detail," he said with a smile. "I'm certain you understand. One can never be too careful when one has access to the fortunes of the Dolly Mae."

Nic lifted his chin to let them know he understood, but his eyes remained on the three who now dismounted. Mr. Dell didn't bother to introduce them. Reluctantly Nic turned and led the way to the mouth of the mine. Everett followed along, clearly moping.

Once there, the men of Mr. Dell's security detail set up a perimeter watch, one on either flank, rifle at the ready. The third stood beside them. Nic reached out a hand. "I'm Dominic St. Clair. I didn't catch your name."

The man glanced from Nic's eyes down to his offered hand and then away. "No need to be exchanging names, sir. Far as I know, this isn't a social call."

"Pay him no mind, Nic," Mr. Dell interjected. "Rinaldi's job is to protect me. He's rather single-minded about the task. Come. We are most anxious to see the mine."

Rinaldi. Nic looked from the men on either side back to the man, Rinaldi, behind Mr. Dell. Nic didn't like having them here. He'd spent enough time with men of his ilk to know that the wrong move—even by accident—could set them off. He reached out and took Everett's shoulder.

"Stay close to me, Ev," he said lowly. They entered the mouth of the cave, an opening that was a little over six feet tall, and paused to light three lanterns.

The surveyors touched everything as they went by, the timber braces, the rock, the dirt. They took clumps from walls and ceiling, crumbling it in their hands, studying the texture, muttering among themselves. Forty feet back, the tunnel turned to the right and ended ten feet farther. Here the glint of gold glistened in a diagonal line between two tiers of black rock. One of the surveyors lifted a lantern close to it and whistled lowly. "Whoo-we, she's prettier than any gal in town."

The others with him chuckled. "Some of that in your pocket, you could have any gal you fancied."

"Hey!" Nic said. "Far as I know, this is all still in my name."

The men hesitated a moment, glancing at him, then moved on with their work in silence. The mine felt more claustrophobic than usual, being in the company of seven men and the boy.

One of the surveyors lifted his gaze and bent, peering up above him, then down the four-foot hole that followed the angle of the vein. He lowered himself down and picked at where it disappeared into the rock below, roughly in the direction of Sabine's property. "No end in sight," he muttered at his companions, eyebrows raised. He and the others swarmed over the exposed line, tossing geologic terminology back and forth, speaking a different language for a time. They took measurements and samples and, with Nic's permission, a small chunk of the gold ore.

The leader showed it to Nic. "All right with you if we take this back to our office for analysis? We'll pay you for any gold we extract, of course. It's simply to measure the grade of ore that this mine is likely to produce."

Nic nodded once. After only a week and a half of mining, it grated to have anyone else haul out even a few dollars' worth of gold. It surprised Nic, this protective surge within. Behind him, two of the surveyors had moved on to talking about what they'd do first in terms of structural support, widening the tunnel immediately in order to get the maximum numbers of men and machinery in here.

Nic shook his head. He didn't want to spend years down here, right? It would be good to sell this place, get Everett established with a proper family, and move on. Somewhere. He glanced down at Everett but looked away when the boy lifted his gaze toward him, those doleful eyes boring deep. Nic shook his head. In time, Everett'd see this as gain. Necessary. Logical. He'd see it as a man would. Nic leaned back against the far wall, watching the men work, but his mind was in another place, another time. Back at home, in Philadelphia, when his father demanded he take his sisters west to Colorado. He had desired clear things for Odessa—for her to find a cure for her consumption. But for Nic and Moira, it was far less clear.

Father had wanted Moira to be removed from society and the stage that called her ... as if the move would take away those desires from her heart. He wanted Nic to stop fighting any challenger ... as if moving West would magically make any opponent disappear. Father had always been good at addressing problems on the surface; it had been Mother who could get at the dreams and delusions that both drove and clouded her children's judgment. But by then, she was long gone.

"St. Clair?" Mr. Dell moved in front of him, his brow knit in wrinkles of concern. "You all right?"

"Fine, fine," Nic said, straightening and shaking his head. "You fellows done?"

"We're done." He smiled. "And I can tell you we are quite pleased with what we've seen here. Might you escort us to Mrs. LaCrosse's property? As I understand it, there will be far more work to be accomplished there. We'll need a good portion of the day to obtain the data we need to finalize our offer."

Sabine stood at the window on the morning of the survey, both wanting the party to arrive in order to be done with it and yet dreading it, wishing something would occur to keep them away for a while longer. She loved this view, through the wavy glass. It made the valley something of an oil painting, depicted in vivid greens of the pine and cottonwood of the Gulch, the deep blue of a sky that was heavy with coming rain, the brown of the rocks upon which this cabin had been built. When everything else had failed her, this she could count on. Home and God, her only two rocks.

All winter, she longed for home. All spring, she anxiously willed the snows to melt and recede, so she could return to this place for the summer and fall. It had been her life for ten years now, since she arrived as a young bride. She'd so hoped to come to love her husband in time, as her father promised she would.

At least she had fallen in love with her home.

Was Nic right? Might she find someplace else where she could live year-round? Someplace beautiful? Someplace safe? Here, on the rocky, open slope, nothing and no one could approach without giving her enough notice to reach for her rifle in time to meet them.

Her hands tightened around the rifle when she spotted the first man on horseback round the bend on the path from the Vaughn place. Seven more figures quickly followed. Sabine glanced down at her rifle. She knew how the town talked, of "Crazy LaCrosse up in the Gulch." They said it was her Indian blood that drove her to want to kill any white man. But it was only here on her land that she became so protective. Down in town, she was the model citizen, suitable to be the schoolteacher. She knew that there was a campaign to bring in a white teacher. It was simply proving difficult to lure any woman here to teach over a shortened year; in these parts, fathers were only willing to let sons go to school through the winter and spring, and the girls were an afterthought. Sabine had tutored several girls into the summer at times, girls who wished to go to finishing school or even teachers college. Earlier that summer, she'd received a letter from one of her students, now teaching in North Dakota. Even now, the thought of it brought a smile to her face.

Sabine set down the rifle and moved to open the door. She fought the urge to step back inside. "Sabine," Everett called, "we're here to check out your husband's old mine." As if she didn't know. As if she hadn't spent all night tossing and turning, thinking about it.

"Is that right?" she asked gently. She'd miss Everett if they moved in opposite directions. Of that she was certain. She put her hand on the boy's shoulder, feeling stronger somehow with him near as she looked at each man in the group. She paused over the tall one, who looked at her with hunger in his eyes. Rinaldi. She felt her stomach clench and twist. He was the one who had taken to following her down the boardwalk whenever he spotted her in town. Over the summer, his flirtations had moved to taunts when she failed to reciprocate. Her eyes moved to Nic, who returned her gaze under a furrowed brow. He'd noticed her hesitation. Was her fear that obvious?

"Gentlemen, the mine is over there," she said, pointing to the entrance in the hillside. "Everett, why don't you come in and share a glass of tea with me while they see to their business?"

The boy looked up at her and smiled. "Oh, Sabine, I kinda want …" He longingly looked after the group moving off.

"Go on," she said.

They moved off as a group, Everett trailing behind, but the last two—Rinaldi, with his twisted grin and improper gaze, and Nic, his jaw muscles tightening and eyes hardening in his direction—lingered a moment.

"Let's get on with it, Rinaldi," Nic growled, shooting a look from him to Sabine and back again. "Mr. Dell is far ahead."

"On my way, Mr. St. Clair," he said, still staring at Sabine. "Mrs. LaCrosse." He tipped his hat, then slowly, ever so slowly, moved his eyes off her and onto the path ahead.

Nic gave her a rueful look that said, *I'll want to know later what that was about,* and then followed him up the path. His body moved in the easy, rocking motion of a man comfortable in the saddle.

Sabine stared after Nic. It felt nice to have a man look after her. Only Peter and Sinopa had done that for her.

Or was it that they were the only two she had ever allowed to do so?

CHAPTER TEN

Nic wondered why Sabine had refused to accompany them down to town the next day, saying she'd be along at the appointed hour. After the visit from the surveyor's team, and Rinaldi's clearly unwanted attention, she'd seemed to take a step back, refusing to tell him what had happened. Was Rinaldi a past beau or a threat of some other kind? Every time he thought of it, his heart raced in protective concern for her.

You have no business entertaining thoughts of Sabine LaCrosse, he told himself for the hundredth time. He was about to sell the mine and leave. There was no time for a romance to develop, even if he was interested and she happened to be interested too, which he hadn't yet ascertained. It was an idle, foolish distraction, this idea of Everett and Sabine and him somehow being together forever. She had her life. He had his. Everett would find his way too, in time.

Daisy stumbled as they left the Gulch path and hit the main road into town. Everett swung around behind him, holding firmly to Nic's waist, as the horse pulled up short.

"She's thrown a shoe," Everett said.

"Ahh," Nic growled, swallowing a swear word. "Hop off."

Everett did as he was told, and then Nic swung his leg over and lowered himself to the road. He leaned into the mare's hind quarters until her weight shifted, and then he lifted her hoof, easing it up as Everett ran back to retrieve the missing shoe. Nic felt along her fetlock, and was relieved to find that nothing else appeared to be wrong. He sighed and said, "At least we're early. Let's head on over to Jed's and see if he can reshoe her."

Everett hesitated. "Maybe God doesn't want us to do this—sell the mine."

Nic scoffed. "You a believer in God now?"

The boy shrugged a shoulder, the tinge of a blush at his cheeks. "Me and my dad, we've always believed in God."

Nic softened when the boy mentioned Peter. He reached out a hand and put it on Everett's shoulder. "This is a good thing, Ev. You'll see."

But the child wouldn't return his gaze. Nic held his breath, ignoring the sense of betrayal in his chest. Was it for the child or for himself that he was so keen to sell the mine? Then he swallowed hard. He hadn't asked to become guardian to Everett Vaughn. Peter had gone and gotten himself killed—that was no fault of his. No, he could sell this mine, put money away for Everett that he'd never have seen otherwise, find him a good home, and move on. This was just another stop for Nic on a very long journey home. These people intrigued and moved him, but they were not part of his future. He had to get to Odessa, find out about Moira … the money from the mine would allow him to do that with his head held high. His sisters never need know that he had spent and gambled his inheritance away, just as their father had feared he would.

They walked through town, Daisy moving more easily behind them now that she was relieved of her burden. "I'll want you to fetch some supplies at the mercantile," he said to Everett, "while I'm at the meeting."

"Yessir."

They passed a new block of small, hastily constructed buildings, all raised over the last two weeks. A livery. A laundry. A restaurant. The town was bustling, far busier this day than when Nic had arrived.

"Well, lookie there," Jed boomed, spotting them as they entered the stable gates. "Thought for sure you'd end up a dead man before the month was out." He came over to thump Nic on the back.

Nic glanced at the child, who blanched at Jed's words. Jed followed his gaze. "Didn't mean no disrespect, son," he said. "No, no, Peter was as fine as they come, a saint among us. This one"—he slapped Nic on the back again—"is a mere mortal, far as I can tell." He looked beyond them to the mare. "Now what's come against that mare of yours?"

"Threw a shoe," Nic said. "We were wondering if you could see to her in the next few hours."

Jed studied him and lifted his chin. "You goin' to meet with the men of the Dolly Mae now?"

Nic frowned. How could the old man know that already? Although he supposed talk of mines and their production was on everyone's lips. "I might be," he said.

"Hold on there, friend," Jed said, cocking his head to one side. Did Everett lean slightly forward, sensing an ally? "I'd tread mighty carefully with them folk," Jed went on. "What're they offering you?"

"I'm really not at liberty to—"

"What are they offering you?" he insisted calmly.

Nic clamped his lips shut for a moment and studied him.

Something about his expression made him want to trust him. What did it hurt? "Fifty thousand."

Jed nodded and looked down at the ground. "A handsome sum. Handsome. But I happened to know the owner of the Dolly Mae, back when it was nothing but a claim like yourn."

"And?"

"And, they gave him a handsome sum too, then proceeded to mine a thousand times that out of that there earth." He gestured in the direction of the Dolly Mae.

"They're offering shares as well."

"That's good, good," Jed said, nodding. He sighed and sat down on the end of a log, upended to be a stool of sorts. He gestured to two other logs, and after Nic and Everett sat down, he leaned forward. "But I'm tellin' ya, it's likely they'll get much more out of the Vaughn mine."

Nic scowled. "But an operation like theirs is apt to retrieve far more gold than I could ever get at on my own. No, it's best to take the money and the shares and let them have at it." He glanced over at Everett. "Go see the mare into the stable, Ev."

"But I—"

"Go," he said sharply.

Jed kept his eyes on Nic as the child left them. Then he looked over Nic's shoulder, down the street, as if to make sure they were still alone. "Those men," he said in barely more than a whisper, "they are not honest sorta men, 'spite what they seem."

"What does that mean?" Nic growled.

Jed hesitated, as if he were offended by Nic's response, and then said, "They swindled my friend Flaherty. Didn't even pay 'im the second half promised. Cited *details* in that contract of theirs that they said they could use against 'im."

"But that mine paid out in the millions. It makes no sense."

Jed nodded. "I know it. But you've got a bigger problem."

"What's that?"

"The Dolly Mae is even more powerful than before."

Nic waited.

"Once that sort wants somethin', it's mighty hard to dissuade 'em. They're like a terrier with a rat, that's what they are."

"So … what would you advise?"

Jed leaned back and thought on it a moment; then, "Why not go and fetch your own 'vestors? Create your own company? Bring some men in here with pockets as deep as those of the Dolly Mae?" He tucked his head. "And hired guns to defend 'er."

Nic laughed under his breath. "You think I can do that? Just mosey on down to Denver and find my own investors? And who's to say they wouldn't try and swindle me, just the same?"

Jed looked him steadily in the eye. "Maybe. Look, it ain't none of my—"

"No, it's not," Nic said, rising. "Please, see to Daisy. We'll be back after our meeting." He beckoned to Everett, who was waiting in the dark of the stable doorway.

He looked back at Jed and felt a pang of contrition at the hurt expression on the older man's face. "Look, I was a little—"

"Don't mention it," Jed said, with a dismissive flip of his hand. And then he turned his back and entered the stables.

❀

Sabine rode down the Gulch beside the creek, closing her eyes and listening to the water rise and splatter, rush and fall. Above her, the wind wove through the white pines, making her think of her days as a small child at the reservation in Montana. There the trees had had a similar sound and were accompanied by the billow and snap of the worn tepee wall. To her, it was the sound of home.

She'd wanted this time to herself, not to have her thoughts clouded by Nic's input or Everett's chatter. Her father would have wanted her to seek Jesus' guidance for her next steps. She closed her eyes and imagined his heavily accented voice, gone so long now. *Jesu, Jesu, we must always zeek Him. Look for Jesu, ze Holy Father, ze Holy Ghost, Sabine. Zey are all around you. Zey never leave you. Never.* Sabine looked up to the treetops, their leaves rattling in the wind and thought of God, all around her. *Is this what You want me to do, Lord? Move on? Let this place go? Are You urging me forward? Away from this place?*

She breathed in and out, waiting, but hearing nothing.

Sabine had always thought she'd grow old here, be buried in the town cemetery along with old miners and fellows down on their luck. If she left, where would she go? She had heard good things about Denver and Fort Collins. On the other side of the Rockies the winters were supposed to be a bit milder. And Nic was right; she'd enjoy a nice house with a nice view that she'd never have to leave.

She sighed as she reached the end of the path and entered the main street of St. Elmo. The law office of Jeffrey Hohn, where she was to meet Nic and the men of the Dolly Mae, was just ahead. When she saw Richard Rinaldi shift from his position and reach to take her reins at the hitching post, she resisted the urge to wheel the horse around and hightail it for home. She pretended confidence but refused to meet his eye.

"Sabine," he said in greeting, eyeing her leg a bit too long as she pulled her boot from the stirrup. "You going to marry me, quick, before you make your fortune inside? Wouldn't mind having a piece of that, as well as a piece of … well, you know." His eyes moved down her body in a suggestive fashion.

She ignored him as she dismounted and moved past him, but he reached out and grabbed her arm. She stiffened, waiting, but refused to look his way. His companion, standing beside the door, looked down the street one way, and then another. He wasn't going to intervene.

"You don't even have the decency to respond?" Rinaldi growled lowly in her ear. "Don't tell me *you* think you're too good for *me?*"

Slowly, she moved her head and met his gaze. "Too good for you?" she said sweetly. "Why yes, Mr. Rinaldi, in more ways than you can imagine." She wrenched her arm from his grasp and climbed the steps. "Open it," she commanded the second man, who stood in front of the knob, arms folded. "Or tell your employers there's no deal."

Grudgingly, he moved aside, turning the knob for her. The men rose from their chairs at the table, Nic first, and after a second's hesitation, the men of the Dolly Mae and the attorney, Jeffrey Hohn. Quietly the door closed behind her, and Sabine took a deep breath. She was temporarily shielded from one level of threat, leaving her to negotiate only that threat before her.

"Please, Mrs. LaCrosse, be seated," Mr. Hohn said, pulling out a chair, beside him.

"We're so glad you could attend our meeting," Mr. Kazin said. Across from him, Mr. Dell nodded.

"Thank you." Sabine unpinned her hat and laid it on the table, smoothly taking her seat. She looked at Nic across the table as the three men sat down, but his eyes told her nothing. Perhaps they had just begun their talks.

She waited and hoped Nic would stay silent too. Her father had taught her that it was always best to speak last in negotiations, not first.

She was thankful when Mr. Hohn opened a folder and extracted some papers. "You'll see here that we've taken the liberty of drawing up the proper documents, ceding both your properties to the Dolly Mae Company."

"Hmm, that *is* a liberty," Nic said, accepting his set from Mr. Hohn and picking up Sabine's from the table as she started to reach for them. He hesitated over them, looking in her direction as if to say, *Is this all right?*

She nodded. Together, unified, they would be stronger. And he'd promised not to agree to anything, not today.

The fellows of the Dolly Mae exchanged worried glances, then looked back to Nic as he compared both sets of documents, flipping to the second page. Sabine hid a smile and assumed a demure, patient posture in case they looked her way.

After perusing page three, Nic looked at Mr. Dell, then Mr. Kazin. "You are offering Mrs. LaCrosse forty thousand dollars less for her property than you are for mine."

Mr. Kazin cleared his throat until it grated at Nic's nerves. "Yes, well, our survey team was able to find positive proof that the vein is clearly on your property, Mr. St. Clair. There is an assumption that the vein will continue at its current angle, which would make it extend under Mrs. LaCrosse's property. But there is no proof that it actually does."

"True," Nic said with a nod. "But you said, Mr. Kazin, that you are in need of Mrs. LaCrosse's property to build the size of structure and supports you need to actively work the Vaughn mine, did you not?"

"We need the acreage," Mr. Dell put in, clearly a bit flustered. "But we are paying you for the space and the guarantee of quality ore. For Mrs. LaCrosse, we are only assured of the space itself. And land in these parts, without ore, is hardly worth a dime an acre."

Nic sat back, as poised as the seasoned gambler he was. "But Mrs. LaCrosse has the good fortune of having land adjacent to mine, which should be worth considerably more. And if this mine produces what you think—my, my, you gentlemen are in for quite a payday."

Mr. Dell let out a small, scoffing laugh and threw up his hands. "But of course. If we did not hope for that, we would not be here at all."

"Of course," Nic repeated, nodding in a friendly way. He lifted one hand. "But given that you *do* hope for that, if you truly hope for that, the only fair thing would be to give Mrs. LaCrosse the same terms as you have given me."

Mr. Kazin and Mr. Dell exchanged another short, alarmed glance, and both began to voice their retorts at the same time. Mr. Hohn tried to interrupt, tried to soothe the matter, but they ignored him.

Nic waited them out, not looking at them, but only at Sabine.

There was something about Nic's presence that both made her heart beat faster and calmed her at the same time. He let a small smile curl up the corners of his mouth as the two businessmen rattled on. Finally they were silent. Nic looked Mr. Kazin's way.

"We cannot do it," Mr. Kazin said, flushing at the neck. "It simply isn't done that way!"

Nic looked to Mr. Dell.

"Perhaps you are too new here, Mr. St. Clair," he said as he glanced Sabine's way. "Mrs. LaCrosse knows how it is." His mouth opened and closed, as if he were considering words, then swallowing them, then trying again. "Not only is Mrs. LaCrosse's land … *unverified*, but she is not in the same *position* as others to negotiate."

Nic's brow lowered and all trace of his smile disappeared. Sabine watched him, allowing him to rise to her defense, feeling his protection wrap around her shoulders like warm, supple leather.

He placed his hands on the table in a wide *Y* fashion, fingers splayed, and stared down at the wood between them for a long moment. Then he looked at each man. "I guess you face a puzzling situation, gentlemen. You know for a fact that the Vaughn mine carries a wealth of gold…." He paused, allowing his words to settle like a hook in a fish's jaw. "But you won't see an ounce of it if you don't deal fairly with the lady. She gets the same deal as me and Ev or there's no deal at all."

Mr. Dell stared at him, frozen, caught. "Everyone knows that a woman can't expect the same as a man. If Mr. LaCrosse were here—"

"But he's not. And he's been declared dead. Right?" He looked quickly to Sabine, as if worried that they should have discussed the matter before, and then he visibly relaxed as she nodded. "So Sabine is the rightful owner."

"But, Mr. St. Clair, it is not only the matter of Mrs. LaCrosse being *female*," Mr. Kazin tried.

"No? What else?" He lifted a brow. "Is it that she is a teacher? Are teachers not allowed the maximum value on their property either?"

Sabine tried to keep her head up. He knew what they were saying. They all knew what the men were trying to say. She didn't have the right to the full value of her land because she was—

Mr. Kazin cleared his throat and lifted his head high. "Mrs. LaCrosse is of mixed blood. There are some that would insist she go to a reservation. That is where people of her descent are allowed to own land. Nowhere else—"

Nic shoved his chair back and stood, then walked around the table and picked up Sabine's hat and handed it to her. "I believe we must decline your offer, gentlemen. We came here believing you intended to deal with us in good faith."

Sabine swiftly drove two hatpins into her hair and rose.

Mr. Kazin and Mr. Dell both rose with her. "Wait," Mr. Dell said, a placating expression on his face. "I think there's been a misunderstanding."

"A misunderstanding?" Nic said, retrieving his hat from a peg by the door. "What, that you intend to dishonestly purchase land? Mrs. LaCrosse owns her land as clearly as I do. We're done here." He turned his back to them, one hand coming to her lower back as the other reached for the knob.

"Sixty thousand," Mr. Kazin said.

Nic froze and then smiled at her victoriously, but Sabine was a mass of nerves, sick to her stomach. All she wanted was *out*. Nic's small smile faded.

"For each of you," Mr. Kazin added.

Nic shot her another look, begging her with his eyes to consider the offer.

But she couldn't. Not now. Everything in her told her to get out. Escape.

Nic sighed, then he turned his head and looked at the men. "We will confer and get back to you tomorrow."

"No. If you leave this office, the offer is rescinded," Mr. Kazin said, punctuating his sentence with a sniff.

Nic raised alarmed eyes to meet hers. *He means it,* his eyes said.

Sabine shook her head again. The room was closing in on her. All she wanted was to get home to her cabin. How had she ever thought she could leave it?

But still Nic hesitated.

"Let's go," she muttered, reaching for the knob herself, unwilling to stand here a second longer.

"Mr. St. Clair," said Mr. Dell. "Perhaps we might have a word with you alone."

"Sorry," Nic said, placing his hat on his head in the open doorway as Sabine rushed to untie her horse. "We're a team. If you don't convince both of us, you're out of luck."

CHAPTER ELEVEN

Nic's tone, as he exited the law office, had been full of bravado and confidence, but as they left, he seethed with fury at Sabine. They made their way to the stables in silence and picked up his horse and found Everett. Then they rode down Main Street and took the path up the mountain. Why had she not taken the deal? It was more than what they had hoped for!

"Will you slow down a little, Sabine?" he called out to her, when they were well out of earshot of anyone in town. Daisy was slower than Sabine's mare, which was carrying far less weight up the Gulch. She pulled up on the reins but did not turn. Nic wished Everett weren't here, but he supposed the boy had as much right to hear this as he did.

In a couple of minutes they were side by side on the path. Nic took off his hat, wiped the sweat off his upper lip with the back of his wrist, and then looked over at her. "What was that about?"

She sniffed. "I thought you said we weren't going to agree to a deal today, no matter what."

"They offered us sixty thousand dollars, Sabine."

"Sixty thousand?" Everett said.

"Sixty thousand *each*," Nic went on. "I never thought they'd go that high."

"The offer will be there tomorrow if we want it."

"No. He said if we walked out the door it was rescinded. And he meant it." He sighed and put his hat on his head, slowly straightening the brim. "Don't you see? It's how men negotiate such things. The gamble. That was what I was trying to tell you—we had to take it then or we weren't going to get it again."

"Yes, well, I decided I didn't want it."

She spurred her mare forward, but Nic stayed with her this time. "Can I talk to you a minute? Alone?"

She grimaced but then dismounted and headed toward some trees, leading her horse.

"We're almost to the cabin," Nic said to Everett, also dismounting and holding the horse as the boy moved into the saddle. "You go on up. I'll walk the rest of the way."

The boy reluctantly continued toward the cabin, and Nic turned to follow the faint trail that led to towering, thick aspens in heavy leaf. Sabine looped her horse's reins over a branch and reached up to unpin her hat and hair, running her fingers through it as if it was a relief to feel it fall across her shoulders. Nic paused for half a step, savoring her beauty. All at once he could see her an Indian maiden, in a buttery soft leather dress, rather than her severe Western dress, all corset and stays.

She was exotic. Enticing. And completely aggravating. He steeled himself as he strode forward.

"You realize that this is Everett's chance at a future," he said. "A life outside of this mountain town. An education."

"You realize," she mimicked, "that maybe *this is* Everett's best future. Staying here with you. With me around the corner. Fresh air. Mountains." She paused and looked out toward the valley and beyond, then back to him. "You think God had you here by accident when the boy lost his father?"

"You think God orchestrated all of this?" he scoffed. "If you only knew how I've handled fortunes before, you'd know that God would avoid entrusting me with another. Let alone a *child*. I am hardly the sort that anyone would choose to father his son."

She paused for a moment. "I think," she said softly, "you'd make a perfectly decent father."

He was taken aback by the abrupt turn of tone, and he studied her big brown eyes, so intently meeting his own gaze. Her lashes were thick and long, as if they'd been plucked from the coat of a minx. "You can't possibly mean that, Sabine. You hardly know me."

"I know," she said, laying a small, soft hand on his chest—did she feel his heart thumping wildly beneath it?—"I know enough."

He stared at her, longing to kiss her, but his mind was trying to pick up the tail of their argument. He was angry with her, right? What had he been about to say? "Sabine, I—"

"I have to go," she said, pulling her hand away, leaving a cold spot on his chest where it had been. She raised a boot to her stirrup, then easily lifted herself up and into a sitting position. She squeezed her mare's flanks and the horse walked down the path.

"Where are you going?" Nic called after her.

"It's an old Indian trail," she said over her shoulder. "Leads to my place."

"Sabine!"

She pulled up on her reins as if she regretted it already, and turned to look back at him.

"Will you at least come over tonight? For some supper? So we can—"

"No," she said, shaking her head. "I can't. I'll see you tomorrow."

He called her name again, but she ignored him as she pushed her horse through the huge grove of old aspens, disappearing among the trees. Nic sighed. He fought off the desire to take the path behind her, catch up with her, and force her to see his way of things, and instead he turned and trudged up the hill to the Vaughn cabin.

Everett was outside, splitting kindling with a small ax.

He reached for a bigger one, centered a log on top of another, and then, measuring the distance with his eye, arced around and slammed into it, dead center.

"That woman has been on her own too long," he muttered.

"I know," Everett said. "My dad used to say the same thing."

They chopped wood in silence for a while. Then Everett said, "You were pretty mad at Sabine?"

"Still am, I think. She lost us a lot of money."

They continued to chop again.

"She a good teacher, Ev?"

"Yeah, I suppose. Never had 'nother."

Nic glanced down the Gulch to the tops of the towering grove of aspens, wishing he could see her one more time.

What was he supposed to do now? Mine all winter? Alone? And for what?

They didn't go down in the mine that afternoon. Nic was in no mood for a pickax and shovel and pail and being caked with dirt in every wrinkle and crevice. He paced back and forth between the cabin and the creek for a while and started for Sabine's several times but came to a stop each time.

The woman wanted to be alone.

Far be it from him to intrude.

He paced to the creek again. He hadn't felt this kind of frustration since … the ship. Since he launched into that taunting, nasty sailor and found himself strapped to the main mast and whipped. Since then, he'd been able to find avenues of release, or ways around the anger that would work him up. He didn't want to hurt Sabine— he'd never want to hurt her—but as the afternoon wore on, he was so wound up inside he couldn't stay still. He was like a toy his father had once given him; he'd wrapped a string round and round and when he pulled it, the toy spun away across the floor, vertical but whirling.

Nic reached the bathtub by the creek and stood there with one boot on the side wall, only half seeing the water rush by. Remembering how his mother used to calm him by making him splash his face with cold water ten times, he flipped the creek-side wall into place, trapping the water inside. He yanked off his boots and hat, trousers and shirt, and jumped into the cold bath, underwear and all. The cold made him gasp, but he allowed himself to stay under for a moment, feeling the icy water chill away the heat of his frustration. He emerged and took a gulp of air, letting out a small cry then. His skin was a mass of gooseflesh.

He forced himself to remain in water up to his armpits and looked up to the trees that waved in the wind, giving him glimpses of the blue sky above, then hiding it. Why was it that he had to think

this through, again and again? What was driving him? Forcing him
to the edge of fury?

He thought back to the meeting. The banter. The offer. Turning
his back, walking out that door, getting more frustrated and angry
by the moment.

Then that moment by the grove, when she made him feel like he
was spinning again, half drawn to her, half furious with her, confusing him, more than he had ever been before by a woman.

Control.

He wanted to control it. Decisions. Money. Sabine. Everett. His
future. His life itself.

But he could not do so.

Nic sighed, cupped his hands in the water, and splashed and
rubbed his face several times. He wanted to stay there, in the water,
thinking it through, but he was too cold. His teeth chattered. If he
stayed in the water much longer, he might lose his senses and never
get out. On shaking legs, he stood, got a grip on the wall, and hoisted
himself up. He dried off, then reached for his hat, covering his wet
head from the wind before pulling on his shirt and trousers. He
gingerly picked his way up the path, carrying his boots, and ignored
Everett's questioning gaze as he looked up from stirring a pot of stew,
by the smell of it.

They ate in silence.

That night, for the first time in several days, Everett cried in his
sleep.

Nic lay in the other cot, one arm tucked under his head, listening to him whimper and cry out in his dreams. And he felt the knot
of the day's frustration slowly rebuild.

What are You doing with me here, Lord? he asked the wood-planked ceiling, feeling awkward about speaking to God, but knowing nowhere else to turn.

Everett's crying turned into sobbing. Nic glanced over to him, a dim outline in the warm red light of the fireplace's coals, then back to the ceiling.

Is Sabine right? Did You really bring me here to help this boy? Why me? I'm clearly doing him no good. Get me out. Show me the way out. Amen.

Sabine stared up at the ceiling of her small cabin. It was covered in yellowing newsprint, with water-spot circles from leaks in the roof she'd need to fix before much longer. Another winter of dripping might lead to bigger trouble. She'd kept the fire fed, feeling as though the night were somehow darker, lonelier. She wished Sinopa were here, solely for the feel of another person inside this place.

She let out a sound of exasperation and rolled to her side, staring at the fire. The afternoon wind had whipped into a nighttime howl, whistling through the chinking of her log walls and making the fire flicker. Among the flames, she imagined Nic, with his blue-green eyes, sandy hair, and strong chin. Today, something had shifted between them. What was that? And what had she been doing, laying a hand on his chest like that? The last thing she needed was the complication of a man in her life. Especially that man.

Sabine pulled the wool blanket higher, not really cold, just wanting to muffle the noise. She was just getting drowsy enough to sleep, when she heard an odd sound outside. Her eyes flew open.

She listened hard, trying to distinguish what she heard. Might it be Nic, come to see her, work out their differences? But Nic would've called out, warned her, angry though he might be.

All she could hear was wind and her pulse pounding in her ears.

There. A horse's hoof on stone. She was sure of it.

Sabine moved her blanket down and eyed the latch on the door. It was locked with the peg. If anyone tried to open it, she'd see the crossbar move. She glanced at the window to the left of it. The curtains were pulled shut, and it was too small for anyone to get through.

But that wouldn't keep them from busting out the glass and pointing a rifle in her direction.

She grabbed her gun from beneath the bed along with a case of shells and scurried to the door, placing her ear against it to try to hear what was going on outside.

Pitch from a log popped in the fireplace, making her jump. She clamped her lips shut and listened again. Two or more horses. Men's voices, in loud whispers. Nothing discernible.

They were coming after her. No one arrived at a person's house this late in gold country without a call of greeting. Unless he wanted to risk getting his head blown off. The only reason to arrive in secrecy, under cover of darkness, was one: attack.

Her hand trembled as she pulled back the chamber and checked to make sure the rifle was loaded. She grimaced as it made the loud, familiar *ca-thunk* and cracking *clink* as it slammed back in place. But then she brought her head up. *Good. Let them know I am ready.*

Fast footsteps in the gravel in front of the door warned her of a man's approach. There was no knock. No taunting call, meant to instill fear. Just a full body slam against the door, making it tremble and even crack in one spot.

Sabine glanced up in startled surprise as a man in a black hood stared through the crack.

She scrambled away as he reached through the hole, grasping at her as another pounded out the glass of her window with the butt of his rifle.

She aimed at the hole in the door as the man withdrew his hand, and when he pounded against it a second later, she fired.

Nic sat up straight in his bed when he heard the echoing retort of a rifle shot.

He cocked his head, listening for a second, but there was no more. He dashed out of bed, yanking on his trousers, then his boots. He threw a log on the fire. Everett was asleep now, no longer dreaming. He'd be scared all alone, but there was nothing to be done about it. He had to wake him up.

"Everett!" Nic pulled on a jacket and reached for a gun. "Ev!"

The boy sat up, trying to focus his vision, by the looks of him. "Trouble over at Sabine's, I think," Nic growled, handing him the rifle. "You lock the door behind me and sit against it until I get back, you hear? Don't let anyone in but me. Got it?" He reached for a blanket from the bed and wrapped it around the boy's shoulders. "Ev?"

Everett's brown eyes were sharp now in the sparking light of the fire. He nodded.

Another shot echoed through the Gulch.

Nic's eyes met Everett's. "I'll be back soon."

"Promise?" the boy whispered, looking up at him, the gun huge in his small hands.

Nic cast about for an answer. How to promise what he could not know? "I'll do my best," he said. "But I have to go to Sabine. You stay here and be brave, all right?"

The boy nodded, his hair a mass of spikes going in all directions, the product of his rough dreams.

"Lock it behind me," Nic repeated. "I'll be back as quick as I can."

Outside he waited until he heard the peg in the hole and the thump of the boy's back against the thick door. And then he set off at a dead run toward Sabine's.

He panted hard as he ran, struggling to see the path in the dim moonlight. He knew it was only a five-minute walk to her place; why did it seem that this was taking twice as long? No more gunfire split the air. Was that good? Or bad?

Nic hunched over and ran the last few paces as quietly as he could, stopping beside a tree to assess what had transpired and to catch his breath. Two men in black hoods were outside Sabine's cabin. He could see them in the moonlight. He frowned. There were holes in her front door. They were trying to break in.

One man sat down heavily on the edge of the narrow front porch. Was he wounded? Nic hoped she had at least winged him. It would give him one less man to take down. The second backed up and ran at the door, crashing into it with the bulk of his shoulder. He immediately spun away, just as Sabine fired again. "Get out of here!" Sabine screamed from inside. "I'll kill you if I have to!"

As if to emphasize her words, she shot through the door again.

Nic frowned as a third man came into the clearing, carrying a lit torch. Did they intend to burn her out? Or trap her inside? He clenched his teeth and slowly reached for his pistol, a six shooter. Could he get them all with the six bullets? Would it be enough? It comforted him to know Sabine had a shotgun inside. If he could get to her, they could fight their way out together.

The third man handed the torch to the second, who was still sitting down, and reached for a sheet of metal. Then he climbed on top of a tree stump beside the cabin and atop the roof. Smoking her out, Nic quickly decided. He had to move. One way or another, Sabine couldn't make it in there for long.

He edged through a group of pines, keeping his eye on the man who stood beside the front door. The other two were distracted. But that one might well catch sight of him. The third had reached the chimney. A shot rang out—likely Sabine firing at the man on her roof. The man above swore and laughed with the man by the front door, and then Nic could hear the scraping sound of metal on stone. He was sliding the sheet into place.

Sabine had only a few minutes until she would be forced outside.

Nic moved slowly, not wanting any of the three to see him until the last possible moment. He edged forward, from one tree to the next, until all that was left was open space between him and them. The man on the roof was making his way down. It was now or never. Nic ran forward, stopped, and took aim at the tall man by the door. Just as he squeezed the trigger, the man on the roof spotted him and shouted out. The tall man dodged, but Nic hoped he had managed to get a piece of him.

The man on the porch was running toward their horses. To a

gun? And the man on the roof took aim at Nic, who threw himself to the ground and rolled as a bullet hit the dirt beside him. He glanced at the man and rolled again and again, the bullets getting closer and closer to him as the shooter unloaded one shot after another. At six, he stopped rolling and came to his feet, guessing that the man on the roof would have to reload. He strained his eyes, trying to see the tall man, but could not spot him. The other two were now on horseback, and the first threw his torch on top of Sabine's roof.

Smoke was pouring out from under her eaves. The torch's fire caught and spread rapidly, fed by dry timber and the fierce wind, a tongue of orange licking its way across within seconds.

Nic shot at the men, making one of the horses rear, but then he saw that all three were on their horses, reeling them around and retreating. Whoever they were, they did not want their identities discovered.

Sabine.

He ignored the men disappearing into the darkness and ran the rest of the way to the cabin. The fire was building now. It wouldn't be long until the ceiling collapsed inward.

"Sabine!" he shouted. "Don't shoot! It's Nic! The men are gone, Sabine. Get out! Get out now!" He tried the door but it was locked.

Sabine did not answer.

"Sabine!" he screamed. "Sabine!"

He backed up and ran at the door with everything he had in him, making the hole just large enough to squeeze half his arm through. "Sabine!" It was hot, even here. His eyes stung from the smoke and he blinked rapidly, trying to see inside. He had to get her out of there.

Unless she was already dead.

He groaned and shoved his arm further in, ignoring the splinters of wood scraping his skin. There. The peg. He grabbed it and pulled it out, lifted the latch, and the door swung open.

He backed up half a step from the wave of black smoke that poured out. "Sabine!"

He bent over and moved inside, ignoring the flames covering the ceiling, dropping curled, blackened newsprint down upon the floor. He caught sight of her foot and then her white nightdress. She was unconscious.

Feeling as if his back were about to burst from the heat like a fat sausage over an open fire, he gathered her into his arms and rushed her outside. He gulped in the clean air, even as he laid her on the dirt, carefully setting her head down. He stared at her, clearly visible in the hot light of the cabin, and saw that she was not breathing.

"Come on, Sabine, please," he said, touching her cheek. "I ... Everett can't take it, not another person close to him, dying. Come on, woman, take a breath. Just one breath."

The cabin ceiling collapsed then, falling in two pieces.

When he looked back to Sabine, she moved. "Sabine?"

She gasped and then choked, coughing for a terribly long time. But at last she opened her eyes and looked up at him, as if he were an apparition. "Nic?" she asked, her voice strangled.

"I'm here," he said, taking her hand and bringing it to his chest. He grinned in elation. She was alive! She was going to be all right!

She frowned and looked over to her cabin. "They ... they burned it?"

He nodded. "I'm sorry. We can help you rebuild. I know how you loved that place. You were lucky you weren't inside when it came down."

"You … you pulled me out?"

He nodded again and then pushed her hair from her face.

She closed her eyes and gave in to another weary fit of coughing.

"Come on," he said, picking her up again. "I'm taking you home. We'll figure out what to do come sunup."

He was carrying her out of the clearing when she said, "Wait. One last look." He turned, and they stared at the cabin, the flames lessening now. She stared at it for a long moment, her eyes wet with tears, and then she turned her face to his chest and closed them.

Whoever they are, Nic vowed as he walked down the path, *I'll find them.*

Sabine's head lolled back, over his arm. He paused and set her down, holding his own breath as he did so. She was breathing. But she was unconscious again.

Sabine blinked her eyes and stared at the ceiling. It wasn't hers.

She sat up fast, and spotted Nic asleep on the floor, with his arms crossed, head on a rolled-up blanket. She looked down. She was in her nightdress, covered in soot. In the other cot was Everett, softly snoring.

For a moment she thought she was in a dream, but then the terror of last night came back to her. The men. The guns. The smoke. She had just decided to burst out the door, shooting anyone in her way, when the smoke overtook her. She had collapsed and dimly watched the flames eat through her ceiling before she fell under the spell of unconsciousness.

Sabine glanced over at Nic again. He must've heard the gunfire and come and rescued her. Somehow. Dimly, she remembered being in his arms, watching her cabin burning, but no more. Where had the intruders gone? Who were they? She remembered their low voices, their laughter, the sound of her front door splintering, the footsteps on her roof, and shivered.

Quietly, she tiptoed over to the bucket of water, desperate for a drink. Nic's eyes popped open, and he raised his head. "You all right?"

"As all right as I can be," she whispered with a croaky voice. She could feel his eyes on her as she bent over the pail, lifted the ladle, and drank, then drank some more. She placed the ladle back on its perch on the lip and moved to the door, unable to meet Nic's gaze. Quietly, she lifted the latch and moved outdoors, her still-burning eyes met by a brilliant pink sunrise seeping across the valley.

He'd think she owed him now. Coming to her aid like that. Risking his own life. What would he demand as payment?

She crossed her arms. It was cold out here, this early. And she, with nothing but a nightdress.

He came out after her then, rubbing his head and his face as if still trying to awaken. He carried a jacket with him and she turned away, feeling discomfited by his attentions. Still, she accepted the coat when he reached her and he settled it around her shoulders.

Sabine took a deep breath, waiting for him to speak, and inhaled the scent of him—smoke and pine pitch and saddle leather. It was a good smell, not like her husband's had been. His had been alcohol and old sweat and rotting teeth.

"Pretty morning," he said softly, standing beside her, crossing his arms as if trying to stay warm. She supposed she had on his only coat.

"It is," she returned. "No matter what happens in the night, the sun rises in the morning."

"True," he said.

They stood there in companionable silence.

"Sabine, I'm sorry about your place."

She shook her head and glanced down to her toes. Not even a pair of shoes for her to wear … "It was only a house. In a way, it's a relief to be done with the bad memories of what happened there. Fitting, somehow, that it burned to the ground." She cocked her head and glanced at him.

"You know who those men were last night?"

"No. But I can guess who sent them."

"Who?"

She gave him a small, incredulous smile. "Who would want to scare me off?"

He lifted his chin, no trace of a smile on his face. "You think the men of the Dolly Mae would go to such great lengths?"

"There's a reason they came to me and not you last night, Nic. You were ready to take the deal. I'm the obstacle."

He stared at her a long moment and then rested his chin in one hand. "Men can be ruthless," he said, looking her way. "But we're hardly a match for them, Sabine. What do you want to do?"

"Hold them off. Find another buyer, if we must. Or our own

investors. But I won't let my beloved land—or Peter Vaughn's—go to men who are underhanded."

He caught and held his breath. "It won't be easy."

"No. I suppose it won't."

"It might not even be possible."

"Maybe not. But we have to try."

He thought on that for a while; then, "What about Everett? We're putting him in danger, messing with men of this sort."

"We're showing him what it means to stand up for what's right. We're teaching him to demand the full value of his land, if someone wants to buy it. We're teaching him to be a man. It's what Peter would've wanted."

"Peter? Or you?" he asked carefully.

"Both of us."

Nic rubbed the back of his neck, as though it hurt. "You'll have to hole up here with us. Unless you have some other safe place you can go. We can hang up a couple blankets between the beds. Give you privacy. Or I can sleep out on the front porch if you prefer."

She looked down at her feet and then out to the view, embarrassed to be discussing such intimacies. "Thank you. We'll find our way." She looked up and met his intense, lingering gaze. She wished she could read what he was thinking. What he wanted from her, if anything.

He pulled away as if he was reluctant to be known so intimately and moved up to the house. "I'll get some coffee on," he muttered.

"Nic."

He turned and looked over his broad shoulder at her, waiting.

"Thank you. I owe you my life."

He gave her a small smile and a gentle shake of his head. "You owe me nothing, Sabine. But I find myself hoping …" He broke off, shook his head as if thinking better of his words, and then moved away.

"What? What are you hoping for?"

He turned around slowly, until he was facing her. He lifted his hands out, palms up. "I'm hoping that someday you won't feel like you *owe* me anything, but after yesterday I found myself wanting …" He squinted and looked down at the ground.

She sighed and said, "What? Just tell me."

He stilled and lifted his eyes to stare into her own. "Since yesterday, Sabine," he said lowly, "I keep finding myself hoping you'll want to *give* me a little bit of your heart. Not because you feel like you *owe* me anything. But because you hope for the same from me." He laughed then, seemingly at himself, lifting his eyes and hands to the sky.

She stared at him and then, realizing her mouth was hanging open, abruptly shut it. "Oh," she said softly, belatedly.

"Right," he said. His eyes hardened and he turned away from her and walked up the hill to the cabin, never looking back again.

Sabine wanted to call out to him, make him wait, make him clarify what he meant, but she knew. And she wasn't ready for more than that. It was all too much—losing her home and now discovering that a man was falling in love with her. Her eyes narrowed and she looked out to the valley again. What if it was all another ruse? Was he looking to make her fall in love with him so he could control her land too, sell it to anyone he wished?

No, that's not right either. She could feel God's gentle nudging, setting her back to His way of thinking. She shook her head and lifted her hand to her temples. Nic knew who she was, knew what she was—nothing more than a *half-breed* that other men dismissed—and yet he was still drawn to her. Was it possible? Possible that she might be finding love, after all this time? She'd given up on it. Never thought she'd find a man like that.

Not that she knew enough of *him*, yet.

But what she did know, she liked, she admitted to herself. Liked very much. She tried to swallow, but found her mouth dry again.

She scanned the sky changing hues before her eyes. Perhaps, in time, her next steps would become clearer too, like the last colored vestiges of sunrise giving way to the blue skies of day.

CHAPTER TWELVE

After lighting the lamp, Nic straightened and watched Sabine approach. "What is it that you think you're doing?"

She was in his trousers, belted at the waist with a piece of rope, and one of his shirts, which hung in big folds from her torso and arms. The sleeves were rolled up. She'd wound rags around her feet since she'd lost her shoes in the fire and pulled her hair up into a loose knot. "You didn't expect me to stay in my nightdress all day."

"No," he said slowly. Despite her silly appearance, he didn't know if he'd ever seen her look more fetching. "But what are you doing here?"

She had a determined look on her face. "I want to help in the mine."

"Sabine, you're not even in proper clothing. And a mine is no place for a woman."

She shrugged her shoulders. "We need some cash to purchase new clothing for me. And there are plenty of women who mine in these mountains. It looks as if I'm to be one of them. At least," she hesitated, "for a while."

He studied her a long moment and then sighed. Another set of adult hands would be welcome down below, woman or no. And she was right—they would need funds to purchase her new clothing.

"And if we're to try and find our investors, we need to expose more of the vein. The farther we can dig and show them it continues on, the better offer we'll get."

He studied her. She stared back, expectantly. Everett watched them both.

"Do you always get what you want, Sabine?"

"It's not often I ask for anything."

Nic paused another second, then bent and picked up an ax. He handed it to her. "Don't say I didn't give you the opportunity to get out of this. Lord knows, I'd take the first chance to get out of it."

She smiled and followed him into the mine.

Nine hours later, Sabine straightened and groaned. Her arms and shoulders ached. Her back hurt. There was a fine layer of dust on every inch of her, including the inside of her nostrils. She looked over at Everett, clearly as exhausted as she was. He sat on a boulder in the corner of the mine tunnel, watching them both with dull eyes. Nic was six feet down in the beginnings of their shaft.

All that work for a lousy foot of gain. The three of them had toiled all day long. Was it still even light out? She walked to the corner and peered down the passageway and glimpsed blue sky. They probably had another several hours of daylight, but she didn't know if she could plunge a shovel or lift a pickax one more time. She returned to the shaft where Nic was still whacking away at the side, trying to square up the shaft.

Nic looked up at her and grinned, his teeth brilliantly white against the backdrop of his dirty face. "Don't tell me you're giving up already." He wiped his forehead of sweat, leaving a smear of dirt across it.

"I'm not giving up," she said, instantly moving the pickax in her hands.

He lifted a hand a little in her direction and shot her a curious look. "Hey, I was only teasing. It's tough work. I'm about to call it quits. We need to shore up this shaft with some timbers tomorrow. To say nothing of the time it will take for us to clean up."

She eased her stance, feeling embarrassed by her reaction. Why must she always be so defensive?

Nic stepped on a crossbeam already in the shaft, and Sabine reached down to give him a hand up. He lifted one brow in surprise, then took her hand. In a second, he was up, beside her, and she quickly let go of his hand, self-conscious under Everett's gaze. All day they'd bumped into each other as they dug and handed up pails full of dirt to the child above. Every time, it sent a surge through Sabine's body, making her scalp tingle.

He looked down into the shaft, surveying their work, panting a little, and she noticed his full, well-formed lips. What would it be like to have him kiss her? She felt her face flame. What had come over her?

He looked her way as Everett trudged past them, obviously noting her discomfort. "Tired?"

She gave him a small smile. "I think I might sleep tonight."

"Think we've cleared enough away to win over a new investor?" He didn't even try to cover his wry smile.

"Maybe after another thirty days like today," she said, glancing down.

"You ready for another twenty-nine days?" he asked.

"I am if you are. But I'd like a couple sets of clothes, so I can have a clean set each day."

"Me too," he said, with a nod toward her attire. "So I can wear mine."

She gave him a rueful smile. "Sorry about that."

His eyes softened. "It's all right. Have to admit, you look pretty charming in my clothes. Better than I ever did in them."

She smiled again and turned, afraid he might kiss her right then. She wanted him to kiss her. And yet she didn't. She bent to pick up the pails. "I saw that you have some eggs. What if we fry them up with salt pork and skillet biscuits for dinner? Tomorrow we should go and find any chickens left over at my place."

"Sounds good to me."

They moved toward the light at the end of the tunnel, and Sabine took her first free breath of air. She hadn't known what it was like, to be in the dark for so long, so dirty, breathing stale air. She'd never offered to help her husband; he'd never asked. It would get worse as they went down, she knew. She'd heard the stories of old miners around St. Elmo.

Outside, she caught sight of Everett to the right, wearily trudging toward the house, head down. But then her eyes were on the trail that led past the mine, and to her house. Or where it had once stood. She paused, looking at the trees that parted and the brown trail that disappeared around a bend.

He stood there with her, in silence for a while. Then, "Need to go see it?"

Still she remained where she was. Part of her wanted to see it. Part of her didn't. There was part of her that wanted to believe it had all been a terrible dream. That the cabin was still there, waiting for her. And her things. Her diary, her books, the few treasures she had amassed over time. To be without them—to be forever without them … it was too sudden. Too much of a rip, like a lightning bolt splitting a tree in half, leaving one side to grow, scarred, the other to shrivel.

"It might help—" he began.

"No." She shook her head and moved toward his cabin.

He caught her hand, gently pulling her to a stop. And she turned back. He gazed at her with compassion. "I could go with you."

"No," she repeated. She withdrew her hand from his, slowly, then turned and walked away.

"When you're ready," he said, catching up with her. "If you need me …"

"Yes," she said. "I …I know."

He followed behind her a step, so he could watch her. She moved gracefully, even distracted and in his clothes. His eyes followed down her lithe body to slim hips and slender ankles. She was impressively strong for such a small woman. There was a part of him that hoped that the day's work would convince her to return with him to face the men of the Dolly Mae, corrupt though they may be, to see if they could salvage their deal. Surely she wouldn't want to continue their dig. Would it not be best for her to sell and begin to rebuild, somewhere else, somewhere new?

And yet there was a part of him that caught his breath at the thought. What if she left, went on to some other place, far away? Would they ever be able to discover what seemed to be growing between them? He shook his head. He had to focus on what was real, not what might be. That was how he was of best use, to her, to Everett, to himself. *Get your head out of the clouds*, he heard his father say, as he had so often said in Nic's youth. *You can't be any earthly good if your head is always in the heavens.*

He paused, broke off his pace behind Sabine, letting her go ahead. Memories of his father came flooding back, along with the promises Nic had made to him—to look after Odessa and Moira. Yet he still hesitated to contact Odessa even though he was but a couple of days' ride away. He lifted a hand to his head and stared to the valley floor, envisioning each of his sisters. Would they forgive him his absence? Would they welcome him, when he had so utterly separated himself? Was it even worth the effort of trying?

Perhaps it would be best for them if he stayed away. If he didn't disrupt their lives.

No, that didn't settle right either. *Stand up and face the consequences,* he heard his father say. How many times had Father said that to him? Nic closed his eyes, picturing his father's expression of disgust or dismay or dissatisfaction. It pained him, even now, years after he had passed away. Why did it still plague him, what his father thought of him? How he felt judged and found wanting, again and again?

It would've been better if my brothers had lived and I had died.

Even as he thought it, it rang hollow in his heart.

I'm weary, Lord, he said silently, lifting his eyes to the skies, *of feeling guilty for living. Of feeling unworthy. Of feeling nothing but failure. Show me. Show me the way out.*

The response wasn't in words but an urge. A desire that began inside, at the core of him, but clear in its pull. *Come. Walk with Me.*

That's how Nic would put it, if he had to tell someone else … and he sincerely hoped he wouldn't.

His head came up and he looked down the path. Sabine was looking back, a question in her pretty brown eyes.

"Coming," he said, responding, though she hadn't called out any question.

She turned and walked, not waiting.

Nic looked back out to the valley. Something was shifting inside him. Something forceful. Something foreign and bigger than him, like the power of the seas themselves.

And he wasn't sure he liked it.

The hymns were challenging, to be sure.

As Moira practiced that afternoon, preparing for the evening's sing, she stopped and rested her hands on the piano, staring at the words and music before her. The hymn had been her maternal grandmother's favorite. She still remembered being in the portly woman's lap, staring at the black-and-white notes that, when she placed fingers to keys, became a rainbow in sound.

> *Abide with me; fast falls the eventide.*
> *The darkness deepens; Lord, with me abide.*
> *When other helpers fail and comforts flee,*
> *Help of the helpless, O abide with me.*

She rested her head against the music stand. *Help of the helpless,* she thought, *I need You.* It seemed that every hour of daylight was measured against Daniel's absence. His departure made the seconds become minutes, the minutes hours. While outwardly she recognized the importance of his desire to resolve whatever tortured him from the past, it left her floundering in her present. How could he so callously walk away from her?

Her thoughts moved to a time when she was sought after, pursued. The stage … all those men clamoring for a glance, a sweep of her hand … But her audience had disappeared within a fortnight, thinking only of the next woman to adorn their local stage. She thought instead of Gavin's mother's letter, her friendly tone. Could she possibly mean what she'd written? Then Moira considered Daniel and the longing she felt deep within for his return. But he seemed farther off than ever.

What to do, whom to rely upon? Only You, Savior.
Only You.

Moira raised her head and focused on the words, found her fingering.

I need Thy presence every passing hour;

What but Thy grace can foil the tempter's pow'r?
Who like Thyself my guide and stay can be?
Through cloud and sunshine, oh, abide with me.

She sighed and closed the lid of the piano, covering the keys. She needed to get out. "Odessa?" she called up the stairs. "I'm going out for a bit. For a walk." Her sister bade her well and she moved out of the house, through the front door, and to the hot sunlight of midafternoon. She didn't wear a bonnet. She wanted to feel the heat, to lie down somewhere she could close her eyes and see the sunlight flit in red-gold patterns against her lids, like she had as a child.

She walked to the creek. Five hundred yards up, she could hear men working. Some singing. Some shouting. Mostly hammers and saws. There, the men of the Circle M—those who had seen Bryce and Odessa and the rest through Reid Bannock's attack—had been allotted five acres each. Six of them were building an enclave of sorts, a village of homes that they could bring a young bride home to, perhaps eventually raise children.

She could see it in their eyes. Their furtive glances. They wondered if she might stay, perhaps be that potential bride for them. And with Daniel's departure, a few had been more forward the last couple of days. Gently, she dissuaded them. Her mind and heart were set on a certain sheriff, foolish though she may be....

Moira looked up to a giant oak, sprawling across the creek. She sat down with her back against the curve of it, watching the sunlight sparkle atop the water, and then she closed her eyes to envision it dancing across her eyelids. It was comforting, to hear the men in the distance, working so hard on homes they hoped to fill; the dancing, tinkling waters of the creek; the rush of a thousand leaves as a gentle breeze washed down off the mountains.

Abide with me; fast falls the eventide, she hummed. *The darkness deepens; Lord with me abide.*

"Moira," a voice said in wonderment.

Her eyelids flew open; the respite fled. She blinked, recognized a couple of the men who had been working on the Circle M these past weeks. The man shook his head. "I *knew* I knew your voice. I'd heard it before. You're not Moira St. Clair. You're Moira Colorado."

CHAPTER THIRTEEN

Moira rose, feeling caught between the two men and the giant tree at her back.

One moved a step back and turned halfway, obviously not wanting her to feel trapped. But the other leaned forward from the waist, studying her face. He shook his head in wonder and then nodded. "You're her. I'll never forget that voice. I was in Telluride when you were singing once, last spring." He gave her a slow, conspiratorial smile and raised one brow. "But you weren't singing *hymns* then."

"You must have me confused with another," she said. She pushed past him and walked swiftly toward the house.

"Donald …" his friend tried, sounding as if he hoped to dissuade the man from following, but he stayed right beside her.

"They said you died. The papers reported you were burned in an opera house fire. Is that what happened to you? Why you wear the scarves? The veil?"

"Donald!" his friend called from behind.

The stable came into view as she strode forward. Tabito looked up. She took a relieved breath as he glanced from her to the man beside her and back again, then immediately began walking toward them, concern etched in his face.

But still Donald persisted. "Why are you hiding, Moira? You

have one of the most famed voices in the West. Why, you could set up on a stage in Conquistador and pack the house every—"

"Please. Leave me be." She stopped and faced him. "You don't know me. You don't know anything about me."

"Everything all right, miss?" Tabito asked, joining them.

"This man is bothering me," she said. "He is … confused." She kept walking as Tabito reached out and grabbed Donald's arm. Her heart was hammering in her chest.

She hurried into the house, ignoring Odessa's call from the kitchen. She ran up the stairs and closed the door of her bedroom, resting her forehead against it. Then she moved to her bed and drew her knees up. It was a miracle, really, that no one had recognized her until now. Bryce and Dess had shielded her from the reporters that came to the ranch to interview them, but the journalists' focus had been on the hook of their story—the conquistador gold find and a rogue sheriff. They never guessed that there might be another; that Moira Colorado had survived the tragic opera house fire. They never asked how Reid Bannock came to hold Odessa; they never guessed that Dess had traded herself, almost sacrificed herself, for Moira.

If they found out, they'd surely return for the rest of the story. Moira shook her head. *They must not find out.*

She could not bear the scrutiny. The publicity.

She lifted her pillow and pulled out Francine Knapp's letter. Maybe it would be best if she left for a while.…

They slept on opposite sides of the curtain, but he could feel her there. He imagined her asleep, on her side, head on the pillow, her face a mask of peace. It curiously drove him, that desire to see any trace of angst or dissatisfaction melt from the wrinkles of her forehead and mouth. But he resisted the urge to peek.

Would not selling to the men of the Dolly Mae give her some permanent peace, regardless of how it might grate at first?

A horse whinnied outside the door, and Nic sat up. He grabbed his rifle and moved over to the window, glancing over. Everett and Sabine were still fast asleep. Outside, a horse bent to nibble at long grasses by the cabin. He peeked a little farther. The sheriff. And another portly man he did not know.

Nic eased open the door, hoping to allow the others to continue their rest, but both stirred at the creak of the hinge. He winced and then edged outside, lowering his gun and rubbing his head with the opposite hand. "Sheriff," he said.

"Dominic," Sheriff Nelson returned, dismounting.

Beside him, the other man lumbered to the ground as well. He straightened his shirt and jacket and reached out his hand. "Parson Brookings," he said.

Ahh, the local clergyman.

The sheriff took a couple of steps forward and shook Daniel's hand. "You folks have some trouble up here in the Gulch?"

"Trouble?" Nic said, putting on a blank look. "What sort of trouble?" From the beginning, Sabine and he had both known that alerting the local authorities would only bring further difficulties down on them—and possibly Everett. That was the way of things in this part of the country. If you wanted justice, you saw to it yourself. Once in a blue moon, the sheriff picked up the slack. But with a company the size and influence of the Dolly Mae giving their side of the story ...

"Word reached us late yesterday that Sabine LaCrosse's cabin was afire the night before last. A man from the other side of the valley reported seeing it burn. We've been by there this morning. Nothing but ashes. Have you seen her?"

"Yes," Nic said. "She's here. With me."

The parson shifted his considerable weight to the other foot and coughed. A red tinge worked up his neck, and his eyes narrowed.

"Now, hold on," Nic said, lifting a hand. "I'm only being neighborly. I assure you that nothing untoward is going on. Everett's here with us."

"You may not know, Mr. St. Clair," the parson said with a sniff, "that I am the school superintendent as well as the local pastor. We simply cannot have our teacher living in … such conditions. It's not right."

The sheriff's red mustache twitched. "Care to tell us what happened?"

Nic paused. "No. No, Sheriff, I don't suppose I do."

The sheriff nodded and dug his boot toe in the ground. "I see. Anyone hurt? In the fire?"

"No, sir. Not that I know of." Other than the man Sabine shot.

The sheriff studied him for a long moment. "I'll need to see Mrs. LaCrosse for myself. You know, to make sure she's all right."

"She's all right," Nic said, lowering his gaze. Did the man think he had hurt her?

"Yes, well—"

The door creaked open again and Sabine emerged, a disheveled sight in one of his clean white shirts, hanging loose, and pair of pants, hair a tumbled mess.

Never had Nic seen her look more beautiful.

He glanced at the sheriff and parson, knowing what they would think. The men paused, seemed to catch their breath. *So they noticed how glorious she was too.*

"Nic saved me," Sabine said, looking up at the lawman from ten paces away. "My place caught fire. I would've died there had Nic not come running and pulled me out."

The sheriff and parson looked from her to Nic to her again. The sheriff said, "I know what that place meant to you. You plan on rebuilding?"

"Perhaps," she said, shifting her eyes to Nic.

"Surely you realize you've put me in an impossible situation, Mrs. LaCrosse," the parson put in. His mouth worked as he searched for the right words, thought better of them, and then formed another sentence. "I've fought to keep you as our teacher, these last two years especially. But this ... St. Elmo is doing her best to be a civilized town. A town of morals. If word reaches—"

"I resign, Parson Brookings," she interrupted. "You still have a few weeks to find a suitable replacement. I'm certain that all will be relieved when you find a more *educated* woman to fill my position."

"Sabine, now see here, it's not about that at all," he grumbled, frowning. "You've done a decent job, these last few years. I—"

"No, Stuart, stop," she said. "You and I both know that if a *white* woman had her house burned down, and her kindly neighbor rescued her and took her in for a few days, the superintendent would not be so quick to judge." She paused, took a breath, and seemed to soften. "I recognize that you've protected me from those who wanted me removed long ago. I'm grateful for that. But this seems as good a time as any to move on." She glanced at Nic. "We're looking to sell our properties together."

"But you turned down the Dolly Mae offer," the sheriff said.

"She ... *we* didn't like how that offer came about," Nic said. "We want to deal with men we can trust."

"Ahh," the sheriff said, lifting his chin. "I may know of some others who would be interested. Want me to bring them by in a few days?"

Other investors? Nic's heart started beating faster. He had a good sense about the sheriff. He'd likely bring them people Nic'd like too, hopefully not like this blustering parson. He glanced over at Sabine, and she met his gaze. She was open to a meeting.

"We'd appreciate that, Sheriff," Nic said. "Bring 'em by in three days; we'll be ready for them."

"Will do," he said. He paused and looked at Sabine again. "I don't suppose you know anything about a man with a bullet wound, do you?"

"Depends on the man," she returned evenly.

He gave her a small smile. "This man said he was minding his own business, when someone shot at him. Winged him in the shoulder. Funny thing is, the man reeked of smoke. Could barely be in the same room with him."

Nic's eyes narrowed. "You know him, Sheriff?"

"Nah. He's new to town. In fact, Doc fixed him up and then he took off. Couldn't find him again last night."

"Hmm," she said. "Story like that, I imagine there's more to it."

He studied her for a long moment. "Yes. I believe you're right."

He put on his hat again and looked back to her. "You hear more about that story that you think relates—will you come see me?"

"I will."

He followed Parson Brookings to their horses, mounted, and looked back at them. "I'm just down the hill if you need me," he said. "I'll see you folks in three days."

"Sheriff," Nic said, nodding in parting. "Parson Brookings."

Sabine gazed after them, stoic, as they turned and rode away. Nic studied her. He could watch her all day. Her guileless expression hardened as she turned to him.

"You all right?" He reached out and pushed back an errant piece of hair over her shoulder, and she looked back at him.

"Do you think I'm all right?" A tinge of tears made her eyes shine, surprising him.

"I think you've suffered a blow losing that job. But maybe … it frees you up to go elsewhere, if we sell the land. Find a new position, if you want it. With people who not only accept you, but really want you as their school's teacher."

She studied him a moment longer, then turned toward the open doorway.

Everett peeked out. "Who was here?"

"Sheriff came by to make sure Sabine was all right," Nic said, winking at her. He turned to the boy. "You hungry for breakfast?"

"Yeah," Everett said, rubbing his eyes. "I want pancakes."

"That," Nic said, "I think we can manage."

"And after that," Sabine said, "I'll head to town to purchase some clothes."

"Want me to go with you?" Nic asked.

She shook her head and then looked up at him. "It would be good for me to be alone. Consider what just happened. And where I might go next."

He tried to hide his frown. There was nothing spoken between them. No reason for him to protest the idea of her going anywhere without him, insist upon his protection. Hadn't he been thinking the same thing this morning? That if they sold the land, they'd be free to go anywhere they pleased? But there was something different about hearing her say it.

He turned away before she could make out his expression, discern what he was thinking. Everett was looking out the door again, waiting on them.

"Pancakes," Nic said, rubbing his hands and pretending to be more lighthearted than he suddenly felt. "I think I might eat ten myself. How many will you eat?"

"Twenty," the boy said, grinning. It felt good to see the child smile again. But his smile didn't last long as he looked past Nic to Sabine, who was still standing outside. "She comin'?"

"She'll be along," Nic said, gently shutting the door. "She just needs a bit of time to herself. She's not used to sharing a place with two men."

She was exiting the mercantile, crossing the street, when he rode up and blocked her way.

Rinaldi.

She stood still, waiting, hoping some of the passersby on the boardwalk would sense her hesitation and see if she was all right.

But they all moved on, either unaware or uninterested in getting involved.

Rinaldi circled her, still on his horse. "Came down for some new boots, I see."

"Boots and other things," she said. She shifted the packages in her arms. The gold dust had been just enough to cover all she needed.

She moved to the right, but he edged his horse around, dismounted, and grabbed her elbow. "Come with me," he ordered, pretending to smile and tipping his hat toward two young women who passed by and gazed their way. He pulled her toward the alley beside the Merc and then blocked her way.

"You have no right—"

"You couldn't just agree to the offer they gave you, huh?"

She clamped her lips shut. He towered over her, but Sabine refused to back away. It'd give him too much pleasure, she knew. It had been the same with her husband. "It was a good offer," he said.

"Not good enough."

He took a breath. Then, "You cut down my partner."

She stared up at him, incredulous that he would own up to it. "You burned down my house and tried to kill me."

"It wasn't yours. It was your husband's."

"It was mine."

"Come with me, Sabine," he said in a monotone. "Take the offer."

"That deal has come and gone."

"I happen to know the offer might still be on the table. If you sign, so will St. Clair."

She looked down, to her right, then back into his cold gray eyes.

"I don't take offers from men who would burn down my house with me in it. Something about that makes me not trust you."

Rinaldi scoffed and looked up the mountain, in the direction of the Gulch. "Does your partner agree with that?" He said the word *partner* as if it were something unsavory, unclean.

She followed his gaze, thinking of Nic, working inside the mine today, of Everett, wearily filling yet another pail of soil to carry to the pile outside. How dare this louse disparage either of them. How dare he insinuate …

She drew in a long, slow breath through her nostrils. "My *partner* respects my opinion. And my opinion is this …" She reached out and poked the despicable man's chest. "You and your bosses are the worst kind of predators. Had you come to us with an honest offer, had you not dealt such an underhanded blow, we might've taken the deal. But now? No." She shook her head, ignoring his startled expression. She pressed on. "No. Never. The Dolly Mae Company can find another valley in which to roost. They will not have ours."

He backed up a step and looked down at her, his eyes wide. Then his expression hardened. "You don't want to do this, Sabine."

"I do."

"It won't bode well for you. I'm giving you fair warning. I've heard tell that you might be entertaining other investors."

"And if we are?"

He cocked his head. "I wouldn't be sleeping too soundly tonight."

"Get out of my way," she said. "I'm leaving."

He slowly stepped aside but leaned down and grabbed her arm again, speaking lowly into her ear. "You realize this isn't the end of it. You can hide behind St. Clair, but not forever."

"Let me go," she ground out through her teeth.

He casually let her go and then moved to his horse and swung up into his saddle. "I'm coming to see you tomorrow, Sabine."

"You step foot on my land or Nic's, know that I'll have a rifle in hand. And you'll get far worse than your friend got."

He let a slow smile spread across his face. "You always did have spirit. You go on back to St. Clair, now. Tell him the offer still stands. Chances are, those other investors won't offer you half of what the Dolly Mae can give you."

"Chances are, we'll trust anyone more than you and your bosses."

He was no longer smiling. "Tell him, Sabine. Tell him it's best to take *our* offer."

But no answer came to her on the wind through the trees.

She turned away and strode down the street to her horse, hurriedly securing her packages to the saddle. Why was she so stubborn? Even after the fire. Why not take what she knew they could get and move on? Why hold on, hoping these new investors would pay out decently, risking not only her life, but also Nic's and Everett's?

She glanced up the Gulch, picturing the yawning mouth of the mine. She hated every minute she was in that hole. She hated the grit and grime, the darkness, the punishing toil that left her arms and shoulders and back aching, begging her not to repeat the punishment the next day. The only bright spot was being there with Nic and Ev.

But still, she resisted. It wasn't right, giving in to the men of the Dolly Mae. It was too much like her years with her husband, giving in to abuse, thinking it was all she could expect out of life.

There was something better ahead.

Wasn't there?

CHAPTER FOURTEEN

The sheriff had sent word that he'd need a few more days than he thought. He was waiting on an investor from Denver to arrive in town. Nic, Sabine, and Everett redoubled their efforts to expose as much of the vein as possible, but the day before, the vein had abruptly come to an end. And to make matters worse, water had begun to seep into the twelve-foot-deep shaft.

"I don't know what to do about that," Nic had said, staring down into the hole as he climbed out, the bottoms of his trousers soaked and muddy. "That's going to take a pump of some sort."

"So we'll get a pump," Sabine said.

"Sabine," he said, trying to control his agitation. "We're obviously hitting a water table. This is so far beyond my level of expertise, it's ridiculous. What if it's an underground lake? A mining company might be able to handle it. But you, me, Everett?" He let out a humorless laugh and threw up his hands. "We're done."

"No," she said. "We cannot be done. The sheriff's bringing those men here in two days. We need to do more than sit around and wait. We need to find the vein again."

"I'd wager the surveyors of the Dolly Mae had a pretty good idea the initial vein petered out about there," he said, gesturing toward the shaft. "You can be certain they knew about the water too. They took enough samples and did enough testing to have a good idea of what lays between us and China."

"So they knew. I don't see how that helps us."

"It doesn't."

"Then what do you suggest we do?"

"We could put in a well. Have some fresh artesian springwater," he said, exasperated.

She glared at him. She knew he was tired. But so was she. And this was important. Their future. "What if these new investors don't want to do that much testing? What if they're not as prepared to gamble on what lies beneath this water table?" She dug into the soil around a big boulder and brought up a pail of soggy dirt. It felt three times as heavy, wet.

Everett ignored their argument and cast down a bucket beside her. Sabine filled it with more mud, then Everett hauled it upward on its rope.

"This is like bailing water from a leaking boat. It's ridiculous," Nic said, gesturing toward the boy.

Sabine ignored him, yanked the pick from the wall beside her, and then felt it connect, just beyond the edge of a large rock. She pried it downward.

Nic sighed and began to climb down. "Hold on. Let me do that."

Still angry, she pulled on the rock, using her wet boot as leverage against the wall.

Panting, she gave up, but she frowned at the hole she'd left in the wall. It was spurting water.

Nic stared down at her, still several feet from the bottom. "Sabine, give me your hand," he said firmly.

She reached for him, but at that moment the boulder gave way, and a massive burst of water pushed against her. She went down into the mud at the bottom, getting a mouthful of dirty water in the face, but the boulder, thankfully, moved in the other direction, and narrowly missed her foot. Sabine came up and tried to scramble to her feet. She couldn't get any decent footing, slipping again and again.

The shaft rapidly filled with water, rising to her chest in thirty seconds. But then it was sinking. Sabine tried to make sense of it. She could see the water coming in. Where was it exiting? She felt behind her, noticed for the first time a sucking sensation.

Oh no. "Nic …"

But as she said his name, another hole in the shaft suddenly appeared, caving in on itself, spilling water outward. She struggled to find her footing and balance between what was raining down upon her and what was pulling behind her. The whole thing was becoming an underground river. "Nic!"

He grabbed her hand, but it was muddy and wet and immediately slipped from his grasp.

"*Sabine!*" Everett yelled from above.

She reached out, but there was nothing to grab. All was slick and slimy. She grasped for the nearest timber on her side of the shaft. "Nic!" she screamed, now fearful as the new hole gaped wider, a growing chasm pulling her toward it.

"I'll be there in a second!" he called. "Ev, throw me a rope! Tie it to a timber up there, good and tight!"

But she couldn't hold on, no matter how hard she tried. One foot slid and she went down to one knee again, chest-deep in water.

There the current took her, like a sail in the wind, backward to the hole. She wanted to scream, but her face was awash in cold water. She reached out, grasping, touching nothing but dirt clods that gave way in her hands like putty. The current was strong, so strong, it tugged her toward the hole, now just inches away.

"Sabine," Nic shouted, hovering above her then, a rope around his waist, reaching out with one hand. "Grab my hand. Grab it *now*."

She pushed with all her strength, and their fingers met, but the current was too much to resist. She plunged back into the water and her body turned. She fell headfirst down a shallow waterfall and through a tunnel beyond.

Sabine nosed upward through the dark waters, hoping, praying there would be a space for her to breathe. She reached up, feeling her way, searching, before she dared to surface, but there was nothing, just a long tunnel, full to the top. The water was pulling at her, fast. How far? Would she ever surface? Or would she die in this underground river?

Her lungs began to burn and she knew that her moments left were few, but then the current slowed. Cautiously, she reached up again, and felt air meet her hand. She rose and gasped, paddling in the water, and felt, rather than saw, the chasm of space. The echo of bubbling water reverberated around her. She gulped air. Her new boots, full of water, pulled her down. Forcing herself to remain calm, she paddled forward, hoping to reach the edge, or at least shallows, where she could rest.

There. Sharp, crystallized rock met her fingertips and she winced. But she was glad for the pain, glad for something solid, tangible, known.

Even if she was in utter darkness.

"Hello!" she called out through chattering teeth. Not that she hoped to hear anything back. Just to find out what she *could* hear.

Her voice reverberated through the cavern. It was bigger than she thought.

Right. The tunnel is to my right, she told herself as she turned, not wanting to get disoriented in the pitch dark. She pulled her body out of the water on the shallow ledge and curled her legs into her chest. *It's on my right. The way out is to my right.*

But she could hear the surge of water pouring in, the rush and power of it. She'd felt it, driving her onward, through what? A ten-, twenty-foot tunnel? Or was it longer?

Her teeth chattered and her body trembled.

Never, in all her life, had she felt more alone.

"Sabine!" Nic screamed, reaching down and through the water, vainly hoping she would be right there, reaching back. But there was nothing, nothing but cold, sucking water, rushing faster and faster through one side and out the other. Both holes yawned wider like the mouths of two monsters.

Everett screamed her name from above. Nic glanced up. The child's face was a mask of horror.

Nic racked his brain, trying to find a solution. He took a firm hold on the crossbeam and ducked low, to try to see the tunnel that had opened up, where Sabine had disappeared. *Stop the water. You have to stop the water.*

Of course. He turned and made his way to the boulder, nearly losing his own footing. Then he took a deep breath, went underwater, and tried to lift the stone.

At first it didn't budge at all; it was extraordinarily heavy. *Please, Lord,* he found himself praying. *Help me move it. Help me save Sabine. For Everett's sake, if not my own. For hers.*

The rock shifted out of its shallow pit. He came up out of the water, gasping for breath, trying to avoid the stream of water as he maneuvered the rock back into place, back into the wall from which it had come. Water cascaded in around it, the hole now much wider than the boulder. "I need some rocks, Everett! About this size," he said, showing the boy what he needed. "Toss 'em down to me, one at a time."

"What about Sabine? We have to go after her!"

"That's what I'm trying to do." He glanced up at the boy. "If she's alive, she's someplace where she can breathe, through there," he said, throwing his thumb over his shoulder. "Our only chance is to lessen the flow for me to go after her and pull her out."

"What if she *can't* breathe?" the boy asked, his voice so tremulous, so full of sorrow it almost made Nic want to weep.

"If she can't breathe, Ev, she's already gone." He clamped his lips together. "So come on. Toss me those rocks. Quickly."

The boy disappeared for a moment, undoubtedly over to the rock pile, and tossed the rocks down to him. Nic caught one and then another and another, each time placing them slightly behind the edge of the boulder, building up a temporary wall. Anything to slow the flow of water. In a few minutes, they had most of it sealed off.

Nic shook his head. "I'm not sure how long that will hold. I need some timber, nails, a sledge hammer."

The boy disappeared. In a moment, he handed down a plank. Nic positioned it against the far wall and against the boulder, making him trust that the rock might actually stay in place. He took the next three planks and fashioned a barrier against the rest of the wall, leaving a two-foot gap behind. "Ev, now start dumping dirt back there. Right here." He gestured toward the gap. "If you can get about twenty pails full down here, we'll cut off a lot of this flow. You'll be making a dam."

As the boy set to putting dirt back into the shaft, Nic turned to the other tunnel. It was easier to see now, since the water was lower. "Sabine!" he called. He cupped his hands around his mouth. "Sabine!"

He heard no answer, only the continual flow of water, like a stream that had overflowed its banks. "Throw me down another rope, Ev," he called up. In a moment, the rope landed in the water beside him and he plucked it out before it could get sucked away. Swiftly, he tied one end of the rope to the one that Everett had tied above. "Sure that rope's secure?" he called.

"Yessir."

Nic pulled off his boots and emptied them of water, eyeing the wall of stone. It was spurting out in a few new areas, and Everett's mud seemed to be doing nothing to stem the flow, just washing away. He had to hurry. He threw one boot to the top, then the other, not wanting them to weigh him down. Next, he checked the hitch knot at his waist to make sure it wouldn't give way, then the other that connected with the second rope. It brought back his days on the *Mirabella*, tying knot after knot.

"Okay, boy, this is how it's going to go. I'm going down there," he said, gesturing toward the new tunnel, "and I'll go as far as this rope will let me. If I can't come up for air at the end, I'll haul myself back. You make sure it doesn't come undone, all right?"

The boy nodded.

"Ev, if something happens and I'm not back in ten minutes, you run for the sheriff, all right? He'll see to you."

"You come back," the boy said, his expression one of blind panic. "You come back!"

"I'll do my best, Ev. Say a prayer for me while I'm gone." With that, he edged into the tunnel, feeling his way with his stocking feet. Below, the stream grew stronger, pulling at him. He frowned, then took several deep breaths, and let the water carry his body along a tunnel. Several times he reached upward, feeling for air, a space for air, but found nothing. The only good thing, he supposed, was the rush of water. All this water had to be going somewhere, spilling into something.

He was about to give up, thinking that the rope would pull tight, thinking he couldn't wait much longer to breathe, let alone fight his way up current, when he popped to the surface. He gasped for air and tried to make sense of the echo of his own sputtering in a wide chasm.

"Hello?" a voice called.

Nic laughed. "Sabine! I'm here! Sabine!" Their voices careened so fast and echoed so clearly around the chamber, he couldn't tell where she was.

"Nic? Nic!"

"Wait! I'm here. Come here to me, Sabine. We have to get back before it's too late."

He heard splashing and suddenly she was near him, reaching out, grasping his forearm, then wrapping her arms around him. She was laughing, giggling like a girl, laying her head against his wet shirt. "You're here. You came for me."

"We have to go," he said, reluctantly pulling himself away. "Back in that tunnel, as fast as we can."

"Back through?" He could hear the doubt in her voice, even though he couldn't see a bit of her.

"Yes, it's the only way. We stopped most of the water, but I'm not sure how long it will hold."

"How long do you suppose the tunnel is?"

"I don't know. Twenty, thirty feet? Here." He took her hand and placed it on the rope. "I'm going to stand here, keep it taut for you. It'll be easier for you to pull yourself along. When you get to the end, yank on the rope three times. I'll know you're safe and come after you."

"Promise?" she whispered.

He hesitated a moment. "Promise." He reached out and found her head, cradling it in his hands. "Go," he growled. "Don't stop. Go as fast as you can. For you. For Everett. For … me."

She moved out then. He could feel her making her way along the rope, inching forward, until the rope sank down below the surface. "I'll see you on the other side," she said in a whisper. But her promise carried over the waters as if she were right beside him.

She took a couple of deep breaths, and then went under. He felt comforted, each time she pulled. So strong was she. He wanted to think of her on the other side. Alive. She'd see to Everett. Together, they would find their way.

How many others had he failed to look after properly? This time, at least, he would have done what he could.

He pictured the mine shaft again, and their makeshift dam. How long would it hold? Surely long enough to get Sabine to safety. *Please, God, let it be long enough. Watch over her, Lord. Help her.*

Nic laughed under his breath and listened to the sound of it echo around the chamber. "Since when have I become a praying man?" he asked the darkness.

CHAPTER FIFTEEN

I'm not going to make it. The current wasn't nearly as strong as the one that had swept her down and into the cavern. But fighting against it, rather than allowing it to carry her, was a whole other matter.

She had to hurry. She didn't have much air left. She kicked and yanked herself up the rope, moving constantly, and yet feeling as though she were treading water. *Help me, Lord. Help me. Help us both get out. It's my fault. My fault that Nic's back there.*

And then her hand met air.

She pulled forward, and her face broke the surface.

Everett shouted, "Sabine! Sabine!" He grinned from ear to ear and she smiled, but her mind was on Nic, behind her.

She glanced at the wall. Water was spurting everywhere, Nic's makeshift dam about to burst. She pulled herself to where the rope was attached, stood up and turned. Three times she yanked at the rope. Was that an answering yank back? *Please God, please God, please God ...* she chanted silently. *Help him. Help him get through.*

She eyed the dammed wall again. Was it her imagination or were there more rivulets and spurts of water since she came up? "Come on," she whispered. "Come on, Nic." She looked to the rope, watched it tighten as he pulled forward, imagined his strong arms and felt hope surge inside her.

Three rocks tumbled down from the wall and Everett cried out. Water rushed through.

Sabine carefully made her way over, staying out of the worst of the current that had pulled her under before, and bent to feel for some rocks below. Nothing but mud. She chastised herself for thinking, even briefly, that her small hands might stave off the flow, knowing that to put herself in front of it might send her sliding down the tunnel again, endangering both Nic and herself.

She looked back to the cavern and rope. Still, he pulled. He was coming! Getting nearer!

Two more rocks fell down as did a plank from across the boulder. More rocks creaked in protest. Another plank, the one that spanned the shaft and was leveraged against the boulder, began to bend, splintering in the center.

"Sabine!"

Everett threw down another rope, and she tied it around her waist. She climbed to the first support beam, which was mostly out of the water. "Come on, Nic," she whispered, willing him to appear. "Come on."

The support beam cracked and the boulder edged outward, allowing a solid sheet of water to cascade over it and down through the tunnel that Nic was climbing.

"No!" Sabine cried, staring at the rope. What did it feel like for Nic, to be pummeled by such force? "Nic, come on! You can do it!" she cried, as if he could hear her. She willed the rope to move, wishing she could force it to tell her if he had been swept away, or was nearer than ever. Why didn't he appear? Where was he?

With a groan the third support plank gave way, the power of

the surge pulling out the huge long nail that Nic had pounded into it. Sabine lifted herself higher, but even as she did so, her heart sank. Nic's rope was entirely underwater now. Was the lifeline even there any longer? It was impossible to see in the swirling, muddy, dark water. The boulder rolled and a massive wave rolled through the shaft, cascading across, rolling, foaming, and then rushing outward.

"Sabine," Everett cried, reaching down toward her. Tears dripped down his face, much like her own. Wearily, she pulled herself up to the next board.

But then Everett was looking behind her, his eyes widening, not in terror, but glee. "Nic!"

"Nic?" She turned and looked over her shoulder. Nic came up, sputtering, trying to grab a bit of air, then went under. He pulled himself across the shaft, still connected to the rope.

Oh, thank You, God. Thank You, thank You, thank You, she said silently. She moved down a step, trying to reach for him, but he waved her away. Clearly too short of breath to speak. But his eyes were clear. *Get up there. To safety,* they said. *I'm coming too.*

She turned and climbed with renewed vigor, reaching the top quickly and then turning with Everett to watch Nic. The entire shaft was in danger of collapse. He had to get out as fast as possible.

"Here!" she called, throwing another rope down beside him. He grabbed hold and wrapped it around his waist, abandoning the first. And then he began to climb.

When he reached the top, his hair slicked back like her own, his teeth chattering, she and Everett pulled him over the ledge, laughing in hysterical relief. He lay on his back, panting, and

Everett hugged him from one side. Sabine took his hand and looked down at him. She shook her head. "I thought I'd never see you again."

He smiled and reached up to touch her cheek with the back of his hand. "I feared the same."

"*I* thought I'd be heading to that orphanage in Buena Vista," Everett said.

Daniel rode up with Glen to the Conquistador site, aware that with all the temporary carpentry and sawyer help, there might be a few fugitives among them. He'd studied the wanted posters, committing faces and details to memory. Most outlaws fled to Texas or as far as Mexico—as the Westcliffe First Bank & Trust robbers were rumored to have done—once their pictures and names began to circulate. But it was easy enough for a man to grow a beard— or shave it off—and go by a different name if he wished to stick around. Those were the most lethal sorts: the ones who didn't fear getting caught.

The workers watched out of the corners of their eyes as Daniel and Glen rode by. Many kept their eyes averted in deference, but a few stared back. Several who knew him from the Circle M lifted their hand or shouted in greeting.

The tiny town was taking rapid shape. The post office was entirely enclosed and roofed. Two men were inserting glass-paned windows. Four others were putting together roofing trusses on the ground before hoisting them atop the mercantile. A bell, still in its crate, stood beside the church location. Daniel smiled, thinking of it ringing, welcoming worshippers. He might come and worship there himself, once they got it going. On the edge of the block, all four walls were up at the sanatorium and roof trusses were in place. Several men were balancing on beams high above, receiving more lumber to start filling in the roof.

Daniel looked the men over, but as he passed, he closed his eyes. *Had that last man—? Was he—? Did he look like—?* He wheeled his horse around, ignoring the confused expression on Glen's face, as he studied the sanatorium crew again. He didn't see the man who had triggered his memory. Was one missing now? He thought back, trying to place how many had been working on that one wall before, certain there was one fewer.

He was imagining things. Believing what he wanted to believe. The idea that he might run across Mary's remaining killer here so soon after he became sheriff, hundreds of miles from where she had been murdered … He scoffed at his wild imaginings.

Bryce was on-site, looking over plans with an architect. He smiled when he caught sight of Daniel and offered a wave before he left the other man, who was still staring at his blueprints. Daniel asked Glen to introduce himself among the men and get a good look at each of them. Daniel reached out his hand as Bryce neared, and he shook it. "Good to see you, Daniel."

"And you."

"What brings you out to Conquistador today?"

"Getting familiar with your crew," he said lowly. "Wanted to make sure there weren't any wanted men among them."

"Fine by me," Bryce said, his eyes scanning the street.

"How's Moira?" Daniel asked.

"Why don't you come on up to the house, ask her yourself?" he said, lifting a brow.

"Maybe after a while. How is she?"

"Fine," he said, then paused. "She was singing for a bit, but she's quit." His voice dropped. "Two carpenters recognized her as Moira Colorado."

Daniel's head came up. "If that word gets out …"

Bryce met his gaze. "Newspapermen love that sort of story."

Daniel sighed. "I've learned it doesn't matter where we go or what we do, if we don't resolve our past, it will affect our present and future."

"Wise words," Bryce said, cocking a brow. "Spoken as someone wrestling with his own past, present, or future?"

Daniel studied him. Had Moira told him? He kept his expression carefully blank. "All three, I think. I have my fair share of skeletons," he allowed. That reminded him…. "Bryce, do you have a man on the crew that is in his forties, heavyset around the shoulders, brown hair, but balding a little?"

Bryce frowned, thinking it over, and then gave him a wry smile. "I probably have ten or more that fit that description."

"Do you mind if I do a walk through your little town? See if I locate a man I thought I recognized?"

Bryce gestured forward. "You're the sheriff, Sheriff."

They shook hands and Bryce set off down the street, leading his horse. A few minutes later, Glen whistled and lifted his chin, then nodded to his left. The sanatorium. Had he found the man that Daniel had spotted earlier? His heart skipped a beat and then pounded forcefully. He'd seen to it that the wanted poster for his wife's escaped killer—yellow with age, now—had been one of many that he and his deputies looked at that morning. The three men had shot him questioning glances when they got to that one, depicting a heavyset, brown-haired man wanted for a woman's murder, but none dared ask him about it.

He hurried forward, watching as Glen slid to the left side of the building, slowly drawing his pistol. Daniel tied up his horse and gestured toward his own dark brown hair, then pointed toward the back of the building with two fingers. *So he spotted a balding man too.*

Daniel held his breath and nodded his agreement, then eased his own gun from its holster. He moved down the opposite side of the building, his eyes running over each man's face. As they passed, work slowed to a stop, the sounds of sawing and hammering fading as each man stilled, watching what was unfolding before them.

Daniel frowned as he reached the last man. *He wasn't here. Who had—*

"Stand right where you are!" Glen shouted. "Raise your hands above your head."

Daniel whipped around and found his deputy, his revolver pointed at a tall brown-haired man with a handlebar mustache. He tried to swallow, but couldn't. "What's your name?" Glen shouted.

Daniel climbed through the joists of the supporting wall in front of him and made his way over to the man Glen had captured. His stomach was a knot. He'd missed this one, so focused was he on finding the man who killed Mary....

"Michael Hambry," the man said.

Daniel reached over and took the man's gun out of his holster, as Glen pulled one of the man's hands behind his back. "Ever been up near St. Elmo, Mr. Hambry?" Daniel asked, trying to get a hold on himself. He stared into Hambry's light-colored eyes, an odd contrast to his dark hair, remembering the poster he'd seen and thinking it was all the more likely that they'd captured their first wanted man.

"Can't say as I have," the man said in a snide tone.

"Well, you bear a striking resemblance to a man wanted for murder."

Nic accepted a mug of coffee from Sabine and watched her as she moved back to the stove to turn over the flapjacks. Everett sat on the edge of the bed, bouncing a little. "I am so, so hungry."

"You're always hungry," Nic teased him.

"Dad said it's because I'm growing," Everett said. A shadow crossed over his face at his own mention of Peter.

"Your dad would be proud of you, Ev," Nic said gently. "You've been doing a man's work around here. And yesterday—you helped me and Sabine get out of that hole."

Everett smiled, but then he shook his head. "I don't want to be that scared again."

"Me, neither."

Sabine put two flapjacks on a plate and set it on the table in front of Nic. She put a thick pat of butter on top and then, smiling slyly at Everett, a spoonful of honey. His eyes got wide and he hurried to his chair, picking up his fork as he sat.

She then poured herself a cup of coffee and sat across from Nic. "The sheriff's investors are due tomorrow."

"Yes, they are."

"Don't you think we ought to go up to the mine? See if we could do some work? Make it look a bit more presentable?"

He covered a smile. "You think we can make a tunnel filled with mud and rock and water more presentable?"

She looked away, as if embarrassed, and he was immediately sorry for his teasing. He reached across the table and took her hand. He was a little surprised that she allowed it. "I understand your desire. But yesterday ... Sabine, only by God's own hand did we survive." He paused, wondering over his own words. "I'm not anxious to be in there again. Let's let it ride. It's like my gambling days. You blow on the dice and let them fall as they may. They might not offer what we want for the land. They might offer more. We might not accept. But right now, I want to steer clear of the place that almost cost me you."

Still chewing his food, Everett watched him.

Sabine looked up and into his eyes. "All right," she said softly.

It struck him then. Between almost losing her yesterday and the pleasure of waking today, knowing she was on the other side of the curtain ... It was right there. Had been for days. *I love her. God help me, I love Sabine LaCrosse.*

She studied his face as if she could see the realization come over him. He wasn't ready for her to know. *Not yet.* He withdrew his hand from hers, rose, and turned away. "I need to step out for a bit. I'll be back." He pulled on a light coat to ward off the morning chill and then moved through the door, carefully closing it behind him.

He walked up the hill above the cabin until he was looking down at the moss-covered roof. A tendril of smoke curled and rose from the narrow chimney pipe, and he thought about Sabine sitting at the table, perhaps staring out the window after him, lost in her own thoughts. And Everett, happily munching away. Was it Sabine he loved? Or this sense of family he'd stepped into, almost by accident?

He put a hand on the back of his head and looked out to the valley. He'd been with many women before, some he'd fancied. But never had he proclaimed love for any of them. He had missed a couple, wondered about a few, but never longed for any until Sabine. Standing out here, he felt torn, wanting to be inside, beside her, reaching out and touching her even as a part of him writhed against what felt like increasing numbers of tethers tying him down.

Nic sat down, hard. *In love. So this is what it feels like.*

Down below, the door of the cabin creaked open and then shut. Everett walked past the house and down a faint trail. Immediately Nic knew he was heading to his father's grave site. *He must be missing Peter.* Was he as at ease in Nic and Sabine's care as he seemed?

Nic rubbed his eyes and face and then rested his chin on his forearms, looking out to the mountain valley. *You've cobbled together a sort of family here, Lord. On purpose?*

He heard no response, only the gentle breeze in the trees. His eyes scanned the mountains, some rolling and covered in pines, others fearsomely rugged and thrusting upward above the tree line, as if striving to reach their Creator. He thought of his father, who always professed belief in God but never really talked about Him. He thought of his mother, praying beside his bed each night. What would they think of Nic, here in Colorado, so near Odessa but still wrestling with something inside him that kept him from going to her?

The door down below creaked again, and Sabine walked out, looked around, saw him, then climbed up the hill. She sat down beside him, pulling up her knees and hugging them to her chest. She looked fresh and clean in her new skirt and blouse.

He held out his hand and after a half breath of hesitation, she slipped hers into it. They sat there for a while in companionable silence, staring outward. Then Nic said, "You think you can leave this place? For good?"

"I think so," she said. "Sometimes it's good to make a change."

"Where would you go? If you had a fortune in your pocket?"

She thought on that for a bit, then glanced at him. "I … I don't know. What about you?"

"Day by day, Sabine, I find myself hoping that wherever I go next, it'll be near you and Everett."

She smiled a little and looked to the valley, as if a bit embarrassed. But she kept her hand in his.

"I've had a fortune in my pocket before," he said. "A few years ago, when my father died, and I split the proceeds from the sale of his publishing house with my sisters."

She sucked in her breath. "You have sisters?"

"Two," he said, smiling gently at the thought of them. "Odessa— she was sick with the consumption, so we came out here so she could get well."

"Did she?"

"Yes. Married a rancher near Westcliffe. Bet they have a baby by now."

"Westcliffe? That's not far. You haven't sent her a letter? Don't you want to go see her?"

"Been a little busy since I arrived," he said, sidestepping her question.

"And the other?"

"Moira. Last I heard she was in Paris, singing on the opera stage there. But it's been a couple of years."

"Paris," Sabine said, lifting her brows as if that city were as far away as the moon. "My only sibling is Sinopa."

Nic nodded. "Do you miss him when he goes?"

She shrugged. "We make no promises to each other. But he has been here for me when I needed him most."

"I wish my sisters could say the same about me."

"You failed them?"

He thought about that a moment. "I'm not certain they would say that. But my father would. He would have wanted me to stay close to them. Yet I took my share and traveled."

"Where'd you go?"

"Europe, then the islands. Ended up in South America. Spent most of my inheritance by the time I got there. Then lost the rest when I was shanghaied. Eventually I got back to the States and here I am," he said, shrugging his shoulders a little.

"Here you are," she repeated, accepting his tale as if he were telling her about what had happened down in St. Elmo, not the far reaches of South America. She wasn't like most women, pestering him with detailed questions. She seemed to accept him as he was now, what she knew of him. It was enough for her, it seemed. And there was something reassuring about that.

"Sabine, I'd like you to meet my sister Odessa. Do you think you … you would be willing to come with me for a visit? You and Everett?"

She smiled at him. "I'd like to know your sister. Both of your sisters."

"You don't want to find another mine property?"

She let out a light laugh. "After yesterday, I don't care if I never step into a mine again. I only hope that the sheriff's friends will be able to offer us enough to move on, see where God is leading."

"Where God is leading," he repeated softly. "Do you believe God is leading us? All of us?"

"I believe He shows us where to go. But it's often only a few paces at a time."

She sounded content with that. Nic, he wanted to see several miles down the road. He sat there, looking at the mountains, considering the idea of God leading him anywhere. He supposed God had been nudging him all along, here and there. He clearly remembered making a few decisions that felt defiant of anything his father or God would've approved of. He had reveled in those decisions at the time. He had been angry, so angry then.

Where had that anger gone? Increasingly it seemed like a distant memory.

She lifted his hand and peered at it more closely. "Where did you get these cuts? And this knuckle," she said, touching a swollen joint that no longer bent, "what happened to you here?"

He hesitated. Would she fear him if she knew? He met her gaze, and finding only acceptance there, cleared his throat and said, "I used to fight, in the ring. Gambled my way from one corner of the country to another. Lost a few. Won a lot more."

She had stilled and stared into his eyes. "When did you last fight, Nic?"

"On a ship heading up the coast of South America, about four months ago," he said. He looked away, suddenly too fearful to continue looking in her eyes. "There was a sailor aboard, taunting me. We fought. And I was tied to the mast and whipped."

"Whipped?"

He nodded. "Thirty lashes. And left to stand tied to the mast through the night." He tucked his head to one side. "It wasn't all bad. There was a coal boss aboard that spoke to me of God. I didn't want to hear it then. But more and more, his words made sense to me. God has a claim on me. Has all along."

Something had shifted in her. She was pulling away, in more than the physical sense. He held onto her hand as she stood and turned to face him. Her face held a new kind of fear that he'd never seen there before.

"Sabine," he said. "I'm not that same man I once was. I know your husband … I'm not that sort of man. I was angry for a long while. Took it out on anyone I could. But not anymore. Not since that voyage … I'd never, ever hurt you. I swear it."

She pulled back a little. "He used to swear he'd never hurt me again," she said softly, glancing toward the creek.

"I will never hurt you, not even a first time. I promise it." He let her go then.

She pulled her hand up and crossed her arms. Then she looked into his eyes, searching them as if she was trying to figure out if she could trust him.

Everett was running along the path below them. "Sabine! Nic! Nic!"

"We're up here!" Nic called. But then he saw what had the boy concerned.

Rinaldi was back.

And he wasn't alone.

CHAPTER SIXTEEN

Rinaldi's head turned as if following Everett's gaze on the hill. He rode up with two others right behind him. Sabine's heart kicked up its pace. Nic stepped in front of her as Rinaldi's horse pranced before him.

"Well, isn't this cozy? The drifter and the schoolmarm, playing house."

"What do you want?" Nic said.

Rinaldi dismounted and stood in front of him. He had a good six inches on Nic, but Nic did not step back, even as the man moved closer. Sabine slipped a hand around one of Nic's arms, felt the power of it, and wondered if the confrontation would end in a brawl. It made her hands sweat, the thought of seeing Nic fighting. She never wanted to equate anything about her dead husband with this new man in her life.

Rinaldi pulled a piece of paper from an inside jacket pocket and slowly unfolded it. "I want you to sign this. Her too," he said, letting his eyes linger on Sabine.

Nic shifted slightly to break off the man's gaze. He took the papers, still staring impudently up at Rinaldi, and unfolded them slowly. His every action said, *I will not be rushed or pressured by you.* Sabine absorbed some of Nic's strength in standing up to Rinaldi, who was frowning at Nic, ignoring her. Sabine hid a small smile.

Nic glanced over his shoulder at her and then turned to pass her the papers. Everett finally reached them, scrambling into their circle. "It's a new offer," Nic said in a monotone. "Seventy thousand for each of us. Half up front, half in a year. Points tied to earnings."

Sabine took a step forward, so they stood shoulder to shoulder in front of Rinaldi. She shook her head and held out the sheets to him. "I told you in town. I don't trust men who would burn a woman's home down." She glared up at him. "Especially when I was the woman in that burning cabin," she said.

Rinaldi turned back to her. "It's a good offer," he said slowly. "More than fair. Take it."

"And if we do not?" Nic asked.

"You don't want to do that," Rinaldi said, his eyes shifting slowly from the boy over to Nic and Sabine. "Not if you're not ready for all-out war." He backed up a step and lifted his hands. "Why not take it?"

Sabine let out a scoffing laugh. "Everyone in town knows how the men of the Dolly Mae robbed the original owner. Many promises were never fulfilled. It's hardly a secret, Rinaldi."

"I'm afraid I can't let such idle gossip go unchallenged," he said. "Not about my employers." He nodded toward the papers, still in Sabine's hand. "Sign them and be done with it."

"You know that the sheriff is bringing his own investors up tomorrow, don't you? That's the reason for the pressure from you now."

"Pressure?" Rinaldi said, one eyebrow lifting. "This is not pressure. This is more money than either of you have ever seen, or will ever see again. Take it, and we'll all go to dinner tonight at Amy's Restaurant in town to celebrate."

"Tell you what," Nic said, pulling the papers from Sabine's hand and tapping them against Rinaldi's chest. "You go and tell your bosses that we'll get back to them tomorrow evening."

Rinaldi shook his head. "No. The deal is only good if you sign today."

"We're not signing today."

"Yes, yes you are," he said, eyeing Sabine again. He glanced down at Nic. "Now."

As he said the last word, the two men on either side of him moved in, grabbing hold of Nic's arms. Everett yelled and pulled on the arm of the nearest man that held Nic. The man shoved him to the ground. Two others rode up the hill, but Sabine was concentrating on Rinaldi, who picked the papers up from the ground and then advanced toward her. She retreated as he came around Nic, who struggled against the two men, but could not get free.

Sabine lifted her hand and forced herself to stand her ground. She closed her eyes and waited until he neared, seeing in her mind's eye her husband coming after her. *Help me, Lord. Help me.* Those days were long over, she reminded herself; why did she cower like it was happening now? She wished she had her rifle. From behind the gun sights, she never felt weak, exposed, vulnerable.

Shield me, Lord. She prayed Rinaldi didn't see her fear. A man like him fed on such emotions like a bear drawn to spawning salmon on the river.

Rinaldi grabbed her arm and shook her. "It's a good offer, Sabine.

Sign the pages and be done with it. No harm needs to come to you or yours." He glanced over at Everett with a menacing look.

"Let go of her!" Nic shouted. He writhed and kicked at one man, shoving him away, but before he could free himself of the second, the first was back.

Rinaldi looked at him and then back to Sabine. A slow smile grew across his face. He pulled her in front of him and gave Nic a sneer. "This rattle you, St. Clair? Me, with my hands on your woman?"

"We have company, boss!" shouted a man down the hill.

Sheriff Nelson rode out of the trees, a deputy beside him. He scanned the group, and as he did so Rinaldi and his men let go of Sabine, Nic, and Everett. "You folks all right?" he called to Nic.

"We are now." Nic turned and climbed the hill, taking Sabine's hand and leading her away from Rinaldi. He circled Everett's shoulder with his other hand, giving the child a reassuring look. They walked down toward the sheriff. The sheriff withdrew his revolver from its holster.

Rinaldi and his men followed—Sabine could hear the crunch of gravel behind them. Would there be a firefight? She feared for the sheriff. If they could get to the cabin's front door, she might be able to reach Nic's rifle, shove Everett into safety....

Sheriff Nelson studied Nic, as if looking for silent clues as to what was truly transpiring.

"You come up here to make sure your fish don't slip the net?" Rinaldi taunted the sheriff, as he entered the clearing.

"Came up here because I received word that you might be pressing a deal," the sheriff returned. "What Sabine and Nic decide to do with their properties is up to them. And I'm here to make certain it is up to them. You fellows move along now. You're on private property."

"You don't want to do this," Rinaldi said lowly to the sheriff.

"I don't?" His face held no trace of alarm.

"You know how it works in this valley, Sheriff. You don't want a hundred men employed by the Dolly Mae to all be against you...."

He glanced at his deputy and back to Rinaldi. "We're striving to make St. Elmo a reputable town. We let you run roughshod across her citizens, we're not doing our job."

Sabine moved slowly toward the door, pulling Everett along. She and Nic shared a glance. Nic said something to Rinaldi, obviously buying her some time. In a moment they were by the door. In another she eased inside, daring to take her first full breath since Rinaldi had ridden into the clearing below the cabin. "Get down, beyond the window, Everett."

"But I wanna see what—"

"Do as I say," she snapped in fear. She pulled a revolver from a small desk drawer and handed it to Everett. "Anyone but Nic, the sheriff, or his deputy come through that door, you shoot him. Understood?"

The boy nodded, eyes wide. She knew Peter had taught him how to use the gun, but she hoped he wouldn't have to do so. She edged the door shut slowly, hoping not to rile any of the men outside, and reached above it for the rifle, which she loaded. She cracked open the door and aimed at the nearest of Rinaldi's men. They'd taken Nic's revolver and flung it to the ground up above the cabin. At least the sheriff and deputy were still armed too. But they were outnumbered, two to one.

"What are you going to do?" the sheriff asked Rinaldi. "You kill me and my deputy, there will be a posse after you, Dolly Mae men or not. Dell, Kazin, they don't want that kind of attention."

Rinaldi glanced from the sheriff to Nic. "You know his boys will never offer you what we've offered. Take the deal, St. Clair."

"As I told you before," Nic said, "I might do that. But not until after tomorrow night, once the sheriff's contacts have a chance to survey the properties and make us an offer themselves."

Rinaldi's jaw muscles worked, and he pulled off his hat, wiped the sweat from his brow, eyed the sheriff once, and then looked at his men. "Let's be on our way, gentlemen. There is nothing else for us here." He mounted his horse and looked down at Nic. "Don't say I didn't warn you."

Nic said nothing in response. In minutes, Rinaldi and his men were gone. The sheriff and deputy dismounted, and Sabine and Everett came out of the cabin. Nic reached out to shake the men's hands. "Glad you fellows arrived when you did. It would not have ended well for us."

The sheriff nodded to Sabine. "I wouldn't stay up here tonight if I were you," he said. "The Dolly Mae bosses might resort to extreme measures. Don't want to see any more cabins on fire. Why don't you come down? Spend the night in the hotel?"

Nic hesitated. It had taken most of their gold dust to outfit Sabine again, after losing everything. And the St. Elmo Hotel didn't run cheap, making what they could off of miners yet to stake a claim. And they'd need two rooms.

But the sheriff was right. It wasn't safe here. Not tonight. Visions of Sabine's cabin caving in, firelight dancing off the surrounding trees like giant shadowed ghouls came back to him. Had that only been five days ago?

"You and Everett could bunk with me," the sheriff said, obviously noticing his hesitation. "Then there'd only be one hotel room to pay for."

"Thank you, but no," Nic said firmly. He didn't want to owe the sheriff, and he didn't feel comfortable leaving Sabine alone in the hotel. It'd be best if they were in two rooms, within shouting distance of each other, should anyone dare to attack them there.

"Suit yourself," the sheriff said with a shrug. He nodded toward the cabin. "Why don't you gather your things? We'll see you safely to town."

Sabine gathered her dress, trousers, shirt, and a hairbrush, tying them up in a blanket, and then helped Everett collect his things too. They reached town by noon and sat down at Amy's Restaurant for a meal. Afterward, Everett walked across the busy street to a scrap pile beside the lumber mill, and Nic and Sabine followed. Dozens of chipmunks hopped and crawled over and under the boards.

"Amy feeds 'em scraps," Jed said to Sabine and Nic when he spotted them watching the boy. "Been doing it for a couple years, so the little varmints don't know what to do when she has no bread left at the end of the day."

Everett held out his hand. A chipmunk ran into it, sniffed for food and found none, and so moved on.

"Heard you folks are in for some good money on your claims," Jed said.

Nic met Sabine's gaze, then looked back to him. "We're hoping so."

"Smart of you, to come down to town tonight," Jed said lowly. "Don't be out past nightfall, I'm tellin' ya. Best to turn in early." His shaggy eyebrows lifted in sincere admonition. He wasn't threatening them; he was simply warning them of what he knew to be true.

Sabine looked down the busy street. Wagons and horses moved in both directions. But across from them, about a block down, two men leaned against the side of the bank building, staring their way. Watching them. She turned to Nic.

"I see them," he said quietly.

Jed didn't follow her gaze. "You're playin' it right. Just keep on doin' what you're doin'. And stay in public places. Those Dolly Mae boys, they can be rough at times. But they don't want no messes."

"Thanks, Jed," Nic said, reaching out to shake his hand.

"Anytime! Take care, folks." He waved across the way to Everett, rousing him from his fascination with the chipmunks.

"Ev, let's go choose a book from the mercantile. It'll keep your mind occupied tonight," Sabine said, "when we're cooped up in the hotel."

"All right," Everett said enthusiastically. "Can I choose it? Maybe one of those Western dime novels?"

"Maybe," she said. She left a light hand on his shoulder and they crossed the street, Nic right behind them. At the store, he stayed outside, keeping watch while they did their shopping. She was about to go out and ask Nic for the coins she needed, when he arrived, added a couple apples, a loaf of bread, and a wedge of cheese to the pile on the counter. Supper. It'd save them some money. He paid and escorted them out.

"Straight to the hotel," he said in a low voice.

She glanced around his shoulder but saw nothing. Still, she moved as he directed. In a few minutes, they arrived at the St. Elmo Hotel and checked in, opting for a room for Everett and Nic, and a second for her.

The woman at the desk looked over her spectacles and down her nose when Nic requested the rooms be side by side. "Mr. St. Clair, we are a reputable hotel." She glanced at Everett, and over Sabine, and her scowl grew. "A block down, you'll find the Brass Horseshoe. They'll gladly—"

"It is for Mrs. LaCrosse's *safety* that I must be next door," Nic said tightly. He tapped on her log book. "Nothing untoward will be transpiring upstairs. Please, we'd like our two keys as soon as possible. We are all in need of a rest."

The woman looked all three of them over again and then reluctantly dipped her pen in the inkwell and wrote in their names. Then she turned to pull two keys off a board filled with hooks and turned back to hand them over. "Room 208 and 209."

"Thank you," he said, his tone clipped. Sabine imagined him as he once was, the son of an Eastern publisher, dressed in fine clothing. Educated. Refined. She wished she could have seen him there as he once was, know that part of him. Because try as she might, she couldn't picture him anywhere but here. In her part of the country. With her. He paused at the staircase and gestured for her to go before him, clearly a gentleman. Few had ever treated her that way. They'd been polite, especially as a schoolteacher to their children, but it was the barest of civilities.

She walked up the stairs, turned, and found their first room. Nic bent, slid the key into the lock, and opened it, remaining in the hall. It was a decent room, with fresh wallpaper, a dresser with a pitcher and washbasin, and a bed, neatly made. The window was open, relieving some of the afternoon heat, but Sabine could see the dust from the street below flowing inward. She dropped her makeshift satchel on the bed and turned to Nic and Everett in the hallway. "I think I'll rest for a bit." She shook her finger at Everett. "Now you get some reading done, young man. Don't be just staring out the window, watching the town."

"I will," he promised solemnly.

Nic gave her a tender smile and then leaned forward a bit. "Lock it behind us, all right?"

She nodded and went to close the door.

Still he hovered. "You'll be all right? You haven't been alone since … well, since the fire."

It was her turn to smile at him. "I'll be all right, Nic. Send Ev with some of the food later on."

"I will." He paused, began to say something, then closed his mouth. Then he gave her a little wave and turned to follow Everett to the room next door.

Sabine shut her door, turned the key in the lock, and then pocketed it. She moved over to the wall that separated them and, feeling a little foolish, laid her cheek against the rippled paper and listened to the muffled voices. She closed her eyes, imagining Everett bouncing onto one bed, then gazing out the window, and Nic lying down on his bed. To be so close to them, and yet parted, felt odd. But then she felt ashamed, even thinking it. They were not a family. Nic had not yet even professed love for her.

But he loved her. She could see it in his eyes. She heard it in his words. He hated being separated from her, as clearly as she hated it herself.

Could she—was it possible?—that she was in love with Dominic St. Clair?

She moved from the wall to the bed and lay down upon it, suddenly weary. But not tired enough to sleep. Only enough to doze off for a bit …

It'd been four days since the ranch hand Donald had decided she was Moira Colorado, in spite of her denial. How long until word reached the newspapers?

Moira stood at her window and twisted a handkerchief. She needed to go. The train would arrive in the Westcliffe station in but two hours. She wanted to be there in time, but not too early. She slipped a watch from her dress pocket and checked the hour, then took a deep breath. It was time to face her sister.

As quietly as she could, she swept down the stairs and set her two valises at the bottom, then moved into the kitchen den, where she knew Odessa was reading during Samuel's nap.

Her sister looked up, lowering her book. "My, don't you look lovely. Where are you off to?"

Moira swallowed and moved over to the settee, sitting down beside her. She reached over and took Odessa's hand. Odessa's eyes narrowed.

"Dess," she began, "I'm going to be gone for a while."

"What?"

"I'm going to New York for a visit."

"New York!"

"Yes, I received a letter from Gavin Knapp's mother a while ago, and—"

"Gavin Knapp? Your child's grandmother?" Odessa blinked in confusion.

"She invited me to come. So that I might know her, and her me, and maybe someday, that the Knapps might know their grandchild."

Odessa shook her head as if trying to catch up with her thoughts. "When? When are you going? You *are* returning?"

"I am leaving today. Right now, actually. I didn't—"

"Right now?" Her volume went up and Moira shushed her.

"I didn't want this to create upheaval. I knew you wouldn't be fond of the idea."

"Fond?" she sputtered, clearly upset, as well as fearful.

Moira rose. She knew this could be an endless argument and there was no point to it. She'd made up her mind. The sound of a wagon pulling into place outside filtered through the curtains. She glanced over her shoulder, as if she could see it, then back to Odessa.

Odessa rose, her face ashen. "You are running, Moira."

"Running?" Moira scoffed. "No. I've come to realize I've been *hiding*. That is what I aim to remedy. My injuries are what they are. What I make of my life ahead is up to me. I cannot wait on a man to define it for me."

Odessa looked to the window and back to her. "What of God? What about His desire for your future? The baby's?"

Moira paused for half a breath. What *of* God? Who was she to say this wasn't what He wanted for her? Yet doubt remained. She let out her breath, dismissing her own niggling concerns. "Does God not go anywhere we go? Is there any place that He is not?"

"God is with us, wherever we go," Odessa quickly replied, "but there are certainly places we go that He'd rather *we not*."

Moira glanced at her. "I am not heading to the saloons, Dess. I'm coming back. This is not a repeat of past journeys." She stepped across to her sister and took her hands, begging with her eyes for understanding. "I have some money, the gold. The thought of New York fills me with hope. A little distraction never harmed anyone." Her eyes widened. "Why don't you come with me?" she cried, feeling like a giddy girl again. "Wouldn't it be lovely to run our hands over fine fabrics and order a few dresses? Perhaps call on some of our old acquaintances? Oh, I want a proper dinner at a restaurant that serves courses, with silver cutlery and china and crystal goblets. Don't you?" She let go of Odessa's hands and splayed her own outward. "Just a bit of our old life. The fine things. A taste of it. A glimpse. Please, Dess. You and little Samuel can come with me."

"I can't do that," Odessa replied in a whisper. "I have responsibilities here, and you know how the air in the East affects me." She looked slowly up at Moira, her eyes so like her younger sister's. "And Moira, *this*, what I have here with Bryce, Samuel—they've *become* the fine things in life for me. I thought ... I thought you had come to that too."

Moira stared back into her eyes. "I did ..." She let her lips close. She wasn't ready to share details about Daniel's rejection. Not yet.

A knock sounded at the door. "Cassie," Moira called. "Can you tell him that I will be out in a bit?"

"Yes, ma'am, Miss St. Claire," the girl called.

"What about your baby?" Odessa asked in a hush.

"What about it?"

"Is it wise, to be traveling? For the baby, and for you? People know of the gold, Moira. They know of your connection to us. It could make you ... vulnerable."

"I'll hire a guard," she said, meaning it. "Please don't fret over me, Dess. I'll be sure to not take foolish chances." There was no use, telling her about Francine's mention of returning to her career. If news got out about Moira Colorado, there in New York—

Odessa shook her head, her eyes clouding.

"Please, Dess. Don't be sad. I'm not leaving forever."

"No?"

"No!"

"How long will you be away?"

Moira shrugged. She truly had no idea when she would come back. What if she decided to stay, so that her baby might know his grandparents? Become heir to their fortune? What if ... there was some opportunity for her to still sing? "I don't know. A month, maybe through the winter. I think New York would offer far more distractions than this valley, come snow."

"Through the winter? I had thought ... I dreamed of you having the baby, right here at home. Sharing in that joy with you."

Moira sighed and lifted a hand to her head. "I don't know, Dess. I'll know, in time. I will stay in touch. I promise."

"What of Daniel?" Odessa said quietly.

"What of him?" Moira said, turning away.

"What if he returns for you—only to discover that you are not here?"

Her eyes moved to the window. *Daniel.* The thought of leaving him behind tore at her. But she steeled herself against it. He had left her. He had made her no promises. Even if he came back to her today, she would still struggle over his decision to be sheriff. He could get shot. Die.

No, she'd had enough of death, from her brothers to her parents to Gavin. She wanted *life*. Dreams that she could capture, even if she couldn't capture the man that she loved. Now that she'd decided to go, her heart pumped with excitement, the thrill of rediscovered freedom and choice. She would go to New York and find out about the Knapps, the family Gavin refused to introduce her to, and see where that led her. For her baby. For herself.

She could always return. Always.

"Daniel made his choice," she finally said, turning to her sister. "I'm making mine now." She gave her sister an awkward hug before sweeping out of the room, lest Odessa come up with the ten arguments that, had Moira given her time, might've dissuaded her from going at all.

CHAPTER SEVENTEEN

Nic barely slept. He spent most of the night prowling around the hotel room, watching the empty street below, listening for any sounds of alarm from Sabine next door. He didn't know how long he sat in a corner chair, staring at their shared wall, thinking about her slumbering on just the other side. When the sun rose, they would travel back up the Gulch, let the surveyors do their work, and hopefully receive an offer. Would she decide to move on without him? Or Everett? *I don't want to be without her, Lord. I don't ever want to be without her.*

He glanced over at the boy, who was snoring lightly. The tears had abated in his dreams. Was it possible that he, Dominic St. Clair, might be a halfway decent stand-in father? He'd never be Peter, for sure, but could he do right by Everett? Do what he could to lead him into adulthood?

Nic laughed at himself, softly. *I'm just now coming to some semblance of peace with myself as an adult. Now I want to be a father and a husband?* He'd never considered himself suitable husband material, let alone a father. On and on his mind went, racing ahead, arguing for one road, and then another, thinking of one problem and then several solutions—churning over those difficulties he could not solve. He was just beginning to doze as the town came awake, a heralding rooster a block away, a rumbling wagon full of lumber, another with metal milk cans rattling together.

Everett stirred, then stretched and rose to a sitting position on his bed. Nic peeked at him and then closed his eyes again, wishing for a few hours of slumber at least. He took a deep breath, held it, then released it. He supposed it was impossible now. The day was beginning, whether he was ready for it or not.

"Nic?"

"Hmm?"

"If we sell the mine today, what will happen to me?"

Nic opened his eyes. He slowly sat up, facing the boy. The child's legs dangled from the bed. "I've been thinking about that, Ev. If we sell your dad's place, we'll put a good chunk of money into savings for you, for when you're grown up. And I can help you find a good family to live with. Or, I've been thinking … if you're willing …" He paused, looking for the right words. "What I mean to say is, there's a part of me that wouldn't mind having you stay with me. If you don't mind."

Everett's eyes widened, and he smiled. "You mean, you'd keep me?"

Nic smiled back. "I guess we'd keep each other."

"And Sabine? Sabine too?"

Nic's smile faded. "I don't know about Sabine, Ev. She and I have to figure things out. But you and me—if you don't mind living with me, I kind of like having you around. You're a good kid."

Everett pushed off the bed and stepped over to him, throwing his arms around Nic. Slowly, Nic wrapped his arms around the child's thin body, hugging him back.

"Does this mean you'd like to stay with me?" Nic asked, his voice muffled a bit against Everett's shoulder.

The boy let him go, backed up a step, and gave him a solemn nod.

"Well, then," Nic said, offering Everett his hand. "I guess we're partners."

"Will we mine some more?"

"Hmm, I think I'd rather get out of the mining business. Would you mind staying aboveground with me? I've always been pretty good with a hammer and saw."

"I like building. My dad and me ... we built the cabin."

Nic nodded. "You did a fine job on that. I didn't make it through college, but I took a few classes in architecture that I liked. It was the only thing I *did* like about college," he said conspiratorially. "Maybe I can find work, building houses."

"Or maybe even hotels and banks!"

"That would be fine. Fine indeed." He considered the child in front of him. "Will you mind it much? Leaving this place? You've been here since you were little."

"It'll be all right. As long as I'm with you and Sa ... with you," he quickly amended.

Nic smiled. It was clear the child was envisioning them as a new family, with all three of them. His father had always said that a three-legged stool was strong....

A gentle knock sounded on their joint wall. Nic stood and leaned close, imagining Sabine on the other side. "We'll be over in a few minutes," he said loudly. There was a muffled response of assent. "Come on, kid," he said to Everett. "We need to get dressed and head on down to breakfast."

Everett hopped off his bed and scrambled over to his small

bundle of clothing, shaking out his rolled trousers and a shirt. Nic did the same, dressing beside him, and then pulling on his boots. They moved over to the basin, which Nic filled with water from the pitcher, and each of them washed their faces and patted down their hair.

Taking care of the boy was surprisingly easy, comfortable in fact. Even … satisfying? He shook his head in wonder. What had happened to him?

Daniel was watching a stable boy brush down his horse outside the sheriff's office in Westcliffe, when a hired carriage came rumbling down the street. With distinctive markings, the cab was often parked outside the rail station.

The boy turned and watched as the carriage came to a stop. The coachman climbed down and opened the small door, and a man in a top hat—a top hat; how long had it been since Daniel had seen someone in one of those?—emerged. He glanced over at them and sniffed, covering his nose and mouth with a white handkerchief. "I am Bradley Grubaugh, from the *Rocky Mountain News*. I assume you are the sheriff."

"I am."

He glanced down at Daniel's plain shirt with some disdain. "May we speak inside?"

Daniel shifted his weight to his other leg. "Probably have more privacy out here, if that's what you're after, Mr. Grubaugh." Behind him was the office and inside, the lone jail cell that held his prisoner from Conquistador, who had stubbornly refused to say much at all.

"Fine. Thank you," the journalist said. He turned and handed the coachman a coin before the carriage rumbled off. He followed Daniel to the corner of the building, out of the flow of pedestrian traffic.

"How can I assist you, Mr. Grubaugh?"

"I've just been out to the Circle M."

Daniel waited. What business had he out there? Still trying to figure out another angle to the conquistador gold story? Or perhaps a piece on the fledgling town?

"I was informed that a Miss Moira St. Clair lives there."

Daniel did not blink. "And?"

"And my informant presumes she is actually the songstress Moira Colorado who was believed dead in a fire, up in Leadville. Are you familiar with the story?"

"I am," he said, struggling to focus on the journalist, rather than get lost in past images of flames, searing heat that had left blisters on his hands, the billowing, black smoke … Moira inside …

Mr. Grubaugh sniffed and wiped his nose with a handkerchief. "The people out at the ranch weren't very helpful. They said they have only known the woman who has been living with them as Moira St. Clair, Mrs. McAllan's sister. They said she has a beautiful voice, but they have never seen her onstage."

Daniel struggled to stifle his smile. It was the truth.

"I once saw Moira St. Clair at the Opera Comiqué in France," the man went on. "She was magnificent. I never saw this 'Miss Colorado' in our own mining camps of Colorado, but it's hard for me to believe she might've fallen to such base a task as to sing in those establishments."

"Quite," Daniel said.

Mr. Grubaugh studied him. "My informant said that *you* might know the whereabouts of either Miss St. Clair or Miss Colorado."

All trace of amusement faded. "Whereabouts? Was Miss St. Claire not at the Circle M?" He tensed, waiting for the answer.

"No," the reporter said, lifting his eyebrows. "A hired hand told me she packed her bags and took a train out yesterday."

"A *train?*"

"Why, yes. A train. Do you know wh—"

Daniel did not wait for another word. He unwrapped the reins from the post and flipped a coin to the stable boy, who was still holding a brush in his hand. Then he mounted, wheeled his horse around, and set off for the Circle M at a gallop.

Daniel moped around the Circle M until dinner, ate his supper in silence, and then paced the porch outside, as if by simply remaining where he had last seen Moira she would appear.

He understood how headstrong Moira could be.

He understood that he had helped open a door for her to go.

But he didn't understand how Bryce and Odessa could just stand back and see her leave. Did they not know what danger a woman traveling alone might be in? Especially if someone found out who she was? His deputies' comments about her being a target, as partial heir to the conquistador gold, rang through his mind.

He ran his hat through his hands in an agitated circle, staring at the purple sky coming alive with stars. Over and over, he'd run it through his mind. He wanted to go after her, beg her forgiveness for ever leaving her side, and ask her to come home. But he had responsibilities here now as sheriff.

Deep down he knew she wasn't coming back.

Not tonight.

Maybe not ever.

He clenched his hat so hard the brim curled into a tight coil.

Swallowing hard, he moved to leave the porch. He was halfway down when Odessa came out, with Bryce right behind her. "Daniel?"

"I have to be off," he said over his shoulder. "Thank you for supper."

"Daniel, she said she'd be back."

He stilled, at once caught between hope and fury. *Don't say anything.…* But he couldn't help himself. "How could you let her go? Bryce? After all that went down here this spring? Don't you know she might be in danger?"

"Daniel, listen," Bryce said, putting a warning hand out.

"I … I can't," Daniel said. He moved the rest of the way down the steps, pausing by his horse. "I'm sorry," he said, shaking his head. "This is my fault. Not yours. Her leaving …" He shook his head again.

"What will you do?" Odessa asked, coming to the porch rail. He was glad he wasn't close to her. Seeing her green-blue eyes, so like Moira's, had been torture all evening.…

"I don't know. I want to go after her. But my place is here."

"A man has responsibilities—" Bryce began.

"And one of them was to your sister-in-law!" Daniel bit out.

"Now, look …"

Daniel sighed. "I'm sorry. I'll go. Before I say anything else I regret." He put his hat on his head and mounted up. "You'll let me know? If you hear from her?"

Odessa nodded. Bryce looked angry.

There were no more words. Daniel wheeled his horse around and set off toward town, hoping he could navigate by starlight and the vague, pale outline of the road.

Nic guessed that the trio of finely dressed gentlemen having breakfast across the restaurant might be their potential investors. He was sure of it when Sheriff Nelson arrived and greeted them all, shaking their hands. He had barely been able to eat, his stomach in knots. By the looks of it, Sabine was struggling too. Everett ate everything on his plate, then some of theirs as well. There was so much he wished he could ask her, so much he wanted to know. But everything was happening too fast.

The sheriff stood up with the three businessmen when they were done but then spied Nic across the way. He came over to greet them. "All set for our meeting this morning?"

"Ready as we'll ever be," Nic said, glancing at Everett and Sabine. "We'll meet you outside and ride up together?"

"I think that's safest, yes," the sheriff said. "Hired a couple of temporary deputies, just in case."

Nic frowned. He had relaxed a bit this morning, when the night passed by so uneventfully. But the sheriff was right; he needed to be on his guard, especially with the investors accompanying him up the Gulch. The waitress came by. "What do we owe you?" Nic asked.

"Oh," she said with a smile. "Your bill has been taken care of by the gentlemen who were sitting in the far corner."

Nic glanced over to the empty table where she gestured.

"Don't worry, Nic," the sheriff said. "No assumptions made, just buying you folks some breakfast." He settled his hat on his head and checked his pocket watch. "I'll see you outside in about forty minutes."

As they set off, the sheriff handed Sabine a rifle. "I know you probably lost yours in the fire. It'd be good to have every sharpshooter armed," he said with a smile.

She smiled back. She breathed easier with a loaded weapon at her side.

They rode up the Gulch with the three investors—who seemed like respectable, nice men—their two surveyors, a pack mule with all their equipment, the sheriff, deputy, and two additional deputized men.

They rode through the trees, across the creek, so low this time of year, the air growing cooler the higher they climbed. Would she be able to find another place that felt so good, so right to her? Her eyes shifted to Nic and Everett. Were their paths about to divide? Or grow closer together than ever before? What would it be like to be a family? Was it even possible?

In time they reached the Vaughn place. Nothing looked disturbed since they had left it the day before. They climbed higher and dismounted right beside the creek, where the horses and mule could graze and drink while tied to the aspens that bordered the water.

They walked over to the mine entrance and Nic lit several lanterns. He gave her a long look that said, *You ready?* And when she gave him a nod, he entered the tunnel they hadn't returned to since they had so narrowly escaped the water two days prior.

"You want to wait out here, Everett?" Sabine asked. She feared it would be too much for the boy, being where he had almost lost Nic and her, so soon after losing his father.

But he shook his head. "I want to go with you."

"All right," she said. She bent and lit the last lantern, following the men who had gone in already. She glanced over her shoulder. One of the three deputies took up position at the entrance. She had seen the other two take up positions farther out, on either flank.

She and Everett found the men at the end of the second tunnel, peering down into the still flowing shaft. "Ah, you opened up a new channel for an underground river," said one of the surveyors.

Briefly, Nic told them what had happened to Sabine and how they had gotten out.

They all turned with wide eyes toward her. One of the investors, the portly Mr. Woodveis, smiled in wonder at her. "Well, you are quite a woman. Quite a woman, indeed."

They turned back to the cliff face, examining the crevice where they had extricated most of the gold. The surveyors began extracting samples, measuring ore quality with a portable kit, and nodding in satisfaction.

"You think the vein continues?" Mr. Woodveis asked Nic. "What makes you so certain?"

"Well, the men of the Dolly Mae believed it was true too. Their surveyors said, judging from the plates you can see here—" he paused to trace the first with his hand— "and over there too, there's a good chance that it might follow all the way down the mountain. Geologic forces remained consistent. No reason it shouldn't be there. But then that's the guessing game of gold mining, right?"

"Right," said the taller, broader Mr. McManus. "And if it follows those plates, that's where it would descend beneath Mrs. LaCrosse's property, correct?"

"Correct," Sabine said.

"Any idea where that water exits?" the second surveyor asked. "Or does it stay belowground, best you can tell?"

"There's a large pool on the other side of my property," Sabine said. "As the snows melt, a waterfall from above feeds it. It flows all summer. The water is crystal clear. I'd guess it's about fifty feet lower than the mine entrance. My guess is that river might feed it and exit there."

Mr. McManus smiled in satisfaction. "If you're right, Mrs. LaCrosse, then this water issue will be easily resolved. We can use the water as a hydraulic source to quickly open up the mine, then drain it down to a level we can easily manage. We'll only need to secure enough property for a drain field."

"And make certain we don't flood St. Elmo," said Mr. Woodveis with a jowly laugh that made his belly rise and fall.

Everett frowned and Sabine wrapped an arm around his shoulders. It was the nature of the big mining companies to take such actions. It was why they could get a thousand times more gold that Nic, Sabine, and Everett would ever see. But it meant their beloved Gulch would never be the same again. They would need to move far from this place.

The two surveyors were speaking in hushed, excited tones to each other. Mr. McManus went over to chat with them, his low voice rumbling across the tunnel. Sabine wandered over to the two other investors, sheriff, Everett, and Nic, who were all peering down the shaft.

And that was when they heard the explosion, felt the earth tremble. A second later they were all knocked off their feet.

CHAPTER EIGHTEEN

Sabine came to and blinked, but she could see nothing. She coughed and looked around, trying to gain any glimpse of light at all. Nothing. Only black the color of tar.

Cave-in, she registered at last. *The mine has caved in.* After an explosion. Dynamite, by the sound of it.

"Nic? Everett?" She couldn't breathe, the air was so thick with dust. She fought off the desire to give in to panic. Where were they?

"Mrs. LaCrosse?" asked a deep voice. "Mr. McManus?"

A man moaned, from about ten feet away. One of the surveyors. No one else responded.

"Nic! Everett!" Sabine called again, hearing the note of hysteria in her own voice but unable to stop it. They had been right by the edge of the shaft. She crawled across the ground, in the direction of the sound of rushing water, praying she would come across one or both of them. Nothing. Nothing but rock and dirt beneath her hands. And then the shaft. She leaned over, smelling the fresh scent of water, feeling the mist billow up and bathe her face, giving her the first clear breath possible.

But the men were gone. Nic. Everett. The sheriff. Mr. Woodweis. Mr. Avery, the third investor, a mouse of a man. "Nic!" she called down the shaft, knowing it was hopeless. "Nic!"

Mr. McManus reached her, touching her shoulder. "Sorry," he said. "Let me help you up, Mrs. LaCrosse."

Wearily, she rose, but her knees felt weak, as if they might give out at any moment. "They are gone?" Mr. McManus asked in his low, kindly voice.

"Down the shaft," she said, hating the weakness of her voice.

"So … they might be in the cavern where you found yourself?"

"Or worse," she said. Drowned. Knocked unconscious by the blast, swept into the current and through the cursed tunnel.

"Step lively, Mrs. LaCrosse," he said. "Let us choose to believe they are all right. But first, we must ascertain the degree of our cave-in. Would you be so kind as to take my hand so we don't lose each other?"

She reached out and found his hand, wide and warm, grandfatherly. It gave her some strength. Perhaps he was right. Perhaps Nic and Ev were still alive.… They moved forward slowly, tentatively, down the tunnel toward the entrance, taking a left at the corner. She stubbed her toe on the first boulder. "Oh, no," she muttered. "Hello!" she cried. "Can anyone hear me?"

Was there anyone on the other side? One of the deputies? Or had they been killed by the explosion?

"Hello, there!" called Mr. McManus. "Hello!"

They both held their breath, listening.

Hoping the deputies who'd been on duty could hear them, they shouted again. But then the report of two rifle shots, in quick succession, silenced them "Whoever trapped us in here meant to do it," Sabine whispered in shock. "And now we have ten feet or more of mountain between us and the exit. Maybe as much as thirty feet, if

the whole entrance caved in. Do you know how long it took Peter
Vaughn to excavate that far?"

Mr. McManus said, "A year or two?"

"Two."

"But we wouldn't need to pull out that much rock. Just enough
to let us through."

"So that someone can shoot us on the other side?"

Nic had hit the far side of the shaft so hard, he almost passed out.
But then he fell and landed in the water below. When he came up,
he called out for Everett. The boy was right beside him, sputtering
and gasping. "Take a deep breath!" he cried, right before they were
sucked through the tunnel. It was all he could do. He had never even
asked Everett if he knew how to swim.

He held him firmly with one hand, stroking with his other, willing the tunnel to end, the cavern to arrive. Everett struggled against
him, clearly panicking, wanting to rise, grabbing hold of rocks, slowing them down.

But then he stopped struggling.

*No, no, no, Lord. Please, Lord. Not this one. Not this child. He's
innocent! Innocent! Save him, Father. Save us both.*

A moment later, they were out, popping to the surface. Nic wept
as he pulled Everett into his arms. "Everett! Everett! Come on, boy!
No. Please God, no …"

He pushed through the chest-deep water toward the edge of the
pool, ignoring the other voices in the cavern as he lifted the boy onto the
ledge. "Ev, come on. Come back to me. Please," he said through his tears.

Panting and weary he lifted himself out of the water, partially landing on Everett. "Come on, Ev!" he cried. "Take a breath!" He moved away, and as he did so, Everett coughed and from the sound of it, spewed water from deep within.

"Everett? Ev!" Nic said, pulling him into his arms. He could hear the others, splashing their way toward them.

The boy coughed again, fearsomely, and then said, "Nic? What happened?"

Nic laughed and yanked him up to his chest, now crying and looking up, even though he could not see anything. "Oh, Lord. Thank You. Thank You, thank You."

"Sabine! Sabine!" he shouted.

"I think she was farther back in the shaft, Nic," Sheriff Nelson said.

"Drew," Nic said. "Glad you made it."

"You too."

Where was Sabine? Was she was all right?

"Are you okay, Everett?" Nic said, pulling his attention back to those he could reach. He was so thankful, so grateful, that Everett wasn't gone forever.

God had spared him. Again. And Everett too.

Please be with Sabine, Lord, he prayed silently.

"Mr. St. Clair?" asked a small voice beside him.

"Please, call me Nic," he said. "Mr. Avery?"

"Yes."

"Mr. Woodweis?"

"He's over here, gone," the sheriff answered for him. "Drowned on the way through. Sounds like we almost lost Everett."

"We did," Nic said, pulling him close.

"Uh, Nic?" Everett asked.

"Yeah?"

"Can you let go of me now?"

Nic laughed and loosened his grip on the boy. "Sure, sure. But stay right here beside me, all right? It's darker than a mother's womb in here."

"I might be able to help with that," Drew said. They listened to him strike a flint over and over again. Finally a candle was lit.

"You carry a candle with you?" Nic asked.

"I work in mining territory. I'm never without it. Lucky for us it was in an oilcloth."

They all breathed a sigh of relief and looked around at their dripping wet companions, glad not to be alone, but at a loss as to how they'd get out. Nic looked beyond Mr. Avery to the plump body of Mr. Woodweis on the shore of the small cavern pool, his legs still in the water. Nic shivered when he realized that could've been Everett....

The sheriff stilled and stared up, beyond Nic. Quickly, he moved around the group and held up his candle. The warm light was blocked by stalactites. The shadows its light cast danced in eerie fashion. The cavern was vast. But the closer he got to the far wall, the more the light danced. Against flecks and chunks of gold. "There's your vein again," the sheriff said in wonder.

Nic met Mr. Avery's astounded gaze.

"You, Mr. St. Clair," Mr. Avery said, "will be a very wealthy man." He turned to look Nic in the eye, adding, "If we ever get out of here."

Nic rose and stood beside the sheriff, staring in awe at the fifteen-foot-high wall—thirty feet high at the apex—and the beautiful gold streak running down it, two feet wide.

"*When* we get out, Mr. Avery," Nic corrected. "When we get out."

Moira was thankful that she had purchased tickets for a special first-class sleeper car in Denver, shortening her transit to New York to just four days and four nights. The train still stopped but half as often. A couple of times, the sleeper cars were transferred to new engines, keeping them moving at the fastest rate possible.

She remembered their long, arduous journey out to Colorado the first time; six days in uncomfortable, dusty, smoky cars. Odessa's terrible wheezing … it was a miracle they had arrived at all. And that made her think of Dess, and sweet baby Samuel, Bryce, and … Daniel.

Daniel. Did he even realize it yet? That she was gone? Not that this was about him. This was about her. Her baby. Her past. Her future.

She ate and sat and slept alone—the most continuous amount of time she'd had to herself since her days in Paris. And even then, she'd been surrounded by servants, most of her days and evenings filled with social engagements and appearances. The solitude of the train was a strange, and yet welcome, experience.

She finished her luncheon in the dining car, staring out at the endless plains that passed by outside, fields warmed by the high, bright sun. She could feel the stares of passersby, but she ignored them. She knew her veils gave her an air of mystique; she also knew that if any of those intrigued by her visage got a look beneath, any sense of mystery would disappear.

The group of four, at a table across and down from her, were loudly urging their companion on to something. She glanced up and studied them. A well-dressed man smiled and rose from his table, walked over to a small piano in the corner, and sat down. He pulled music from his coat pocket, set it in front of him, and began to play.

Moira's breath caught. "The Veil Song." One of her favorites, from Verdi's opera *Don Carlos*. She closed her eyes and fought to keep from swaying with the slow crescendo of it, the hint of the chorus already in her mind. She didn't know how long she was humming along when she abruptly opened her eyes and glanced around, wondering if anyone had noticed.

But all appeared to be engaged in the pianist's work. He was a small, mousy, nondescript man, but he was quite accomplished. Moira had to grip the table to keep from rising, walking over to him, and singing. The play was about an ill-fated love that ended in devastation. Moira laughed under her breath. No wonder it was a favorite of hers. Like its protagonist, she had longed to be with her one true love, but the selfish machinations of others kept them apart—like those of Reid Bannock.... She only hoped her story would have a happier ending.

She looked out the window again. Another day would soon be over. How many would she spend striving after the unattainable, rather than accepting what she had? She sighed and gave her head a little shake. She was merely weary. Overwrought. Sleeping on trains was difficult, far from the quiet nights of the ranch. Perhaps this night would be better.

She rose and set her napkin on her chair.

And that was when she saw it. A piece of paper in front of her, with "Moira Colorado" written across it. She looked up and around her quickly, to see who might've slipped it onto her table, but everyone was staring toward the pianist, not at her. Holding it closer to her, she unfolded it and took a peek at what was inside. It was one of Gavin's old posters, sent to towns ahead of her during her tour to help publicize her appearance.

I know who you are. I think you're still beautiful. Will you sing for me?

A chill ran down Moira's back. Again she glanced around, but there was no one looking in her direction. She gathered her bag and shawl and rose, exiting the dining car as fast as she could. She looked over her shoulder and then down the hallway of the sleeper car.

It was empty.

She saw no one who looked ill placed, no one moving as if to follow her. She rushed down the hallway, keeping her hands out to steady herself as the car rocked back and forth around a bend. With shaking hands, she pulled a key from her pocket and tried to get it into the lock. "Come on," she whispered, feeling as if the eyes of her enemy were upon her. *"Come on."*

Finally, the key slipped in, she turned it and opened the door, thankful that the steward had already been there to turn down her cot and light her small oil lamp. With some agitation, she managed to get the key back out of the lock, slammed the door, and threw the bolt into place. She backed away from it, as if she thought someone might crash through. But no one came.

Her knees felt weak. Moira sank to her narrow cot. The room was nothing more than two beds, a desk, chair, and small window. But it was hers alone.

What was she to do? Go to the conductor? And tell him what, exactly? That someone was following her, claiming to know who she was? What peculiar kind of threat was that?

She rose, pulled the heavy wooden chair to the door, and jammed it underneath the knob. Whoever was following her, whoever thought they "knew" her, would have a hard time getting through the door now. And if they didn't want to get her, what did they want?

Moira stared at the door for hours, until her eyes grew heavy with sleep.

Common sense told her no one was coming, not with neighbors on either side and no easy escape route. But fear kept her rooted in place. She adjusted a pillow behind her back and pulled a light wool blanket to her shoulders, intent on keeping watch until daybreak.

But in time, she drifted off to sleep....

CHAPTER NINETEEN

"What are you doing, Mrs. LaCrosse?"

"Sabine. Please. If we're going to be trapped in this mine together, facing death, I'd prefer you call me by my first name."

"Sabine?"

"I'm looking for rope. There used to be one over here...." She reached out, wishing for any bit of light. Her hands met the wall, then, feeling along it, found the hook, awkwardly driven into the tunnel wall. She smiled as her hands closed around the prickly woven twine of the rope that had saved her and Nic before. She hoped it was strong enough to do the job again.

"We need another section," she said, "if my plan is to work."

"Plan?" She heard his voice shift from her left side to the right.

"Careful where you walk!"

He coughed, and by the sound of it, the action was more from nervousness than the dust still circling in the air. "What are you planning?"

"We can't dig ourselves out. Even if there was someone outside of the tunnel digging toward us, it might take weeks to clear a path. Fortunately that water below us might give us a way out."

In the dark she couldn't read his expression. And he was deathly quiet before saying, "Are you mad?"

"I think not. I believe it's our only avenue of escape. Through the tunnel and then onward, out to the spring on my lower property."

"That's a big gamble."

"Yes. Yes, it is."

He sighed. Then, "What about our surveyor?"

The man hadn't said a word since the cave-in. Sabine had thought him swept away with the others. "Is he unconscious?"

She listened as he moved toward the other man and assessed his condition. "Never mind. He's gone."

She swallowed hard, then pulled down the rope and tied it around her waist. "Feel around the floor. See if you can find a second rope." She knotted the rope, again and again. Then she reached down and felt for the timber just at the top of the shaft. Clawing at the soil, she tunneled out a space behind it. Then she slipped the rope around the timber, tying it tight as her anchor in case anything went wrong.

"Ah. Found one," Mr. McManus said in satisfaction.

Sabine smiled. "That's good. Very good." She waited, feeling her impatience rise as he moved slowly toward her. She had to know about Nic and Everett. Were they alive in the cave? Or would it be horribly silent when she reached it, all of them drowned?

He dropped the rope between them on the ground with a *thump*.

"All right, so this is my plan. I've tied the rope to my waist—"

"Sabine—"

"I've attached it to my waist," she repeated. "I'm going through the tunnel below again. Hopefully, I'll reach the cavern and find some of our ... party. Then I'll take this second rope—" she paused to place it on to her shoulder—"and use it to go through wherever that second tunnel is that drains to my spring pool."

"But—"

"If I'm right, and if it's large enough to fit through, we'll all have a way out."

He was silent for a couple of seconds. "Our way out. Or our entry into a deeper tomb?"

"Our *way out*," she insisted, rising in front of him. The rope was heavy on her shoulder. Could she swim to the cavern? It was their only chance. Mr. McManus was clearly reluctant. It was up to her. And having been through it before, it was far less terrifying.… "I will go through. You'll feel me tugging as I swim. I think it will take a good thirty, forty seconds. Count it out with me so you know. One-Mississippi, two-Mississippi."

"Three-Mississippi," he joined in.

"Good. When I reach the cavern, I'll turn and give you three yanks on the rope. So you'll know I've made it. Here, let me show you." She reached out, found his hands, and gave him a section of the rope. "Three clear yanks, got it?"

"I believe so."

"Then I'll attach the second rope and go on through the next tunnel. Give it some time. Probably fifteen or twenty minutes, all right? If we're successful, we'll have a rope train to safety. We'll let you know by yanking on the rope six times. Then you'll know it's your turn to come through."

He paused. "It's an audacious plan, Sabine."

"It is."

"If we get out of here, I'll owe you my life."

"If we get out of here, Mr. McManus, all I'll want is a check for my land."

He laughed softly. "We can arrange for that too." The trace of a smile left his tone. "Three clear yanks. You're there. Six, and I'm to come through myself?"

"Six clear yanks. If you're unsure, give a yank. We'll think of one yank as a question mark. Two as a 'don't come.' All right?"

"All right," he said. His voice sounded as if he was pretending more assurance than he felt. "Three that you're all right and the way is clear. Six as an invitation to follow."

"Right." She reached out to him. "Take my hand. What's your given name, Mr. McManus?"

"Michael," he said. He found her palm and she shook it.

"God be with you, Michael. I'll be glad to see you again in the light of day."

"As will I, Sabine."

She climbed down the shaft, reaching for supporting timbers she half remembered, then forced herself into the icy waters. Her skirts billowed around her and she wished she had worn her trousers today. She took several breaths and then was under.

She prayed she'd surface alive.

Nic heard the bubbles first, then the sounds of someone breaking the surface. He looked up at the pool and saw, in the dim light of the candle, a woman's face. "Sabine?" He pulled his arm from around Everett, who was shivering uncontrollably, and stood up.

Sabine tread water, then moved toward him. She smiled. "Nic! Everett!"

She appeared as a vision, rising out of the pool. He met her halfway, sweeping her into his arms and hugging her to him, lifting her, dripping, out of the water. But then a surge of fury swept through him. "Why did you come? Why have you endangered yourself?" he said, moaning, cradling her face.

"The tunnel has collapsed. There's twenty feet of rock between us and daylight. Nic, there were gunshots. This is the only way." She backed away a step and untied the rope from around her waist. Then she tied it to his. "Stay right here. Mr. McManus is waiting on you." She looked toward the tunnel, then yanked three times. Then she pulled the other rope off her shoulder and tied it around Nic's waist too. "What are you doing, Sabine?" he asked in utter confusion.

She pulled the other end of the second rope around her waist and started tying it. "I'm going on, Nic. I think we know the only way out."

"And that is …?"

"Through there," she said, with a swoop of her head over her shoulder.

He looked in confusion to the far wall. "But we have no idea if that way is passable!"

But then she was swimming away from him. She paused, ten feet off. "If I get through, I'll tug six times, letting you know it's safe to come. Send the same signal to Mr. McManus. If I can't make it, I'll haul myself back."

Nic frowned. "Wait," he said, lifting his hand. "No, Sabine. *Sabine.*"

"Three times means all is well. Six times means come ahead. Got it?"

"Sabine!"

"Do you understand?"

"I understand."

"Then understand this too, Dominic St. Clair. I'm in love with you. Like I've never been in love. I love you. Do you hear me?"

How could he not hear her? Her voice echoed around the chamber. But as clearly as her words reverberated, they seeped deep into his mind, his heart. *She loves me.* "Sabine, I—"

But she was already gone.

Sabine swam, feeling lighter without the rope over her shoulders, but conscious of the rope that connected her to Nic. *Tell me, Lord. Tell me if I need to turn back. Give me the strength to make it if I can. For Nic. For Everett. For me.*

She kicked and crawled her way forward, through a bending tunnel that narrowed alarmingly, then widened again. Just as her lungs started to burn and she was considering turning back, she caught a glimpse of light. The black waters faded to a deep blue, then a blue-green. She was close.

She redoubled her efforts, kicking madly, pushing off the mineral-laden rocks, ignoring the cuts on her hands, focusing only on the light. The light. The Light.

She rose, breaking the surface, and resisted the urge to shout in triumph. She had not the air to do so anyway. She gasped and smiled and gulped in more air. She had made it. There was a way.

Sabine swam to the edge of the spring, turned, and yanked on her rope six times.

"Come on," she whispered. "Come out. You can make it. Please, Lord, help them out."

A cracking branch right behind her made her whirl and sink back into the waters.

Someone was in the woods.

She pushed back into the tall reeds that surrounded the pool, praying she wouldn't be seen, praying no one would hear her chattering teeth.

"She's out!" Nic shouted, feeling the tugs. "She's made it!"

He turned toward the tunnel that led back to the mine and tugged on the rope that Mr. McManus was holding. "Everett," he said to the boy, "you go first. You're so cold—you need to get to sunlight and dry air as fast as possible."

The boy came out to him, teeth chattering, his whole body visibly shaking. "I … I don't know if I can swim that far."

"You can do it," Nic said, placing a hand on either side of his face. "You just take a deep breath, and pull yourself along the rope. Sabine's on the other side waiting for you."

"Is it … is it a long way?"

Nic tried to hide his grimace. "It might be. I don't know, but it seemed to take Sabine a bit. But she made it, Ev. You can too. Can you be brave?" he asked. "Show me what you're made of?"

"Yessir," he said solemnly, his jaw bouncing up and down with tremors.

Nic hugged him for a moment, then urged him forward. "Go, Ev. To the end of the rope, then take three big breaths and kick like everything."

The boy did as he bade, and then he was gone.

Mr. McManus popped up behind him, sputtering and coughing. "Sabine … she's off again?"

"Out the next tunnel already," Nic said with some pride. He reached out to steady the older man when he stumbled.

Sheriff Nelson was wading out to them. "If it's all right with you, I'll go next. Make sure Sabine and the boy are not running into any trouble, considering those gunshots."

"Good idea," Nic said, feeling badly that he hadn't thought of it first. All he could think of was getting the shivering child to warmth. "Take care of them, Drew. Tell them I'll be along shortly."

"I will." He took several gulps of air and then disappeared under the water, tugging so hard along the rope that Nic had to adjust his stance in order not to be pulled off his feet.

The water was a heavenly, pearlescent green. Sabine glimpsed Everett's hands as he came out of the tunnel. She could hear someone behind her—maybe on horseback? She did not dare to look. Had they figured out that there might be a way out through the waterways? Or were they merely looking around, making sure they were alone on the property?

Everett was rising, just eight feet away from her. She slipped under the water as quietly as she could and gestured to him to come to her, putting her finger to her lips. Did he even have his eyes open? She remembered being a child, learning to swim, and her father teaching her to open her eyes. It didn't come naturally.

But he seemed to catch sight of her and sense, if not see, her lead. They rose together, and she prayed he would not be too loud when he took his first breath of air. They broke the surface and she quickly put her finger to her lips again, urging him to be quiet. His eyes were wide, but he concentrated on her, mouth wide, panting. She pulled him to her, hugging him, and then they moved back, among the reeds. They were a foot into the cover, then two, when she stopped. She prayed the swirling mud would settle and not alert anyone looking that there was something—or someone—among the pool's grasses.

She could feel someone else yanking on the rope between her and Nic. But Sabine dared not expose herself or Everett again. The sheriff came up then, and Sabine whispered, "Look out!"

A gun fired, making Sabine wince and squeeze her eyes shut, waiting for the pain of a bullet. In her shoulder? Her head? But nothing pierced her.

She opened her eyes to see the sheriff whirl and dive back under.

The rope pulled at her, dragging her and Everett forward, making the tall reeds above wave.

No! No, no, no!

She heard the splash of boots in the water just behind her, two steps, then three. A hand clamped around her hair, pulling her upward. She gasped and turned to see who had a hold of her.

"Well, would you look at this!" Rinaldi crowed, ignoring Everett, who pounded at his arm and screamed for him to let Sabine go. "A little Indian squaw and her runt."

Moira awakened with a start, and once she saw the chair, still securely in place, she looked out the window. She'd ignored the bell for supper and had fallen asleep again. It was a moonless night, but here and there she could see brush and hills within the few flickering lights emanating from the train.

For a long moment she wondered if she had dreamed the incident in the dining car. Surely no one had followed her onto this train with an old playbill in hand. For that to be true, they would have had to be watching the ranch for some time, waiting for just the right moment. And passage on this particular train was a luxury. Who had that kind of money in their purse without careful planning?

She shook her head, as if she hoped to shake loose the dream cobwebs inside.

She had almost convinced herself that she had dreamed the whole thing when she saw the glass knob of her door begin to turn.

Someone was trying to get in.

CHAPTER TWENTY

Nic frowned, feeling the tug of the rope again, as if the sheriff might be returning, but then it stopped. What was happening on the other side? "Here, take these ropes," he told Mr. McManus, pulling at the knot with fingers trembling with cold. At last it gave way and he yanked it off, wrapping it around the other man's waist. "Something's wrong out there. I have to get to Sabine."

The surveyor broke the surface from the other tunnel, and the men on the bank of the pool shouted in celebration. But Nic's attention was ahead of him. He took a deep breath and went under, stroking hard, and growing alarmed when the rope grew slack in the darkness. He prayed that somehow, some way, the rest would make it out. But something had happened to Sabine and Everett. He could feel it. *Please, Lord …*

At the end of the tunnel, his lungs burned, bursting to escape, but as he was rising to the blessed blue-tinged light of the pool above, strong arms reached out and encircled him, pulling him up and backward into the tunnel.

Nic came out of the water and gasped for air. "What are you doing?" They were in a dimly lit cavern, with just enough air space for their heads, both treading water now.

"Shush," Sheriff Nelson demanded in a harsh whisper. "There's a man outside who just tried to kill me. Would've shot you too."

"Probably the same people who tried to kill us inside the Vaughn mine," Nic guessed.

The sheriff nodded, adding, "He likely has Sabine and Everett too."

Nic's brow furrowed in fear. There was nothing but a fight to the death ahead of them. *No mercy.*

He groaned. "How would they know we're here? Trying to escape?"

"I'd wager those Dolly Mae surveyors knew there was an underground lake and figured it extended through a cavern system underneath Sabine's property too."

Nic blinked. How could he have been so stupid?

The sheriff let out a sound of surprise and then took a deep breath and went down, coming up with Mr. McManus. Briefly, they told him what had transpired.

"Well, what are we to do now?" sputtered the man. "We can't survive in here much longer. Either the cold or the lack of oxygen will kill us all."

"We have no choice but to go out, all together," Nic said. "You have a gun?"

"It's pretty waterlogged," he said. "Not sure it'll fire."

"Let's hope it will," Nic returned. "I say we all three move out at once, each heading in a different direction. He can't kill us all. With luck, he won't hit any of us, if we stay deep."

"Somebody has to stay here and warn the others," Mr. McManus said.

"That's true," the sheriff said.

"All right," Nic said to the older man. "You stay here and warn the others. Tell 'em to come out in twos, swimming away from each other when they get to the outside."

"They should swim toward the edge," the sheriff said. "There are banks full of reeds. It'll give 'em some cover as they come out of the water."

"I will. Good luck, gentlemen," Mr. McManus said.

"I'll go left, you go right," Nic said to Sheriff Nelson. Then he took a few deep breaths and dived in.

He steeled himself for what was ahead. Years in the ring had prepared him for this moment, when he would do whatever he had to in order to save the woman and boy he was coming to love. *My family,* he thought. *Lord, help me make it through this, and I'll make them my family for good.*

He reached the tunnel's mouth and slowly edged out and to the left, aware the sheriff was right behind him. He grimaced at the power of the current that pushed him faster than he wished to emerge. With any luck, his brown shirt and dark trousers would blend in with the rock. He kicked, leaving the current, and held on to the rock for a moment. He exhaled some of his precious air, trying to stay down a few moments longer. He heard no firearm blasting, even through water-filled ears, and his heart pounded with encouragement.

Please, Lord, please hide me. He pulled himself along the slippery, slimy rocks toward the bank of reeds and then let his body rise gradually among the outer portion of reeds. His eyes and nose were above the water, and his nostrils flared, sucking in the oxygen, while he blinked and looked about, careful not to splash. The pond appeared to be empty. Slowly, he turned and looked to the other side.

Nothing.

There. The sheriff had just come to the surface too and was look-ing around. After a moment, he spotted Nic. He gave him a little shake of the head, indicating he didn't see anyone either.

Sheriff Nelson pulled up hands full of nutrient-rich mud and slowly spread it across his head and face. He was instantly less visible. Nic followed suit, although his darker hair and skin was less notice-able than the sheriff's red hair and pale complexion. Sheriff Nelson motioned to head toward the other end of the pool, and Nic followed his lead. Behind him, the sheriff pulled out his gun, dropped the bul-lets from their chambers, blew inside with quick huffs, and put the bullets back into their chambers. Nic hoped it would work—that the gun would fire, if need be.

Nic moved down the pond slowly. The water became shal-lower, and soon he was pulling his way along, legs floating behind him.

"Stop where you are!"

He stilled, hearing a voice almost directly above him.

"Why, Sheriff, you really do need a bath," said the man.

Rinaldi.

Nic prayed he wouldn't spot him too.

"Come on out of the water now," Rinaldi barked, pointing a gun in Drew's direction.

Slowly, Nic swiveled his head to eye the sheriff. The man rose, as if defeated, then whipped out his gun toward Rinaldi. Shots fired above Nic's head. Three times and he heard the sickening sound of Sheriff Nelson's body falling among the reeds and shallow water. But he used the moment to gather his feet beneath him, then rose and roared as he surged forward, cursing the sucking power of the mud that slowed him down.

But it mattered not. Adrenaline surged through him, making him feel stronger than ever before. Rinaldi had just shaken loose of Sabine, throwing her to the ground, and was bringing his gun around to take Nic down when Nic tackled him, striking at the man's belly with his shoulder.

Dimly, he felt the shoulder pop out of place, and for a split second his vision clouded. But then he spotted Everett, his face drained of color. Fury surged again through Nic, sharpening his focus. He rose up, still partly atop Rinaldi, and struck him twice in the face with his good arm.

The man blocked the third blow with his right and then struck Nic with a left, knocking him off.

Nic rolled and came to his feet, immediately coming after Rinaldi, pummeling him as fast as he could, knowing there were probably others on their way, if they'd heard the gunfire, if they weren't here—

—*already.*

He stilled when he felt the cold ring of steel at his temple and saw Rinaldi rise and take a step back, a grin on his face. The monster was panting so hard, he put his hands on his knees and stared at Nic, then shook his head. "Lots of fire in you, for coming out of such cold water."

Nic ignored him. His eyes shifted to the right, to the one who held a gun on him. One of Rinaldi's cohorts.

"Don't you move," said the man beside him.

Nic slowly raised his hands, as if surrendering. Then, as the man took a step closer, Nic backhanded him and bent to give him

a swift sidekick, knocking him to the ground. The gun went flying, but Nic's attention returned to Rinaldi, who was once again
lunging at him. The taller man struck hard, hitting Nic with a
tough right that almost sent him whirling. Then he grabbed him
and picked him up, ramming him into a tree.

The breath was knocked out of Nic, but before he collapsed, he
pulled his head back and rammed it into Rinaldi's nose. The man
screamed out in rage and backed off a few steps, blood pouring from
his nostrils.

Nic leaned back against the tree and tried not to panic as his
lungs refused to cooperate for a moment. At last he was able to take
a breath. And another, even as he became a little woozy. Slowly, his
vision cleared and he saw that Rinaldi had pulled his gun and had it
pointed at Sabine and Everett.

Nic froze again.

Rinaldi grinned, blood dripping down his lip and through his
teeth, giving him a ghoulish appearance. Sabine and Everett were
clinging to each other, weeping.

"I think," Rinaldi said, "you're gonna pay for that, St. Clair."

"Who's there?" Moira screeched, staring in horror at the door, pulling
her blanket to her chest like some sort of protective shield.

The knob reached the end of its axis.

The lock held.

"Get away!" Moira yelled, growing angry in her fear.

The interloper released the knob and it rotated back to its original position.

It did not turn again.

Moira threw the blanket aside, now furious. She would not be bullied. By anyone. She'd had enough of it with Reid. Even with Gavin's slier methods, pushing her to do things she didn't care for. From here on out, her life was her own. No one else's. And this man—whoever he was—was not going to rob her of that.

She glanced around the tiny compartment, looking for a weapon of some sort. Everything was too bulky or too soft. Remembering her umbrella with its sturdy hand-carved handle, she dug to the bottom of her valise and pulled it out in victory. Holding it tightly in her right hand, she went to the door, and before she could second-guess herself, unlocked it and yanked it open.

Moira took a step back and tensed, ready to bludgeon whoever was outside. How dare he invade her privacy, prey upon her, attempt to frighten her, even try and enter her room! How dare he! She whipped her head around the corner, looking one way, then the other. Nothing but the swaying, flickering lights of the two gas lamps in the hallway.

There. At the end of the hall, a door was just closing. He was going to the dining car.

Moira turned, grabbed her key, and hurriedly locked the door, then ran after him, nearly falling once when the train car lurched over a particularly bad track connection. By the time she reached the door, she felt her first moment of hesitation.

"You will not be bullied, Moira St. Clair. See this through," she ground out in a whisper.

She hauled open the connecting door, pausing when the night air rushed through the compartment, and clenched her teeth against the jarring noise of train tracks, wheels, and metal fittings. She stepped in, relieved as the racket behind her eased.

But she stilled and felt her heart pound painfully.

The dining car was completely dark.

Three others on horseback arrived at the LaCrosse property, each carrying a lantern, and took a look around the group before dismounting.

"Everything all right, boss?" asked one.

"Right as a straight flush and a pile of money on the center of the table," Rinaldi grinned. "But we're not alone. There are some serious gamblers still in play." He nodded at Nic, Sabine, and Everett. "They came out of the tunnel, and up and out of the spring. Two of you head to the pond to keep watch. You should find the sheriff's body in the reeds across the pond. Bring him."

"The sheriff?" asked one blankly.

"Go," Rinaldi answered in irritation, waving him off.

He looked back to Nic and slowly pulled his own gun from its holster and approached. Nic tensed, and the pain in his shoulder screamed, though he did his best to hide it. Rinaldi circled Nic, looking him over. "Where'd you learn to fight like that?"

Nic ignored him. Rinaldi halted behind him, then punched his dislocated shoulder.

Nic gasped and fell to his knees, holding his arm in front of him. He fought to stay conscious. The pain, miraculously absent during the fight, was now upon him, worse than ever before. He blinked and looked over at Sabine and Everett, still weeping and holding each other, refusing to look his way. Why was that? Were they afraid they'd see him die? He had to stay conscious, for them if not for himself. There still might be a way out.

Two more horses approached.

Mr. Kazin and Mr. Dell. They looked about with alarm on their faces, from Sabine and Everett to Nic, then over to the two men who dragged the sheriff's body into the clearing and dumped him.

Mr. Dell took off his hat and wiped his upper lip with the back of his hand. "This is not quite what we discussed, Richard."

Rinaldi grimaced and glanced his way. "It's not quite what any of us thought could happen, Mr. Dell. Who would have guessed that these river rats could make it through the caverns? We're only lucky that I thought to come over and check it out."

"And now what are we to do?" Mr. Kazin said, imperious as ever. "Kill them all?"

"You were more than happy to see them die inside the mountain," Rinaldi responded, eyes back on Nic.

"It is one thing to fake a cave-in, another to shoot at close range," Mr. Kazin retorted. "They took a chance going into that mine. We only hastened what could have happened naturally."

"Hastened?" Nic said with a hollow laugh. "You tried to *murder* us."

"Yes, well," Mr. Kazin said, sniffing, "regardless of how you put it, you are very much alive now, aren't you, Mr. St. Clair? And you, Mrs. LaCrosse."

"Very much," Nic responded drily.

Mr. Kazin dismounted, and Mr. Dell followed suit. "Bring her," Mr. Kazin said to a man beside the sheriff's body, gesturing toward Sabine, then walking over to Nic. Behind him, the man grabbed Sabine's arm and yanked her to her feet. Nic had to force himself to remain where he was, well aware that neither Rinaldi's eyes nor his gun ever left him.

Mr. Kazin reached inside his coat pocket. He looked over his shoulder to Mr. Dell. "Bring the pen and ink, please."

"These," he said, holding out two sheets of paper in front of Nic's face, "are the deeds to both your mine and Mrs. LaCrosse's. You shall sign them over to us now."

Nic scoffed. "For what reason would I do that? As soon as we sign them, you'll kill us."

"This is true," Mr. Kazin said, raising a brow. "One way or another, you have seen the end of your living days. We can kill you and lay claim to the properties before anyone else even knows you're gone. But it'll be much cleaner if we have your signatures."

"I'm sorry," Nic said. "But I missed why we would want to make anything easier for you."

Mr. Kazin stared at him for a moment, then at Sabine, and then slowly looked over at Everett and back. His inference was clear.

"Sign the documents," Kazin said lowly, "and I'll see the child to the orphanage in Buena Vista. If you refuse—" he paused, letting his words sink in—"he'll die alongside you."

CHAPTER TWENTY-ONE

Nic moved to strike Mr. Kazin, and Rinaldi instantly rammed him in the shoulder again. Sabine winced and turned away, well aware of how such a blow would affect him. She heard him moan and fall back against the tree. Tears streamed down her face. The violence, the blows. *Too much, Lord. I cannot take it.* Her mind cascaded back to Henri, her husband, how he had become expert at bruising her where no one else could see. Until that final day when he broke her arm and battered her face. It was then that Sinopa returned to her, cared for her. And Henri disappeared forever …

She was trembling, shaking as hard as she once did when she feared Henri's approach. But then her eyes met Everett's. He was twenty paces away, arms wrapped around his knees, peering over at her, his forehead a wrinkled mass. He was afraid, so afraid.

Immediately, Sabine's waves of fear turned into white-hot anger. Never before had she been so angry. With a cry of rage she grabbed the pen from Mr. Dell's fat hand and rammed the tip into Mr. Kazin's cheek. "Run, Ev!" she screamed, even as she lifted Rinaldi's arm and ducked. He fired at the same time, but the bullet went high.

Nic plunged back into the fight, incapacitated as he was, and Sabine joined in his attack on their tormentor. A gun went off, and then another. She waited, thinking that at any moment a bullet might pierce her chest or head as Rinaldi's men gathered themselves to take better aim, but then there were other men about them, entering the fray, exchanging blows. The others! The others had made it out of the tunnel. *The tide is turning. There is hope,* she thought, slapping away a tiny pistol in portly Mr. Dell's hand.

She looked to the side, searching for Everett, hoping he was gone, but then he was flying at Mr. Kazin, who was hunched over, gingerly trying to pull the stuck pen from his cheek. The boy hopped on the tall man's back and pulled backward on his neck, as if he meant to strangle him. The man grabbed hold of him and savagely tossed him to the ground. But Everett came skidding to a stop six feet away and rounded, as if to come at him again.

Another two guns fired in rapid succession.

Beside her, Nic and Rinaldi crumpled to the ground. Sabine's gaze flew to them. Who was hit?

Before her, Mr. Dell, hovering over his pistol, as if he had been about to reach for it, clutched his chest and then fell on his face, into the dirt.

Then she saw Mr. Kazin raise his hands, his face grim in defeat. He was giving up. They had won.

Her eyes went to Nic and Rinaldi.

Rinaldi, too, had his hands up and was rising.

But Nic was motionless on the ground before him.

Moira opened her eyes as wide as possible, as if she might be able to suddenly see in the dark. Was he here? Could he possibly see her?

Her pulse thundered in her ears, a dull, muffled *whoosh* audible even over the *clickety-clack* of the train tracks beneath her feet. She felt behind her for the wood-paneled wall, and then edged to the right, where she knew the piano was. She wanted to know no one was beside her or behind her.

She bumped into the piano bench with her right knee, then edged farther in. With a sweep of her right hand, she knew the corner was empty. Before her was the piano. That left only a space to her left where he could come at her. If he was coming after her. If he was here at all.

Maybe it had been the conductor, on his way to the engine.

But he wouldn't have tried her doorknob.

She waited, willing her breathing to ease from quick frantic pants to a slower stream, still listening for any movement at all, since she could see little.

A favorite hymn of her grandmother's ran through her mind.

> *God, my Lord, my strength,*
> *My place of hiding, and confiding,*
> *In all needs by night and day;*
> *Though foes surround me,*
> *And Satan mark his prey,*
> *God shall have His way.*

Father, have Your way here, now, she prayed. *Give me Your strength. I am Yours. Claim me, Lord, as I claim You as my God. With You by my side, who can harm me?*

She straightened and felt a pervading sense of peace surround her.

A sound made her turn her head toward the passageway.
Someone else was coming.

Mr. McManus knelt beside Sabine and reached out to feel for Nic's pulse.

Everett came to her and she gathered him into her lap, but still Mr. McManus did not turn.

She closed her eyes and held her breath. *Please don't let him die, Lord. Please don't let him die.*

"He's alive," Mr. McManus said. But there was no trace of joy in his voice, only a grim announcement. Clearly, Nic was in mortal danger.

"So is Drew," the deputy called, beside Sheriff Nelson. The deputy was on the other side. He'd turned Sheriff Nelson over. His shirt was bright with blood.

"We have to get them to the doctor," Mr. McManus said.

"And these men into the jail cell," the deputy added.

"Do you think they'll survive the ride down the mountain?" Sabine asked in a whisper.

No one heard her. The men left in their party scurried to secure the would-be assassins, tying them behind horses. They would have to walk.

"Quickly, Sabine," Mr. McManus said. "We must bind their wounds, keep them from losing any more blood." Sabine and the deputy surged into the task, ripping pieces of fabric from her underskirt to create bands that could go around and around the men's wounds.

One of the sheriff's investors and the deputy climbed atop the two largest horses and then motioned to the others to bring the sheriff and Nic. Mr. Avery and Mr. McManus carried the sheriff first, holding him between them like a hammock in a tree. "Go, go," Sabine urged. She and Everett climbed on a third horse. The others silently agreed to hike down behind them all, keeping a close watch on the men who had almost killed them.

"You think this is over?" Rinaldi sneered as he walked behind the first horse.

"It is for you," Sabine said. She looked at the deputy. "If he does anything suspicious at all, kill him."

The door opened, and with it came the warm, welcome light of a lamp.

She glanced around the train car as it illuminated the space, and saw that no one else was present. Moira turned back to the man with the lamp—the diminutive pianist.

His hand was over his heart, his mouth open. "Heavens, miss, what are you doing here in the dark?" His eyes moved to the umbrella, still clenched in her right hand. "Are you all right?" He scanned the rest of the car, as if seeking what had frightened her so.

Moira sank down to the piano bench and slowly released the umbrella. She'd been holding it so hard that her hand ached.

"What were you doing in here? Alone? And at such an hour?"

"I could ask the same of you," she said.

"I couldn't sleep. Sleeper car, my foot," he said with a scornful sound. "We'd be better served stopping at the railroad hotels. I came in here to play some piano." He stepped forward, gingerly. "Name's Benjamin Bonser. My friends call me Ben."

"Nice to meet you, Ben," she said, accepting his hand. "I'll vacate so you might resume your piano playing. I enjoyed it after our noon meal."

She moved off the bench and he smiled, set the lamp atop the piano, and then took a seat. "Stay, if you like," he said. "Apparently you had difficulty sleeping too?"

"Indeed," she said. Her eyes slid up and down the car once more, just to make certain they were alone.

The man who had tried to enter her compartment was likely the same one who had slipped the poster onto her table. He sought to provoke or control her, somehow, by wielding his knowledge of her identity over her.

There was one way she could diminish that power.

She could acknowledge her identity herself.

A slow smile spread across her lips. "Ben," she said quietly. "Remember that song you were playing at supper? Do you still have the music?"

The ride down the Gulch had never seemed so torturously long. All the way to the bottom, Sabine kept wondering if they would lose one or both men.

"Is he gonna die, Sabine?" Everett asked, from behind her.

"I hope not, Ev," she returned.

"If he does, can I live with you?" he said.

"Right now, let's hope for the best and pray God delivers them, all right?"

He nodded, his head bouncing against her back. The poor child had to be lost in grief, the loss of his father so fresh, and now potentially Nic. She swallowed hard around a ball in her throat. She could not cry again now. To do so would mean never stopping. She concentrated on the wind in the trees, the thousands of fluttering leaves of the aspens, the clouds high above, curling and spreading and curling again.

They picked their way down the trail, relying on the light of the lanterns. Had it been just this morning that they had all ridden up the Gulch, the thrill of potential and plans thick in their minds? It was too much to absorb. She opened her eyes wide, suddenly aware of how weary she was—almost near collapse. She had to stay strong for Everett, for Nic. She had to see this through.

She looked out again to the valley, to the silhouette of trees against a starry sky. She could smell the smoke from fireplaces about the valley. She used to imagine her neighbors fixing dinner, eating together, playing a hand of cards, climbing into their beds at night. Now, as their horses descended, all Sabine could sense was the smoke, entering her lungs, making her want to cough. She wanted to be away from this place, free of it. Far from the memories of Henri and his ways, which were like the smoke—encircling, stifling, choking. She wanted to be with Nic, who was more like the stars, circling, dancing, moving forward.

Sabine moved her head, daring to look beyond Mr. Avery to Michael McManus, who held Nic in front of him to keep him from tumbling from the horse. She knew it had to be hard, holding the weight of the unconscious man, but he held Nic tight. She glanced back at Mr. Kazin. Blood still streamed down his face and neck from the puncture wound she'd inflicted with the pen, and he stared back at her, his eyes dull with rage.

That's right, she said to him silently. *You're only fortunate I didn't have my rifle when I realized how much I loathed you.*

She turned back around, knowing Everett was watching her. She would find a way to make Kazin and Rinaldi and the rest pay.

But it would mean little if Nic was not with them.

Their horse stumbled and Everett's arms shot around her waist. He leaned hard, then righted himself. "Sorry," he muttered.

Sabine glanced down at his hands, in a knot now in front of her.

Then she reached down and covered them with one of her own. "It's all right, Ev," she said. "Somehow, some way, this will all turn out all right."

She looked ahead to Michael's back again, and Nic's body, swaying before him.

But were her words anything more than a lie meant to soothe them both?

CHAPTER TWENTY-TWO

Once it was known that Moira was aboard the train, the passengers were atwitter. The result was that she was hardly alone after that, giving her the welcome insulation of people from morning until late at night.

The only thing that nagged at her was that one of the men at her dining table—or hovering about as she sang with Ben's accompaniment that evening—could be the one who had tried to get into her compartment. But try as she might to determine who it was, no one gave her a further clue. Every man appeared to be a gentleman, never peering too long or asking too many questions. More than five were traveling alone, which to Moira's mind made them likelier suspects than others, but their utterly polite ways made Moira feel paranoid for doubting any of them.

Had the interloper somehow escaped the train?

She still spent the next night fully dressed, and with the chair lodged under the knob, but no one came to her door.

Moira awakened the next morning, accepted a pitcher of warm water from the steward, and peered outside. The train was slowing. A grin spread across her face. They were rounding a curve in the tracks and for a brief moment, the skyline of the city was in view. Her heart picked up its pace. The thought of being surrounded by people, of meeting the Knapps, of being amidst so much life felt good, right to her.

Clearly God meant for her to come here.

Why else would she feel so deliriously happy?

"He's waking up," said a grizzled voice, tinged with jubilation.

Nic tried to open his eyes again but they felt heavy, as if sandbags covered them. He shifted his eyes back and forth and then forced them to blink. Bright morning sun blinded him and he closed them again.

"Nic," Sabine said. He wanted to smile and laugh in relief at the sound of her voice, but he could not seem to make himself do anything at all. She came to him then, sitting so close that he could smell her, the wild, woodsy scent of her. She took his hand in hers, and he could feel the strength of her small fingers, warm and dry. "Ev," she called toward the far end of the room. Where were they? Why couldn't he open his eyes and see them? "Ev, come over here. He's waking up."

He concentrated hard, focusing on this one task, and at last, his eyelids fluttered open. They closed again, but at least he could glimpse them, these two he had come to love. He smiled, or tried to smile anyway.

Everett was grinning and Sabine was smiling, her eyes wet with tears. "Nic, Nic," she said, rising, "you've come back to us." Then she leaned over and gently, slowly, placed a warm kiss on his forehead. Her fragrance surrounded him, and he longed to rise and pull her into his arms and kiss her in return. But he could do nothing.

"Just sit tight," came the grizzled voice again, along with a pat on his arm. The pat sent a surge of pain up his arm and through his dislocated shoulder. His eyes shot open.

"Oh, sorry about that, young man. We got it back into place, but it likely hurts like the dickens still, eh?" The doctor glanced at Sabine, and she moved away so he could examine Nic's eyes, first one, then the other. He brought a lamp closer—lit even though the room was flooded with daylight—and did the exam again. "Yep," he announced, "it'll take a few days, but he's on his way."

Three faces filled Nic's line of vision—Sabine, Everett, and the doctor—and then he closed his eyes, giving in with some relief to unconsciousness again.

The deputy, with his feet up on the desk and hat over his eyes, said, "You keep walking that path, you'll wear a track in the boards."

Daniel paused and looked up at the ceiling. Glen was right. He'd been pacing for hours.

"What has you so tied up in knots, boss?"

He looked back and watched Glen put his feet down on the floor, rock forward in the chair, and rest his arms on the desk, waiting on Daniel to speak. Then he looked past him, to their prisoner, still stubbornly refusing to speak. The man appeared to be asleep.

"It's Moira," he said, with a tinge of a groan. "Miss St. Clair."

"She your sweetheart?"

"Thought she was, once. But she left."

Glen pursed his lips and nodded, thinking that over. "Does she plan to return?"

"I don't know for sure." He leaned back against the wall and crossed his arms.

"So … what's holding you back? Why not go after her?"

Daniel pulled his head to one side. "Responsibilities. To you boys, the job …"

Glen studied him. "Something else?"

Was he so transparent? He frowned and looked at the floor, then back to Glen. He ignored the prisoner, still unmoving. "My wife was killed, some time back," Daniel said lowly. "I thought I might've seen him, that day we captured him in Conquistador." He nodded to the back.

Glen stared at him. "Here? You think your wife's killer is here?"

Daniel shut his eyes and ran his hand through his hair, feeling the heat of embarrassment on his neck. It sounded foolish when he said it. Was he a fool?

"Stranger things have happened.…"

"No. You're right. But it's a long shot."

After a moment, Glen said, "So, you let Miss St. Clair go, because your wife's murderer might be about?"

"I didn't let Miss St. Clair do anything," he defended. "She did it on her own."

"But she might not have done it if you had been more … attentive?"

Daniel shot him a look that said he'd gone too far. The deputy leaned back, put his feet on the desk, and lowered his hat over his face again, as if to say he was done with the conversation. Daniel turned and leaned against the window frame, staring outside. It was a quiet night in Westcliffe. Even the saloons seemed to have few patrons entering and exiting.

Was Moira there in New York, yet? What would happen if she

passed by a saloon, unaccompanied? Even Gavin Knapp had not allowed her to travel alone. But now she was alone, without a chaperone. Because of him. Because he had walked away.

He sighed heavily, Glen's words running through his mind, over and over. *So you let Miss St. Clair go, because your wife's murderer might be about?* Might be about. Or very well might not be.

How long would Daniel let the shadows of the past darken the hope of his future? He took the job because he knew he'd be good at it, in spite of Moira's concerns, in spite of her fears, protests. But he took it, if he was honest with himself, for one primary goal: to find Mary's remaining killer and bring him to justice.

Daniel brought a hand up to his face and rubbed his temples. *How long, Lord? How long, until I trust You and Your timing again?*

He knew God's justice frequently did not match man's sense of timing. And a thought darted through his mind. What if Mary's killer, imperfectly remembered, was somewhere far away, even in jail? Or dead?

I'm chasing a ghost.

And I've let my second chance at love, a full life, walk away.

Nic awakened again the next day, feeling far more alert. He blinked several times, and while his body felt unaccountably weary, he could move his head. He gazed upon Sabine, sleeping in the corner in a chair, her long hair falling out of a knot and partially over her face, and at Everett in the other corner, curled up in a winged-back chair.

He didn't want to disturb either of them, but he needed to move, and he was desperate for a drink of water. Slowly, he curled his toes and tightened the muscles in his legs. All seemed in order there. But he could feel the tight bandages around his waist. Had he been shot? Dimly, he remembered the firefight at the pond, Rinaldi, Sabine, and Everett …

Nic lifted the sheet and blanket that covered him and positioned his head to look. White bandages were wound around his torso, making him appear partially mummified. Two red splotches, each about five inches in diameter, spread out across the white, like intersecting planets.

Shot twice. I was shot twice. No wonder his body wasn't as anxious to move as his mind was.

A man about his age came in then and gave him a gentle smile. He glanced over at Everett and Sabine, then back at him. "Good to see you awake," he said in a whisper, reaching out a hand. He gestured over at the others with a tip of his head. "They will be too. I'm Dr. Deck."

"Doc," Nic said, wincing a bit as he shook his hand, wincing a bit at the pain in his torso.

"Easy, there," the doctor said, gently settling his hand. "It'll take a while, but you'll heal up in time."

"I hope so," Nic said, looking over to Sabine. She was stirring.

The doctor felt Nic's forehead and then took his pulse. "You're a little clammy, but that's typical with bullet wounds. No fever, which is good. And your pulse is decent. Except when you look over at her," he added in a quieter whisper. "She's a fine-looking woman. You're a lucky man."

"Yes I am," Nic said. He remembered her words in the cave, just before she so bravely set out to look for the next tunnel, a tunnel that ultimately led them all to freedom, to life. She loved him. She *loved* him. And he loved her. He shook his head at the wonder of it.

"Sheriff's lucky too," the doctor said. "He's in the other room. Similar wounds. But like yours, the bullets passed clean through. You two kept me busy, but I think you'll both be all right."

"We owe you much, Doc."

"Just doing my job," he said with a shrug. He raised a brow. "But I tell ya, I could use a good night's sleep. Think you can stay out of any further gunfights for a few days?"

"I'll do my best."

The doctor poured him a glass of water and helped him sit up so he could drink some of it. Then he set down the glass and left the room, presumably to check on the sheriff.

Sabine woke then with a start and rose quickly. She looked lovely, her hair disheveled. Nic longed to reach up and pull it loose, see it cascade across her shoulders. "Nic! Oh, Nic, you're back," she said, moving toward the cot on which he lay.

"Never left," he said, hiding his desire to wince again as she took his hand and lifted it to her cheek.

"I was so afraid," she said, looking into his eyes.

"I was too," he said. "Afraid something would happen to you or Everett." He shook his head. "I couldn't tolerate that. I know … I know it must've been tough, seeing me fighting like that, Sabine. I could see it in your eyes," he rushed on. "Brought back some bad memories, huh?"

She looked away, still holding his hand, and then nodded quickly.

"Look at me, love," he said quietly. He waited until she met his eyes again. "I have a history of fighting. It's been who I am for a long time. But something's happened to me here, since I got back to the States again, really …"

"You don't have to—"

"No, let me finish. This is important. For us. God has been working on me, softening my heart. Healing me. Getting me ready for you. I was angry at Him for a long time, which made me angry at the world. But it was only when we were in danger, when you and Ev were in danger, that I wanted to fight again. I'm going to do my best to be a man of peace. Of peace. The only thing that will move me to fight is defending you, Ev, myself. All right?"

She nodded again.

He caressed her pretty face. "Sabine, you said you loved me in that tunnel. Did you mean it?"

Her eyes searched his. "Yes," she said softly.

"I'm so glad," he said with a smile. "Because I'd like to marry you. As fast as possible. I can't do this properly, get down on my knee and all, but I can't wait another minute. Would you do me the honor of being my wife, Sabine? I am in love with you. And I'll do my best to always show you that love."

Sabine grinned and her eyelashes grew wet with tears. She leaned down and kissed him, softly, slowly. "Yes," she whispered when her face hovered a feather's width from his. "Yes."

"I can feel you looking, Ev," Nic said, as she pulled away. He glanced over at the boy, who squirmed in his seat at having been caught spying. But Nic smiled. "Come over here." He reached out his other hand.

Everett moved over to them, as if expecting punishment.

"Take my hand, Ev."

The boy did so, and Nic looked from Sabine to Everett. "Ev, in case you only caught our kiss, Sabine just agreed to marry me. That makes me about the happiest man in Colorado. I know I'll be the happiest if one other person agrees to something."

"What?" Everett asked.

"Would you be willing to be a part of our family, Ev?" Nic asked. "Stay with me and Sabine. Let us raise you?"

Everett smiled.

"I take it that's a yes?"

Everett nodded.

Nic sighed, wincing this time. But he couldn't keep his grin from returning. He closed his eyes, holding on to both their hands. "You two have made me so happy. We have so much ahead of us. So much. But right now, I need to go back to sleep...."

Inside her lovely hotel room, Moira turned and watched as the steward set down her valises. She planned to purchase a few more dresses while in the city. Slowly, she pulled off her kidskin gloves and then opened her purse to pull out a coin and a letter to the Knapps. She slipped both into the young man's palm.

"Might you post this for me, please?" she said.

"Certainly," he said with a nod. "It will go out this afternoon."

"Wonderful. Thank you."

"Here's your key," he said, holding it up for her to see, then setting it on the low table beside a settee. "Supper is served in the dining room downstairs, beginning at six. Would you like me to make a reservation for you?"

"No, thank you. Might you simply send up a bowl of soup and bread?"

"Certainly. Now or later?"

"Hmm, if you could send up maids to fill my bath, then I'd like my supper an hour or so after that."

"I'll see to it, ma'am."

With that he exited. She followed behind and, after peering down the hall to make certain it was empty, locked the door. It was a far sturdier door than the one on the train. Here, after a bath and a meal, she could get a good night's sleep. She was desperate for it suddenly, the rush of adrenaline that had been flowing through her veins on the train depleted like water leaking out of a broken bottle.

She opened the curtains and stared out of her fifth-floor room to the vast Central Park, spreading in a huge rectangle before her. It was a beautiful view, but she found herself remembering the last time she had been in this city, staying in Gavin's apartment, falling for his charms. She had entered the city a virgin; she left as his lover.

What might have happened had she been able to resist him? Refused him? What if she had swallowed her pride and returned to Odessa and Bryce instead? She turned to the mirror above the dresser and slowly unwrapped her veil to study her reflection. Her hair was growing longer now. There was still a patch over her ear where it might never grow again, the burns leaving her skin wrinkled, raw, and angry. But in time, the hair above it would grow long enough to cover it. Perhaps she could even wear it in curls and down over her shoulder as she had when she was a girl. Then it'd cover the burns on her neck as well. Or perhaps she'd always wear her veils. She was becoming comfortable in them, finding a layer of security when they were wrapped about her head and neck.

Her eyelashes and eyebrows were growing back, enhancing the St. Clair eyes that all three siblings had inherited. Her nose was long and straight, her lips full. If something could be done about her hair … a wig. Her eyes opened wide. When she'd thought of a wig before, she'd given up on it immediately. Westcliffe had no selection; she would have had to special order it, and the humiliation of going through that process in front of the proprietor at the mercantile would have been too much to bear. But here in the city, where no one knew her, she wouldn't have that embarrassment. What was to stop her?

It would be no different than donning a wig as a character in an opera. A slow smile spread across her face and she arched a brow. She always favored red wigs. "Heavens, Moira," one of her directors had once said. "That auburn makes your eyes scream at me like sirens to a sailor. We're going to put it on you every moment possible."

Auburn, hmm. After a night's rest, she'd set out for the wigmaker's shop. With luck, she might have it in hand before the Knapps summoned her to come and meet them.

CHAPTER TWENTY-THREE

Moira entered the grand breakfast room, which was elegantly appointed and filled with guests seated at tiny, round, white-cloth-covered tables. She made her way to the concierge in the corner.

"Two today, madam?" he asked, glancing over her shoulder with one arched brow.

"No, a table for one, please," she said, staring right into his eyes, daring him to be anything but polite. "My name is Miss St. Clair."

"Right away, Miss St. Clair," he said with a sniff, writing something down on his tablet. He moved off and she followed him through a sea of fine dresses and suits, feeling the sly glances and stares as she passed. Even here in New York, it was rare to see a young woman unescorted.

The concierge pulled out a chair for her, and once she sat down, helped her push it in. He then took her napkin from the table, unfolded it with a snap, and carefully laid it across her lap. Moira looked down with some chagrin. The way her skirts had settled, the bump of her belly was clearly visible. She picked up the small menu, carefully avoiding looking into the concierge's eyes. He dipped his head, then left for the front.

Moira stared at the words on the menu, not reading them, only pretending, unable to concentrate under the weight of the room's stares and wondering who else might have seen the curve of her pregnancy.

A waiter arrived with coffee and orange juice. How long had it been since she had orange juice? Since … the last time she was here. With Gavin, dining with Gavin.

"Ready to order, Miss St. Clair?" the waiter said.

She glanced up in some surprise at the use of her name. But that was common in a hotel as fine as this. "A soft-boiled egg and toast will be adequate," she said, handing him the menu, still unread.

"Would you like bacon with that?"

"No, thank you." The way she was feeling, it would take everything in her to get her simple order down her gullet.

"I'll have that for you right away, Miss St. Clair."

The slim man moved off, and Moira reached for her orange juice. She lifted the small glass to her lips, staring straight ahead, and nearly spit out the mouthful of sweet, pulpy liquid.

Four tables away, a man immediately moved his eyes to a newspaper spread before him.

But Moira had seen him before. *On the train.*

She swallowed hard and dared to look again. Tall and broad shouldered. Brown hair and murky eyes. He was turned slightly away from her now, apparently engaged in his paper. Or was he pretending as she had with her menu? A muscle twitched in his cheek, as if he were clenching his jaw.

She knew he had been on the train. *You're making too much of it, Moira. Leaping to conclusions.*

On a train full of well-to-do people bound for New York, it would not be odd to run into a good portion of the passengers here in this hotel, a day after arrival. But she knew him from somewhere else too. Where? One of the mining camps? She wracked her mind, trying to place him.

Slowly, he lifted his eyes from his paper and met her stare. A hint of a smile lifted his lips, and Moira immediately broke her gaze. What was she doing? If he was not the interloper, he'd consider her brazen stare as flirtation. And if he was the man who had been following her on the train, trying to get into her room—

The waiter returned, with a steward beside him, blocking her view.

She hadn't seen that man on the train after she followed him, after she met Benjamin Bonser and let her identity be known. She was certain of it.

"Your egg, miss," the waiter said, setting down the soft-boiled egg in an elegant china stand. "And your toast," he added, setting down a second plate. "Is there anything else?"

"No," she mumbled, shaking her head, willing the waiter and steward to stand aside, but not wanting them to go at the same time.

"A letter and a telegram have arrived for you, Miss St. Clair," said the steward, stepping forward. He held out a tray and Moira took the two pieces from him.

"Thank you."

"You are quite welcome."

"Is there anything else you need at the moment, Miss St. Clair?" the waiter asked again.

"Well, I … no. Not right this instant," she said.

The two frowned at her, glanced at each other, and then left. Once they were gone, Moira dared to drag her eyes back to the table four away from hers.

But the brown-haired man was gone.

Four days after the shooting, the doctor insisted Nic stay where he could keep a close eye on him, but let him leave with Sabine for short walks. Today they were to meet with Michael McManus and Mr. Avery—both now fully healed from their own misadventures in the Vaughn mine and the aftermath that ensued—and sign the deal for transfer of ownership. Sheriff Nelson would join them as well.

They walked slowly with Sheriff Nelson and Everett down the street to the attorney's office and let the lawman enter without them. "Give us a minute, will you, Sheriff?"

"Sure, sure."

Nic tried to shake off the bad memories of the last time they had walked in … the Dolly Mae men's offer, and what occurred when they declined. He glanced down at Sabine, who held lightly to his arm. "You all right?"

She nodded.

Then he looked at Everett. "You okay too, Ev?"

He reached out and put a hand on his shoulder. "You sure you're good with this? Us selling your dad's property?"

Everett looked Nic in the eyes. "I trust you, Nic."

"Thanks for that, Ev. I'll do my best to never betray that trust." He lifted his brows. "You're about to be one of the richest kids in Colorado."

The boy smiled and his eyes widened. "Can I buy my own rifle?"

Nic smiled. "I think we might be able to manage that." He reached for the door and opened it for his wife-to-be and boy to enter, then followed behind. The lawyer, Sheriff Nelson, Mr. McManus, and Mr. Avery stood, and shook Nic's hand in turn, each nodding toward Sabine. The sheriff gestured for Sabine to take a seat, pulled up a chair for Everett, and then they all sat down.

"We're certainly glad to see you and the sheriff are recovering so well, Nic," Mr. McManus said.

"No more than I."

"Yes, well," he said, barely covering a smile that he shot toward Mr. Avery. "The good thing about our travails is that we were able to ascertain how deep and long that gold vein really is."

Nic nodded, saying nothing, waiting for them to go on, but his mind was back in that cold black chamber, remembering the way the gold sparkled when the sheriff lit the match.

"There's a wealth down there, for sure," Mr. Avery put in, leaning over in excitement. "And we have an adventure story we can tell our grandkids someday to boot." He paused as he glanced at Sabine. "We owe you two our lives. Without you, and Sheriff Nelson, I'm not certain we would've made it out at all."

"I've come to believe that it was the hand of God," Nic said, leaning back a little. "But I'm glad we all did what we could."

"Indeed, indeed," Mr. McManus said, opening a portfolio with papers inside and sliding them across the table, one set before Sabine, the other in front of Nic. "And it is our honor to make you this offer. Given the amount of gold up on your property, we'd like to offer you one hundred thousand dollars, for each of your properties." His glance turned to Sabine. "In addition, we shall grant you points that would continue to accrue after we pull out more than two hundred thousand dollars in gold. One point for the next hundred thousand, two for next, and three points beyond that."

Nic fought to keep his facial expression controlled. He'd played enough poker in his time to know he couldn't afford to tip his hand yet. He stared at the papers as if reading, but the words and numbers blurred before him. This was more than enough to begin their life together and assure Everett that he could take as much schooling as he wished—or launch a business when he came of age, for that matter. "It's a strong offer, gentlemen," Nic said. "Would you mind if we took a moment to confer?" He gestured toward Sabine and Everett.

"Not at all, not at all," Mr. McManus said. "You three stay here. We'll step outside."

They rose and departed, clearly hopeful as they bustled out the door. Sabine turned to him, her smile making her brown eyes dance. "A hundred thousand dollars? Each?" she whispered.

"We can put ninety in for Ev, divided up among several different banks for safety. He can have it when he's older. That still leaves us plenty to buy property and get settled anywhere you wish." He lowered his voice. "And I can buy you a proper wedding ring."

Sabine smiled and looked down at her lap for a moment, then back to him. "So? Shall we accept?"

"We will. But I'm going to edge our friends up a bit higher yet. Just sit tight, all right?" He rose, went to the door, and looked down the boardwalk, gesturing to the men who stood chatting a few paces away. They all returned to the table.

"Well?" Mr. McManus said. "Do we have a deal?"

"Can you take it up to one hundred and twenty each?" Nic said, carefully keeping his expression neutral.

Mr. McManus blinked twice and then looked at his partner

and the attorney, then back to Nic. "We can't do one hundred and twenty, but we could do one hundred and five."

"One hundred and ten and you have a deal."

Mr. McManus smiled. "One hundred and ten," he said, reaching out a hand.

Grinning, Nic stood to shake it.

They left the attorney's office with several hundred dollars in "goodwill money."

Nic wrapped an arm around Everett and offered his other to Sabine. It was getting late to accomplish all he wished to do. If they hurried, they could get down to Alpine and find some wedding clothes, as well as a ring.

"Nic! Hold up a sec."

Nic looked over his shoulder and pulled Sabine and Everett to a stop. They turned to face Sheriff Nelson, who was standing with a messenger boy and an open telegram in his hands. With one look, Nic realized the sheriff wanted to speak only to him and Sabine.

"Hey, Ev, why don't you go see if there's a rifle at the Merc that catches your fancy."

Everett's eyes widened in excitement. "All right!"

"We'll come and find you at the Merc. Stay there, okay?"

The boy did not wait for another word. He tore down the boardwalk as if a fire-breathing dragon were on his heels.

Nic smiled and looked back to the sheriff, who was moving closer to them. His smile faded.

Drew stopped in front of them. His color was better today, but his face was grim. "We just received a telegram from Westcliffe. Sheriff down there thinks he has our man—the man who killed Peter Vaughn."

CHAPTER TWENTY-FOUR

The sheriff excused himself, and Sabine pulled Nic off the boardwalk and around the corner of the building.

Nic took her hands in his and stared at her in shared misery. "I'm sorry."

"No, shh," she said, lifting the tips of her fingers to his lush lips. "This isn't your fault, Nic. We need to see justice done. For Ev. For us."

He looked at her with his green-blue eyes that reminded her of the deepest rivers of her youth. "I wanted it to be today, Sabine. To be married. But with this … it mars what should be a perfect day."

She gave him a tender smile. "We've waited this long to find each other. What's another week or two?"

He looked rueful. "An eternity."

She smiled fully. "An eager groom, are you?"

"More than you know," he growled, looking as if he planned to take her in his arms and kiss her, right there in the middle of town.

She laughed under her breath. "Come, beloved," she said, hooking her arm through his. "Let's go find our boy and buy some supplies. We have a journey ahead of us."

"In more ways than one," he said with a groan.

Moira choked down half her egg and a bit of toast and forced herself to drink the last drops of juice. Even the thought of the bitter coffee turned her stomach, so she never lifted the cup, no longer steaming, to her lips. For propriety's sake, she sat there for a few minutes longer, nibbling at her toast and pretending to chew. But between the idea that man might still be lingering about, watching her, and the telegram that she assumed was from home, and the note, clearly addressed by Mrs. Knapp's looping, long script, her mind was on anything but food.

She rose at last, careful to arrange her skirts before doing so, and was walking through the lobby, when Ben Bonser and his wife, Abby, approached her. She smiled in relief to see their friendly faces, accepting Abby's hands and then Ben's.

"You are looking rested," Abby said in admiration, stepping back and looking her up and down.

"Am I? Well, it is a relief to be off that train." Despite the stress of the morning, she had managed to sleep last night.

"We were wondering if you might join us for dinner tonight," Benjamin said. "There are a couple of friends I'd like you to meet."

"I just may," Moira said. Company for dinner was a fine idea, especially if she was being watched … and if she was not yet welcome at the Knapps'. "Abby, you must give me the name of your favorite dress shop in town."

"Ahh, Madame Bouverie's boutique is lovely."

"Hmm, I've had an unfortunate experience there," Moira demurred. That was where Gavin had taken her to fit her for gowns as Moira Colorado. "Is there another?"

"Truly?" Abby said in dismay. "I've never heard a poor word

about her work. Well then," she went on, brightening at her second choice. "Go to Madame Champlain's on Eighteenth and Broadway."

"Thank you," she said, turning, "And Benjamin, I'm certain you understand my plight as a woman traveling alone. I am in need of an escort. Do you know of a service here in town?"

The small man's eyebrows shot up and then lowered as he nodded in understanding. He locked his hands behind his back and looked down at the floor, thinking. "Quite, quite." He lifted his head after a moment. "Have the concierge call for the Brown Cab Company and explain your situation. They serve only the finest in the city. I'm certain you can have your driver accompany you anywhere you wish to go."

"That's a good idea. Thank you. So I shall see you two here in the lobby this evening?"

"Eight o'clock?" Abby asked.

"That will be lovely."

They parted ways, and Moira made her way to the hotel lift. An operator closed the doors behind her, flipped a fifth-floor marker, and threw the switch. After a slight lurch, they moved up the cable, reached their destination, and the operator opened the doors and gestured to the empty hallway before them.

Her room was only seven rooms down. Yet she hesitated.

"Miss? Do you need an escort?" the operator asked her.

"No, no, thank you," she said, moving at once. As soon as she heard the gates close behind her, she fought the urge to run. She scurried to her door, slipped the key into the lock, and turned it. She slammed the heavy lacquered door behind her, wincing at the sound, but glad to have it closed and bolted. Her eyes flitted about the room. Empty, as expected. Slowly, her heartbeat returned to normal.

She went to her bed, already made up by the maids, and lay down for a few moments, her telegram and note clutched to her chest. Then she sat up and opened the telegram first.

> *Miss Moira St. Clair, New York City*
>> *Please notify us of your arrival STOP Anxious to know*
> *of your safety STOP Would like to know anticipated return*
> *STOP*

>> *Daniel Adams*

Moira's eyes ran over the words again, reading between the phrases. So he knew now that she was gone. That he didn't hold her future in his hand. No man would ever do that again, she reminded herself. Only God, God could hold her future.

What do you think of this, God? Does this mean he cares? Or that he merely feels responsible for me?

She was glad that Daniel was feeling some discomfort, even pain, at her departure. Feeling a measure of what she had felt when he left her. It was good for them to have some separation, distance, to sort it all out. She sighed. At the same time, she longed for him, wishing he was here, to hold her in his big, warm arms and cradle her to his chest. Why did love have to be so tangled and difficult?

Wearily, she swiped her finger under the flap of Mrs. Knapp's envelope and slid the heavy card out.

Dear Miss St. Clair,

I trust you have arrived safely and are settling into your lovely hotel. I must beg you to wait to visit, as I am ill and have taken to my bed. It is nothing serious, but I am too ill to receive company. Might you come next week? Please send word back at your convenience. It distresses me to delay our meeting, my dear. But I will be more myself after I convalesce, I'm certain of it.

Francine Knapp

The delay in meeting Gavin's parents was both a frustration and a relief for Moira. On one hand, she was eager to see them, discover their commonalities with a man she once loved, and forge a relationship of some sort—if not for her, then for her baby. On the other hand, the whole idea of it would take every ounce of acting ability she had within, for she would have to pretend confidence where she had none left. Gavin had seen to that. *My parents would never approve of our union. I am meant for someone ... more.* He'd always considered her lacking, even before he remade her into Moira Colorado. She had loved him. But he had not truly loved her in return.

Moira swallowed hard, staring into the mirror, then slipped her gloves on, picked up a light, lacy shawl for her shoulders, and went to the door. She paused there a moment, worried that the tall brown-haired man might be outside. She shook her head in frustration with herself—*Moira St. Clair will fear no one any longer! God is beside her!*—and moved out into the hallway, turning to lock the door. She refused to search the passageway. If he was there, she would face him. *Besides*, she thought, *a loud scream should bring others running.*

With the door locked, she turned and lifted her chin, then strode confidently toward the elevator. She heard no footsteps behind her and the way before her was empty, as it had been that morning. Perhaps the man was nothing more than another from the train. She was being silly, leaping to such conclusions. Surely the man who had dared to try to get to her on the train had given up. What would he have to gain, pursuing her here? But still, she sifted through her memories, trying to place where else she'd seen him.

She rang the bell and tapped her foot, waiting for the lift to arrive. It hadn't been just on the train; she was sure of it. And he'd had an old poster....

After a few minutes, the lift came to a squeaking halt, bouncing a bit before her within its cage. The operator opened a door, then the metal bars of the outer gate. He smiled. "Where to, ma'am? The lobby?"

"Yes, please," she said. She stepped to the back of the car and waited for him to close both the gates and the door, then set a switch.

"Please hold the rail, ma'am," he said over his shoulder.

Moira had just grabbed hold when he flipped a lever and the lift began its descent with a lurch. Her free hand went to her belly and she fought the urge to cry out in surprise. It hadn't been quite so rough the first few times. Perhaps she simply was suffering from a general case of nerves.

They reached the bottom and Moira emerged into the busy lobby. Elegant couples strode by, all intent upon their own meetings and plans for the day. Spotting the concierge at his desk, Moira moved across the polished floors and waited behind several others for her turn.

Within twenty minutes, the concierge had motioned for a bell-man, who bent down to listen to him speak into his ear, and Moira left the hotel behind the young man. Outside the bellman whistled for a Brown Cab, one of several carriages who waited in line around the corner from the front of the hotel. The cabbie pulled up on the reins of his white horse, tied them around a metal horn before him, and then quickly lumbered down to the front walk. He pulled off his hat and gave her a short bow. "Billy Samson, at your service, ma'am."

"Mr. Samson," the bellman said with a superior sniff, "this is Miss Moira St. Clair, a distinguished guest of this hotel. She is in need not only of transit from here to several shops and back, but she is also in need of an escort. Miss St. Clair is a celebrity of an international nature and might draw some undue attention should she be recognized. Are you up to the task of watching over her?"

"Indeed," Billy said, casting her a wry look, never once looking at her veil, only her eyes and down in a quick assessment. "She's but a wisp of a thing. How hard can it be to keep her safe? I could put her on my shoulder and carry her out of any mess she might get into."

"Mr. Samson," the bellman said, as sternly as a headmaster to an errant student, although the cabbie was clearly older than him by ten or more years. "Miss St. Clair deserves only your most utter respect. Am I guaranteed that you will give her that?"

The cabbie's expression fell. "Of course, sir. I'll treat her as fine as my grandmother's china." He was certainly large and willing.

Moira hid a small smile, thinking that he would do. The bellman slid Moira a look, asking her if she was all right with this one. Moira smiled and placed a coin in his palm. "Mr. Samson will take good care of me, I'm certain of it," she said, slipping past him. She took Billy's hand and climbed into the carriage, then swept her skirts to one side in order to sit. It was good she was going to a dressmaker. If she didn't get some new gowns, she'd soon be popping buttons, given her bulging belly.

Billy shut the small gate and winked at her, then turned to nod at the bellman. A moment later, Billy was before her in the driver's seat. "Where to, Miss St. Clair? It's a beautiful day. Care for a turn around the park?"

Moira glanced down a side street and glimpsed the expanse of green. "No, thank you, Billy. Please take me directly to Madame Champlain's. I'm in need of a few gowns."

"Right away, miss," he said, moving out into the flow of traffic, between a large armored bank wagon and a string of carriages of various sizes. The street was a cacophony of sounds—horses' snickers and whinnies, street hawkers' cries selling fish and nuts and bread, drivers' shouts to *beware!* and *get out of the way!* and *coming through!*

Moira sank back into her seat and tried to absorb all she was seeing. When she was younger, the constant movement, the tide of humanity, the pulse of so many in such a small space thrilled her. Today it merely felt overwhelming. She lifted a hand to her temples, a headache threatening from the wings.

"I'll have you there in a jiffy," Billy said over his shoulder, apparently catching her move with a quick glimpse she missed, or the gift of a second sight.

She smiled and glanced down at her lap, then to the side, watching people as they passed. A young couple, obviously in love, a mother and grandmother dragging tired children behind them, and numerous men in top hats, striding purposefully along, apparently on their lunch break or returning from it to one of the thousands of offices around them.

Moira looked up. Buildings here rose to eight or nine stories tall, casting the street in shadows during all but the hours of eleven to one. She shivered, suddenly longing for the wide, open fields of the Circle M and the mountains in the near distance. She shook her head. What use was such a fanciful thought? She was here, in New York. And she would make the most of every moment she had.

Billy turned a corner and then another, then pulled up on the reins, saying lowly, "Whoa," to his horse. He clambered out of his seat, opened the small door beside her, and offered his hand. "Miss?"

Moira stared at the huge store before her. It was not the small, intimate affair that Madame Bouverie's had been. This was a large building, with dozens of headless mannequins wearing dresses in every color imaginable.

"It's a fine sight, isn't it?" asked Billy. "The ladies all swoon at such a thing. The back rooms are filled with a hundred seamstresses, ready to make a replacement for those that are purchased today or to tailor anything you purchase." He studied her a moment. "Would you rather go to another shop?"

"No, no," she said, finally rising and accepting his hand. She climbed down the step and let go when she was on the walk. "You'll wait for me here?"

"I won't leave this spot. Unless you wish for me to accompany you in there," he said, frowning.

Moira smiled. "I doubt they allow men inside. Out here will be fine, Billy."

She turned and strode to the door. A young woman opened it for her. "Welcome to Madame Champlain's," she said in a thick French accent.

In two hours' time, Moira had been given tea and delicate sandwiches and had tried on more than twenty gowns. She quietly mentioned her pregnancy to the female tailor assigned to her, and the young woman neither glanced at her ringless finger or mentioned it again—she merely steered her toward one fine gown and then another. The dresses, with full, gathered skirts and Empire waists, would disguise her burgeoning belly and yet flatter her slender arms and narrow shoulders. After fitting her for each of the five she eventually chose—and carefully averting her eyes from the scars on Moira's leg, shoulder, neck, and head, then helping her dress again—the seamstress guided her toward a rack with several corsets, especially made for pregnant women.

Moira shook her head. "I think not," she said. She couldn't imagine compressing her baby, making the child fight for breath. On the ranch, no one wore such things. Her own mother, in Philadelphia, had scorned the use of corsets, especially for anyone pregnant. The seamstress frowned in disapproval.

Moira glanced back at the rack. Undoubtedly, the gowns would look better on her with a corset beneath, but she would wear her own underclothes, regardless of what the young woman thought. "No," she said firmly.

After making arrangements for the shop to send the gowns to the hotel, Moira moved out of the store and through the massive doors to the busy street again.

Billy started when he saw her, immediately pulling the grain bag from his horse's head and moving to set it in the back. "Find what you were looking for, miss?"

"Yes," she said in delight. "Five of them. It will be lovely to receive them."

"Indeed, indeed," the man said, helping her into the carriage. "Where to now, miss?"

"Oh, uh," she paused, then slipped open her purse to pull out a piece of paper. The seamstress had given her the name of the finest wig shop in the city. She handed it to Billy, hoping he knew how to read. He nodded and handed it back to her. "Right away, miss."

They were pulling out into the flow of traffic again when Moira's eyes locked on a man in the shadows across the street. A large red coach drove between them then, and when it passed, the man was gone.

But it had been the brown-haired man from the hotel lobby. And the train. She was sure of it. She turned in her seat and searched the far walk in vain. There were simply too many people, too many wagons and coaches and men on horses....

"Everything all right, miss?"

Moira sat back in her seat again with a sigh. "I appear to have someone following me," she said to his back.

He straightened and glanced over his shoulder. "Want me to set him straight, miss?"

"No. He disappears as fast as he appears. But I've seen him several times."

"Do you know who he is?"

"No," she muttered, "I have no idea."

Billy scanned one side of the street and then the other. "Want me to take you back to the hotel?"

"No," she said. "We shall see to this next errand. After that, perhaps I'll take you up on that turn around the park. I am in need of a dose of ... nature, I believe."

"As you wish, miss."

Moira unwound her veils with some trepidation. The older gentleman ignored the scars above her ear, much as the seamstress had ignored the scars on her leg and shoulder. *Why is it that I can let these people see them, but not Odessa, or ... Daniel? If only they could look upon my scars with the same distance.*

She closed her eyes for a moment, missing Daniel so much it shot a physical pain through her. She opened her eyes and stared at Mr. Tennesen, fighting to keep her composure. She tried to swallow but found her mouth too dry. Mr. Tennesen was focused solely upon his business. With swift hands that belied his age, he tucked the remains of her shorn hair in a net, then reached for the first wig. "Now this, this is the fine auburn you chose." He settled the front of the wig on her forehead, then swiftly tugged it down the back. He moved to settle the long curls about her shoulders. "My, you were right, Miss St. Clair. The color is beautiful on you." His eyes widened as he stared into her face. "I've never seen eyes as beautiful as yours.

Truly." Part of the wig swept up in a knot, part of it remained down. "You see how nicely that covers your neck and ear?" he asked.

He was referring, of course, to her scars. She nodded. There was something comforting, familiar in the dark red hair. It was as if she were again on the stage, and a costumer was giving her various options for her character. She blinked several times, staring at her visage, the relief of being hidden, even more so than when she was in her veils. But it felt … wrong, somehow. False. Truly like a costume. And wasn't she ready to be embraced as Moira St. Clair, now? At least to a certain extent?

"Might we try that one?" she asked, pointing to a subtler blonde wig that closely matched her natural hair color.

"But of course," Mr. Tennesen said, reaching for the next. He pulled it atop her head, settled the coils around her shoulders and stepped back, head cocked, to study her image along with her. Chin in hand, he lifted a brow and nodded. "It is a lovely match."

Moira slowly smiled. It was as if the fire had never occurred. As if her hair had miraculously grown back. It would take several extra coils on one side to cover the scars on her neck, but once he had showed her how it would look, she was convinced that it would do the trick nicely. As much as she loved the auburn, this, *this* was more her.

"This is the one," she said to Mr. Tennesen, meeting his gaze in the mirror.

"A fine choice," he said. "I'll wrap it up immediately."

"No," she said. "I'd like to wear it out, please. And might you make me another? It would be good to have two."

"Certainly."

She rose, paid him for the two wigs, then hurried out, aware that the sun was growing low in the sky. Had she really spent hours shopping in only two stores?

She slowed as she reached the exit. Outside, a man stood looking into the window display. Beyond him, just three paces off, was Billy, staring hard at him.

The brown-haired man's eyes slid toward Moira, a curious look of accusation in them. Then he turned and walked down the street.

It was him. Fury rushed through her. Emboldened with Billy standing right there, she rushed after him. "Hey! Hey, you! Stop!"

He glanced over his shoulder, but not at her. He kept walking, picking up his pace.

Catching up to her, Billy grabbed her arm. "Miss St. Clair—"

"What do you want?" she cried after the spy, as the crowds swallowed him. "Why are you following me?"

She fought the urge to jump, to see over the heads of the others. "Do you see him?" she asked her much taller guardian. "The man who was just here?"

Billy shook his head and shrugged his shoulders helplessly. "He's gone, miss."

The brown-haired man had disappeared again.

CHAPTER TWENTY-FIVE

As soon as Nic heard that Peter's killer was being held at the jail in Westcliffe, he knew the time had come at last to go and see Odessa.

Now that they were there, at the entrance of the Circle M, on the verge of seeing her, Nic hesitated. He whistled lowly and cocked his head. "Well, this is about the prettiest ranch I've ever seen," he said. Still dotted with snow at the very top, the towering mountains were a crimson-purple in the early evening. The valley grasses were turning brown, and with autumn soon upon them the sagebrush was becoming dry and brittle, but there was a sense of lush abundance within the shadowed hills and wide, fenced patches of land before them. In the distance, a huge herd of horses set off running across the field, making their own horses prick their ears and shift in agitation.

"Easy, easy," Nic said, bending low to pat Daisy's neck. He looked over at Sabine and Everett, and said, "Ready?"

"Are you?" Sabine asked.

"I think so. Hopefully Odessa will forgive me my long silence."

"She will when she learns what has happened for you these last months," Sabine said, reaching out a hand shyly to him.

Nic smiled and squeezed it. He hoped she was right.

He was about to urge his horse forward when he saw someone galloping down the road toward them, from the direction of what he assumed was Westcliffe. They had just come through a small fledgling town called Conquistador. Was the man heading there? But as he neared, he began to slow as if he meant to turn into the Circle M gates too.

Again, their horses shifted nervously, with the other horse's approach. The animals were weary from the journey, clearly eager to be relieved of saddles and the burden of human weight, free to run in the fields before them.

The man pulled up. He was a large, striking man. A star on his lapel caught the soft sunset glow. The sheriff. "Hello," he said, nodding toward Nic and tipping his hat toward Sabine. "I'm Sheriff Daniel Adams. You folks heading into the Circle M?"

"We are," Nic said, reaching out a hand. "I'm Dominic St. Clair. This is my fiancée, Sabine, and our son-to-be, Everett."

"Dominic St. Clair." The sheriff smiled and reached over to take his hand, slowly shaking it, while looking him over in delight. "Though I could've picked you out in a crowd, with eyes like that," he said. "Remarkable that all three of you share the color."

"You know my sisters?" Nic asked. They all started moving through the massive Circle M gate and down the lane.

"I do."

"Moira? She's *here?*" Nic said in excitement. Last he'd heard, she was in Paris.

"She was. She left a little over a week ago." A shadow passed over Daniel's face that made Nic wonder if he carried more than a passing interest in his sister, but Nic didn't press him. Another sheriff? Nic would've guessed she would've sworn off lawmen forever after Reid Bannock. "Odessa is going to be some kind of glad, seeing you again. She's worried about you."

"I know. I've done a poor job keeping up with correspondence." It was enough, to admit that.

Daniel said nothing. His eyes shifted over to Sabine, Everett. "You folks been on the road long?"

"A few days. We had joint properties, up past Buena Vista. Just sold them to a mining company. Figured it was time to look for a new place to settle. But I couldn't move on before checking on my sisters."

Daniel nodded. He had an easy way about him, quiet, contemplative, that Nic immediately liked.

In a few more minutes they crested a hill and Nic could see the grand, main house, with stables and other outbuildings stretching beyond it. His eyes widened.

"First time at the Circle M?" Daniel asked, surprise in his wide brown eyes.

Nic nodded. "Last I saw them was their wedding. They married up in the Springs. I never got down here." He looked back over the ranch and then to Daniel again. "I knew Bryce had enough to provide for Odessa. Didn't know his ranch was the size of Montana."

Daniel smiled. "Come. I know just where to find your family this time of day."

They rode down the lane and straight to the house. He shot an encouraging look at Sabine and Everett, though his own heart pounded. Would Odessa embrace him? Or slap him? Laugh or cry? He inhaled, calming himself. His sister couldn't remain angry with him for long. They were blood. Kin.

He hoped.

Bryce came out on the porch first, to see who had arrived.

"Daniel," he greeted the sheriff with a nod, then glanced with some curiosity at the others. But then his eyes shifted back to Nic. "Dominic?" He rushed down the stairs as Nic dismounted and wrapped him in a big bear hug, pounding his back. "Nic, brother, your sister is going to be so glad to see you. Let me go and get her—"

But then she was there, at the top of the stairs, her arms around a small towheaded boy who looked to be about a year old. *She has a baby. Odessa has a baby.* He grinned and his heart flew with exhilaration as he slowly climbed the stairs, eyes on his sister. "Dess," he said, sweeping off his hat. "I'm so sorry it's been so long. Will you—"

She let out a little cry, as if she finally believed her eyes, and crossed the remaining distance between them. She wrapped her free arm around Nic's neck and clung there until the baby started to squirm and complain. "Nic, Nic," she said. "I'm so happy you're here." The baby squawked, and she backed away and touched his cheek, tears in her eyes. "Oh, you are well. And here. At *last*. You don't know how long I've waited for this."

"Me too, Dess. And who is this?"

"Why, this is Samuel McAllan, your nephew," she said, jostling the baby. His frown eased into a smile, punctuated by a few widely spaced baby teeth.

"And this is my family-to-be," Nic said, turning to gesture toward Sabine and Everett, who had quietly followed him upstairs. He proudly introduced them all. Sabine and Odessa stood together for a moment.

"A new sister," Odessa said, taking Sabine's tentative hand. "Oh, Nic, she's beautiful. And a son!" Her eyes moved to Nic, but blessedly, she didn't probe further. He'd fill her in later. "Aren't you a fine young man," she said. "I bet you're hungry."

"Yes, ma'am."

"Well, let's go in and get you something to eat. There's plenty left over from supper." Bryce headed in and Odessa waited at the door, watching as Sabine and Everett filed past.

"Where's Moira off to?" Nic asked. "She coming home soon?"

Odessa's elation left her eyes as they shifted to Daniel. Daniel hesitated before her, and Nic looked back. "Dess?" Nic asked.

"Moira left over a week ago," she said, glancing at Daniel again with reproach in her eyes.

Nic frowned, worried over the unspoken conversation happening between his sister and the sheriff. Why the concern? "Where'd she go?"

"To New York," she said. "She heard from the family of Gavin Knapp, a former beau. They wanted her to come and meet them."

Nic turned back around, alarm surging through him. He didn't like how either of them were acting. Moira had been in Paris and London for years, why were they so worried now? Surely, she could make her way around a city on her own. And who was this Gavin Knapp?

Daniel shifted, uncomfortable in the face of Nic's obvious agitation over Moira. It brought up everything he himself was feeling. *Moira, Moira, where are you?* She had not answered his telegram. Why? To punish him? Or was she in some sort of trouble?

"You folks have a lot to catch up on," he said, hat in hands.

"So I'll get along. But I wondered … Have you received word from Moira?"

Odessa's expression softened. "Just one telegram. The day after she arrived."

Daniel took a deep breath and let it out slowly. So she was safe. She just didn't feel compelled to send a telegram to him. Not that he blamed her.

"You sent a telegram to her?" Odessa guessed.

"Yes."

"I'm certain she's been busy since she arrived. You'll probably hear from her soon."

"Yes," he said, feeling the emptiness of the word. He didn't anticipate a telegram. Not really. "Odessa," he said, before she could turn away and join the others. "Why did she go?" he asked quietly. "What does she want with the Knapps?"

"I'm not certain," Odessa said after hesitating. "I think she wanted a glimpse of her old life. Perhaps so she can more fully embrace this chapter. Gavin—because it ended so poorly …" She shook her head, as if she were sharing too much. "I think Moira is seeking healing. In many ways. Hopefully, in New York, she can find a portion."

Daniel nodded and turned his hat in his hands again. "I'm going after her. I shouldn't have ever let her go."

"Oh, I don't know, Daniel. Maybe it's best you let her return on her own."

"I let her go before," he said miserably. "Back when I had no claim on her. Back when she was with Gavin. If I'd stepped up, done what I needed to …" He shook his head. "So much might've been different."

She gave him a look of compassion and reached out to place a hand on his arm. "It might've been different. But you might not have discovered that you loved my sister. Truly loved her. Nor that she loved you."

He stared at her, hard. Love. *Love.* He'd let love slip from his fingers. Let her go, to New York, where she might face danger, unprotected …

Daniel set his hat on his head. "Nonetheless, I'm going after her. I'll be on the morning train."

Odessa frowned. "She might not be ready to come back, Daniel. You know how Moira is."

"I know how she is. I'll let her see her business through. But I want her to know she won't be alone. That I'm there for her, whenever she needs me, however she needs me."

Odessa's frown moved into a smile. "Then God go with you. I hope you return soon. Both of you."

He squeezed her hand and then turned to go. He was out on the front porch and walking down the steps when the door opened behind him again. "Sheriff?"

Daniel paused and turned. It was Nic.

"Sheriff, may we come and see you tomorrow?"

Daniel hesitated. "Certainly. But I'm heading out on the morning train. Going to New York. After your sister."

It was Nic's turn to hesitate. He closed the door and walked to the top of the stairs. "You have intentions when it comes to my sister."

"Intentions, yes. But bigger than that," he said, a smile spreading across his face. "Dreams. Hope."

Nic smiled then too. "Those are good things."

"Indeed."

"Well, I'll look forward to getting to know you better upon your return, then," Nic said, reaching out a hand. Daniel shook it. "But we have some official business with you before you leave. Everett, back there," he said, hooking a thumb over his shoulder. "Sabine and I intend to adopt him, once we're married. But he's Peter Vaughn's boy. I think you have his dad's murderer in your jail, right?"

Daniel paused and turned fully around to face him. He'd heard from Sheriff Nelson that the boy and his guardians were heading down to Westcliffe to identify him.... His eyes widened in surprise. "That I do. Maybe once he gets a look at Everett, he'll start talking. He's been stubborn. Refused to speak other than to ask for a lawyer, who said to wait for the judge. Judge is due in any day now."

A muscle in Nic's cheek twitched. "Perhaps Everett identifying him could move him to confess. Can you take a later train?"

Daniel paused before saying, "First thing tomorrow?"

"We'll be there."

CHAPTER TWENTY-SIX

Moira's stomach rolled as Billy turned the corner and drove through the gates of the Knapps' massive estate. She was here at last, for better or for worse. At least the anticipation of their meeting would soon be over. The lane meandered for a full quarter mile and was lined by perfectly pruned oak trees, each perhaps fifty years old. At the end of the macadam sprawled a massive, gothic mansion of gray stone, with two towers that bookended the building between them.

She closed her eyes and took long, slow breaths, trying to calm her flighty stomach. She reminded herself of the many times she called upon the powerful nobility in England and France who lived on estates much like this one, who received her with joy. *You have the social graces to manage this awkward situation,* she told herself, *no matter how long those skills have lain dormant.*

"You all right, miss?" Billy asked over his shoulder.

"Yes, Billy. Thank you," she said. Ever since her afternoon of shopping—and her run-in with the brown-haired man—Billy had been present every moment she had had need of him. Fortunately, since that day, the man had not presented himself again. Perhaps he had given up, seeing as how Moira refused to cower when he neared. Perhaps he was like Reid Bannock had once been with her, preferring her meek and yielding. Perhaps he had recognized her, and thought that since she had donned her veils, she was now someone who could be controlled. Manipulated.

She flipped a coil of her blond wig over her shoulder and tilted her face up to the sunshine. It felt good to be free of the veil, even if it meant that she had to bear the heat and weight of the wig. For periods of time she could imagine herself whole again, unfettered by scars. Even when she gazed into the mirror, she could pretend for a while. The hairstyle was not entirely appropriate. Most kept their hair swept up in a loose bun nowadays. But the wig dresser had convinced her that a few extra strands about her neck, coiled *just so*, would be comely. And he was right.

She'd been recognized by several guests at the hotel who knew her as Moira St. Clair, having seen her on the stage there or met her at grand galas teeming with crowds of Europe's elite. None were friends, only people she'd met in passing, but two had asked her to consider singing. She'd declined the invitations, of course—she was not yet prepared for that—but it felt good, to be noticed, to be wanted again. If they wanted her, surely the Knapps would as well.

Billy pulled up to the house and immediately climbed down to help her out. A butler appeared at the massive front door and stood with his hands behind his back, waiting on her.

Moira lifted the skirts of her new turquoise gown with one hand and accepted Billy's hand with the other. Once down upon the wide flagstones of the front walk, she watched as a small, graceful woman appeared in the doorway. She knew her immediately as Gavin's mother. She had the same fine bone structure and piercing gray eyes. The woman moved toward her immediately, hands outstretched.

"My dear Moira," she said. Moira stretched out her own hands. "At last you are here."

"I am very happy to meet you," Moira said, smiling. "Thank you so much for the invitation."

"It is our pleasure, my dear," she said, smiling back into her eyes. She released her and gestured inside. "Please, have your man bring in your trunk. You planned to spend several days with us, did you not?"

"If it's all right with you …"

"Of course, of course!" she said, clasping her hands together. "It will be a delight to have so much time together. I've nothing else planned."

"It's very gracious of you."

Francine led her through the grand foyer and up a massive curving staircase, the balustrade in polished stone. A gigantic chandelier, holding perhaps more than a hundred candles, was in the center. Gas lamps dotted the wall, flickering with light. At the top, they turned and walked down a wide hallway to the very end. "I wanted you to have this room," Francine said with a tender smile. "It was always Gavin's favorite."

Moira shoved aside a desire to ask for another room. It was odd, to be shown to Gavin's favorite, when she was nothing more to him than a spurned lover, a temporary professional partner in the business of the stage. His mother behaved as if she had been his wife and would be comforted here in this masculine room, surrounded by his old things. One glance told her that many of the pieces of furniture and artwork from Gavin's apartment had been moved here after his death. She could not control a shiver. She turned to ask if there was a smaller apartment, something that might not remind her so much of the Knapps' lost son, but Francine's face, so open and hopeful, made her clamp her lips shut.

"It's beautiful," she murmured.

The butler arrived, showing Billy the way with her trunk, and Francine turned to go. She paused in the doorway. "Perhaps you'd care for a moment to yourself. I will await you in the parlor to the side of the stairs."

"Thank you," Moira said.

Francine gave her a small smile and then disappeared around the corner.

Moira turned to the small table where she'd set down her purse, and drew out a coin. The butler now waited at the door to show Billy out.

Billy glanced his way and then to her as she handed him his pay. "Sure you're ready for me to leave you here all alone, miss?"

"I'll be fine, Billy," she said. He really was sweet, the way he'd taken to watching over her. "I'm with … family."

He put the coin in his pocket and hesitated a moment longer. What gave him pause? "Do you want me to come for you tomorrow, miss?"

"I don't think that will be necessary, Billy. I imagine the Knapps can send me back to the city in one of their carriages." She looked over to the butler and he nodded once, in grave agreement.

"All right then," Billy said at last. "You look after yourself, miss."

"I've become fairly adept at it," she said with a smile. "I'll have the concierge find you when I return to the city, all right?"

"All right. Good day, miss."

"Good day, Billy."

At last he was gone, and the butler with him. Moira shut the door quietly and then leaned her back against it. Her eyes scanned the long room again. The ceilings were high, and two windows stretched upward, three times her height. She walked the perimeter, then down past the windows and to the turret, and looked through the wavy glass of its lone window to the courtyard below. In a moment, Billy appeared, climbed into his carriage, and set the white mare in motion.

Moira exhaled a long breath. Now she was truly on her own.

Daniel paced back and forth, awaiting the arrival of Nic, Sabine, and Everett. One of the deputies had been assigned duty as temporary sheriff in his stead. So if he could see to this business with his prisoner, all would be ready for the judge, due in town this afternoon. And then he'd be free to go after Moira. Now that he'd made his decision, he could barely wait.

"Up on your feet, Robinson," he said over his shoulder to his prisoner, watching Nic and the others approach through the window. "You're about to find your tongue."

Chandler Robinson had risen only to be led to the outhouse thrice a day, or to pace his small cell. But now Daniel could sense Robinson behind him, rising, wrapping his fingers around the cold bars. Waiting on his accusers.

Had the man truly killed that boy's father for nothing more than to take his supplies? Daniel was cast back to finding Mary, sprawled across the floor of their cabin, bloody, lifeless. For what? A few dollars in the larder… He clenched his teeth.

Nic tied up his horse out front and helped Sabine off her horse. Everett came around, hesitating.

"You mind your manners, Robinson," Daniel warned lowly, pushing away from the window and walking toward the door. He opened it, just as Nic was raising his hand to reach for the handle.

"Come in, folks, come in."

Cleveland, the deputy on duty, rose from his chair.

They filtered inward, but Daniel's eyes were on Everett, the boy who had seen his father killed. He stepped in front of the boy and laid a hand on his shoulder. "Our prisoner, he can't hurt you, boy. But if he's the one that killed your father, we need to know it, straight away. You understand me?"

Everett nodded soberly. He appeared pale and anxious. He glanced over Daniel's shoulder.

"This way," Daniel said, nodding to the left. It was but a few paces more, but then they stood, still, suspended.

"That's him," Everett whispered. "That's the man that shot my dad."

"You sure?" Daniel asked, standing beside him, arms crossed, staring at his prisoner.

"I'm sure," Everett said, leaning a bit in his direction. Daniel reached out to loop an arm around his shoulders, turning his face away. It was enough, that.

"Rules of the road," Chandler snarled, with his fingers still laced around the bars. His voice sounded foreign, odd to Daniel, after days of silence.

"Excuse me?" Nic said. Daniel's eyes darted to the right as Nic approached the cell.

"Rules of the road," Chandler said in cavalier fashion, lifting his chin. "It's a tough territory here. The weak fall prey to the strong. No harm meant by it. Merely survival."

Nic drew closer. "Survival, eh?"

Chandler was lifting his head, studying him, when Nic reached through the bars and grabbed a fistful of his shirt with one hand, and the back of his head with the other. "Survive this." Swiftly, he pulled him against the bars, ramming his head again and again against them.

"Nic!" Daniel cried, along with Sabine. "Nic!" He snaked a hand out to stop him. Dimly, he felt his deputy, Cleveland, moving behind him, several seconds late.

Chandler hovered midair, blood trickling from his nose and brow; then, knees collapsing, he crumpled to the ground by the bars.

"Mr. St. Clair!" Cleveland yelled, tackling Nic to the ground.

Daniel looked over and saw Sabine haul Everett to the corner and shield him with her body. He grimaced, seeing the utter terror on her face. Behind him, he could hear Nic wrench away from Cleveland with a guttural yell and rise, reaching through the bars again. He heard Chandler's screech of terror, the sickening crunch of bone against bone.

But he could only watch Sabine, trembling, eyes wide as she looked beyond Daniel, then turned to cover Everett again.

CHAPTER TWENTY-SEVEN

"What in the Sam Hill is going on here?" thundered a new voice behind him.

Daniel wrenched his eyes away from Sabine.

Cleveland threw his arms around Nic and bodily lifted him from the ground, turning him from the cell and dropping him. Nic sprawled across the floor and then rose on one arm, panting.

Daniel gazed toward the cell and shook his head, spying his bloody prisoner as he bent down to get a better look at the man. *Great,* he thought. *A week in custody with barely a word spoken and now this.*

In the distance, he could hear the long, lonely whistle of the train. Fifteen minutes until it left for Denver again.

He slowly rose to his feet, turning to the stranger as dread settled in his stomach. "Judge Basinger," he said, assuming, by his dress and carriage, that he was the long-awaited messenger of the court. He reached out a hand.

Mouth open, the smaller man numbly reached out his own. "You the sheriff here?"

"Sheriff Adams," Daniel said.

"I'd hoped to find order restored here in Westcliffe, Sheriff," the man said, indignation tingeing every word.

"Yes. I did too," Daniel returned. "By and large, it has been."

Nic moved over to Sabine and helped her up, and then the boy, as the prisoner came to his feet and wiped his bloody nose with the back of his hand, glaring at them.

"My deputy here will see to your needs," Daniel said, putting a hand on Cleveland's shoulder.

"Where are *you* going?" the judge sputtered.

"To New York. I have personal business there and need to be on that train you just arrived on," he said, gesturing toward the station with his hat. "This boy here is the eyewitness who saw the man in our cell—a man also wanted in Denver and Fort Collins—murder his father. These folks are his guardians. All right? Need anything else from me?"

"Yes, of course there's more. You can't leave right now," Judge Basinger said, shaking in indignation. "I didn't travel all the way down here to be handed off to a deputy. Is this how General Palmer is running his towns?"

"I don't know General Palmer. But like it or not, it's how I'm running it."

"Well, *I* know the general. And I'll have you removed from office," the judge said, shaking a finger at him.

"Listen, Judge, this was my fault—" Nic put in.

"No," Daniel said. "I don't need you to shoulder my responsibility." He shook his head. "I've been looking back, trying to fix my past for too long, whether it was five years or five minutes ago. It is what it is. I aim now to focus only on my future. On what might be." He looked over at the judge. "Do what you have to do, Judge, and I'll do the same."

And with that he left the sheriff's office and headed to the train station.

Moira moved down the staircase, relishing the luxury of the Knapp home, with all its fine appointments. There were fresh flowers in every room and delicately tufted carpets down the center of the hall. She reached the polished floors of the foyer, then moved toward the parlor, which was beautifully decorated in French blue and white decorative moldings that reminded her of Queen Palmer's music room in Colorado Springs.

Francine rose from her wing-backed chair, and a tall, distinguished man turned from staring out the window beside her. Gavin's father, he had to be. They both strode over to her. Francine took her hand in both of hers and turned toward the older gentleman. "Henry, I'd like you to meet Miss Moira St. Clair. Miss St. Clair, this is my husband, Mr. Henry Knapp."

"Moira, please," she said, nodding back at him as he gave her a smart, short bow. He had wide mutton chops that were a dark gray, and thick, wavy hair that had obviously once been as dark as Gavin's. But Gavin had really favored his beautiful mother in looks, while gaining his father's height.

"I'm glad you are here, Moira," Henry said.

"Thank you," she said, studying him closely for even a hint that said he didn't mean what he said. "I must say, I never dreamed I would be."

"Quite," he said, lifting his brows.

Moira drew back a bit.

"Please, come and sit, my dear," Francine said soothingly, gesturing toward a chair beside hers. Henry took a chair on the far side of a small conversation table between. "There is so much I wish to learn from you, I barely know where to start."

"You'll have time, Francine. Give the young woman some breathing room," Henry said with gentle reproach. A maid arrived and poured tea for them all, handing out the cups and departing.

"Might you start … you see we miss Gavin very much…." Francine brought her knuckle to her lips. Then after a moment's pause, gave her a bright smile. "Please, tell us how you two met."

Moira was moved by the woman's tenderness and felt a pang of sorrow again over Gavin's death. For the next hour, she spoke of the crossing from Europe and, circumspectly, Gavin's gentle pursuit. At one point, she was relating the harrowing storm, and how water was rushing in and Gavin hit his head, but their friend saved them both. *Daniel. Daniel, always there …* She caught herself and grimaced. "It was that night that Gavin's headaches began. I believe he was seen by a physician when we arrived here. At least he said he did." She shifted in her seat, feeling guilty for not recognizing the severity of his symptoms, although she was not at fault. Would they see that?

"Our physician did see to Gavin," Henry said gravely. "But as wondrous as the medical sciences are, it does not make them fortune tellers. He could not have known what was happening within. On the outside, he appeared as well as ever."

Moira nodded, feeling a breath of grace flow through their conversation. She glanced over them both with a small smile. There was something about them that reminded her of her own parents. Was it simply their age? No, it was more than that. The love they obviously shared. A tenderness. Henry's businesslike manner was so like her own father's. She settled back against the chair for the first time. "I want you both to know that I loved your son. The road we took together is not a road I would choose again. We made several grave mistakes. But I loved him."

Francine nodded, eyes wide. Henry remained motionless.

"And what of the child you carry?" Francine said gently. "He will be a Knapp."

"I'm afraid he will be a St. Clair," Moira said, as carefully as she could. "Gavin did not wish to marry. At least not me."

"I don't understand that!" Francine said, setting down her coffee cup with a clatter. "As much as I loved my son, he was a cad when it came to women."

"Francine—" Henry said with a frown.

"No, truly! He cavorted about with one after another. It was not how he was raised."

"He … he told me that he did not believe you two would approve of me."

They both paused.

"He said it was one thing to be a singer upon Europe's finest opera stages, but when we went West …" She sighed and set down her cup, settling her hands in her lap. "As I said, were I to do it over again, I'd do it differently. But I cannot go back."

"We were told …" Henry cleared his throat and began again. "We were told that you and Gavin presented yourself as husband and wife."

Moira sighed. "Yes, and I wish it had been the truth. Gavin considered it a convenience. A business matter." She felt the heat of a blush rise along her neck.

"He put a ring on your finger?" Francine asked, face drawn.

"For a time, yes."

"Oh, my dear, I am so sorry." Francine shook her head.

"With wealth comes privileges," Henry said, rising and moving to the window again. "I too am sorry that our son felt it was his privilege to abuse his association with you."

Moira paused. She was so surprised. Never, in all the times she had imagined their meeting, had she expected them to apologize for Gavin and his choices. "Gavin was a grown man. I was a woman grown. Neither of us behaved as we ought to have behaved. But I thank you for your kind apologies."

The grandfather clock began to bong noisily, covering the awkward silence that then ensued.

Sabine rushed outside, gasping for air. The splatter of blood, Chandler Robinson's blood, on Nic's hand sickened her. It was almost as if she could smell the metal odor of it. She leaned her head against the wall, trying to dispel the memories of her own blood spraying across the wooden floor of her cabin, the awful tearing of her lip, the difficulty chewing for days afterward when her teeth felt loose in her mouth.

"Sabine?" Nic asked, coming outside.

"No," she said, shaking her head, and moving around the building, into the alley. "Please, just give me a minute," she said, putting her hand up in the air, halting his progress toward her.

"Sabine, I'm sorry—"

"I know. I know," she said, her eyes closed. "I understand. There was a part of me that wanted to hit him too." She opened her eyes and stared at Nic, the man she loved. "Please. Can you wash your hands?" she pleaded.

He glanced down at his hands, saw the blood, and his frown grew deeper. "I'm sorry, my love. I know it's difficult, you seeing—"

"Please. Just go wash your hands, Nic. Then we'll talk."

He hesitated, then left her to pace in the alley for a while. He returned, hands in his pockets, and leaned a shoulder against the side wall of the sheriff's office.

"Where's Everett?"

"He's sitting out front," Nic said, nodding in the general direction. "He didn't want to be inside. With *him*." He paused for several breaths, waiting on her to speak. "Want to tell me what this is about?"

"I ..." She lifted a hand to her temple. "You know it's difficult for me, any violence at all. I'm reminded of some of my most difficult days. Today ... I don't know if it's because I'm so tired, or there's so much to consider, between meeting your family and facing Peter's killer ..." She shook her head and sighed. "I was back, back in my cabin, somehow. The sound of you pulling Robinson into those bars reminded me of my husband, I think, and one terrible day when he struck me with a crowbar."

Nic's cheek muscle twitched, but he remained deadly still. "A crowbar?" he asked, so quietly she barely heard him.

She glanced into his eyes and then away, knowing she might cry if she stared into them too long.

"Sabine." He hadn't moved closer, but he was upright, with one hand outstretched to her. "Please. Come here."

She forced her feet into motion, moving to him. She did not fear this man. She feared a man in memory. This man, this man before her, was good. Different. He'd never strike her, with hand or tool.

He wrapped her in his arms, slowly, and she could feel his breath in her hair. Gradually, she grew relaxed against him.

"I will never, ever hurt you," Nic promised. "You know that, right?"

She nodded, feeling the truth of his words deep within.

"When I strike others it hurts you somehow. I'm sorry for that, Sabine. Will you forgive me?"

She nodded again.

He pulled back and lifted her chin with the knuckle of his index finger. "I'm trying, my love. Truly. I really am much better than I used to be," he said with a wry start of a smile. "I've been a fighter my whole life. But I'm trying to do what my father always urged me to do, use my brain," he said, tapping his temple, "as well as my brawn. But you, Sabine, since you came into my life … you and God are teaching me to use my heart too." He took her hand and placed it on his chest, where she could feel the dull, steady beat of it. "Give me more time to get used to using all three, all right?"

"All right," she whispered.

Cleveland, the deputy, appeared on the front porch. "Mr. St. Clair."

Nic turned and looked at him.

"I'm afraid the judge wants you in the holding cell. He's considering bringing you up on charges."

Nic tensed. Sabine pulled back and looked up into his eyes with alarm. They were going to put him in the same cell as Peter's killer? "Nic …"

He closed his eyes, drew in a deep breath, and then opened them to stare at her. "It'll be all right, Sabine," he said softly. "I promise." Then he lifted his hands in surrender to the deputy.

CHAPTER TWENTY-EIGHT

"Come now, Judge," Bryce said the next morning, hands on his hips. He gestured over to the cell, where Nic was handcuffed to one side, and Chandler Robinson to the other. "You can't really blame Dominic for his actions. That louse was taunting a child over the death of his parent!"

"Foul behavior, indeed," said the judge soberly from behind the sheriff's desk. He dipped his pen in the inkwell, signed a document, and set it aside to dry, then looked up at Bryce. "But surely you want order in this town as much as the next citizen."

"Indeed. But he was hardly wandering drunk down the street," Bryce said, lifting a hand.

From the cell, Nic admired his brother-in-law's tone, reasonable, but insistent. He'd do well to emulate him. He hadn't slept all night, with Peter's killer just a few feet out of reach. Even now, his blood surged at the thought of the handcuffs coming off, a moment's lapse in attention when he could leap over and teach the murderer what justice really meant....

His eyes shifted to the deputy on duty, Glen, alongside Sabine and Odessa, who hovered beyond Bryce near the entrance. His wife-to-be and his sister. He could not act as he used to. He had to find a new way. A new way ... *Lord, give me Your ways. Teach me to trust in Your timing, Your ways. Let me leave justice to You.*

The judge sighed heavily, as if what Bryce was asking was its own trial. "I suppose a night's imprisonment is enough punishment. I will release him to your care," he said, pointing a finger at Bryce. "If he does anything like this again … I will be looking to you."

"Understood, Judge."

"That's it?" Chandler barked. "A man beats me and he's let off after a night on a cot? I've been here more than a week!"

Nic sat up and stared over at him, trying to remember the words he just prayed.

"You, be quiet, now," the judge said to him. He looked over at Glen. "Release Dominic St. Clair."

Glen ambled over to the cell, unlocked the door, then came over to Nic and unlocked his handcuffs. "Don't give me any trouble," he said lowly. He took hold of his arm, and keeping himself between Nic and Chandler, ushered him out of the cell, locking it behind him.

"Now, let's get this hearing over with," the judge said. "You brought the boy?"

"He's outside," Sabine said. "I'd rather he only be in here when the prisoner is locked inside the cell."

"Understood. Bring him in.…"

In short order, the judge had taken down Everett's detailed story about the day his father was killed, then Chandler Robinson's story. Chandler denied ever being on that road, of course, even though he'd practically admitted to the crime the day before. But Everett positively identified him, pointing at him in the cell with a trembling finger. "He's the one, Judge. The one that killed my dad. My dad had his hands up. He wasn't fighting them or nothing. And that man shot him dead."

Sabine took him outside, tears streaming down his face, and the judge went through telegrams from Denver and Fort Collins, as well as the wanted posters that listed Robinson's name. "Bring the prisoner out here," he said to Glen. "And you," he said, nodding to Bryce, "take Mr. St. Clair outside."

Bryce moved a step closer to Nic and studied him, but Nic was already on his way outside. He wrapped Sabine and Everett in a hug. "It's almost over," he said lowly. "This is almost behind us. Come on, let's go back to the Circle M."

Everett paused on the front porch of the sheriff's office, watching him go.

Nic looked back. "Come on, Ev."

"You're not going to wait?" Everett said. "To find out his sentence?"

Nic returned his gaze. "We can wait if you want. That's your right, son. But one thing that God's impressed upon me yesterday and today is that I can't take justice into my own hands." He threw up his hands and shook his head. "We all belong to Him, from the cradle to the grave, whether we know it or not. I do. Sabine does. You do. Even that man in there, Robinson. And He'll see justice done in His own time and in His own way. Now if we trust Him, that's all we have to think about. I'm not saying it's easy," he said, lifting a brow and shaking his head again. "I'm just saying it's what I think we're to do. Make your best call."

He turned and walked with Sabine over to one of the two wagons from the Circle M. He helped her up and into it, and then smiled when Everett appeared beside them too. "You're not going to wait?"

"Nah. Odessa and Bryce can tell us what happened. I belong with you."

Moira dressed for dinner the next night and pulled on long white gloves in a delicate kid leather that Francine had given her. They were entertaining several of their friends after supper, and they'd hired a pianist to play. "Will you sing a song or two, Moira?" Francine had asked her.

She was so enthusiastic and kind, Moira could hardly turn her down. "One or two," she said.

"Marvelous, dear," Francine said, clasping her hands. "Marvelous!"

Moira moved away from the mirror and strode to the windows to look upon the grounds. She felt as if she were living in a world straight out of a novel. How had Gavin been so wrong about how his parents might receive her? They were more than gracious to her, and seemed to truly like her. Today had been filled with warm conversation and a few laughs. All in all, it was going far better than she had ever imagined it might. It would feel good to sing tonight—to show them what had drawn Gavin to her most, her talent.

Down below she spied two men walking along the edge of the gardens, near the shadows of the trees. She squinted and moved to see through another pane, one that was a little less wavy, giving her a clearer view. They were getting close to the house, leaving her line of vision—it was clearly Henry Knapp, with his wavy, gray hair and distinguished gait, but who was he with? Tall, broad shouldered … She drew in a quick breath.

Impossible.

The man from the train? From the streets?

She turned and rushed to her door, then down the hallway and stairs. Lifting her skirts, she ran past the dumbfounded butler and yanked open the door.

Henry was there, hand reaching for the knob, surprise etched in his face.

She drew back and gasped.

"Moira, my dear, where are you off to in such a rush?"

Recovering, she edged past him and looked over to the gardens that extended from the south side of the house. "Henry, forgive me, but I must know. Who accompanied you on your stroll?"

"Accompanied me?" He shook his head. "I'm afraid I was out on my own. A bit of fresh air always helps me to think more clearly in the late afternoon," he said, patting his chest.

She frowned and thought back. The tall gray-haired gentleman had been in a dark charcoal-colored coat too, right? Or had it been brown? "Were there two other men in the garden with you? Or perhaps across from you?" Her eyes went to the vast garden, with its neat hedgerows and perfectly pruned trees. It was over five acres wide and doubly deep.

"No, no," he said, peering at her as if he thought she had bumped her head and might be a bit dizzy. "It's a rather large garden, but I saw no one else while I was about."

"No one at all?"

"Only Mansfield, our gardener," he said, one eyebrow arched. "But I do tend to get lost in my own thoughts," he added with a charming smile.

Moira lifted her chin and drew in a deep breath. "Forgive

me … I only thought I saw you walking with a man I once … knew."

"Ah." For a moment, she could see he thought her excuse dubious, but then he quickly covered it. "It's getting a bit chilly out here, my dear. Shall we return inside?"

"Yes," she mumbled, turning toward the door. "I am so very sorry for coming upon you like that, Henry."

"Not at all, my dear," he said, tucking her hand into the crook of his elbow. "Not at all."

Moira settled into the evening, feeling as though she were back home again, surrounded by beautiful, insightful, witty conversationalists, people who truly appreciated the arts. Over and over again she was told that she was in the hands of the finest hosts in New York, and measuring by the amount of champagne and caviar that was served, the Knapps appeared to be living up to their reputation.

Only one thing gave her pause. Several couples came up to her and expressed their condolences over "her loss," and "dear Gavin," murmuring about what a fine man he had been and how fortunate she was to share her life with him, even for a short time. It took her aback, their full embrace, and that none seemed to be chagrined at the clandestine nature of their relationship. Could it be that this was how the upper crust of society dealt with such affairs? She didn't remember anything like it from her days in Philadelphia; perhaps her parents had simply shielded her from such sordid details. Surely Gavin's was not the first affair in this circle, judging from how they all reacted to her and folded her in, as if she were truly one of them.

The pianist played Chopin and Beethoven, then a bit of sprightly Mozart, upon the request of several giggling women who hovered about the grand instrument in the corner.

After a bit, Henry tapped his crystal flute with a tiny spoon, drawing everyone's attention. "Ladies and gentlemen, thank you for joining us here tonight. As we expressed to each of you, it is a special night for us, given that our dear Moira has come to visit us. With her soon to bless us with our first grandchild, this gives us cause for twice the celebration. But we have a special treat in store for you."

Moira almost choked on her swallow of champagne at his words, but forced a genteel smile. How could he speak of her, her child, so brazenly? As if it were the most natural thing in the world?

"But we have a special treat for you tonight," he repeated. "Gavin fell in love with this girl not only for her beauty, but also for her incredible talent. Many of you have heard of Moira St. Clair, an opera phenomenon in France. I would wager that many an opera house would pay a pretty penny to have her return. But fortunately, she's here with us, and they'll be hard pressed to take her away from us now." He raised his champagne flute. "To Moira St. Clair, our son's beloved."

"To Moira St. Clair," said the room full of people in unison.

Moira could hardly keep her breath. Was this really happening?

"Won't you honor us with a song, Moira?" Henry asked.

"Of course," she said, feeling that it was the very least she could do. She strode forward and the crowd parted for her, clearing a path to the piano. She whispered the title of a lovely song from her favorite opera to the pianist, and when he nodded, she turned to face the room. She took a deep breath, and at just the right moment, let her voice rumble and hover in its deepest register, then climb to thrilling heights, as if she'd been rehearsing all week.

Everyone in the room appeared speechless for a moment when she finished, as if they hoped to hear just a bit more, but then the crowd erupted in applause. She sang several more songs before the time came for the guests to depart.

Moira moved to stand beside Henry and Francine, thanking each for coming. When only their closest friends were still in attendance, a chubby, short woman came up to her and clasped Moira's hands. "Gavin couldn't have chosen any better, my dear. But I must ask. Why did you not take his name? The Knapp name would open many a door for you."

Moira frowned. "His name?"

"Moira had already established her following on the stage before she met Gavin," Francine put in, drawing her friend toward the door. "It is common for those in the public eye to do the same."

"You must be so proud," said another man to Henry, shaking his hand and putting a hat atop his head. "A gem like that in the family will shine for a good long while."

In the family …

She forced a smile, her mind cascading through comment after comment through the evening. Could it be …had they …?

"It is such a shame Gavin is not here with us," said the last guest in the room. She was tall, slender, elegant in silk of a fine deep blue. "But having his bride with us is almost like having a glimpse of him again, isn't it?" She smiled kindly at Moira, offered her cheek for Henry to kiss, and then walked with Francine out the door.

Moira remained where she stood. *His bride.*

They all believed her to be the widow of Gavin Knapp. They did not accept her as she was, a used and discarded mistress. They accepted her as the widow, the survivor of a tragically short marriage.

A marriage that never occurred.

She looked about the empty room. It was all wrong. She was simply falling for the same charms that had first drawn her to Gavin. He wasn't different from his parents. He was the same. Masters in manipulation ...

She had to get out of here.

Francine returned to the doorway of the grand drawing room, with Henry right behind her. "Sit down, dear," she said to Moira. "We need to speak of this matter."

"No," she said, shaking her head. "I will not live a lie. I thought ..." She shook her head more vehemently. "I don't know what I thought. But this, this charade—I will take no part in it. I lived my life for a good number of years playing a role. But I don't want to do that anymore."

"Please," Francine said. "Hear us out. Any wise woman would do as much."

Moira considered her words. What was the harm of hearing their rationale? Francine was right. She was no mere girl; she was a woman. She ought to behave as one.

Numbly, she walked to a settee and perched on its edge. Her host and hostess sat on two chairs across from her.

"Really, Moira, you needn't look like we're two cats about to pounce on a pretty bird," Henry said, leaning back into his chair.

"It was the only sensible solution," Francine said. "We couldn't introduce you, and embrace our grandchild, and let it come out that you and Gavin shared no more than a sordid affair."

"I … I loved him," she said.

"Of course you did, dear," Francine enjoined. "We understand that. But we're thinking of your options at the present, your future. Our grandchild's future."

Moira didn't like how she said *our grandchild*. A tone of possession dripped from every syllable.

She rose on trembling legs. *This can't be happening.…*

"You will sit down, Moira," Henry barked.

Moira's eyes widened, but she did as he directed. No one had spoken to her like that since she was a little girl.

"Henry, please," Francine said, reaching out a hand to him.

He rubbed his temples tiredly, reminding her of Gavin. It was happening again, all over again. How could she be so stupid? *Oh Lord, how could I have fallen for such empty promises again?*

"You will not move until you've heard us out," Henry said, stretching out a finger to her. "You owe us that much."

Owe? They thought she was in debt to them?

"We just reintroduced you to your public," Francine said, her features again full of hope and kindness. "Once the baby is born, you will be free to take the stage again. Here in New York or elsewhere. We will do nothing but support you."

Moira hesitated. There was a lovely promise in those words … but at what cost? Her eyes narrowed. "The stage is hardly a place for a mother. The late nights alone—"

"We'd help you in every way," Francine said. "We've thought it all through. You could live here, with us, and we'd care for the baby while you are traveling or in the city."

Traveling or in the city. That was at least six days a week, longer if she went to other cities to sing.

It was clear now, what they wanted. The baby.

She had known, but hoped, even distantly—

"You will want for nothing," Henry said. "I can open far more doors than Gavin ever could. Would it not be the best for everyone? If you left the child here with us, leaving you free to pursue your dreams?"

Moira took a deep breath. "More and more," she said quietly, "my dreams have been for more than the stage. For love. Of a *good* man. Of family. I came here so that I might know you. To establish a relationship with you so that my baby would know his grandparents. My own parents are dead. So you were his—or her—only chance at that. But I see now that I was wrong. Gavin seduced and used me, and now you intend to seduce and use me in a different way, all for the goal of keeping my child as your own."

She rose again, trembling now in fury. At them. At herself. "I'm sorry. I cannot be a part of your charade."

Francine's mouth dropped open. "It is too late," she said, standing now herself. "The decision has been made. A marriage certificate will be here tomorrow."

"A marriage certificate?" Moira sputtered. "Gavin and I were never married!"

"It is but a trivial matter," Francine said, with a flick of the hand. "Consider it done."

"Listen," Henry said, rising. She took a step back, but he stayed where he was, reaching out a conciliatory hand. "This is all in the best interests of your baby. If not for yourself, Moira, won't you consider doing it for the child?"

She hesitated at that. They were right, in some measure. Askew in their thinking, but perhaps on the wrong track for the right reasons?

"Born as a Knapp, this child will have every opportunity in society. Money will never be something that confines him because he will be the heir to a great fortune."

"You speak as if you already know this child will be a boy!" she spit out in irritation. "Will you still lay claim to the babe if she's a girl?"

"Of course," Henry sputtered.

But not with quite the same fervor, Moira thought.

"Gavin himself had amassed a small fortune. It's all yours to use as you wish," Francine said soothingly. "Think of it as that which would have been yours, had he done the right thing in the first place."

"I don't have need of his money," Moira said, shaking her head. They were confusing her with their logic.

"So you intend to live with your sister forever?" Francine probed. Her tone said it all. The spinster sister, fallen in disgrace. "Will your community embrace a child born out of wedlock?"

Moira lifted her brows. "I doubt it will be easy. We'll bear the brunt of some scorn. But at least it will be honest."

"All this talk of honesty," Henry said, striding over to a small table to pour himself a scotch in a short crystal glass. He glanced back at her. "You never hesitated to live a lie when you were parading about as Gavin's wife in the West." He took a slow sip.

"I did hesitate. I did not like it. But he convinced me it was best.

For my safety. For the business." Her words sounded shallow, hollow, foolish, even to her.

"You've been through so much, Moira," Francine said, reaching out to take her hand. Moira watched her do it as if she were taking the hand of some other woman. "Won't you spend the night and make your decision in the morning? Sometimes the light of day brings renewed clarity."

Moira hesitated. She was so kind....

Run, Moira. Be away from these people.

The voice was clear in her head, reverberating in her heart like the echoes of a pealing bell. Not her mother's. But God's.

She lifted her chin and gave Francine a small smile, pretending, taking on the role of the dutiful daughter-in-law. "Perhaps you are right. I do need to give it some thought. But I believe I need a little breathing room in order to do so. Would you be so kind as to call a carriage for me? I'd like to return to the city tonight."

"It's far too late," Francine said. "The road is dark."

Be away.

"He can light a lantern," Moira said, moving toward the door. "Did not your own guests all depart after sundown?"

Henry turned to watch her walk, making no move to stop her. Perhaps she was being paranoid, overly suspicious.

"Moira, just one more night," Francine pleaded, her face stricken.

They were truly relentless, teaming against her, utilizing every emotional and mental trick possible.

"You can come to the city and call upon me," Moira said, looking back. "We will talk further of this. But I'll feel more comfortable there."

The hairs on the back of her neck prickled. Someone was behind her.

She turned, and her eyes widened in terror. The man from the train. The one who had been following her.

She backed away and pointed at him. "This man needs to be arrested," she said to Henry. "He's been following me. He tried to get into my compartment on the train! He meant to accost me!"

Henry set down his glass and strode over to them. Moira dared to take in a breath, gaining strength with his support, but then he grabbed her arm and handed her to the burly brown-haired man.

"Enough," he said. "Take her to her room. And lock her in."

CHAPTER TWENTY-NINE

Moira struggled against the man, but he clamped his hand over her mouth and lifted her bodily, carrying her out through the empty foyer and up the stairs. She clawed at his hands, but the gloves given to her by the Knapps—gloves that she now realized cleverly disguised any missing wedding band—kept her from truly hurting him. She kicked and writhed, but only succeeded in wearing herself out. By the time they reached her door, she was panting, her heart beating wildly.

The man pushed her inside and slammed the door shut. Moira saw Francine right behind him. She ran over to the door, but heard the key slide the bolt into place just as she reached it. "Please," she cried, pounding on it with the palm of her hand. "You can't do this. Please! Let me out!" In vain, she turned the glass knob. "Please!"

It was a nightmare. A horrible nightmare. She sank to her knees, her lovely new skirts billowing about her in a deflated ball of creamy silk. She lifted her hands to her face and cried for a while. When her tears were spent, she rose wearily and went over to the dark window. There was nothing visible outside, other than the five-foot span lit by the front gas lamp by the door and several gas lamps in the garden, each spilling their warm light in orbs about them.

Moira reached for the window latch and yanked on it, then pulled the window open. She peered outward. No ledge on which to balance. And she was more than eighteen feet off the ground, if she dared to climb up and through the windowsill. She considered shouting, crying out for help, but realized that it might bring the wrath of the Knapps down on her. And whose ears might she reach? At this hour, and on property this vast, only servants in the Knapps' employ would hear her.

No, she would wait. Someone would come to call upon the family. And when they pulled up outside, she would open and scream for help. She took deep breaths of the cool night air, trying to calm herself, to think through her various means of escape. It would not be easy. By the sound of footsteps outside her door, she knew she was already under guard.

She tiptoed across the room and peeked through the keyhole.

He sat across from her door, in a chair, gazing at his fingernails. He glanced up, as if hearing her, and she sprang away from the keyhole.

The Knapps had sent the man to follow her, to make sure she came to them, one way or the other. For aid? For protection? He'd used the old playbill, hoping she wanted her identity to be kept a secret. Perhaps the Knapps thought that would be useful to them? She thought back to Francine's original letter, subtly putting together her identity with that of Moira Colorado, planting the seed in her mind that she might not be the only one who could do so....

Moira paced for a bit and then wearily sat down on her bed. *I've been so foolish, Lord,* she moaned in silent prayer, falling to her back in the soft, luxurious folds of the coverlet. She closed her eyes, wanting him to feel closer. *Forgive me, Father. I've fallen prey to my own old sins. I desired so much, Lord. I wanted acceptance. And accolades again.*

She reached up and pulled off her wig, letting it flop to the bed beside her. She rubbed her head, feeling the short hairs as they ran through her fingers. *I wanted to be seen as beautiful again. I wanted to be admired. Acknowledged.*

You are beautiful, Moira. Nothing makes you more so than being one of My own.

She groaned. *I have difficulty with accepting how You define beauty. I am scarred.*

So was I. In your scars, you will find strength.

Moira frowned. *I need strength, Father. I need an escape.*

Trust in Me, child. Trust in Me. And wait.

Daniel paced the car from one end to the other.

Despite the cost he had opted to take the same luxurious line that Odessa told him Moira had taken, getting him to New York a couple days faster than the other, but he could not make use of the sleeper compartment. He was a mass of agitation, furious at himself for letting her go. Not that she had asked his permission.

But something was wrong.

Moira. Moira. Moira. Over and over, her name ran through his mind.

Deep within, he could sense the trepidation of what was to come, like the slow turning of a whirlpool, threatening to suck him down. *What is it, Lord?* He hadn't felt such warning from God in years. He hadn't felt his Lord this close at all, period. Not since before Mary died ... Not since the day he'd tracked down one of her murderers and in turn, killed him.

He reached out a hand and rested it on the cold wooden frame that surrounded the window. He peered outside, seeing nothing but a vast, moonless sky and a thick seasoning of stars. The train car rocked beneath his feet, but Daniel stayed where he was, staring outward.

"I acted rashly and sinned deeply," he whispered. "And given the opportunity, I might've done it again." He shook his head, feeling the deep shadow of shame cover him. "Forgive me, Lord. Forgive me." His foolish pull, the old need to track down Mary's remaining killer and bring him to justice, had driven Moira away. He knew she was ahead of him, scared, searching for something, because he hadn't given her what she needed. Had he done so, had he turned down the sheriff's position—if only to assuage her fears—she'd be safely at home, and he with her.

He rubbed his face, feeling the sickening pull of warning at his gut again. "Protect her, Lord, whatever she is facing. Protect her. And make this train go faster," he groaned, slamming the windowsill with the palm of his hand.

She was ready when they came. She'd lain awake all night, planning it out. She knew Francine would wish to play the role of the benefactor captor and would arrive with food and warm water in which to wash. When she heard the key in the lock, she sprang to her feet and moved to about ten paces off, in order not to surprise them.

The door swung inward and a maid walked through, bearing a tray full of food. "Morning, ma'am."

"Morning," she returned. She glanced at Francine coming in

behind the maid, a steaming pitcher of hot water in her hands, just as she expected. "Here, let me take that from you," she said graciously to the maid, walking several paces toward her, reaching for the tray. She quickly lifted it, setting the food and glasses in motion, falling toward the maid, who cried out in horror.

Moira reached over to Francine and wrenched the steaming pitcher away from her, then splashed the scalding water in an arc toward the brown-haired man. He bellowed in pain and turned from her, his hands on his face and chest. The hot water dripped from him, and steam rose from his shirt.

But Moira was already in motion, lifting her skirts and running past him and down the hall. She was nearly at the top of the steps, reaching for the railing, when a hand snaked out and grabbed her arm, wrenching her backward.

She slammed into his chest, knowing before she turned who it was who had her.

Henry. He held onto her easily, with an iron grip that belied his age.

"Come now, Moira. This can be a simple, pleasant experience. Or it can be less genteel. The choice is up to you."

"You are keeping me prisoner!" she cried, glancing down to the foyer, hoping someone, anyone heard her.

He laughed. "Silly girl. You are our guest, of course." He pulled her around and dragged her down the hall. The brown-haired man came running, obviously livid, and took her from his boss.

"There now, Sully," Henry said with a chiding laugh. He straightened his vest and jacket as Sully tried to keep hold of Moira. "Bested by a mere wisp of a girl, were you?"

"It won't happen again, sir."

"See that it doesn't." Henry turned and walked down the stairs, as leisurely in his pace as if he were out for an afternoon stroll.

Moira faced forward and saw Francine waiting, hands knotted before her, in the hallway by her door. "We will bring you more food and water, now that that spat is over," she said. The maid passed by, already on her errand.

"Please!" Moira cried out to her, over her shoulder. "Please help me!"

Sully clamped his wide hand over her mouth and carried her inside the room. He dumped her upon the bed.

"I've explained to the maid that you are not yourself," Francine said from the doorway, "that the pregnancy has made you slightly ... unbalanced. A doctor is en route, of course. He will make you more comfortable."

Moira stared at her, hard. They intended to drug her? For how long? Until she came to term? "You can't do that. It may harm the baby," she said.

Francine paused over that, as Moira knew she would. "The doctor is one of the finest in the field. He will do what's necessary to ease your hysterics and watch over our grandchild."

"Hysterics?" Moira cried, knowing full well that she sounded as hysterical as they accused her of being. She did not care. She rose to go after Francine, but Sully clamped down on her arm before she could take more than two steps.

"Theresa will be back momentarily with the water and food. See to it that Moira does not leave this room," Francine added before she left.

Moira stared at the empty doorway and then turned to Sully. "Please," she whispered. "Listen, I'm sorry about the water. I need to leave. Whatever they're paying you, I'll pay you more. I'll pay double. Please. Won't you help me?"

He studied her. "The Knapps are fine people. They'll see to your welfare, and your child's." He glanced around, hands out. "This is luxury for most people. Doubt you have it this fine at home."

"Don't you see?" Moira asked. "They only want my baby. Once it is born, they'll lock me out of this house as surely as they're currently locking me in."

Sully lifted his chin and looked down his nose at her. "They pay me every week. You don't."

"Listen," she said, urgently casting a gaze toward the empty doorway, knowing if Theresa returned, their conversation would be over. "Did you hear about the conquistador gold that was discovered in June out in Colorado? That was my brother-in-law's ranch. I have a share of the gold. I'll give you more than you've dreamed of if you help me leave here."

He considered her a moment, then shook his head. "Sit down," he said gruffly, and plunked her down in the chair.

Moira shoved down a feeling of panic. She was to trust in God, not man. He knew she was here. He could see her. She could rest in Him. *But, Lord, they intend to drug me! Please, help me, soon. Please.*

She rose to pace, but Sully's hand came down on her shoulder and shoved her back into place again.

She fought to keep from screaming, giving in to the hysteria they claimed had captured her. *Odessa and Bryce know I was coming to see the Knapps. They will come after me. But in how long?* How long until they would recognize that something was amiss, that she wasn't responding to telegrams? How long until they arrived?

Oh, Daniel. If only you were thinking of me, she thought. But she had walked away from him as surely as he had turned from her. Why did she have to be so prideful? So stubborn? Why could she not simply abide, as her Lord had urged her to, and wait for Daniel to return to her? *Impetuous, willful, stiff-necked,* she reprimanded herself silently—

"There now, a new tray," Theresa said, entering the room. "Someone will be along shortly with more water for your bath." She carefully averted her eyes from Moira, as if afraid she might leap toward her again if she met her gaze.

"Theresa, I am being held prisoner," Moira said calmly.

Sully pinched her shoulder.

"I'll be back in a while to fetch your tray," the maid added, as if Moira hadn't said anything at all.

"Send help for me!" she cried.

But the maid gently closed the door behind her.

Sully chuckled lowly. "She believes you're as hysterical as your mother-in-law claims."

Moira sighed and let her head fall into one hand. It was no use even arguing against the unwarranted title of mother-in-law. In this house, the Knapps ruled all.

She supposed they used a cloth soaked in chloroform first, to so completely knock her out. She didn't remember it, but nor did she remember what came after it. Tonics? Pills? Moira dragged her eyes open and tried to still the spinning room. How long had she been asleep? A few hours? A few days? It was impossible to tell.

Dull voices reached her ears, but it was as if she were underwater. She could make no sense of the words.

Lord, Lord, she called, fighting to form the words, even in her mind.

Help me. Save me.

CHAPTER THIRTY

Daniel swung down off the train and hopped to the platform. He looked about for the carriage with the least worn-down-looking horse, and then waved at the cabbie to gain his attention. The young man straightened and smiled, then clambered down to receive his two valises. "That it?"

"That's it." Daniel climbed into the compartment behind the driver's seat.

"Where to?"

He gave the man the name of the hotel where Moira had told Odessa she was staying.

The cabbie hesitated and looked at him. "Beggin' your pardon, mister, but they only let gentlemen in ties and coats through their doors."

"They'll let me through," Daniel said assuredly. "Go."

The young man turned and flicked the reins over the horse and they moved down the street, and through another. He turned and went several blocks, then pulled up in front of the grand, sprawling hotel, at the edge of Central Park. "Nothing but the finest, eh, Moira?" Daniel growled under his breath.

He climbed down and turned. "Wait here a moment, would you? I might need to go somewhere else."

"Sure enough, mister."

Daniel turned and walked up the marble steps, his eyes on the two doormen, who seemed as intent to keep him out as the cabbie had promised. He fished in his pocket and pulled out his tin star, lifting it up to show them. "Official business."

The doorman closest to him hesitated, as if he thought it wasn't enough. Then, "Make it quick. Or come back in a jacket and tie. Sheriff or not, rules are rules."

"Thank you," he said, moving through the hand-carved and heavily lacquered door.

His eyes adjusted to the dim light of the interior, and he moved over to the concierge's desk. "Excuse me, I need to get a hold of one of your guests. A Miss Moira St. Clair."

A movement over the man's shoulder caught Daniel's eye. Had that blond man started when he said Moira's name? He studied him, but the man was merely folding a paper and walking out. *You're acting foolish, paranoid, Adams,* Daniel chastised himself. He stopped watching the departing man and returned his gaze to the concierge, who was staring at him with some chagrin.

"It is not our policy to summon guests, especially when those who come to call are not abiding by hotel dress code."

Daniel slammed down his star on the desk and leaned over it. "Listen, I've just traveled four days straight to get here. Is Moira St. Clair registered as a guest here? This is urgent business. I suggest you do not stand in my way."

The concierge hesitated a moment longer, his eyes flicking over to the hotel manager. But Daniel didn't care. He only wanted answers. And fast.

"We have become somewhat alarmed over Miss St. Clair

ourselves," the concierge said in a low tone, leaning over the desk. "She has not returned in four days."

"You have a guest who has been missing for four days? And you have done nothing?"

"She paid in advance. And went to call upon friends. We assumed she remained there, but most of her things remain in her room."

Daniel frowned. She had intended to see one family, as far as he knew. "Did she go to call upon the Knapps?" he asked.

"I don't know," the man said. "But I can help you find the cabbie who took her there."

"Please," he said, gesturing outward.

They exited back into the brilliant summer day and Daniel blinked and squinted. Luckily, at this time of day most of the cabbies outside were idle, taking their lunch several hours late, talking with friends.

The young man who had brought Daniel here watched with consternation as they passed him by and continued down the line of cabbies, obviously worried that he might miss another fare, but Daniel ignored him, watching only the concierge before him, hoping he might recognize the man they sought. "There!" said the man, pointing. "Five down. The one with the brown carriage and white horse. That's him. He accompanied her for days. She asked for an escort, a guard, of sorts. He was the one I found for her."

Daniel hurried over. The large man looked up, still chewing a piece of bread as he approached. Others ahead of him watched them too, all jealously coveting the next fare.

"You," Daniel said. "Were you watching over a Miss Moira St. Clair a few days back?"

"If I was, what's it to you?"

"I'm Sheriff Adams, out from Colorado. I'm in love with Moira St. Clair. And I have reason to believe she might be in danger."

The man straightened at his last word. "Why do you believe that?"

"Because she hasn't returned in several days. And yet her things are still in her room. Where did you drop her last?"

"Out past the city," he said, gesturing northward with his head. "The Knapp estate. But she was packed for a short stay. Chances are, she's fine, simply enjoying fine hospitality."

"Yes, well," Daniel said, feeling a bit of relief at the news, yet knowing Moira would have at least sent for her things if her stay were extended, "if it's all the same to you, I'd like to see that for myself. I'll pay you to take me out there."

"Hey, you were my fare, mister," said a voice behind him. He turned to see the young man who'd brought him out from the train station.

"How are you in a fight?" Daniel asked.

"I hold my own. Scrappy, my pa calls me."

"Good. You can come with us." He flipped him a coin. "Pay someone to watch over your carriage and horse until we return. There will be two more for you if I get what I've come for."

The young man's eyes widened. "All right. Let me get your bags."

Daniel turned to the other driver, who reached over and shook his hand.

"Name's Billy Samson. I hope you're wrong about Miss St. Clair being in some sort of trouble."

"Me too, Billy. Me too." He settled into the new carriage,

thinking of Moira being in the same spot, just a few days before. But instead of relaxing, he found his sense of trepidation growing. "How 'bout you, Billy? You any good in a fight?"

"Sure," the man said, looking over his shoulder at him. "There was a reason the concierge up there asked me to escort Miss St. Clair about." A grin spread across his face.

"Good. Because we might have to fight to free her."

"Or we might find her on the front lawn, enjoying a cup of tea and a game of croquet."

"I'd welcome that. But are you game to back me up in case we don't find the situation to be quite so ... civilized?"

"I'm game."

"Good."

CHAPTER THIRTY-ONE

Nic walked down Westcliffe's bustling street, whistling, relieved to know that Chandler Robinson had been sent to Denver for his final sentencing. He and Sabine would have to return to Buena Vista in two weeks' time for the trial of the owners of the Dolly Mae. Of course the company had called in high-powered attorneys from Denver, but Nic chose to believe that truth would prevail. In the meantime, he had one thing on his mind: marrying Sabine.

The town was not big enough for a jeweler of its own, but the mercantile was certain to have a bigger selection than anything he'd seen in St. Elmo. He walked along the busy boardwalk, admiring how it was taking shape. The town was full of ranchers and miners and new families on the frontier, fresh-faced and full of hope. Perhaps Sabine wouldn't mind settling here, or in Conquistador, with a fine view of the mountains, or even on the Circle M itself. Bryce and Dess had offered them their choice of lots. He smiled, thinking of Dess, who so clearly wanted her sister and brother nearby. But that was up to Sabine. He'd go anywhere she wanted.

Another block and he spotted the Westcliffe Mercantile, up and on the right. He entered and smiled as the clerk up front greeted him. He paused before a display of trousers, jackets, shirts, and ties. They would be perfect, if he could find a set to fit him. But he could not wait to get to the jewelry case, so he moved on. Slowly, he placed one hand on the curved glass lid, and then another, looking down, into folds of soft fabric dotted with earrings, rings, and fancy cuff links. Men came, he knew, to this territory with such things and used them as currency, exchanging their mothers' and wives' keepsakes for a chance at a greater treasure, so elusive, for so many.

But not for me, he thought in wonder. *How on earth, Lord, did You choose me to be so fortunate? I am far from deserving....*

"Can I help you?" asked the clerk, coming nearer.

"Yes. I need a plain gold ring for me and something special for my bride."

"Getting married soon?" the clerk asked with a smile.

"As soon as possible," Nic said with a grin in return. Saying it aloud made it feel real.

"Well, then," said the man, cocking a brow, "we'd better find you something suitable then. Which do think would capture your bride's heart? An emerald? Or ruby?"

Nic's eyes moved over the rings, looking for the one that was right. "There," he said, lowly, pointing to the lower left of the cabinet. "That's it. That's *it*," he said again in glee.

"Please," Moira said, reaching out to Theresa, as the girl set a tray beside her bed. For the first time in what seemed days, she felt more coherent, but her mind worked and worked to find her next words. "Please," she finally repeated again.

"There's your breakfast, miss. Mrs. Knapp, she's coming to see you in a wee bit," she said. Hurriedly, she turned and moved out of the room, almost knocking over a small table in her rush. Two other maids arrived and set down a washtub. Two men followed behind them, each carrying hefty pails full of steaming water. They never looked in the direction of Moira's bed, but simply poured the contents of each pail into the tub and left. One maid moved to the corner and pulled out an Oriental screen, with ivory panels and black lacquered framework. She set it up in front of the tub, effectively dividing it from the rest of the room and giving the intended bather some modicum of privacy. Dimly, Moira supposed the bather would be her.

She reached up and felt the short hair of her head. Where had her wig gone? Through squinting, weary eyes, she looked about the room and found it upon her dressing table, on a proper stand. So the Knapps knew of her burns now. Not that it mattered. Why had she tried to hide it at all?

The second maid moved over to her and took hold of her blankets. "Come, miss. We're to get you in the tub. Would you care for something to eat first?"

Moira sat up. She didn't bother to answer her question. It took too much effort. To speak. To refuse the bath. It was better to comply and get it over with, then back to bed. She rose on shaking legs and almost collapsed. "Whoa there, I got you," said the maid, wrapping an arm around her waist. She tucked her head under Moira's arm. "Come on. You'll feel like a new woman after a proper bath."

They moved across the room and in short order, undressed her and helped her into the tub. The water was the perfect temperature, and Moira settled in and leaned back, letting the water reach her chest. There was a knock at the door and the maids moved over to it, accepting two more pails of water. "Here you go, miss," said the first maid. "Lean forward and we'll give your hair a fair scrub." Slowly, she poured it over her head. Then Moira leaned back, letting it splash down her face as well.

The maid picked up a bar of soap and moved toward her.

"I'll do it," Moira said, lifting her hand. She was no child, needing a nursemaid. They'd drugged her, not taken her mind in total. And the water seemed to be washing away some of her fogginess. She rolled the bar in her hands, watching as it lathered into billows of bubbles. It smelled good, of lavender, and she set to scrubbing her hair, then her body, and went under for a moment to rinse it all off. She emerged feeling even closer to some semblance of herself. What had they been giving her? And how? When? Never did she remember anyone entering, giving her medication. Only sleep, and drink, and more sleep …

She peered through the crack in the dressing screen, over to where a maid was pulling sheets from her bed and remaking it. Beside her was the tray. Drink. They were drugging her water and tea. That had to be how they were slowly poisoning her.…

No more. It ended today. Somehow. They could not keep her prisoner here until she birthed this baby, still three or four months away. She looked down to her belly and rubbed it. *You are mine,* she told her child silently. *No one will take you from me. Not even your grandparents.*

"Ready for the last pail, miss?" asked the maid, from the other side of the screen.

"Please."

The young woman came in and poured it over her, rinsing her

off, then handed her a thick towel of luxurious Egyptian cotton. Moira stood to wrap it around her body and then stepped out of the tub. The maid handed her a pile of neatly folded underclothes. "Up to dressing yourself, or you would you like help, miss?"

"I think I can do it," Moira said. She was feeling worn from the bath, as if it had sapped her meager energy. But she was feeling more awake at the same time. *Help me, Lord. Help me to make the most of this time. Help me to find a way out.*

"Here's your gown," said the maid. "Ready?"

"Ready."

The woman moved toward her, her turquoise gown in hand. Why dress her in such finery?

Unless Francine Knapp did not intend to call on her alone.

Moira lifted her chin and waited as the maid buttoned up her gown in back, settling it around her. Then she sat down on a pedestal chair beside the dressing table, and the woman carefully combed her hair back, then reached for her wig.

She settled it atop her head and stood back to look at her in the mirror. "There now, the perfect lady," she said in admiration. "Would you care for a bit of powder? Rouge?"

"No, thank you," Moira said.

"Oh, just a spot of color. You're terribly peaked after your days in bed."

Days. So it had been days.

She gave in to the woman's ministrations, and in short order the girl had applied a careful layer of rouge to her cheeks. It was artfully done.

"Much better," said a voice from the corner.

Moira's eyes lifted to the mirror again, and she spied Francine Knapp striding toward her across the room. The male servants and the maids scurried to clean up the tub, emptying it with the pails and carrying the rest out immediately.

Francine paused behind her shoulder, picking up one coil of the blonde wig after another, as if examining the quality.

"So you intend for me to live like this until my pregnancy comes to an end?" Moira asked. She was so tired, she could not move, but her mind was gaining clarity by the moment.

"Is it so terrible?" Francine said wryly. She waved about. "A fine apartment. A luxurious bed. Servants to care for your every need. Most women would envy you."

"I am not most women."

"That, you are not," Francine said wearily. She turned and walked over to the two chairs that were nestled in the turret. Moira could see that her breakfast tray had been moved over there. "Come, my dear. Join me."

Moira glanced over to the open doorway. Might she make it, if she were to run?

"You are far too weak for such a thought," Francine said, staring at her, reading her look. "And there are guards in the hall. Come."

Moira rose, as gracefully as she could on her weak legs, and moved toward the woman, fighting the urge to reach out and steady herself on furniture as she passed. When she reached the chair, she collapsed. A thin sheen of sweat broke out over her whole body from the exertion.

"Here, have some tea," Francine said. "You look a fright all of a sudden."

Moira accepted the cup from her hands, but only pretended to sip from it. The liquid appeared normal, a deep golden brown. And it smelled fine too. But since it came directly from the viper, she would not drink from it. She set it down before her, watching Francine's eyes follow it. *There. You've given yourself away.*

"You need to keep up your strength, my dear. For the baby, if not for yourself. Won't you try and drink a bit more?"

"You're right," Moira said. Again, she feigned a sip, and set the cup down.

"Today we will be joined by our attorney," Francine said. "I do hope there will not be any more messy exchanges between us. Might we not carry forward, as friends, family, really?"

"But the cost for such an agreement is a *life*. My child's."

"Come now," she chided. "We are not threatening to take a life. We are offering to give this child everything."

"I've had everything, Francine." She shook her head a little. "Everything a woman could want, really. And it did not bring me peace, joy. Only love can do that." From a good man. Daniel, not Gavin. From a God who loved her. As she was. Regardless of what she'd done.

"Mrs. Knapp?" said a maid at the door, wringing her hands.

"What is it?" Francine said, clearly irritated by the interruption.

"You have a visitor."

"A visitor? But he is not due until—"

"Not him, mum, but another. Mr. Knapp bade me to come and fetch you."

"Very well," Francine said, rising. "I'll see to this and return to resume our conversation."

"I shall await your return," Moira responded tiredly, as if she could barely stand, allowing the woman to leave her presence.

Francine, as if sensing her sarcasm, lifted her pert nose and walked from the room, every inch the regal woman.

Moira reached for a muffin and forced a bite to her mouth. If she was to gain some strength, have a chance to fight, she would need some food in her stomach. As it stood, she would be lucky to make it to the door without aid. Everything in her called her to return to her bed, nestle into the cool, crisp, clean sheets. Let the comforter settle atop her, slowly warming her as she let her eyelids fall ...

She shook her head. She had to stay alert.

"Theresa," she called.

"Yes, miss?" the maid said, at her door at once.

"Might I have a glass of water? My stomach is too upset for this tea at the moment."

"Right away, miss," said the girl. She disappeared, then returned in short order with a sweating pitcher and a crystal glass, slightly out of breath. "This came straight out of the ice box," Theresa said proudly. "Mr. Knapp, he enjoys his water cold as a dip in a winter pond."

Moira covered a smile. "Well if it's good enough for Mr. Knapp, then it's certainly good enough for me." She gulped down the water and lifted her goblet to the girl again. "May I have some more?"

"Sure enough, miss."

After Moira had finished the water, she handed it to the maid. "You can take those away, now," she urged. "Mrs. Knapp and I will resume our tea."

"Certainly, miss." She bustled out the door and Moira smiled.

Francine would never know that she had taken in liquid, devoid of anything that might harm her further. She looked around for a place to dump her tea. Seeing no other option, she dumped it inside a large Chinese urn of blue and white—possibly Ming Dynasty—and then settled the cup back in the saucer.

Francine Knapp returned, looking a bit … shaken? Moira pretended not to notice. She positioned her head against the back of the chair. "If I'm to speak with your attorney, I shall need a bit of a rest beforehand."

Francine's eyes moved to Moira's empty cup. "But of course, my dear. Theresa! Come at once and help me get my daughter-in-law back to her bed."

Moira accepted the help as if she could barely stand. She was terribly weak and weary, but nothing as severe as she feigned now. There was a shout downstairs and then a terrible pounding upon the door, so loud that they could hear it even here, at the end of the house. The sound reverberated down the polished wooden floors.

Moira pretended a yawn and closed her eyes. "So, so very tired," she mumbled.

"You sleep," Francine said, drawing the covers to her chin. "I will be back to fetch you in a while."

"Sleep," Moira muttered.

The woman hurried across the room and the door shut behind her. Moira heard the key in the lock. And more pounding downstairs, in the front entry. There was something familiar about the shout. A timbre of the voice, muffled and distant as it was …

She forced herself to rise and come to her feet again. She moved across to the windows and looked down into the front area.

She could barely see the edge of a carriage and a white horse. Billy. Billy?

Her heart skipped a beat and surged. Reaching out to steady herself, she moved down to the small window in the turret, the one that faced the front of the building. Through the wavy glass she saw three men at the door.

And one was Daniel Adams.

"Let me in at once!" Daniel demanded, ramming his knuckles against the door.

As soon as he'd seen the blond man from the hotel—the one who had so quickly departed upon overhearing Daniel's quest—beyond the butler, he knew he was in the right place. He was a spy, left at the hotel to do just this—warn the Knapps of anyone seeking out Moira.

"Moira? Moira!" Daniel bellowed, stepping back and staring up at the vast gray monstrosity of a house. Was she somewhere inside? Why would they not allow him to see her? Claim she wasn't here? Unless they intended to do her harm?

"Moira!" he bellowed, cupping his hands around his lips.

The door opened and an older, graying gentleman strode out. "Now, see here. You will cease your demonstration at once!"

"You are Mr. Knapp?" Daniel said. Billy and the young cabbie came to flank him.

Two burly manservants stood to either side of the door, just behind Mr. Knapp.

"You are on private property, sir," Mr. Knapp said. "You must leave immediately."

"I will not," Daniel said. "Not without Moira St. Clair."

"Moira St. Clair?" the man said, raising his eyebrows. "What is your business with her?"

"I'm in love with her. And I've come to take her home."

"I'm afraid you're in for a disappointment. Moira has decided to stay here, with us. We intend to see to her every need. And that of her child."

Daniel rocked back on his heels. Was it possible? Could it be? She'd come, intent on meeting the Knapps, perhaps giving her child a connection to his grandparents.... He studied the older man and steeled himself. "I'm all for family reunions, but I'll need to hear that from Moira herself."

"In time, you just might. But not today. Moira is ... indisposed. May I tell her who it was that came to call upon her?"

"Daniel Adams. Sheriff Adams."

Did the man pause for a moment at the mention of his title? Daniel brushed aside his coat, giving the man a view of the star, pinned to his vest, as well as the revolvers in his holster. Was Mr. Knapp truly ready to come to blows over Moira? "I've come all the way from Colorado. I need to see her, Mr. Knapp. Even for a moment."

The man studied him. "I'm afraid it's impossible today. Come back tomorrow."

Daniel frowned. "I don't think you understand. I'm not leaving here until I see her."

The young cabbie reached out and pulled on Daniel's arm. But Daniel wrenched away, concentrating on Mr. Knapp.

"Sheriff Adams," the young man said.

Daniel looked over his shoulder at him, but the man was looking up, to the top of the building. To the turret. A blonde woman in blue-green stood there, hands pounding against the glass, as if shouting. It was hard to see her clearly, but it was a good bet it was Moira.

"That your girl?" the cabbie asked.

"Yes, it is," Daniel said, drawing his first revolver out and pointing it at Mr. Knapp's forehead. "You," he said to the man, "are going to do exactly as I say."

CHAPTER THIRTY-TWO

Unable to get the window latch to open, Moira screamed and pounded on the window when she saw Daniel. She was moving toward one of the other, larger windows in the room when Sully entered, took her around the waist, and threw her to the bed.

"Stay away from those windows," he growled, leaning over her. His head went up, listening as the noises down the hall and in the foyer grew louder. More shouting ensued, although the words were unintelligible.

"Come 'ere," he said, lifting her by the forearm. He pulled her along to the door of her bedroom and then cautiously peered around the corner and down the hall.

Swearing, he moved back in and closed the door. "Who's coming for you, Miss St. Clair?"

"I don't know," she mumbled.

"Who is he?" he ground out, cruelly pinching her face between his fingers.

"The man I love," she said.

"Perfect." He pulled her in front of him like a shield, then drew out his pistol and placed it under her chin.

Moira closed her eyes. Would this be how her life came to an end? So close to Daniel, tragically separated forever? Unable to give her child even a start at life? "Please," she moaned.

"Quiet."

They heard several others arrive outside the door in the hallway. Someone kicked it in, and there he was, Daniel, holding Mr. Knapp captive at the end of his own pistol. "Let her go," Daniel demanded.

Nobody moved.

"Tell him to let her go," he said, leaning closer to Mr. Knapp.

"Release her!" cried Mrs. Knapp. Moira could see the edge of her skirt in the doorway, nothing more. Was another man holding her? "Please, she is not worth such trouble."

"Francine, are you certain?"

"I am! Let her go!"

Mr. Knapp hesitated, his mouth working, as if he knew the words he wished to say but could not make himself actually form them. Finally, he gave the man holding Moira a quick nod.

The man behind Moira groaned and let the pistol slowly drop from her chin.

With a cry, Moira moved toward Daniel, the room stretching interminably long. It began to spin, slide beneath her feet, and she stumbled. She tried to reach out, grab hold of the table beside her, but it kept spinning out of reach.

"Moira? Moira!" His voice echoed in her head as if through a canyon. "What have you done to her? What's wrong with her?"

Daniel shoved Mr. Knapp through the doorway. He handed his pistol to the young cabbie and rushed to Moira, catching her just before she collapsed. "What did you give her?"

The older gentleman eyed his wife, now in the doorway.

"A mild sedative."

Daniel glanced down at Moira. "It doesn't appear mild to me."

"It should wear off in a day or two. We merely wanted her to stay long enough that we could talk some sense into her. She is carrying our grandchild!"

"She came here, more than willing to make you two a part of her child's life. What did you do?"

"Nothing," Mr. Knapp said. "We only promised her and her child wealth, care."

"That doesn't explain this," Daniel said. "Something happened."

"They wanted me to sign a forged marriage certificate," Moira mumbled. "And leave my baby with them."

"She makes it sound despicable," Mrs. Knapp said indignantly. "We were providing her a way out! A path of honor."

"Except she would be signing away her child."

Mrs. Knapp clamped her lips shut.

"Billy," Daniel said, gesturing the big man forward. "Keep your gun on the guard." He bent and lifted Moira up, then turned to face the Knapps. "I'm taking her out of here now. Give me any cause, and I'll see that you are charged with kidnapping and assault."

He moved forward and through the doorway, then down the hall, never looking back, trusting that Billy and the young cabbie were keeping the others at bay. They swept down the stairs and out past the open-mouthed butler who held the door. He set Moira into the back of the carriage and climbed in after her. His men were coming out, weapons pointing toward the open doorway. But no one pursued them.

"Let's get out of here," said the young man, face drawn.

But Billy was already whipping the horses, sending them lurching forward and away from the Knapp estate.

Daniel struggled to hold on, even as he pulled Moira, slack in a faint, into his arms again. He looked up at the young cabbie. "Anyone coming after us?"

"Not a soul," he said. He turned back around but kept glancing over his shoulder.

"Billy, get us to a physician. Better yet, the hospital."

"Right away, Sheriff."

"Moira," Daniel said, taking her hand the next morning.

She moved her head, as if awakening, and his heart surged with hope.

"Moira, wake up, sweetheart," he urged, caressing her face.

Slowly, she blinked several times and her long lashes fluttered. She stared at him for a long moment, as if trying to ascertain if what she saw was real. "D-Daniel?"

"Yes. I'm here."

She took a deep breath. "You came for me."

"I never should've let you go," he said. "I love you, Moira. With everything in my heart. I was … I was chasing my past. Trying to make something right and only making everything worse."

She considered his words for a long moment. "Me, too, I think."

"I'm hoping, Moira," he said, drawing her hand to his chest. "I'm hoping that you and your baby are my future. When you're better, when you're feeling more yourself, I'll explain everything."

She reached up and cradled his cheek in her small hand. "It's enough, Daniel. Enough that you are here. Thank you for coming after me."

He let her sink back into the pillow and she closed her eyes. But she left her hand in his.

It felt right, good. At last.

Two days later Daniel hired a carriage, and they left the hospital, moving out into a warm, humid summer afternoon. They drove for more than ten blocks, then turned and entered Central Park, climbing a hill. Moira leaned her head back against the seat, watching the broad branches of the trees pass by, a brilliant blue sky beyond them. She felt happy, gloriously free to be out of the confining, austere walls of the hospital.

"It's lovely, but honestly, I can't wait to leave here," she said. "Get as far away from the Knapps as I can. And just be with you."

"First things first," he said, taking her hand in his and gazing at her with his sad eyes. "I need to tell you some things, Moira. Hard things."

She frowned and leaned slightly away, but kept her hand in his. Whatever he had to tell her, it was best that it was out in the open.

The driver pulled up in a small clearing. Daniel rose and then helped her out. He reached back in for a picnic basket and a blanket, and then taking her firmly by the hand, led her up a small knoll. He spread out the blanket and she sat down on it. Her hands were sweating as she waited for him to join her, to speak, to let out whatever he had been holding in for such a terribly long time.

Daniel knelt beside her, and slightly in front, so he could look her in the eye. "Moira," he began tentatively, reaching for her hand, "about five years ago, something terrible happened." His gaze flicked to hers.

"My wife, Mary, was expecting, only a few months off from having the babe. About where you are now," he said glancing downward. He blew out a long breath.

Moira frowned and covered her belly with her hand, fearing what he was about to say.

"We were living in Kansas, homesteading some land. I was away for a couple of days, getting supplies. When I returned …"

She licked her lips and forced herself to remain still, to wait.

"While I was gone, two men had entered the cabin, attacked Mary … and left her for dead. I think … I think she was probably alive for some time after they left. I could tell …" He looked down at his hands. "By the time I got home, she was gone, and the baby with her. I was too late."

His words made Moira ache as if a hollow space had been carved inside her and filled with his sorrow. This, this was what had made him so sad, so silent and watchful, for so long.

"There's more," he said quietly, daring to look her in the eye. "I went after them. Those two. Tracked them down. Killed one, wounded the other. But he got away."

Moira's eyes widened.

"I turned myself in for murder. The judge let me off. Called the act justifiable. Eye for an eye. But it was wrong of me, Moira. Wrong then. Wrong now, for me to still want to make things right."

"But it's understandable," she said. "You were hurt. So terribly hurt."

"I've been on the hunt for that man ever since that day," he said. "In one way or another. It was what led me to Leadville. I figured a big mining town like that with all its gambling and such would draw that kind of man, at some point. At least, it was as good a guess as any other ..." He shook his head and then rubbed his neck with one hand. "I was thinking about moving on when my boss sent me to England for that antique bar and mirror. At that point, I wasn't feeling much. I had a hard time caring about anything, other than showing up for work, putting in my time, and getting to bed. I was moving through my days half alive." He paused, waited for Moira to meet his gaze again. "Until I met you."

Moira shifted. Uneasy, remembering how he had drawn her too, even though he was hardly the kind of man that usually drew her eye. Now he was the only one. She realized he'd always been the only one. Her true one.

"Then you were off with Gavin," he said, giving her a sad smile. "And I beat myself up for letting you go. But I had no claim on you. We were nothing more than fellow passengers on a ship. But then, there you were again, in my life, arriving like a beacon of light in Leadville. And in so much trouble."

"You saved me then too," she whispered.

"But I couldn't save myself." He shook his head again. "I was still wanting to find that man. The other that killed Mary and my child. So I took the sheriff position, thinking that if I could just find him, take care of it, be done with it, then you and I might have a chance."

She waited for a couple of breaths. "And so ... you found him?"

"No. One of my deputies reminded me what God was trying to tell me all along. I was chasing the past, when you were my future. I don't even know if that man is alive, Moira." He looked up at her in misery. "And yet I let you go again, because I was foolish."

"So now … you can let it go? Just like that?"

He smiled. "It wasn't fast. I finally just hit the end. I have to let that man go—leave justice to God—in order for me to claim my future. And, Moira, I hope to God that you will be a part of my future."

She gave him a tender smile. "I hope so too."

"Maybe I ought to simply sign on to one of Bryce's carpentry crews instead of staying on as sheriff."

"Maybe." She lifted a hand to his cheek. "Or maybe you've gained the wisdom to be one of the best sheriffs in Colorado."

He searched her eyes and then smiled. "And what of you?" he asked. "You said you came here chasing the past too."

"I did. I was hungering for a bit of my own family. Grandparents for my child. A glimpse of the 'glory' I left behind."

"And? What did you find?"

"It is … what it is. Places like this—"she waved about her—"will always hold the memories of many chapters in my life. But not the end." She looked at him. "That, I hope, will be with you." She paused. "Daniel, I've been so afraid. So afraid of the scars I carried, the sins I've committed. Afraid that they'd keep us apart forever." Slowly, she lifted a trembling hand to her wig and pulled it from her head. She stared down at the grass before her, unable to summon the courage to look upon him as he gazed at her. Scars and all.

"Moira."

Slowly, she dragged her eyes up to meet his. And all she saw in them was love and admiration. "Believe me when I tell you this, beloved," he said.

She stared at him now, unable to look away.

"You are more beautiful, more perfect to me than ever. Your scars, as terrible as they might feel to you, are simply a part of you. A part of your life. And your life, your *life*, Moira, is more precious to me than my own. I look at you," he said, shaking his head, "and all I see is beauty. Will you allow me that? Will you trust me, when I say that? Because it's true." He rose and cupped her face in his hands. "You are beautiful, through and through. You are beloved. And please, Moira, please say you'll be mine. Forever. Will you be my wife?"

"Yes," she said, her eyelids fluttering, tears spilling down her cheeks. "Yes."

And then he kissed her. Slowly. Passionately. For all the world to see.

But Moira did not care. Because he, her child, and her God were her present. Her future.

Hand in hand, they would see it through together.

EPILOGUE

After they attended the trial of the Dolly Mae owners up in Buena Vista, Nic and his family—past and future—went up to St. Elmo. It took him several days, but eventually he tracked down Sinopa. He didn't think he'd ever seen Sabine smile so broadly as when the two came into town, riding, side by side, that morning.

Now he awaited his bride. He glanced over to Moira and Daniel, who held hands, then to Odessa, Bryce, and the baby. He grinned as he spotted the horse's nose, edging out from the trees.

Sinopa was in front, riding without use of a saddle, and Sabine rode sideways behind him, dressed in a fine ivory leather dress, heavily beaded at the yoke, her hair down about her shoulders. The parson shifted nervously beside Nic, obviously disapproving of the former schoolteacher in full Blackfeet regalia. "Say a negative word," Nic hissed, "and you'll regret it."

The parson snorted, as if offended, but held his tongue. Any thought of him disappeared as Sabine drew closer. He moved forward, Everett right at his side, and waited for Sinopa to pull up on the horse's reins. When he did, Nic reached up a hand. "Glad you're here for this, brother."

Sinopa dismounted, shook his hand and smiled back. "As am I. You understand the importance of this moment?"

"Sinopa," Sabine said, trying to intervene.

Nic smiled. "It's all right, Sabine." He looked at Sinopa. "I will defend your sister with my own life. I will never harm her. I will love her with everything in me. She has a claim on my heart that I don't ever want to disappear. Is that the understanding you seek?"

The brave studied him for a long moment, then nodded once.

The fat parson cleared his throat. The evening was drawing to a close, the sun now setting in the west, casting warm ruby light through the trees. Sinopa moved to the horse and then gently lowered Sabine to the ground. The small group climbed up through the trees on a narrow path, and Nic thought of all the steps he had taken, through so many countries, and all of them somehow seemed to lead here, to this place. A shiver ran down his back as he turned and took Sabine's hands in his. It was holy, this union. This connection between them. How had he not known what love was like, all this time?

The parson opened up a book that looked impossibly small in his round hands, and began to read. Nic managed to respond when he was asked, but in all honesty, he did not hear much of what was said. It did not matter. His eyes were held by Sabine's, as wisps of her brown hair fluttered in the mountain breeze. Her lips moved in response to the parson's question, but all Nic could hear was the chattering of two birds and the wind in the trees, as if those sounds came out of her mouth instead. Behind her, the mountains were aglow, and she appeared as something out of his dreams.

Her dress was impossibly soft, the leather's nap streaked where she had brushed it out after dismounting, and flowed over her womanly curves that somehow echoed the climb and fall of the mountains behind her.

The parson cleared his throat and Nic looked with some alarm at him. Had he missed something? "The ring," he whispered.

Nic widened his eyes in surprise and searched his pocket for a moment before pulling out the silver band, with a long white pearl set in a delicate, scroll-like setting. "You are like a freshwater pearl to me, Sabine." He shook his head. "You came out of nowhere. Surprised me with your beauty, inside and out. I found love when I found you, in the last place I would've expected it."

She watched as he slipped the ring on her finger, then gazed up at him with shining eyes.

"You may kiss your bride," the parson said, raising one hand in gesturing toward her, clearly irritated that Nic wasn't paying close enough attention.

He moved closer and cradled her face in his hands. "Are you sure, Sabine?" he whispered.

"Never more so," she said.

He kissed her, sweetly, slowly, thinking of the night ahead. Of running his hands through her hair. Of helping her out of the soft leather gown. And waking up together. Forever.

The parson, flustered, hurriedly pronounced them man and wife. But they ignored him, only looking into each other's eyes. After a moment, Everett came over and wrapped an arm around each of them and looked up at them with a grin. Then Nic's sisters came and hugged them, and Bryce and Daniel offered him hand-shakes and a kiss for the bride. Sinopa stood back, waiting, then approached to rest a hand on each of their shoulders. "It is done. You are one."

"In so many ways," Nic returned, looking back with wonder at his new wife. "Thank you for becoming my bride, Sabine. You have honored me."

"As you have honored me," she said.

"Do you think you both could do me the honor of some supper?" Everett asked. "I'm starving."

Nic smiled. "Let's go. I'm buying you all the finest meal in St. Elmo we can round up."

"Then where?" Everett asked.

"Home," Nic said, looking at his wife and Everett, then on to his sisters and their men.

But in that moment, surrounded by the people he loved most, under the gaze of the God who'd claimed him from the start, he knew that somehow, he was already there.

... a little more ...

When a delightful concert comes to an end,
the orchestra might offer an encore.
When a fine meal comes to an end,
it's always nice to savor a bit of dessert.
When a great story comes to an end,
we think you may want to linger.
And so, we offer ...

AfterWords—just a little something more after you
have finished a David C. Cook novel.
We invite you to stay awhile in the story.
Thanks for reading!

Turn the page for ...

- **An Interview with Lisa T. Bergren**
  - **Discussion Questions**

DISCUSSION QUESTIONS:

1. It takes Nic a long time to come around to God's way of thinking. What do you think were the most important factors for him?

2. Moira suffers from scars, outward and inward. Which do you think are worse? Why?

3. Moira and Nic are both drawn to their old ways and places where they once found comfort. Have you ever done the same? Discuss why we're drawn to our old ways, even if we know a new way is better.

4. How were Moira and Nic's "prodigal stories" different? And how were they the same?

5. Wealth comes and goes in this series. Both prodigals (Nic and Moira) spend all they inherit, then gain it back in two very different (and sometimes excruciating!) ways. Discuss this factor in their lives—and how it impacts you in your life too.

6. What do you think was the pivotal change moment for Nic?

7. What is it about Sabine that helps Nic get over the threshold to happiness and love?

8. What role did Everett play in doing the same?

9. What was the most moving scene in this book for you? Why?

10. Do you believe that God is calling each of us "home"? What does that look like? Is it internal or external?

CHAT WITH THE AUTHOR

Q: How did it feel to wrap up this series?

A: Very gratifying. These characters have gone through so much, I was eager to see them through to a sense of peace. I got all teary with Nic and Moira in several scenes, which is always a good thing. If I'm moved, hopefully my readers will be too. But then, these days, I cry during commercials and *Extreme Home Makeover*. I swear that by the time I'm sixty, I'll just have to be tucking a handkerchief in my bra like my granny used to....

Q: Odessa and Bryce really take a backseat in this novel. Why did you not write more about them?

A: In my first draft, they actually had a stronger presence in the first third of the book. But their scenes felt flat against all that was happening for Moira and Nic. I decided that in my mind, they were really on a good track now—that the focus really had to be on getting my two prodigals back home. And I think there was more than enough to take in between those two troublemakers, don't you? Odessa and Bryce are present—just more of the "supporting cast members" at this point. And Odessa became my personification of "home" for both Nic and Moira, so I thought it appropriate that she was a bit more in the background....

Q: What motivated you to write about prodigals?

A: I think we're all prodigals, in some fashion. After college, I
had my own prodigal experience, during which I was actually
bartending on Sundays instead of doing anything that my God
would be proud of. I grew deeply depressed, had a come-to-Jesus
experience, and left for the Holy Land. Literally. I went from
bartending to Jerusalem, to visit my cousin who was studying
the life journeys of Paul. After a few weeks in Israel and Egypt,
I returned home—physically and spiritually. And went to work
in an industry that had helped call me home—Christian music
and books.

Q: What's next for you?

A: I'm about to dive into a teen time-travel series, which will take
me back to a time period I love—medieval Italy. Or perhaps
Renaissance Italy. I haven't quite decided on the year. But I
was moved by the passion I saw among teen girls reading the
Twilight series, and since I have a teen and tween, I wanted
to write something for them. I long for them to read about
heroines they can emulate—and heroes that would die trying
to save them (not battling against the desire to *take* their lives as
the vampire heroes do in *Twilight*). So this River of Time series
is my attempt to cover those bases.

Q: What about on the home front?

A: We're currently considering a year away as a family. We're passionate about travel and after I finish the River of Time series, I'm scheduled to begin a series based on characters taking the Grand Tour of Europe. We're wondering if we should take our own Grand Tour ... we'll see! Lots of unanswered questions on that front, but we're leaning pretty hard in that direction. It's exciting to dream about, even if it never comes to fruition.

Q: Anything else you want to say to readers? Where can they find out more about you?

A: The best places are my Web sites: www.LisaTawnBergren. com and www.TheWorldIsCalling.com. I really appreciate my readers and love to hear from them. They can email me at Lisa@bergrencreativegroup.com. I also have eNewsletters on both sites that people can subscribe to, that will give you the lowdown each month. Lastly, I'm on Facebook and Twitter as @ LisaTBergren and @TheWorldCalls. Connect with me via any of those portals—I'll look forward to it!